THE VINEYARD INHERITANCE

Hope Clarke is saved from Sir William Halpen exercising his *droit de seigneur* the night before her wedding to Edward. Halpen's son John, who has loved Hope since childhood, purchases the virginity of Bessie, a simple-minded local girl, for his father and is handsomely rewarded by the grateful Hope for her rescue.

After the wedding Hope and her new husband escape to America and start a new life on Martha's Vineyard, free from the feudal pressures of English law. But their calm is suddenly threatened when Hope's son is born, and he looks remarkably like John Halpen...

THE VINEYARD
INHERITANCE

THE VINEYARD INHERITANCE

by

Elizabeth Daish

Magna Large Print Books
Long Preston, North Yorkshire,
BD23 4ND, England.

British Library Cataloguing in Publication Data.

Daish, Elizabeth
    The vineyard inheritance.

A catalogue record of this book is
available from the British Library

ISBN   0-7505-1618-6

First published in Great Britain by Robert Hale Ltd., 1999

Magna Large Print is an imprint of Library Magna Books Ltd.

Printed and bound in Great Britain by
T.J. (International) Ltd., Cornwall, PL28 8RW

Chapter 1

Fresh rushes lay on the newly damp flagstone floor and the scent of pine logs mingled with the lazy smoke from the kindling in the wide hearth. The fire caught as the breeze from the main door funnelled through the great hall and Ellen Turner called for the boy to rake the half-burned twigs closer to the logs.

The door closed with a thud and she looked round, suddenly apologetic when she saw that the man who stood by the huge table was not Michael, the boy from the yard, but Mr John Halben, the only son of the Lord of Deerwood Manor, Sir William Halben.

'I sent him to take my horse to the farrier as I found him lame,' John Halben said. 'Give me the broom or we'll set fire to the hall.' He flicked the hot ashes back on to the bed of the fire and tapped the dust from the hazel broom.

Ellen watched him and smiled indulgently. 'And what mischief are you after now, Master John?' she said, with the easy familiarity of a woman who had nursed him as a baby and loved him as her own when his mother had died after several miscarriages.

'Mischief?' he asked with one eyebrow raised in mocking dismay. 'Now what mischief could a man like me follow, when there's work to be done here?'

'You don't wear that cloak and those ruffs when you are farming,' she said bluntly. 'Sir William is sick again and there's no knowing when he'll be fit to give orders and it's wrong to leave it all to Furness, the steward, so you should have no time for gallivanting.'

'Is my father mad, Ellen?' he asked quietly. She shook her head vigorously, but he sat on the edge of the table and fixed her with a look that she had come to dread as it meant that he wanted answers to questions to which she alone had the answers. 'I have been back here for three months,' he continued. 'My father blows hot and cold, not least to me, and the yeomen avoid him. He gives them venison one minute and accuses them of stealing the next. Heaven knows how many men he had sent to the gallows while I was away in London and overseas. I saw nothing amiss on the few visits I made here, except to know that his temper hadn't improved while I'd been away.'

'He has been ill for years,' she admitted in a tired voice. 'It was as well for you to be away for so long until you grew more tolerant, or there might have been murder done, but it's good to have you here now, Master John.'

'How do you manage him? For it must be you who keeps the peace and calms him.'

'The apothecary keeps me supplied with laudanum and such concoctions that make him quiet, but the trouble first came not from the head, and it gets worse as he grows old.' She picked up her pot of beeswax and polishing cloths.

'Put that down, Ellen,' he said, and took the pot of thick yellow wax from her hand. 'I have been away in Italy and France and met many men who spoke of such conditions. I went with no whores from the stews as some of my companions did, so unless I have bad blood in my veins I am clean.'

She sensed his concealed anxiety and met his glance. 'You are clean,' she said simply. 'I can swear that you have nothing bad from him except for your temper,' she added with a half smile. 'It is right that you must know that if you are set upon wooing Mistress Hannam from Southampton.'

''Sdeath! How did you know?'

'How could I not know when I nursed you from a babe? You are right to conclude that your father caught a disease from a whore, but it was after you were born and before your poor mother had tainted births which meant that you have no siblings.'

'What will become of him?'

She shrugged. 'God alone will know that, but we must care for him and keep him safe, and now that you are here, there can be no more injustice.'

'No injustice?' The young voice was hard. 'What of the old customs that he says are his right? He flogs men if they anger him and he talks of his *droit de seigneur* which surely died years ago.'

Ellen dropped a cloth on the floor and bent to pick it up, but found her face close to his as he bent at the same time. He took her by the shoulders and shook her. 'I know nothing of that,' she said, with a sullen set to her mouth.

'You lie, my sweet Ellen. You do know of what happened here.'

'I was away and heard something when I returned from Portsmouth where my sister was ill,' she admitted.

He pulled her to her feet and sat her on one of the huge leather benches by the fire. He towered above her and she was aware of his strength and vigour and the latent passion in his eyes. 'Tell me,' he commanded.

'It was last May and Abigail Spence was to be wed,' she said in a low voice. 'The master saw her milking, wearing little more than a shift in the heat and it was as if she lit a fire in him that had long been spent. He told her to come to the manor for a wedding gift, but to come at night the day before the wedding as he had given nothing to the last two brides in the village and he wanted only her to know to avoid envy.'

She bit her lip and John moved impatiently. 'Go on, tell me.'

'When I came back, two days after, Abigail's mother came here and said she was going to speak to the sheriff, but I persuaded her to say nothing as the master had lapsed into childishness again and I knew that he would take away their cottage and their livelihood if she crossed him.'

'Tell me.'

'Abigail obeyed him thinking that she would receive a gift of linen or money, and her mother made her wear her second-best gown. She walked up to the manor in the dusk, saying to her friend who wanted to walk with her that she had been asked to collect fruit for the wedding. When she arrived, the steward let her into the great hall and went away. Sir William was alone. He took her into his bedchamber in the dark and took away her maidenhead, saying it was his right to sleep with any bride in his lands on the night before she married. He told her that it happened everywhere and the girl must look on this deflowering as an honour done to her.

'What of her husband?'

'Abigail was too confused and frightened to say anything at first and they married the next day before he knew what had happened. He took her to bed thinking that she was a virgin, but when he found out, he swore to avenge the violation of his right and had to be restrained.'

'And as I recall,' John said sternly, 'Abigail aborted a monster in September, her husband left for the New World without her, and she is a burden on the parish.'

'I give her what I can,' Ellen said defensively. 'And it was a custom that had roots long before my time; sometimes for good, as they say it often gave good blood to poor families in times of famine and sickness.'

'And more often gave profligates an excuse to slake their lusts on innocent maidens.'

'And have you never taken a girl for your pleasure, sir?' Ellen was indignant.

'Often, but always in sport when the girl was willing and it was for her a pleasure rather than a quick act of horror.' He looked at her with serious blue eyes and she believed him, but wondered, if he wanted a woman, could any refuse him? 'It is good to know that I carry no taint and I must make sure that he spreads nothing more to any who are healthy.'

Ellen absentmindedly scraped away the wax that John had spread on the table edge and rubbed the spot until it shone. She looked up and found that he watched her and showed no sign of leaving.

'Does Mistress Judith expect you, sir?' she asked. 'It's a long ride to Southampton and there's rain in the air.'

'I think I'll stay. The nag is not fit and Mistress Hannam will wait and give me credit for hard work at my father's bidding.'

Ellen's eyes teased him. 'You should take the coach and stay dry. So slow to go a-wooing? No hot blood that pants for a sweetheart's kiss?'

He moved restlessly about the room and thrust a log on to the now blazing fire. He grinned and seized her firmly, planting a kiss on her cheek. 'How can I go when you are so tasty?' he asked. 'Do you recall giving me fresh bread with thick beef drippings and salt when I was a hungry boy? In Italy I hungered for your bread and for the quince preserve you keep hidden away.'

Ellen blushed and tried to sound severe. 'So it was your fingers in that pot last week? I blamed the scullery maid and brought her to tears over it.' She looked out at the now leaden sky. 'Raining at last and the fields need the rain, but young men take no harm from a little shower when they are in love.'

'That can wait.' He sighed. 'Marriage comes soon enough and binds a man down.'

'She is comely and rich and plays pretty

music,' Ellen said lightly.

'She rides badly and plies a needle all day and knows no books or pictures in which I found an interest when I was abroad.'

Ellen sniffed. 'If she had two heads and you wanted her, you would see only beauty,' she said, drily.

'I shall marry her and she shall give me pretty heirs to fill the gap if I die, when our family would have no male to take over the manor.'

'And when is it to be, your marriage? Before your father loses his senses completely and the use of his legs too, if he follows the path of others I have seen?'

'Soon enough,' he said. 'Tell me the gossip and of any bad deeds that they put at my father's door.' He frowned. 'Tell me if there are weddings in the offing. He must never use his power like that again. People in the village have lost their trust in me and my family and I hear nothing.'

'There is one to be at Easter. Do you remember my little niece, Hope Clarke? She will be safe enough. She is betrothed to Edward Fletcher, a young man she has known since childhood. You may know him too?'

'Is that possible? Hope was a fairy child who played tricks on me and rode a donkey as if she was glued to his back.' He smiled. 'I haven't seen her on any of my visits since

I came back. It must be four or five years now so she must have grown beyond recognizing. How does she look?'

Ellen's face was full of pride. 'She is well grown and good and will make a good wife.'

'Poor little elfin child. She will marry and bear countless children and lose her magic,' he said softly.

'She is not a child,' Ellen said indignantly. 'She knows what she must do and she will be happy in her duties.'

'Must do? It sounds like my own plans,' he murmured, then tensed his hands as a voice from the wide stairway came to them, querulous and shaking. 'Does he know? Tell me woman, does he know that Hope is to be married?' John's urgent whisper made her heart ache as she stared up at the dishevelled form that descended slowly to the great hall.

'I have not told him,' she said, 'but he knows from the steward who tells him everything. He will not hold his tongue if there is scandal or hardship over which they can laugh, but she will be safe, I swear.'

'Wine!' called the lord of the manor and slumped into the creaking leather chair. 'You here, boy? Do we expect guests? You look as fine as a court popinjay, if you count Oliver as your example.'

'I was to visit Mistress Hannam in Southampton but the weather turned foul

15

and I have a lame horse,' he said.

'You'll get little pleasure from that yard of pump water. Is there no woman in the village to take to bed?'

'I take no whores, Father.'

'Perhaps not, but there are other ways,' he said slyly. He slurped the wine that the boy brought and poured for him and Ellen left the room to see to her kitchen. It was sad to see the man who had ruled the Manor of Deerwood for the whole of his adult life come to his degradation of body and spirit.

She remembered the old days when his wife was alive and young and the house was bright with company and laughter. Little Hope Clarke had stayed with Ellen at the manor when her mother had new babies and had been petted and indulged by everyone from Sir William to the lowest servant, but now it was as well that Hope lived on the other side of the village and seldom came near the manor.

She selected lavender-scented linen for the guest rooms and sent the girl to sweep the staircases while the master was in the hall and couldn't complain of the dust. She knew that she must call on the apothecary if Sir William was to be fit to receive the guests that his son had invited from London.

She unlocked her medicine chest and saw that she needed more laudanum. The basket of dried leaves and flowers of the Holy thistle were low and she knew that she must gather fresh for the next year if she was to continue treating the venereal disease that ate away a man and turned his brain. The elderflowers would be out and together with ginger, peppermint and the Holy thistle, she could make a decoction that would help the aches and pains in his joints and make the disease less rampant.

Ellen gave orders to the servants and pulled on a warm cloak against the after-rain chill before starting out along the muddy lane to the village. The apothecary asked after Sir William and suggested poultices of wood sage to treat his leg ulcers and agreed that the Holy thistle was best to avert the giddiness and fever that beset Sir William from time to time.

'I must send someone to gather the herb while it is young and in flower,' she said. 'Hope gathered it for me last year and knows where it grows in profusion on the banks of the stream that is salt from the tide, so she may do so now and I can dry it for the coming months.'

She went on to visit friends and to hear the latest gossip, avoiding the cleric who wanted to visit the lord of the manor and could never be sure if he was welcome. This is not the time, she thought, recalling the unkempt and wild look that she had seen that morning. He would shout at the priest and tell him to take away his canting nonsense.

The cottage gardens were blossoming with spring flowers and soft green shoots promised a good crop of fresh vegetables, but one plot remained undug and barren and the cottage windows stared blindly from unheated rooms. No smoke came from the chimney and the air of desolation was complete as if the house was deserted.

'Mistress Turner!' She paused to look back and saw Sarah Rogers at the open door. Ellen was tempted to walk on as if she had heard nothing, but in spite of Sarah being the village whore, Ellen was sorry for her as she had nearly starved during the last cold winter when the worthy men of the parish, most of whom had used her body in the past, now decreed that she was no longer fit to receive parish relief.

'No fire, Sarah? There's kindling in the woods and enough offcuts to keep you warm, free for all,' she said, sharply.

'I had a fever and Bessie brought wet green wood that wouldn't catch fire, but today I am better and can show her what to carry.'

'No food or heat and no parish relief? What can become of you, Sarah? Has your man deserted you? Do you still pleasure men?' In spite of her revulsion she was worried, knowing that Sarah had one talent only and her looks were fading fast and with

18

them her living and the wellbeing of her simple-minded daughter.

'Bessie is all I have, Mistress Turner. The man I had living here who paid me a little for food and lodging, tried to take Bessie to bed and I turned him out, but now I wish he had stayed,' she said bitterly. 'Bessie knows nothing of such things and could earn her living as I do.' She gave a harsh laugh. 'Being without her wits might be better as she could carry no tales to the wives of men who come to her in darkness, and she is pretty, with light hair that falls about her in a tangle of curls.'

'Come to the back door of the kitchens and say that I promised you scraps,' Ellen said. 'Bring a bag and a dish and make a fire before tonight or you will have another fever.'

She went on to the home of her sister, Margaret Clarke, and sat comfortably by her bright fireside, sipping warm ale. 'It isn't far from Easter now,' Margaret said. 'I shall be glad when the wedding is over and I know my daughter is safe.'

'What do you mean?' Ellen asked sharply, as she had tried to keep Margaret from hearing about Abigail.

'Men look at her with lust and she grows prettier with each day and laughs with them as if she is fancy free. Once she is married, she will be safe from such people and made

19

sober with household duties and soon a baby. That will steady them both into a real acceptance of what life is about,' she said, severely.

'Have they a cottage?'

'There is one that needs a lot of work done but Edward is a carpenter and can do that between his own work.' She looked cross. 'He has not started yet and talks of living away from the village. Ever since his cousin went to the New World, he has been restless and talked of nothing but the fine life he has over in America. He has heard no news of him so how can he know if he lives or dies there and if there is work?'

'They have to pay for land,' said Ellen. 'They need ten pounds for a plot of land and wood to build a house and more for a family, so rest your mind, they can not raise that amount for at least five years even if they live frugally. I would miss Hope if she went away but the young must go where they please.'

'Aunt Ellen!' Hope burst into the room and flung her arms round her aunt.

'Don't strangle me, Girl!' Ellen adjusted her cap and smiled. 'I came to see you,' she said. 'I need more of that thistle with the yellow flower that you picked for me last year. The apothecary says that it is nearly ready for picking and drying and you could bring me some from the dunes before the wedding. It doesn't cure the master but it helps keep the disease under control and makes him less angry.'

'You need it picked in sunlight, Aunt, but there will be time if the weather clears for two days.' She laughed and flung back the thick mane of bright gold hair that shone in the firelight like an answering flame. 'It shall be my last gift to you before I am married and lose my virginity.'

'And I shall give you bed linen and some money on the day. Have you a nest made for your wedding night?'

Hope eyed her pensively. 'There is a bed,' she said. 'There are pots and pans and buckets and everything that mother tells me I must have and Edward has ordered a clutch of hens and a pig.'

'You are marrying a good man, Hope,' her mother said reproachfully. 'You will never want if you have him by your side. Craftsmen like him are sure of employment whatever happens to the country and who-ever reigns.'

'King Charles has brought back better times and you can enjoy fairs and the maypole and things forbidden us under Cromwell,' Ellen said.

'He allows far too much.' Margaret pursed her lips. 'It is well known that he fathers bastards and makes no secret of it, giving them royal titles and lands to their mothers.

The church does nothing to stop him.'

'London sounds exciting,' Hope said, to her mother's annoyance. 'Perhaps Edward should take me there and work for the wealthy where we can make a fortune and buy land of our own.'

'It is a wicked place and not for you, my girl!'

'Soon, Mother, I shall be a married woman with a home of my own and not be just your girl.' She laughed. 'Aunt Ellen, Mother thinks I am in danger every time I leave the cottage. There are wicked men behind every bush and bears that will tear me to pieces, so she wants to be rid of me.'

The door rattled and rain began again in hard hurried drops. 'No herb picking today,' Ellen said. She looked out of the window at the muddy path and the grey sky. 'Master John was going to see his betrothed today in Southampton but his horse went lame. He would have been soaked by now if he came home through this,' Ellen said.

'John Halben? It's years since I saw him except in the carriage one day last summer when he came from London, but he didn't see me,' Hope said.

'*Master* John,' her mother corrected her. 'You are not children fighting over a donkey ride now. He is a very rich and powerful man ready to take over the manor when his father is past caring for it, and marrying into one of the best families in Hampshire.'

'I must go back to see what that empty head in the kitchen has done to the rabbits for dinner,' said Ellen. 'I prepared them but I said she must baste them and make sure they don't dry out over too much fire before I make the dumplings.'

A shadow crossed the narrow window and hurried footsteps splashed through the mud. 'It's the coach from the manor,' Margaret said, smoothing down her apron and blushing with excitement. 'Hope, tidy your hair. Tie it back in some order like a good girl and cast your eyes down. Master Halben is coming through the garden.'

Ellen threw the door wide before John could knock and he hurried inside, shaking the rain from his cloak. 'I heard that you were here, Ellen, and brought myself here to fetch you before your kitchen goes up in smoke!' Ellen gasped and made for the door. He laughed. 'Have no fear, your new kitchen maid does as you tell her and the smells from the pots are very good, but a drowned housekeeper would not do this evening as I expect my guests to arrive in time for wine and late supper, so we need dinner early.'

He looked at Margaret and smiled a greeting, then turned to the girl sitting by the hearth, the firelight on her hair, her straight back dignified and still. The hair

23

that was her mother's despair lay unbraided down over her shoulders and John caught his breath. 'It can't be,' he said slowly. 'I can't believe that the child I knew could grow up so … well.'

'She is to be married at Easter,' Margaret said quickly, as she saw the barely concealed admiration in his eyes.

'So I heard,' he said. 'I also am to be wed, madam, so we both join the ranks of the sober and godly.' A slightly ironic smile made Hope look away. 'Come, Ellen, you shall ride back in style. Good day, ladies.' He caught Hope by the hand and kissed it. 'Your husband will be a very lucky man,' he said. 'Will you wish me joy, too?'

'I wish you joy,' Hope said, but the words were stilted as if her tongue refused to mouth them. She watched the coach leave through the pouring rain and turned away to the fire, the hand that he had kissed resting against her cheek.

Chapter 2

'Who is that?' John Halben turned to stare out of the coach at the two women walking towards the manor along the driveway. 'Do they work in the house?'

24

'That's Sarah Rogers and her girl,' Ellen said primly. 'I told Sarah to come to the back door for scraps and a bit of board to keep the wind out of their cottage.'

'Scraps?' John looked back again, as the coach turned to follow the wider path away from the lane leading to the back regions of the manor. 'The woman is sick, Ellen. Look at the way she walks as if every step is an effort. Why does she have to beg in this village? The girl looks healthy enough to work even if her mother is weak.'

'The girl is simple-minded and can't work unless watched, and Sarah has had a fever,' Ellen said, as if that settled it.

'Sarah Rogers? I remember now. When I was a boy, my father tried to make me use her to get experience of women, but I never fancied bedding a woman who stank of other men. Poor Sarah, has she sunk so far? What of the parish? They give to the poor so why does she beg?'

'They'll give her nothing more, and her lodger has left so she has no money.'

His face darkened. 'In Holland, I found that they care better and have hospices for the sick and poor, better than any we have here. They never drive the vagrants from parish to parish to be rid of them as we do here, which only leads them into thieving, but it they are strong, they make them work for an honest living and pay them to survive.

25

If they can do little, they have alms. Does my father know?'

'He says a woman like her can earn her living be she sick or well. I have to make sure he hears nothing of her visits to the kitchens, so I'd be obliged if you say nothing too, Master John.'

'I'll speak to the parish council and make them pay her what she is due and find who stopped her help.' He shrugged. 'What she does for a living is her business and the girl will follow her, I suppose,' he added with casual indifference. 'But now, she needs food or she'll be a further burden on the parish.'

'Yes, Sarah said that Bessie will follow her and become like her and earn enough to keep them both. She is gentle and does as Sarah tells her,' Ellen agreed.

He tapped the roof to make the coachman stop at the main entrance so that Ellen could go to her rooms before descending to the kitchens. 'Give them food and this,' he said, handing Ellen a few coins. 'Tell her that I will see she doesn't starve.' He laughed. 'She does provide a service that can't be had any nearer than Southampton and the men need her, but I don't want to be repaid in kind!'

'No, I doubt if Mistress Hannam would like that,' Ellen said and clambered down from the coach. She went to take off her muddy wooden pattens and change her shoes and hang her cloak to dry before she went into the kitchen.

Sarah was talking to the kitchen maid who seemed reluctant to give her anything. 'You say that Mistress Turner gave you leave but she isn't here and has been away all morning.'

Bessie edged closer to the roaring fire and Sarah unfastened the shabby cloak that hid even shabbier clothes. Ellen noticed that Bessie at least was warmly clad and had a better dress than her mother. 'Give them both good thick broth and bread and make up a parcel of scraps,' Ellen said shortly to the kitchen maid. 'Don't look sullen, just do as you are told and be thankful you have a warm roof over your head.'

The girl turned away to the fire and the cauldron of soup simmering over the red ashes and Ellen pressed the money into Sarah's hand, whispering 'Say nothing of this or Sir William would be angry, but Master John sent it. He saw you from the coach and said he'll speak to the parish about you.'

Sarah gasped with surprise, but shut her mouth when the kitchen maid came with the steaming bowls of thick soup and hunks of rye bread. Bessie said nothing but grunted with pleasure as she tasted the soup and attacked the bread as if she was a starving animal.

'Bessie is really quite pretty, or would be if she had a good wash,' Ellen said.

'I keep her like this until she is ready to work, to keep men from sniffing around,' Sarah said. 'Then, when she is ready I'll wash her hair and make her put on the red dress that you gave me last year, mistress. It will fit her well.' She ate more slowly now and a little colour tinged her cheeks. She looked at her daughter as if appraising a farmyard pig ready for market. 'I want a good price for her the first time and the gentry like a fresh girl who is free of the pox. When I am stronger, I shall ask in Southampton and she can go to the highest bidder.' She sighed. 'I thought she would be a millstone round my neck for the rest of my life, but now she may well be the breadwinner.'

'How can you let her go to just anyone who pays?'

'It's what I had to do. My mother died and my father put me to work as soon as the breath was from her body. I was younger than Bessie,' she said, harshly. 'I was frightened at first but you get used to men and their ways. The likes of us can't choose what we do, mistress.' She tried to look unconcerned. 'They might as well pay for Bessie. I saved her in time from my lodger who wanted her for nothing and who she liked well enough, and there have been others who tried to take her into the hay, so as soon as I feel better, we'll go to Southampton. I can stay with my sister there for a few days until Bessie finds favour and we take a room, or until we have to come back here on the parish again.'

Bessie scraped her dish and smiled. 'Good,' she said. 'More.'

'No more or you'll be sick,' Sarah said. She glanced towards the closed door leading to the main part of the house. 'We'll go now, mistress. We can go by the lane at the back of the midden and no one will see us. Put on your cloak, Bessie; we're going now.' She caught up the bundle of stale bread and scraps of meat and tugged at Bessie's hand to make her follow her, which she did submissively, although she looked back into the warm kitchen with a frown as if she couldn't understand why she had to leave.

'Stop at the bothy and tell the carpenter that you want a piece of board and some sacking for your window. You'll have no trouble from him. He is to marry my niece at Easter and he is a good man.'

Sarah left the kitchen and the lane took them round in a semi-circle to the workmen's huts and the long bothy at the edge of the burgeoning copse where the main work of the carpenter and mason was being done.

29

Bessie sat on the soft pile of sawdust and smiled, running her fingers through the dry powdered wood as if she was a child on a sand dune. The smell of freshly cut wood and the sap from the knots of pine took away the dusty odour from the mason's bench. The carpenter put down his tools when he saw Sarah.

'What brings you here, Sarah? The master is about again and in a fine old tear so it's no use you coming here to put the men off their work!'

'I've been to the kitchen and Mistress Turner gave us food and said we could ask for wood and sacking to put in the window of my cottage. The wind comes in cruelly and I've had a fever.'

'What size is it?' She shook her head and he grinned. 'I can't help you unless I know the size,' he replied patiently. He raised his head. 'The steward is coming this way and he tells the master everything, so you'd best be away before he sees you. I'll bring wood and a saw. Go by the back way through the copse and be quick.'

'You will come, Mr Fletcher?'

'I'll come,' he said, kindly. He thrust a bundle of wood into Bessie's arms. 'That will keep the place warm until I can come,' he added, and went back to his work.

'The master wants the new stools for tonight,' the steward said, as he leaned on the door lintel. He looked round the bothy and seemed disappointed. 'Just the two of you here?' he asked.

'Yes.' Edward Fletcher's voice was nearly lost as he began to saw a plank of wood vigorously. 'The boy had to take a horse to the farrier and then the master wanted more fires laid in the other rooms for tonight.'

'I don't mean the boy.'

'We have no other help since Sir William sent Dick away last week.' Edward stopped sawing and fixed the steward with ill-concealed aggression. 'Dick is an honest man and now I am without a real craftsman. Perhaps you'd like to help me finish the stools, Mr Furness, as it was you who told the master tales about him and made him leave.' He blew away the sawdust.

'You must never talk to me like that,' the steward said. 'I'll tell Sir William that you are insolent.'

'Tell him this.' Edward walked slowly towards the steward holding a pointed awl in his hand. 'Tell him that when you drove him away, Dick was taken on for better pay and under a considerate master and is better off away from this mad house! I am a freeman like him and more skilled, so you can do nothing to me. If Sir William hears tales about me and I leave for work in Southampton, as I can if I must, then you'll be the one to bear the brunt of his anger if

31

he's left without workers.'

The steward looked at the hard set of the young man's jaw and backed away. 'You mind what you say and get on with your work,' he said, weakly. 'You can't afford to leave now that you are to be wed this Easter. Your bride is from this village and wouldn't thank you for taking her among strangers, and you'll need the eyes of people who know her, to tell you what she does when you work.'

'My wife will follow where I say,' Edward replied firmly. 'I've known her all my life and know her to be honest, chaste and true.' The pride in his voice was obvious and Furness smiled derisively.

'Is any woman such an angel?' he said, but he left hurriedly, eyeing the angry man with apprehension.

'That one thinks he knows it all,' said the mason, who had been listening. 'Sarah just about got away in time, but Furness has only to see her once on manor land and she'll be turned out of her cottage and out of the village.'

'He isn't as powerful as he thinks,' Edward said. 'Now the young master is home he has to back down a bit and say less that stirs up trouble. Master John is his father's son in some ways and brooks no trouble from stewards. You must remember he lived here all his life until he went away on the tour and he likes the people.'

'That's more than most of the village feel towards him now,' the mason said. 'They think he might be like his father in other ways and they lock up their daughters when he's around.'

'He's a good man.' Edward squinted along a plank to see that the edge was even. 'If I didn't think I had a future here, I'd be off to the New World tomorrow.'

'How could you? That takes money for land and stock when you get there, and they ask a lot of questions before they take on hands at Southampton, now that the first settlers have made homes and planted crops over there. It will be easier now for latecomers and many want to emigrate, so they can pick and choose who they take.'

'I could go if I wanted it. I'm not a deck hand. Mind you, we'd have to save a bit first, but my trade would take me anywhere,' he added with pride. 'They have plenty of unskilled labour but need more craftsmen.' He laughed. 'When the Pilgrim Fathers set out from Plymouth and arrived in the New World in 1620, only a few years back from now, they were far too green and half of them died. They prayed a lot for help but forgot to take nails and hammers and saws and all the other things they needed to make houses and took few skilled men. They left Holland and Plymouth in late

33

autumn and had to survive the first terrible winter there with little comfort and hardly any food, but now the settlers who go there have learned a lot more from the first failures.'

He shook his head in disbelief. 'I heard that the second batch went out with nothing, as if it would be easy living and the Good Lord would provide for them, but it was hard to find food for an extra thirty or more families, and it led to discontent. Now they take supplies and men who come from working backgrounds, instead of idle churchmen with plenty of religious zeal but no trade. They may not be so holy but they do take provisions and go when the weather is good, to get started in the warm and dry.'

'You ain't a religious man, Mr Fletcher, so how would you fit in? A lot of the Pilgrims were stiff-necked and so had to flee this country because they stuck to their own rigid rules of observance.'

'Plimoth isn't the only settlement. There were others before the Fathers went over, but they live in other parts of New England and a place called New Hampshire. If the names mean they are like here, I could fit in all right. There are ships leaving for America nearly every month now in summer as trade picks up and we exchange cloth and bricks for deerskins, corn and the like.'

'You'd never go?'

Edward glanced out through the open doorway as if suspecting that the steward had lingered to overhear what was being said then, satisfied, he said in a low voice, 'I've been over Southampton way a few times and I've sold a nice few wooden boxes such as ladies like to have to put their fripperies in, safe and sound. I sometimes speak to the sailors and they tell me things that make me wish I could go to America.'

The mason grinned. 'I've talked with them too and believe half of what they say as it sounds too far fetched. It's a wonder I didn't see you! I was there last Sunday, taking small stone crosses and mortars for grinding spices for my sister to sell to the women in the market. I was going to ask if you can make a few small wooden handles with a nice shine on them to fit the stone pestles that go with the bowls and do the grinding.'

Edward laughed. 'Maybe we should set up our own stall and leave His Lordship and all his cronies to stew in their own juice.'

'You'd have to go away to do that, and I don't want to leave the village or my family.'

'Wouldn't worry me.'

'You are going to be wed, lad, and from what I know of your bride, she would have a say in what you do or don't do. She's been born and bred here and is a part of the village, and from what I hear she has a will of her own. Have you ever really crossed her?' He grinned. 'She can hold her own with anyone. My Mary saw her in a temper once.'

'There's been no call for that. We've grown up together and it seemed right that we should marry.' He shrugged. 'We're easy together and fond too, and we know each other's ways. I started making a bride box for her things three years ago and I've made another for my things, lined with cedar to keep out the moth in case we ever want to wander far.' He turned back to his workbench. 'I'll have to leave making trinket boxes as the cottage I've taken needs a lot of work doing and Hope wants things neat, but I'll go along tonight to Sarah and fix that window. Poor slut, she'll die of ague if she doesn't keep out the cold.'

'Best tell Hope where you are and for what purpose. It doesn't do to visit a woman like that unless you want something from her.' The mason grinned. 'If Hope heard where you were spending the evening, she might think you'm getting in a bit of practice.'

'Hope knows that I would never go with Sarah any more than she would go with any other man, either before or after we marry,' he said with pride.

'Some girls are forced to,' the mason said.

'Not Hope. I'd kill the man who took her like that.' His face showed deep emotion. 'Abigail should have been protected, but when it happened, her husband should have avenged her.'

'Against the lord of the manor?'

'Against the highest in the land if need be,' Edward said, firmly. 'The master was wrong by law if not by custom, and should have gone to the pillory.' He tapped the last wooden peg into place and stood the sturdy stool on the ground by the other three that he'd completed.

'That's good and strong.' The mason sat on one and admired the mitred seat of another. 'That should last a lifetime if the master doesn't toss it on the fire when he's in his drink.'

'He wanted six but he'll have to wait for the rest now that Dick isn't here. I'd best take them up to the hall and see if the boy has tended the fires.' Edward Fletcher piled them on the cart and pushed it up to the front steps of the manor. The terrace was empty and he heaved one heavy stool on to his back and walked slowly in though the wide entrance to the hall. The oak door that had hung there for at least a hundred years swung back easily and he propped it back. By the time he had brought in three stools he was breathing hard and sat on one to catch his breath.

'I finished bringing in wood,' the boy said, putting the last log on the pile by the hearth. 'Did you want me to help with the stools?'

'About time you came back,' grumbled Edward, looking up. 'You can help with the last one. I made them too good and heavy but once in place they'll grace the hall well.'

They manhandled the last stool into place and shifted the others to form a wide circle around the fireplace. 'They'll seat two each or even three at a pinch,' Edward said with pride. 'It was Master John who wanted them but his father agreed, so everyone should be happy.'

'They've company tonight,' the boy said. 'Mistress Turner has a hind on the spit and said I'll have to take an hour or so basting it if you can spare me.'

'You can go,' Edward said. 'I have to be away on an errand and I've finished in the bothy for today.' He grinned. 'Don't eat too much in the kitchen and keep your hands off Deb or she'll box your ears like she did at Christmas.'

'She likes me,' the boy said complacently. 'I give her warning when Sir William is about so she can hide. He tried to fumble her when she took him wine and she was frightened. Now, Mistress Turner makes me take him his wine and his water for washing.'

'Be quiet and get down to the kitchen,' Edward said. 'Sir William is coming down the stairs.'

'That's fine work,' Sir William said. He sat

on one of the new stools and ran his hand under the seat. 'As smooth a bottom as I've ever felt,' he said, laughing, and Edward knew that he was half drunk but as yet merry and had not reached the stage when he might be bad-tempered.

'There will be two more next week, sir, but without Dick I am short of skilled hands.'

'Dick?' Sir William sounded as if he had never heard of the man. 'Dick?'

'The freeman who worked with me after he gained his guild certificate last winter. The steward had him dismissed and now I can do only half the work needed for the manor, sir.'

'Thief, was he?'

'No, Sir William, he was as honest as the day is long and now works in Southampton in the boatyards.'

'He had no right to leave me! Get him back!'

Edward smothered a smile. 'The steward got rid of him so he must see to that, sir.'

Sir William peered at him, his eyes rimmed with red and the lids gummy. 'You are Fletcher,' he said with an air of triumph that he remembered his name.

'Yes, sir.'

'And you are to marry the niece of my good housekeeper and nurse.'

'Yes, Sir William,' Edward said, and wished he had merely passed the time of day with his master instead of bringing his attention on himself more closely.

'Pretty is she? I've seen nothing of her family for years, but I remember her as a skinny little filly with a mop of hair.'

'She's well grown,' Edward said, shortly.

'I must see her and give her a present for the wedding,' Sir William said. His eyes were crafty as if he enjoyed what he was thinking and knew that no one could read his mind.

'She is busy helping her mother with the preparations and sewing her wedding dress,' Edward said. 'She will be pleased to hear that you send her good wishes for the future.'

Edward gave a sigh of relief as he saw John Halben standing behind Sir William listening to every word he spoke. They exchanged glances and John jerked his head towards the door to indicate that Edward should leave.

Edward paused outside the open door and heard raised voices, one strong and firm and the other bad-tempered and querulous like a child deprived of a favourite toy, but he could make out none of the words.

In the driveway, he stopped and turned sharply in the direction of the kitchens. Ellen looked hot and the boy stood as far away from the roasting hind as was possible while basting it with fat from the trough under it. His leather apron, usually his protection from dirt in the bothy, was splattered with cooking juices and red patches showed where hot fat had spurted on to his hands. Ellen looked only half pleased to see the man enter the kitchen.

'If you want the boy, you can have him in half an hour or so,' she said.

'It's not that,' Edward said. 'Will there be enough wood for all the fires?'

'Sir William likes to be warm, but the others will find it too hot as the weather has gone quite mild.' She took loaves from the bread oven, thrusting in the wooden paddle and bringing out the crusty bread with the expertise of years. 'I could do with more help tonight but I must make do,' she grumbled. 'Hope might have been useful, but I don't want her here just now.' She gave Edward a searching glance then went on with her work.

'Keep the boy if he's of use,' he said. 'I'll make sure that Hope keeps away while the gentry are here.'

'And keep her away until after the wedding,' Ellen said in a low voice. 'The master has sent for a woman from Southampton who knows his ways, but I worry about him and his state of mind. He has the same look about him as he had before he took Abigail.'

Edward clenched his hands and his face

41

was grim. 'If he touched Hope, I'd kill him,' he said.

'And go to the gallows? You'd leave her with nothing but the pain, Edward.'

'Why doesn't he use Sarah? There are plenty of other women to buy.'

'He hates Sarah as he thinks he caught his disease from her years ago and Bessie might be his. That's why they are not allowed on manor land.'

'I'll go back through the village and ask the Widow More to help you, Ellen, but first I'll see to Sarah's window.'

Edward walked slowly back to his work-bench and selected a few pieces of wood and sacking, then added a piece of glass and some putty he had left from glazing the windows in the new guest rooms that John Halben had insisted were necessary if he was to live at Deerwood Manor for any length of time. He loaded the two-wheeled cart and set off for Sarah's cottage, oblivious to the mild evening and the sound of birds from the copse.

He thought back to his childhood. Hope had been a part of his life even then, and as they grew up they played together, rode the farm horses on Hope's yeoman father's land together and their families took it for granted that they would marry and live the rest of their lives together. When had easy friendship and liking changed for him to a deep and protective love? He pulled the cart over a tree root and picked up the bundle of kindling that had fallen off.

Hope had agreed to the wedding, but seemed in no hurry to be bound to him. He frowned, admitting to himself that he was more concerned that she should meet no other young men at the manor than about his passing fears that Sir William might try to claim the illegal right of the lord of the manor. She was fond of him as she had been since childhood, laughing with him, hugging him and now enjoying his kisses, but there was a kind of innocence still untouched, a feeling that she had yet to be awakened to the pleasures of the flesh.

Edward called a greeting to a girl he knew slightly, a friend of Hope's. She looked at him with bright come-hither eyes that showed clearly her feeling for him. I could take her if I wanted her, he thought with a quickening pulse. She may be a virgin but she knows what she wants. Hope's indifference to the fact that soon they would lie together and indulge in the full passion of marriage was confusing when he saw that other unmarried girls panted after any good-looking lad they met.

'Oh, thank you, Mr Fletcher,' Sarah said when she saw him. He gave the bundle of wood to Bessie who cut the straw binding and laid the sticks on the hearth where a small fire burned. Sarah put two chunks of cherrywood on the flames and Bessie sat on the floor with her hands out towards the glow. She made soft grunts of pleasure and smiled up at the man who had given her such warmth.

'Take no notice of her, Sarah said, sharply. 'She likes you. I think you could do anything with her, but you won't want that before your wedding, and in any case, you couldn't pay enough,' she added with an apologetic smile.

'Don't let them hurt her, Sarah.' Edward knew that his plea sounded false, as he was taking it for granted that Bessie would become a whore as her mother had done and she would suffer sooner or later.

Sarah shrugged. 'I see that you have some wood,' she said. 'How can I help?'

Edward measured the empty window and then the glass. 'If you have a slightly smaller window, I can use this glass,' he said. 'One piece of wood at the top and a sliver at the bottom to hold it and some good putty and you'll be warm and able to look out and have some light.' She lit a candle so that he could see in the darkening twilight and he had it done quickly.

He left the unused wood for the fire and the sacking to stuff into the gap under the door and pushed the cart along to his family cottage where Hope sat with his mother, sewing. She looked up, bit an end of cotton with her firm white teeth and smiled. He watched them from the doorway and wondered what it would be like to go away together, to sleep in his cottage and to make love. He looked away to hide the rising passion in his eyes. Not yet, he told himself. Not until we are wed in church, my love.

Hope sat calmly sewing and talking about the latest gossip in the village while Mrs Fletcher brought them warm ale and cheese and crusty bread. The finished shirt was folded and put in the box that Edward had made and kept in his mother's care until his own cottage was fit for habitation.

'That box is nearly full,' his mother said. 'You'll have enough linen to last you for years, both of you. Hope has filled her chest and it only needs you to get on with the cottage now, my son.' There was a hint of reproach in her voice as if he was not doing his share of the preparations for the future. 'Mistress Warren saw you fixing a window for Sarah Rogers when you could have been painting your own place.'

Hope looked amused. 'That couldn't have taken him long, and poor Sarah isn't a bad soul.'

Edward regarded her with a slightly puzzled air. Some girls would resent the betrothed spending time with a woman of ill-repute and might even suspect him of doing more than putting in a window. He smiled. Such trust was wonderful and it made him even more eager to set up house with her and shut the door against the world.

'Not long now,' his mother said, as if echoing his thoughts. 'Get that place ready and you'll be in clover.'

Hope refused more ale and said she must get back to her own mother. She thought for a moment. 'How is Aunt Ellen going to manage tonight with all those guests at the manor? I could help and sleep in her room if she needs me.'

'No!' Edward and his mother spoke together and Hope looked at them in amazement, then the dimples in her cheeks deepened.

'I'm going to ask the widow up the lane to help. She needs the money and is good with vegetables, or so Ellen says.' Edward spoke firmly, knowing that Hope hated washing root vegetables straight from the fields and caked with mud.

'It isn't that at all,' she teased him. 'You're afraid I might fancy one of the gentry and run off with him.'

'Don't talk like that. I'll take you home,' he said. Outside, he kissed her. 'The sooner we are wed the better I shall like it. I hate this waiting and wanting you.' His hands caressed her body and she shivered but he stood back and took her hand and walked with her under the stars, full of uneasy desires and the muted kind of happiness that goes with yearning.

Chapter 3

The last carriage swung from the long drive into the lane and disappeared between the young-leaved trees, the last horseman mounted and shouted his farewells and the remaining guests who were staying at Deerwood Manor sat down to drink the last of the wine.

John Halben shut the front door of the great hall and turned to watch the depleted company. The cousins from Winchester and the friends from London were gathered round the heavy oak table, the men drinking sack, the ladies spiced ale, and the dogs noisily chewing bones under the table among the rushes that had been strewn fresh that morning.

'No, I find it too heavy and it does nothing to slake my thirst,' John said, when his uncle held up the flagon of sack. He helped himself to ale and stood by the fireplace, his clear eyes reflecting the light from the burning logs. Firelight and a soft spring evening, he thought. How I longed for that when I was far away in noisy towns in Italy and shivering on board the ship that took me to New Hampshire, and how empty it seemed now, back in the shadow of a father who ruled like a tyrant and had such changes of mood that every man and woman who worked at the manor lived in trepidation of what he might decide to do next.

'You should drink sack at least once a day,' his uncle said, as if it was to him a great sacrifice to drink anything. 'All the best doctors say it is specific against the plague.'

John smiled. 'You may drink my share, Uncle,' he said. 'We'll see who gets the plague first. I cast my lot in with those who take exercise and drink ale and water and carry herbs when they go into crowded places, and I keep away from London.'

'In Winchester, just as they did in London, they killed the cats and dogs as they said they carry the distemper,' his uncle went on accusingly, as two dogs fought for the same bone under the table. 'We keep our gun dogs, but let none in the house as you do.' He eyed the visitors from London with suspicion, even though they lived far from the stews of the City of London and never needed to venture further into Westminster City than the village of Knightsbridge.

'We have no rats,' John said, shortly. 'I'm sure that they are unhealthy as they eat

grain and carrion and soil the food in store.'
He gave a lurcher bitch a friendly touch
with his boot as she lay by the fire. 'She's a
good ratter and a good companion and I
wouldn't part with her because someone in
a stuffy committee room who never
breathes country air says that rats do no
harm.'

'They have to blame something,' his aunt
said. 'The numbers of deaths in London
have risen again and the graveyards are full.
I will touch nothing that comes from
London, not even letters from my son who
works in the Navy Office. The girl wipes
them in vinegar before they are opened and
then again as they are unrolled.'

'That's wise,' John agreed. 'I have made
the gardeners grow more herbs and the
servants must wear them when they go to
Southampton and Portsmouth.'

'And you put the stinking bunches in my
chamber,' his father said in a sullen voice.

John regarded him with irritation and
anxiety seeing the return of the morose
humour that everyone in the house dreaded.
Surely tonight when his brother and sister-
in-law were there with their youngest son
and the small daughter who now sat
patiently by her mother, he would behave.
The embroidered waistcoat of green velvet
that had been new that evening was soaked
with spilled wine and now looked a rag with

patches of dull brown under the silken scarlet coat.

He had sneered at John's sober but elegant coat of brown woollen and his plain but spotless shirt and ruffs, accusing him of following the Puritans and wearing the garb beloved of Oliver Cromwell and his like. 'Or does your lady forbid any outward show of wealth, coming as she does from a family devoted to parsimony?' he'd said.

'I was saying,' John's aunt said with an air of reproof at her nephew's obvious inattention. 'I was asking when the wedding will be and what you will wear on that occasion; something to gladden the heart and eye, I hope.' She pulled the elaborate satin wrap closer over her lace collar and regarded her yellow silk shirt with satisfaction. 'Now that we have a king restored to us who sees nothing wicked in fine clothes, if is our duty to follow his example and show the world that we are not a poor relation of Europe any more. I confess that I longed for bright colours and music during the grey days of the Protectorate. There were times when I wore drab and felt I looked as humble as my maids.'

'You are right,' Sir William said. 'All society relaxes now and we may have good sport again.' He laughed and eyed the small girl with speculation. 'There are old customs that need reviving and next spring

I think the hobby horse might be permitted once more, with the maypole dances and the Morris Men.'

His sister-in-law drew the child closer to her and looked uneasy. 'There are some rites best left alone,' she said firmly. 'Merriment lights the spirits but sins of the flesh should remain forbidden.' She tugged the child's arm. 'Come, child, it is time that we retired. Ellen has put a truckle bed in my room for you where you will be safe and quiet.'

John smiled grimly. What will happen to him if I go away again? he asked himself, then pulled his thoughts together. How could he consider leaving the village when he was due to be married and to take over much of the management of the manor? The memory of salt winds and high seas and the sight of strange lands and people nagged at the back of his consciousness and he tried to shake away the desire to travel again.

His uncle sighed and belched. At least his sins were mostly of gluttony and not sex, but in many ways the brothers were alike, wanting their own way at all times and taking advantage of everyone working for them. He heaved himself to his feet and called for his manservant to help him up the stairs, his wig askew and his hose wrinkled.

John watched him go and turned to his

father. 'Do you need help, sir?'

'Not tonight. I shall sleep in the small ante-room by the door where I ordered a fire to be lit and the bed made.' He laughed almost hysterically. 'It sounds like a tryst, an affair of the heart but that is all gone. I am meeting my woman from Southampton and she can leave from that room without the whole house knowing that she came here.'

'There are no sconces for candles,' John said. 'And but a small window for light.'

'It is better so. There will be firelight but I want near darkness. I cannot see her and she cannot see me, but she satisfies me and her man will take her home afterwards.'

'I saw a strange nag by the barn,' John said. 'Ellen said that you have a visitor. I wish you good sport, sir.'

'Not as good as it will be soon,' Sir William muttered with a smile that was as warm as a winter lake.

'What do you mean?'

Sir William wagged a finger in his son's face. 'I rule this place and none may refuse me,' he said truculently. 'The age of glory is back again, my son. His Majesty sets a fine example of what we may do with our women and I value the old customs.' He bent forward, his foul breath making John turn away from his face. 'Have you ever taken a virgin? Have you ever felt the throb of fear and the warmth of unwilling limbs under your touch? Heard the soft weeping and yet nothing said because you have the power to turn her family away in penury?'

'That, sir, is rape if you force the daughter of a freeman or the child of a yeoman!'

'Call it what you will. I call it my right and when I choose, I shall take it,' he said petulantly.

'Already the village is angry over what happened to one girl. I have tried to rebuild the trust we have lost but people sidle away from me as if I was tarred with your brush, sir.' He clenched his hands. 'Old friends who knew me when I was a child now shut their doors and never give me time of day.'

'Not all.' The rheumy eyes were shrewd. 'My housekeeper who dotes on you, would never allow her family to refuse you anything.'

'She knows that I would never ask anything that they had no right to give,' John said simply.

'But she is in my house and owes me everything that she has in life.' He scowled. 'There are younger women who could serve here as well as Ellen and give me more.'

'What do you mean?'

'She never talks of her niece, as if the child is too plain to interest me, or too pretty to be let out alone. I do not like to be left out of her confidence, and I find her medicines tiresome. You have visited the house.'

It was a statement and John knew that the steward had seen him return with Ellen in the coach.

'Hope is to be married. She is the child of a yeoman with land of his own and the family enjoys the respect of all the village,' John said with feeling.

'Yes, she must be ripe for the picking.'

'But not by you, sir!'

'Why not! I could take her by force if she did not come willingly. Two men after dark on the eve of her wedding could bring her here without trouble, when the village is busy in preparation for the wedding, but that would never be necessary. A message to say that her aunt wanted her here would bring her quickly and alone, and the small room has a door leading out to the lane.'

He laughed again and slapped his son on the shoulder. 'You look alarmed, my son! I speak in jest with the longings of an old man who knows that all that warmth and youth is not for him.' He walked slowly to the door leading to the ante-room. 'I must take what I can tonight and imagine that she is comely and pure, and in the dark she will see no ugliness nor my ulcers and sores.'

John climbed the stairs and looked back over the gallery rail to the dimly lit hall. The proud coats of arms and ancient tapestries that graced the grey walls were dark and the dogs lay asleep by the half-dead ashes of the fire. Whatever happened in that small room would go unnoticed and the dogs would sleep on.

He moved restlessly on his bed and stared into darkness, unsure if his father had been speaking in jest or planning a vile abduction. Hope seemed to hover in his dreams, her hair fire-lit golden and her face serious and sweet. He sat up with an oath as he woke to the sound of a cat calling in heat under his window. 'He shall not! He shall never touch her,' he vowed.

The master is still asleep,' the boy said with a grin. 'You'd think a storm had hit the room, tossing the bed linen on the floor and the cushions all over the place.'

'Take him some ale and stay there until he wakes then tell him that his brother's family is leaving soon and would like to speak with him.' Ellen looked annoyed. 'And take that smirk off your face. The master had bad dreams and threshed about in bed,' she said primly.

'We all know what he gets up to in there,' the boy said, and ducked her hand as it tried to find his ear.

'You saw nothing and know nothing, or you'll be out of this house, my lad,' she said.

'Yes, mistress,' he replied with mock humility. 'I didn't see a man and a woman on one nag go in the early hours to take the road to Southampton.' Once again he dodged her hand and tapped on the door of the ante-room before vanishing inside with the jug of ale.

'Not ready?' Squire Halben looked at the longcase clock as it struck the hour of ten o'clock. 'He gets worse,' he grumbled. 'I want to borrow John for a few days to see some bloodstock I'm buying.'

'Must it be now, sir?' Ellen looked anxious.

'Why not now? John has time on his hands and I need an expert eye before I waste any money.' He called to his wife. 'We can't stay. The carriage is waiting and I have business to attend. Tell him I shall expect him the day after tomorrow in the afternoon.'

'But that's the day before my niece is wed, sir, and if he stays in Winchester he'll be away when she goes to church. He promised to be there.'

'My horseflesh is more important, madam,' he said shortly. 'Just make sure he has my message. I shall expect him.'

'Yes, sir,' Ellen said, and bobbed slightly to conceal her annoyance. She saw them leave and hurried upstairs to the room where John had made a study for himself and was lining the walls with books and manuscripts that he had brought back from his travels.

'What's amiss?' he said, with only half his attention.

'The squire asks if you will visit him to

look over horses that he wants to buy.'

'So why the anxious face, Ellen? I shall go willingly, next week or as soon as I have finished here.'

'He wants you, nay demands, that you go the day after tomorrow, Master John.'

'And miss the wedding? That is absurd.'

'I told him of that, but he grew angry and insisted that he would expect you that afternoon.'

'I see.' John Halben put the book he was holding on the escritoire and sat heavily on the tall scroll-backed chair by the table. 'This is an unhappy house, Ellen,' he said, slowly. 'None of us are safe while my father is as he is now. When I go to Winchester I shall see a lawyer and make my last testament and other matters that must be settled.'

'Master John! Are you ill?'

'No, just far-sighted enough to know that he will use everything in his power to have his way in all things.' He regarded Ellen with solemn concern. 'Even you, Ellen, must not feel safe if he is in one of his rages. He could dismiss you tomorrow if he wished, in spite of your long and loyal service.' He stood and walked away to gaze out of the window. 'Especially now.'

'Why now? I have lived with this fear for the past three years and yet I know he depends on me.' She tried to smile but the effort was poor and did nothing to deceive him.

'He has threatened you?'

'Often,' she replied calmly. 'But I recall the good days and the kindness of your mother, God rest her soul, and it makes me strong.'

'My mother was a very wise woman. She saw the way he would go and made over her estates to me during her lifetime in a way that he can never alter, although I believe he tried to turn it to his advantage while I was away. In Winchester, I shall make over the small house by the river to you, and enough money to pension you in your old age so that you will never want. There will be coppicing and commoners' rights and two fields to graze a cow and fowl.'

'Master John.' Her voice was husky and she could do no more than shake her head.

'You were as a second mother, Ellen, and my mother loved you. Now you are my care.' He laughed grimly. 'It is as well that I have means of my own as he threatens to disinherit me if I cross him further.'

'Why are you telling me this today?' Ellen's common sense reasserted itself.

'If I go to Winchester I cannot be at the wedding and I shall be away from here the day before.' He glanced at her set face. 'I see that you think as I do. Hope will not be safe from him and with me gone, he can do as he likes.'

'Not while I live and breathe!' she said.

'And for how long would you continue to live if you hurt him?'

'You must not go!'

'If I stay, after what he said to me, he will know I stay to protect her, so we must plan what to do.'

Ellen went to the door and pushed it wide open then, satisfied that there was no one on the gallery, she closed it tightly and returned to her chair. 'Tell me what to do,' she said.

'The day before the wedding, when I have gone, you must hint to the steward that you need·help with your gown for the wedding and you will ask Hope to come to the manor to fit you.'

'But that will put her in his power!'

'Listen. Hope must not come here. She can go to the cottage where she will live after her wedding and wait there until after midnight, when she can return home in safety on her wedding day. He would not take her on her wedding day as too many people would be close to her.'

'If she is not with me, he will search for her and send that ferret he calls a steward to bring her to him.'

'I shall buy him a virgin,' John said with a rueful smile. 'If it is a choice between Hope being deflowered and the virginity of a girl destined to be a whore, then Sarah's daughter must suffice.'

'He will know,' whispered Ellen.

'They are of a size and he has not seen Hope for months, perhaps years. If you wash the girl well and tend her hair, Bessie will smell sweet. She seldom utters a word and will do as Sarah bids her. In the dark, he will take her to bed and afterwards, when he is sleeping, Sarah can fetch her, using the door to the lane from the small room.'

'He will see her and know,' Ellen repeated.

'No. He knows that he is ugly and his body has wasted and he takes care to hide the ulcers that you dress on his legs. He is still a vain man who hides his body in fine clothes. So that even a whore must never laugh at his appearance, he uses them in the dark.'

'I must tell Edward Fletcher and he can stay with Hope in the cottage to protect her.'

'And have the village say that he took his bride before the wedding? If she stayed until after midnight, and Edward was there, he would see her on her wedding morning before he went to church, which would bode ill and carry a curse for their future.'

'I wish you were here to protect her,' Ellen said, 'but what you say makes sense and Sir William will think he is safe with you out of the way.'

'So what have you to do now, Ellen?' John asked in a loud voice. He pointed towards the door which had opened a crack.

For a moment, she looked startled, then smiled. 'I promised to make my special pies for the wedding feast and must bake them on the wedding eve as the weather is too mild to have them ready too early, even in a cold larder. I'll ask Hope to help me as she will have little to do that night and may be restless. My gown needs a hand to raise the hem as I find it too long for comfort and she is quick with the needle. She can come at dusk if her mother needs her before that time.'

'Wish her joy for me, Ellen. I shall be in Winchester but my thoughts will be here on that day. I must take a present to her today, but if she is not in her mother's cottage, I shall leave it there. It is too late to be made into a wedding gown but she will enjoy it later. I brought back silk from France and I have one length left after giving most to Mistress Hannam.'

'What colour is it, sir?'

'A light cool green with bird's-eye markings,' he said.

Ellen tried not to smile remembering the pale complexion of his future bride which would not take pale green happily.

A tap on the door and the steward came into the room. Ellen picked up her polishing cloth and left the two men, convinced that he had heard everything they had said since he lifted the latch on the door.

John Halben tried to conceal his impatience and distrust as they discussed matters of importance about the management of the home farm. 'You will see my father safe to bed when I am away,' he ordered. 'The stairs are too much for him if he has taken wine.'

The steward smiled as if he held a hidden piece of knowledge that was vastly amusing. 'I shall take care of everything, sir. Sir William has taken a liking to the small room by the entrance and will sleep there for a while.'

John nodded as if the matter was of little importance and dismissed the steward to his duties after ordering the small carriage to take him to Winchester on the following morning.

The piles of books no longer held his attention and John moved restlessly about the library. He packed papers that he knew the lawyer would need in Winchester and sealed the package with wax and his private seal. His manservant packed clothes and ordered provisions from the kitchen for the journey as the inns along the way to Winchester were dirty and best avoided; there had been rumours of plague victims from foreign ships dying in one of them.

He picked up the length of silk and wrapped it carefully in coarse linen before tying it with a white ribbon that was left over from the bunch he brought back from Paris, then called for his horse and put the bundle in a saddle-bag with a heavy purse of money. He saw Ellen again before he left for the village and told her that he was about to arrange the matter they had discussed, then walked his horse slowly from the stableyard and made for the lane by the church as if out for a casual ride.

Taking a devious path, he came to Sarah's cottage and called for her, making sure that anyone passing would think he was on the business of the manor. 'I've come to see that the carpenter made your window safe, and that you have fuel enough,' he said.

'The room is warm and I feel stronger, sir,' Sarah said. He followed her into the cottage and saw Bessie sitting by the fire. She smiled at him and put out a hand, but he avoided taking it in his grasp.

'What I have to say now must never be breathed to anyone. Swear that it will be so, Sarah!' She nodded. 'Swear it,' he repeated.

'I swear it, sir, but after your goodness to us I have no need to promise. It shall be as you wish.'

'I wish to buy your daughter's maidenhead,' he said, softly.

'But she is not clean. I must wash her and comb her hair and make her smell sweet for you,' Sarah said with rising excitement.

'Not for me,' he said, hastily. 'I wish to procure her for someone tomorrow night. She will be docile and speak not a word?'

'If she's had a good supper and some strong waters she will want to say nothing to anyone,' Sarah said. 'She will do as I say and I have already told her that men might want to touch her and do more. She likes men.'

'Take her to the side door of the manor at first dark tomorrow where the housekeeper will find you. She will leave Bessie alone in the great hall for a while in the dark and I think the steward or my father will take her into the small room. When you see them take her, slip away but remain hidden until you think it is over, then fetch her softly so that my father still sleeps. Say nothing and you will be well paid, but he must not know it is Bessie that he takes to bed.'

'Sir William?' Sarah put a shocked hand to her face.

'Yes; my father,' he said grimly. 'I doubt if he will hurt her, and unless she touches his sores he will not infect her as the distemper has burned itself away except in his brain.'

He handed her a large sum of money, enough to make her gasp, and tears fell over her pale cheeks. She wiped her eyes and stared at him. 'You do this to protect Hope Clarke,' she said at last.

'I shall be in Winchester and the good name of my family cannot permit another *droit de seigneur* such as ruined poor Abigail,' he said simply. 'You told me that Bessie was ready to follow you and this might make life easier for a long time,' he added. 'When she goes to Southampton she must have better clothes to attract more money and so this will be a profitable beginning.'

He tried to convince himself that he was doing this to gain the trust of the village again when it was discovered that Hope was not summoned to the manor on the eve of her wedding, but he knew that he could never allow his father to take her in his arms.

Hope was not with her mother and John Halben made his way to the cottage where he was told that Hope was making everything clean and tidy for her wedding night. He walked the horse and listened to the sounds from the woods. A vixen coughed and a crow swooped down on a dead rabbit and the sweet new catkins on the hazels gently powdered him with gold pollen.

She was pulling water from the well, the leather bucket brimming and heavy, spilling the cold water as she drew it over the low wall. John paused to stare at the compact but curving hips and the high breasts that tensed under the strain of the weight she carried. Her thin dress was damp and clung to her as she moved towards the door of the cottage and he followed her, carrying his wedding gift and the rest of the money in the purse.

'John?' she said in a delighted voice. 'Master John,' she corrected herself and set the bucket on the floor.

'When did you ever call me Master John?' he asked, with a faintly rueful smile.

'That was years ago,' she said, and the smooth cheeks creased into laughter. 'I have been told to mend my manners, sir.' She bent to pick up the bucket to hide her sudden confusion and he took the bucket from her and carried it to the kitchen. Watching, she saw how he had grown strong and firm-legged, how his hair still had the curl she remembered and how his hands were the hands of a gentleman, with short nails and white uncalloused skin, but with the force that could handle a stallion or sail a boat.

'Show me your cottage,' he said. 'Your husband-to-be has bought it, I hear.' He glanced up at a damp patch on the ceiling of the small living-room. 'There is a lot of work to be done here, Hope.'

'The bedroom is better,' she said hastily, aware of the air of neglect that Edward had done nothing to dispel over the past few weeks. 'Edward works hard for Sir William and has had little time to mend things here. The kitchen and bedroom are tight against the rain and the cupboards are finished.'

She stood in the open doorway of the other room and blushed at the thought of showing John Halben where she would sleep on her wedding night. Her dowry chest was open and she bent over it. 'Edward made this and one for himself,' she said as if making excuses for him.

'And I have something to add to it,' John said. He put the parcel on the bed and unwrapped the linen, spreading it out over the fresh coverlet. Hope gasped as the silk escaped and eddied over the linen. She put out a hand, touching the soft but heavy material with almost frightened reverence. 'Let me see if it will suit,' he said and held it up under her chin, turning her to the light from the window.

The cool silk on her bare arm made her shiver with pleasure and Hope was aware of sensations that she had never felt until now. 'It's too pretty for me,' she said, softly. 'It's made for a lady, not the bride of a carpenter.'

'It makes your eyes the colour of the hazel wood,' he said. 'Do you remember the day we hung hazel catkins about your neck and hair and crowned you queen even though May Day was forbidden? How we danced and I said that one day I would wed you?'

She jerked away from him, unsure of her own feelings, but knowing that he must have no place in them. 'And now we are to be wed, to real people, good people, and we are not children, playing in the woods.'

'Yes.' He seemed suddenly empty of words. He folded the silk and carefully laid it on top of the linen in the chest, dropping the purse in after it.

'I will wear it when my first child is born; for the christening,' she said.

'I came here for another purpose,' he said as if they had only just met. He shrugged. 'It is difficult to tell you but I must. Sir William has the notion that he can take you tomorrow night before you are wedded.' She gave a muted cry and turned pale. 'You must be careful,' he said. 'Stay here until after midnight and make sure that nobody sees you come here. It will be over by midnight. I have bought a girl to take your place and he need never know.'

'I would rather die than have him touch me,' she said. 'But the girl? Who would sell her body to him?'

'Sarah's girl is to follow her mother. Sarah told me so and wanted a high price for the first deflowering and I have paid well for her maidenhead. I am sure that it will not be discovered, but if Sir William does find out that he raped Bessie and not you, then you and your husband might be in danger. Here, I have money, a wedding gift,' he added, pointing to the wooden chest as she began to protest. 'Take it and hide it in case you have to leave the village.'

'You will be there, at the manor?'

'I cannot be at your wedding, Hope. I am summoned to Winchester and must leave this to Ellen, who knows, and Sarah, who will make sure that Bessie is submissive.' He took her by the shoulders. 'I have to go to my uncle, but that is not the only reason I shall be away. I think I couldn't bear to see you married to any man but me, and I know that we should never have met again.'

'John,' she whispered, tears forming under her closed eyelids as he kissed her gently on the mouth. 'Stay for a while. In such a small time we shall be married to other partners and have to forget two children playing games of make-believe.'

He kissed her with angry, hard lips. 'I will go away with you. We can leave this place, this county and, if need be, this country.'

She placed a finger on his lips. 'We might be happy for a while, but you could never marry me, John, and I want no bastards,' she said proudly. 'You have to make heirs to a fine title and good land and I am a yeoman's daughter with only a small dowry and no land.' She sighed. 'Edward is a good man and will be true to me, and Miss Hannam will be a good wife.'

'I want you! I don't want any woman but you! I want a warm, loving woman not a velvet-dressed dummy.' He embraced her

69

and she sank on to the bed. His hands caressed her and she murmured weak protests and sighs of longing but was helpless in her own desire. Her damp bodice showed the outline of her breasts and he kissed them through the thin fabric. She moaned and he lifted her skirts and parted her firm thighs. His mouth on hers robbed her of the last shreds of discretion and she held him eagerly, desperately, as if she could never let him go. At last they lay together, sweetly satisfied and drained. They lay so for an hour and made love again, more gently and with sad tenderness, then he lifted her from the bed and told her to wash. The linen that had encased the silk now lay crumpled and stained on the bed and he gathered it up and put it carefully in his saddle-bag so that all traces of their love was removed and hidden.

'Goodbye, my love,' he whispered, as he rode away through the woods.

'Goodbye,' Hope whispered and wondered why she felt no guilt, no regret but only a tender happy sadness. She put the silk at the bottom of the chest under the simple cotton shifts and the money with it, smoothed the bed and closed the door after her as she left for the last nights in her mother's house.

Chapter 4

Ellen Turner waited anxiously in her kitchen. The pies were cooling in the huge larder and the gown she was to wear at the wedding, which had been finished days ago, lay over a stool as if someone had just been working on it.

A dog barked and she knew that strangers had passed by the stables and the two chained dogs that guarded them. She took a deep breath and walked slowly out to the terrace where two figures emerged from the shadows. Clouds covered a quarter-moon and the air was misty, making it difficult to see who was there. Ellen dared not call in case it was not Sarah and Bessie who waited in the dusk, but she heard a sound and knew at last that it was Sarah, trying to keep quiet but still unable to stem the hard cough that was left after her fever.

'Is that you, Hope?' she called in a clear voice, and Sarah pushed Bessie forward, pulling away the cloak that concealed all but the face of the girl. 'There was no need for you to come this evening as I have finished the pies and Lucy helped me with the gown, but now you are here, wait in the hall and I'll bring the ribbons I promised your mother.'

Bessie grunted and went into the warm room to escape the sudden chill of being deprived of her cloak, and stood silently by the door of the small ante-chamber.

Ellen's heart beat faster and she was trembling with fear as she went towards the stairs, but she didn't look back until she was hidden by the upper balustrade, then she knelt down and peered between the polished bannisters. The half-closed door to the small room now opened wider and a man came out and took Bessie by the hand.

'The master wants to see you and give you a wedding present,' the steward said and pulled the slowly moving girl inside the room. 'Shall I bring more wood for the fire, Sir William?' he asked. 'The boy brought damp logs and you have no light.'

'Light enough,' Sarah heard. 'Just leave us, Furness. Shut the door firmly and don't come back.'

She expelled her bated breath with relief. The logs had been very damp and she had only just managed to avoid being seen when she had sprinkled them with water.

It seemed an age while she sat there, but at last she walked down the stairs and into the kitchen. The maid was still scouring pots with silver sand in the outer scullery and Michael, the boy, was eating a broken pie that Ellen had put on one side as too damaged to be used at the wedding feast.

'It's good, Mistress Ellen,' he said, half expecting her wrath when she saw him eating it, but she merely nodded and told him to go to bed.

'Deb,' she called from her chair by the fire in the wide kitchen, and the scullery maid came to the door, hands red from her scouring and her face flushed. 'When you finish out there, dry your hands well and take this gown to my room, then come back and you may have a pie.' She saw the girl's surprise and added hastily, 'You may have some ale too, as it is the wedding day tomorrow and you will have to work hard to help with the food.'

'I was going to bed after the pots are done, mistress.' Deb looked sulky and Ellen knew that she wanted to meet one of the stable lads as she did after her work was finished.

'Do as I tell you, girl. There'll be no Wilf waiting by the stables tonight.' Ellen smiled. 'I suggested the Master John take Wilf with him to Winchester as he is good with horses and is clean and quiet.'

Deb's face cleared. 'He'll like that. Do you think if he gets on well with the young master that he might be given a better job? We wants to be married but he says we'll have to wait until he has more money.' She went back to her work and Ellen heard her singing. She shrugged, hoping that John

Halben wasn't riled by the presence of the inarticulate and heavy-handed lad with him, but they had agreed that he must be out of the way tonight and Deb must not go looking for him by the stableyard in case she saw Bessie or Sarah.

She put two more lopsided pies on a dish and poured good strong ale into goblets. As she expected, Furness came to the kitchen and sat himself down as if he owned the place. He saw the pies and reached out for one. 'Help yourself!' Ellen said, with an effort to hide a trace of disgust as he crammed his mouth with the succulent meat and potato and the fine crust that she took such pride in making.

He belched and eyed the goblets with interest. 'You'll need to wash it down,' Ellen said, and took one of the goblets and went to the fire where a long poker lay red hot in the glowing wood. She put spices into the ale and added a powder that she had concealed in a small pocket in her bodice, then plunged the poker into the ale to mull the drink. She handed it to him, steaming and aromatic, and he smacked his lips over it.

'That's good. You make a good pie, mistress.' He eyed her solid but shapely body with interest. 'I wonder you never wedded again. There's many a man wanting a good cook and housekeeper and more.'

'That's what I am, a good housekeeper

and a good cook,' she said, drily. 'I'm paid well and have no man to tell me when to come and go once I have finished my duties for Sir William and his house.'

'What if in one of his rages, he sent you away?' The man's face was tense with an emotion she distrusted. 'You would need a good man then to take you on and give you shelter.'

'I am of use to him,' she said shortly, hoping that the steward would never again try to convince her that she should marry him as he had done two years ago. 'I am loyal and I nurse him like I would my own.'

She took a deep breath of relief as Deb came in for her pie. She took the steward's ale mug and filled it to the brim, heated it again, then gave Deb ale from the jug she had used to fill all the goblets. 'Put the poker in it if you like it, Deb,' she suggested kindly. 'It isn't every day that my niece is to be married, so you must drink and wish her joy.'

'I'll do that, willingly,' the girl said. 'Perhaps next year Wilf and me will be wed, too.'

Furness looked at her red and work-roughened hands and stringy hair and smiled. Sir William might not want his rights with her when the time came.

Ellen watched him closely. 'I wonder where Hope went?' she asked innocently.

'She was to have waited to take some ribbons back to my sister, but when I came to the hall again, she had gone.'

She slapped the steward firmly on the back as he choked on his ale. 'There now, you shouldn't drink in such a haste. That ale is strong and the fumes get down the wrong way.'

'I haven't seen her,' he lied, but glanced uneasily towards the closed kitchen door.

'She'll be at her mother's, dreaming of her wedding night and what they'll do,' Deb said, giggling.

'This ale *is* strong,' he said, shaking his head. Deb giggled again and began to eat her pie. Furness made an effort to stand but sank back on to the stool and leaned against the wall. 'I know I have to do something for the master,' he said, trying to think clearly.

'I expect you've done it all and he needs no help to get to bed tonight,' Ellen said. 'When he uses the small room I have no worries that he might fall down the stairs, so we can sleep easily.'

'I can't think,' Furness muttered.

'Lie on that bench and rest,' Ellen said in a soothing voice. 'Give me your keys and let me lock up, as everyone is here who will sleep here tonight, and the master is quiet.'

She slipped the bunch of keys from his belt and left him snoring. Deb eyed him with a puzzled air. 'I had some ale but I don't feel drunk,' she said.

'He drank with Sir William earlier,' Ellen assured her. 'He hasn't the head for wine that he boasts he has.'

'Is the woman from Southampton in there again?' Deb asked.

'If she is, then I'd best make sure she leaves before the house wakes up,' Ellen said. 'Go to bed, and leave the rest until tomorrow when you'll be busy enough for two.'

Deb wandered up the back stairs and Ellen blew out the candles on the table. In the near darkness of the great hall she listened but heard no sound from the small room. Softly, she opened the door and peered inside. Sir William lay naked on the bed with no covering to keep him warm. Bessie was on the floor by the dying fire.

'Come,' Ellen said firmly, and half dragged the girl from the room, pushing her into her shift as she went. Outside, Sarah emerged from the bushes and folded the girl into her long cloak before hurrying away into the night. Bessie was protesting that she wanted to lie by the fire and Sarah was telling her to be quiet. She seemed quite unmoved by what had happened to her.

Ellen made more noise now as she went back into the room and picked up the bed-clothes from the floor, tucking them round the man on the bed and kicking the smouldering logs into flame. Back in the kitchen she lit two candles and began to bang a large chafing dish on the stones by the hearth until Furness woke and rubbed his eyes, nearly falling off the narrow bench.

'You had a nice nap,' she said, smiling. 'I'd be off to bed now before you drop off again.'

He held his head between his hands. 'That ale has the kick of a mule,' he said, then stared up as if remembering something important. 'I must see to Sir William,' he began.

'There's no call for you to trouble yourself, Mr Furness. I went in when I heard him stir and made up the fire. He was a bit cold as the bed was in a state but he's still sleeping like a babe.'

Furness glanced at her with apprehension but her face was calm and she was smiling. 'Was he alone?' he asked.

Ellen looked surprised. 'Quite alone. Why? Is this another of his nights? If he overdoes it he'll have a seizure.' She folded a sheet that was dry on the airing rack above the fire. 'Go to bed. I locked up and here are your keys. Everything is safe and sound,' she added with satisfaction, knowing that the steward would never dare to confess to his master that he had been too drunk to see the girl off the premises, but would have to make him believe that he had seen to everything quietly, taking it for granted that Hope would be too ashamed to say a word.

'I think I'll take a turn by the stables,' he said. 'My head is aching and I need some air.'

Ellen bit back the words she wanted to say to stop him, then looked at the clock face. 'It's well after midnight,' she said. 'All honest folk be long in bed and today is my niece's wedding day.'

He looked pale as he left the kitchen and walked slowly across the yard by the midden to the copse. Rustlings of small nocturnal animals among the bushes and sleepy birds disturbed by his progress made the only noises and he almost gave up his walk but decided to go further, to look at the cottage where Hope Clarke should have spent her last night before the wedding, in her mother's home.

The cottage was in darkness as if nobody suspected where she had gone that evening. He drew back among the trees as a girl came from the path, looked about her fearfully and slipped into the garden and up to the unlatched door.

Still no sound and he smiled grimly. She would go to bed and pretend that nothing had happened to her. Hope was a proud girl and with luck would keep very quiet now. Abigail's fate would be in her mind and Hope was too sensible to want to be discarded in disgrace by her husband as Abigail had been.

Furness walked back to the manor house, and peeped into the small room. Sir William was snoring and the fire was bright and the room warm. When he wakes, I can say with truth that I saw the girl go back to her mother's cottage, he decided, and grinned. 'As the master will not be there and Master John is away, someone must represent them at the wedding and it might be entertaining to see her face as she takes solemn vows.'

The boy slopped the warm water from the jug as he put it down by the hearth. He knew that something was wrong and went over to the bed. Sir William lay outstretched and the eyes in his reddish-purple face were wild. His hands picked at the bed sheet and when he tried to sit up, he couldn't. 'What's amiss, Sir William?' the boy asked, then ran from the room, calling for Mistress Turner.

'Stop making that noise, boy!' she scolded, and buttoned up her bodice. 'I'm not ready to see Sir William. You know he washes early before I go to him with his leg dressings.'

'He's ill, mistress. He looks demented and can't speak.'

She ran down the stairs and one look convinced her that he had apoplexy. 'Fetch the steward and tell him to ride as fast as he can to fetch the doctor from Southampton. He will need bleeding. I will see to him and keep him quiet until the doctor brings his knife and bowl.'

The boy fled and within five minutes the groom was alerted to bring round a good horse. Ellen was worried. With John away, there was no family to make decisions and yet she knew that the priest should be called. She shrugged. 'If I send for him and the master recovers, that will be wrong, as Sir William says the priest stinks of popery, but if I don't send for him the squire and his family will blame me if he dies unshriven,' she said to herself.

The cupboard of herbs and remedies was well stocked and Ellen selected what she needed. Her hand hovered over the bottle of tincture of wallflower but decided that the plant had far too violent purgative qualities that would be bad now and cause more harm than good. She took powdered flowers of lavender and a tincture of lily of the valley to strengthen the heart and ease the vertigo and soothe the panic that Sir William felt when he found his powers of speech dwindling.

With difficulty, she forced the tinctures between his clenched teeth and soothed his brow with lavender water, then made up the fire again and called Deb to help her change the soiled bedclothes.

'Don't you mind having this stinking thing to do?' asked Deb, as she put the sheets to soak.

'It isn't pleasant,' Ellen said. 'But I've worked for him and for his wife, God rest her soul, for so many years that it is like tending my own.'

'But you smiled as if you enjoyed it, mistress. I can't do that. I show what I feel and I hope I don't have to sit with him in there. I'd rather scour a dozen burned pots than stay in there for half an hour alone.'

'I'll get a woman from the village to come in,' Ellen said. 'Mrs More needs work and she has no babies to deliver and no bodies to lay out so she'll be free.'

Ellen stood at the foot of the bed and looked at the man who had once been a good master and friend, but now was a helpless wreck who had done much harm. Pity mixed with an overwhelming sense of relief made her look away. If he lost his mind and could never speak again he could say nothing about the night and what had happened in that room. He could never harass Hope after she was married and could not boast of his supposed triumph.

'Mistress Turner?' She went towards the door and took the bag that the doctor held out to her. She saw the steward hovering behind him, looking agitated.

'I gave him lavender and lily of the valley and sponged him,' Ellen said. 'He is calmer now but has not regained his speech.'

'I'll bleed him,' the doctor said. 'What

happened? Has he had too much exertion? Had a shock or suffered a blow to the head? I know his history and if it wasn't for you, Mistress Ellen, he might have died years ago, but this is different, and has little to do with his disease.'

Ellen watched the steward out of the corner of her eye but spoke to the doctor. 'Lately, he made a habit of having a woman from Southampton here, and she was here the other night.' She shrugged. 'I refused to have any dealings with her so you must ask the steward. Last night I think he was alone.'

'Was he alone last night?' asked the doctor.

'Quite alone,' Furness said hastily. 'Sir William was in bed when I left him and slept all night. The boy found him like this when he brought water for washing.'

Ellen nodded. 'I looked in at midnight, or after, and he was alone and snoring, but cold as his bedclothes were tossed away, so I made up the fire and tucked him in warmly.' She shook her head. 'He has been restless of late and unhinged at times, needing laudanum, but when I saw him last night, he was not ill.'

'Yes, he was alone and sleeping,' Furness said again and Ellen sensed his relief. She set her mouth in a tight line. Now, Mr Steward, she thought. You can never say that

Hope was here. You can never accuse her of being here or your lies will be brought home to you.

She looked at the face of the sick man. Fury mixed with disbelief contorted his mouth and the eyes were hot and angry. He knows that Furness is lying. He hasn't lost his senses even if he is helpless. Pray God he never regains his speech she thought. Inarticulate mouthings came from the slack mouth and the doctor brought the bleeding bowl and knife to the bedside. Ellen put a thick towel under the bowl and the man's emaciated arm and held his hand while the blade slipped into the engorged vein and the blood began to flow sluggishly into the bowl.

All the while, the hot eyes stared at the steward and the man backed away towards the door. 'Stay close, Mr Furness,' Ellen said. 'After the doctor has finished, I'll need help, as he is heavy to turn without scraping the skin on his back. I must go to the village to fetch Mrs More and then I can go to my niece's wedding with a clear mind.'

'Will you tell her?' asked Furness.

'That Sir William is ill?' She shook her head. 'I think not until after the wedding, as this is Hope's bridal day and must be kept happy.' She gave a half smile and looked into the eyes of the sick man. 'It isn't as if she knows him now. It must be years since he set eyes on her. Once, he was kind and loved her as a child should be loved, but today, she needs no other love than what her husband can give her, and she need have no care for Sir William.'

The red-rimmed eyes closed for a moment as if a passing regret clouded them and the steward looked very embarrassed. 'I'll fetch more hot water,' he said, and left the room.

'That's better.' The doctor straightened his back and Ellen tied on a bandage over the leaking vein putting pressure on it to stop the bleeding. The thin-bladed knife was wiped clean of blood on an old towel and put back in the doctor's bag.

'There's warm ale and a pie in the hall, Doctor,' Ellen said. 'Tell me what I must do for him.' She tucked the bedclothes round Sir William and called to Michael to make up the fire.

'Keep him quiet and sponge him if he is hot,' the doctor said.

'I'll tell the woman who will be here to look after him,' the steward said. He was dressed for riding and insisted that he must save Ellen the trouble of fetching Mrs More.

The doctor nodded. 'Take heed of what he says if his speech improves,' he said. 'Something is troubling him and his pent-up inner rage does nothing to save him.' He began to eat the pie with evident satisfaction. 'If you ever leave here, Mistress Ellen, you may find a home in my house. My wife ails with vertigo and the change of life and we need a good housekeeper and cook.'

'Sir William depends on her,' the steward said quickly.

'He may die, sir, and then what? Mr John Halben is to marry and his bride might have fresh ideas and bring new faces to the manor,' the doctor said bluntly. 'Remember what I say and if not with us then in some other comfortable house, of which I know many, there is a need of someone like you.'

Ellen thanked him demurely and enjoyed the look of anger that the steward gave to his back. Now, she thought, he has nothing to hang over me to make me afraid to cross him in case he turns the master against me. She was suddenly happy and eager to be away to the church to see her niece married and to know she was safe from Sir William Halben and the profligacy and cursed disease that haunted his house. They went back into the sick room and the doctor nodded his satisfaction as his patient seemed less tense.

'Before you leave, Mr Furness, will you help me lift Sir William? He seems to have slipped down in the bed.' They lifted him back and Ellen told the steward to hold him forward while she made the goosedown pillows plump at his back.

'I hope you come to us,' the doctor said. 'You are a good nurse as well as being a good cook. What is this?' He picked up a ribbon that had dropped to the floor as Ellen punched the pillows. It was scarlet and pink, a big bunch of colour that looked as if it had once tied back a lock of hair. The doctor smiled. 'His whore must be good if he treasures her ribbons from the last time she was here.'

Ellen reached across for the ribbon, but the steward was quicker and snatched it away. 'I'll see that she gets it back when I go to Southampton,' he said.

'Burn it,' Ellen said. 'It will only remind him that he is now incapable if he sees it.'

'She may want it returned,' the doctor said. 'Those ribbons are not common pedlar's trash.'

'Good enough for a bride,' Furness said with a sly grin, and stuffed the ribbon into his pocket before striding off to bring Mrs More back, riding pillion on his horse.

'Deb?' called Ellen. 'If you need wood, make Michael bring it in and you must look in from time to time to see if the master needs anything. Don't look frightened; he is helpless and can do no harm. He needs sips of water or ale and you must wipe his mouth. Mrs More will be here soon and she will do everything necessary but she may need help.'

Deb started to whimper and had a slap for it, then Ellen went to change her dress and push the wheel-barrow piled with pies and cake to her sister's house. She paused by Sarah's cottage but decided not to go in as the place looked empty. The ribbon had been one bunch of a matching pair that she had given to Sarah when she found she had too many for the wedding.

A feeling of apprehension grew as she reached the other cottage where her sister was watching the road anxiously. 'I thought you'd never come,' she was rebuked. 'Another ten minutes and the parson will be in the church and Hope waiting to be wed.'

'Sir William was taken ill,' was all that Ellen would say as they hurried through the churchyard and nodded to the people waiting to see the bride arrive. She glanced to the back of the group waiting and saw Sarah with Bessie, standing away from the villagers as if they knew they would not be welcome.

Bessie was laughing and jumped up and down when she saw Hope arrive in her new gown, with a circlet of flowers in her hair. Ellen stared. Bessie was wearing the other bunch of ribbons in her hair as if she too was a bride, and the red dress that Ellen had given to Sarah fitted her full figure and made her look pretty.

Women in the crowd smiled at Hope and

the men eyed Bessie with growing interest. Mrs More, who had begged to be allowed to see the bride before she went to the manor, sat behind Furness on his hunter and sighed with pleasure. The horse sensed his rider's sudden tension and reared, making Furness take his gaze from Bessie. He braced himself and looked at Hope. She was unsmiling and pale and he was reassured. She had the look of a girl with a burden on her mind and he knew that Sir William had taken his right with her. Furness smiled. I'm getting edgy, he thought. Just because the girl wears ribbon like the one in the bed it means nothing. The flower girl wore ribbon and the villagers who could afford nothing new sported a few strands of bright colour, so why not Bessie?

Edward Fletcher heard the bride come beside him and stole a glance at her. He saw her pallor and smiled. At last his true love was aware of the importance and solemnity of marriage and as the priest bound them together she would be his alone, for this day and for the rest of their lives.

The ring felt heavy and cold on her finger as if she had no claim to that hand. Edward took her hand and led her from the church, suddenly too overawed to kiss her. She turned tear-filled eyes to look at his face, almost expected her sin to show.

'I'll be a good wife to you, Edward,' she

whispered. 'I will be true.'

The church bells rang with an unfamiliar but remembered clamour that had been unused in the time of the Republican parliament. The village turned out to eat at trestles set up in the big barn that belonged to Hope's family and ale and cider flowed from huge earthen jugs. Hope's friends gathered round to tease her about her wedding night and she began to smile.

Alice gave her a folded piece of linen in which there was a lining of green leaves. Hope backed away and the girls giggled. In the leaves was a rabbit liver, covered with blood. 'Why?' she asked.

'To prove you are a true virgin,' Alice whispered. 'When I was wed, I didn't bleed and my husband beat me and said I was not whole.'

'Every bride takes this to bed with her,' Susan said. 'If Abigail had done so, she would have a husband now and not beg for alms.'

'But I didn't go to Sir William,' Hope said with a shaky laugh and they all smiled, as if she had made a joke. 'If you don't hurry, the men will have eaten all of my aunt's good pies,' she said. They went away and she wrapped the liver and placed the package in her pocket, remembering the stained linen cloth that John had taken from the bed after their lovemaking.

Dusk came early and Edward took his bride to the cottage and locked the door. He lit candles and Hope gave him more ale. In the candlelight she saw his good face with the honest eyes and firm jaw. If John had stayed away I would be enjoying this, she decided and smiled. John will marry Mistress Hannam and my future is with this old friend, my new husband.

'Come to bed,' he said quietly and doused the candles. Hope lay on the bed and felt the rising desire that she had enjoyed when John kissed her, but as soon as Edward entered her she felt like a stone and endured his lust as if indulging a child. As Edward lay panting and spent by her side, she felt under her pillow and smeared her thighs and the bed with the rabbit's blood. It will be better the next time, she told herself desperately and hated John Halben for ruining her wedding night.

Chapter 5

Hope heated water in the large cauldron over the fire that Edward had made up when he woke. He sat on the bed and watched her as she went from bucket to pot and to fetch a clean shift.

'I must wash,' she said, seeing that he wanted her again for the third time.

Edward sighed and turned away. 'Trouble is, sweetheart, I can't have enough of you.' He looked at the rumpled and stained bed and smiled, his face full of pride. 'I'm sorry if I made you sore, but they say it's always so the first time.'

Gently, she kissed him then put a finger on his lips. 'I am sore, so no more now. We have work to do and I must show myself to my family or they'll think I've run off. I'll wash first and put the bed to rights.'

'Promise me you'll never leave me,' he said, suddenly serious.

'Leave you?' She laughed. 'I've been married for only a few hours and you think I want to run away?'

'I felt a chill of fear,' he told her. 'Promise me.'

'I promise,' Hope said lightly. 'It seems that our lives are bound together now, for good or ill.' She touched his thick hair as if he was child. 'If you sit there in nothing but your shirt you'll have more than a chill of fear,' she said.

'I'll work off my passion by making a small work-table for the kitchen,' he said, struggling into his workman's fustian trousers.

'If you had fears, it should have been the other night,' Hope said. She bit her lip. 'You mustn't be angry as no harm came of it, and

I escaped, but you may hear something from the steward and wonder if what he says is true.' Her eyes were downcast and she felt as if she was living a lie, but knew she must say something before Edward heard anything from the manor. 'Sir William wanted me before my wedding day as he did with Abigail. Aunt Ellen made sure that I hid in this cottage until after midnight when it would be over.'

Edward sank on to the bed. 'What was over? If you didn't go to him, how could it be over?'

'Don't look so wild, my dear. Master John bought a girl's virginity to take my place and Sir William was none the wiser in the dark, with no candles and wet, smoking wood on the fire. Aunt Ellen and Master John arranged it and Sarah's daughter Bessie was there in my place.' She caught his hand as he started up in anger. 'Sir William is old and ill and John Halben wanted no more scandal, so he paid Sarah. There is no harm done as Bessie is to follow Sarah and there had to be a first man who would pay well. John gave us that help because we were all friends as children even if the village has turned against him and his family after Abigail. He loves the countryside and the manor and wants the goodwill of his old friends once more.' It was as if she heard another girl talking, one who was not really involved.

Edward held his head in his hands. 'I owe him a great debt,' he muttered. 'How can any man repay such a gift? I must find him, now.' He looked up. 'You were all alone here until your wedding morning?' She nodded. 'Poor little Hope who was always afraid of the bats, stayed here in the dark, alone?'

She smiled. 'Stay away from the house, or you might meet Furness and have to bear his hints and sneers or fight him, and that would serve no purpose. If he hears the truth, then Sarah and Bessie will suffer and might have to leave the village.'

He nodded. 'It was as well that you told me. Yet I can't stay away if I am to see Master John.'

'He is in Winchester and has been since the day before the wedding, choosing bloodstock for his uncle. Aunt Ellen didn't know when he'd come home.'

'I have much on my mind,' Edward said. 'I'll work in the bothy and come back for dinner at three.'

'And I shall see my mother and look in on Sarah and then pick the herbs for Aunt Ellen as it was too damp the other day when she asked me to go on the dunes. We have food from the wedding enough to make me idle for two days so I can spare the time to help her.'

Hope poured warm water into the big wooden tub and stripped off her shift. It was soothing and healing in the water and she soaked until it was chilled, then dried and dressed and brushed her hair until it shone. I must appear to be a happy bride, she decided. I *am* a happy bride or will be when I have forgotten what happened between us. John is to marry and will give no thought to me and if Edward is as lusty as he was last night, I shall soon be with child and busy working here.

She lifted the new petticoats out of the chest and found the silk. A tremor of longing made her raise it to her face and then she put it back reverently. It must remain hidden until she could handle it with ease: lie hidden as her love must be, perhaps for ever.

She washed the sheets from her bridal bed and hung them to dry on a rope between two hazel bushes at the back of the cottage where the breeze sent soft showers of hazel gold over the wet linen. She burned the now dry liver and the wrapping and picked up a wooden trug that Edward had made of slivers of wood and a knife to cut the Holy thistle, before she set out to the village to meet her giggling friends and to assure them that she enjoyed being married.

Margaret Clarke looked up from the sugar cone that she was scraping to get enough powder to sweeten a lard cake. 'So, you are a married woman now,' she said, and went on scraping.

'Yes.' Hope looked at the earthenware bowl of flour and lard and stirred the mixture with a long-handled spoon.

'It isn't as good as they say, is it?' Margaret said. 'Once wed there's no looking back on games and such, and you'll feel ill with your first when you catch.'

'Not everyone feels bad,' Hope said, and wished she had avoided her mother until her own feelings were under better control and she felt less empty. 'I might not have children. Alice is barren so they say, and there are others I've met who've had only one.'

'Break the eggs,' her mother told her. 'This must go in the oven to be ready for the men when they come for breakfast ale.'

'I thought you had food left from the wedding,' Hope said. 'Who ate all those pies and salmagundy?'

'I'm saving that for dinner. The men like lard cake after working hard since dawn; it fills their bellies and it's cheap.'

'I'll go to see Aunt Ellen later and call in at the bothy as Edward is working there, making a small table for the kitchen. I might take along some bread and cheese as he had nothing this morning before he left.'

She went back to the cottage to fetch the cheese, then remembered that her aunt usually sent food down to the carpenter and the mason so she went on past the cottage and down the lane leading to the estuary.

Fresh cool air tasting of salt and seaweed teased her hair into curling tendrils and she breathed deeply. It was here on the dunes that she had fought John Halben for the next ride on his donkey and he had given in, laughing and calling her vicious little kitten, and here that she had ridden the heavy cart-horses that pulled the plough on her father's land, their broad feathered feet leaving deep holes in the sand.

She watched the breeze stir the dry sand and recalled how the footsteps had faded by the time she rode back from the sea, as her childhood had faded into young woman-hood, her father had died, and John Halben had gone away over the water sailing from Southampton to lands far away. 'Why did you go away, John?' she asked the gulls. 'Why did you come back?' she said bitterly, and watched the birds swooping close to a fishing boat as the crew sent fish guts into the wake as they neared harbour.

Hope climbed the dunes and saw the Holy thistle in bloom. She cut the stems with her knife and filled the trug, pushing down the yellow flowers so that she could add more for Ellen to dry and keep for the whole year. It was ironic that she should tear her hands on the hard stems to make remedies to ease the pains of the man who had tried to ruin her, but Ellen would suffer if there was no respite from his illness.

Sarah watched her pass her cottage and smiled to herself as she drew back so that Hope wouldn't see her. The fire was bright and there was food for dinner, a young rabbit bought from the farm, and a piece of fat pork waited in saltpetre and common salt pickle for other meals, other days. Bessie sat by the fire, refusing to give up the ribbons she wore in her hair and laughing as she tried to tell Sarah that she wanted to go to the manor again.

'Later, Bessie,' Sarah promised, and hoped that when they went to Southampton, Bessie would be as willing as she was now to go to men. The ale that Bessie now drank was heavily laced with laudanum to keep her quiet while Sarah slipped away to the manor. She waited until Hope was gone a few minutes and then followed, using the shorter path through the copse and avoiding the lanes. Cautiously she approached the kitchen door and peeped inside, finding to her relief only Ellen there, folding linen at the big table.

'Mistress Turner,' Sarah whispered and Ellen quickly looked out of the kitchen door and then closed it.

'What is it, Sarah?'

'Did he guess?'

'No, and if he did, he is in no state to say anything.' Ellen told her how the boy had found him and how the steward had been forced to say to the doctor that there had been no night visitor to Sir William and so there was no need for anyone to find out. She went to a closet and pulled out a basket of sewing in which ribbons of all colours lay in neat hanks. 'I'm glad you are here, Sarah,' she said. 'When the doctor was here we found a knot of red and pink ribbons in the bed and Furness took them, saying they belonged to the woman in Southampton, but I think he wants to keep them to use against Hope at some time.'

'Bessie came back with one bunch in her hair and I couldn't find the other.' Sarah looked scared. 'He saw us at Hope's wedding and Bessie was wearing the ribbons then and won't let me take them from her. She is like a monkey with its hand in a jar of sweetmeats that shakes off any attempt to take them away.'

'That settles it.' Ellen looked serious. 'He dare not say anything in the village to make them think that Hope was here, but if he thinks that Bessie took Hope's place then that's another kettle of fish.' She laughed softly. 'This is your name day, Sarah.'

'I was born in October,' Sarah said in a puzzled voice.

'That was a mistake,' Ellen said firmly. 'You mentioned it before the wedding and I gave you ribbons to sell in the village to buy bread for Bessie, but she wanted a bunch to

99

make herself pretty and she took the other red and pink cluster. Here, take these and show them about the village. Sell some and wear others and Furness will be unable to prove who wore them first, the bride before her wedding, or the girl from the whore's cottage.' Ellen looked wicked, and handed over a bunch of red and pink identical to the ones that Bessie wore. 'Take these to Mistress Hamble as a gift from me. Furness will find it hard to believe that our puritan spinster who bemoans the demise of Oliver Cromwell, would lie with Sir William. When they all wear them to church on the Sabbath, he will have at least six women wearing favours of all colours, and if he ever had doubts, then his suspicious mind should be at rest.'

'I shall take Bessie to my sister in Southampton tomorrow, Mistress Turner. We can walk across the two bridges from Eling and take little more than a sack with us. Bessie is strong and can carry it and we can stop at an inn for food after the first six miles.'

'Go and sell or give away the ribbons, Sarah, and God keep you both.'

'I have money enough to last for months, thanks to you and Master John, and when Bessie has new clothes she will earn more.'

'Do you need to go so soon?'

'Yes, mistress.' Sarah gave her a shrewd look. 'I wondered if Bessie would let men take her, but now I know she'll have to be curbed as she has a taste for it. She wanted to go back to the manor today.'

'I know it was dark, but he is ill and scabby and often violent.'

'No, not always. I remember him as a young man when he treated a woman with care if she was willing. The woman from Southampton doesn't cringe from him and those ways don't die unless he's thwarted. Bessie was not dismayed at what he did to her, so she couldn't have been hurt.' Sarah put the ribbons under her cloak and went the way she had come, back to the cottage to put the rabbit in the pot and to make sure that Bessie was there, ready to go with her to sell the bright ribbons.

Hope walked slowly through the glade. It was good to be alone and able to listen to the birds. Sunlight made a filigree of light and dark over her head as the young leaves burst their sticky coats and stretched out to the air. The bushes smelled rank of fox and a vixen called. Two snares held newly dead rabbits and she took them out to give to Ellen before the foxes got at them, swinging them as she walked to the manor kitchens.

'I thought I saw Sarah in the wood,' she said, as she handed the rabbits to her aunt. 'I didn't call to her and she didn't seem to want to speak.'

'Keep away from her cottage,' Ellen

warned her in a low voice. 'Have you said anything to Edward?'

'Only the truth that I waited in the cottage until after midnight and that Bessie took my place with Sir William. Edward knows that John paid for her and feels indebted.' She gave a wry smile. 'He said that no man could do more for a friend. Here are the Holy thistles. There are more that will be ready next week but as yet they are in bud.'

'Thank you, but I may not need more for Sir William. He is sick and unable to speak and I can't tell if his pox will kill him or the apoplexy.'

Ellen told her what had happened. 'I went down to see Edward and now he knows how ill Sir William is, his anger is less hot and he is convinced that a divine justice has befallen the master. Sarah is leaving the village tomorrow so unless the master saw Bessie and regains his senses, there is nothing to fear.' She sighed. 'The doctor is coming again today and I wish that Master John was here. He may come tomorrow with Mistress Hannam. He sent the groom ahead with one horse and will follow with her using one of her hunters to make the pair for the carriage, and leading another for her groom to ride to escort her home.'

'What is she like?' Hope asked.

'Rich and a lady,' Ellen said with a slight curl to her lips. 'Her eyes are everywhere when she comes here, as if planning the changes she'll make as soon as she is mistress of Deerwood Manor.' Ellen regarded her niece with anxiety. 'You look pale,' she said. 'Was everything all right last night?'

Hope began to put the herbs on the table and didn't look up. 'Marriage wasn't as I thought it would be but I think I made Edward happy.'

'That's what a good wife does and you may enjoy it when you get used to it, but I was glad when I had no more of that to endure.'

'Isn't there more to it than friendship and tenderness?'

Ellen eyed her sharply. 'Don't cry for the moon, child. There is more, but few find it except in their dreams.'

'I'll see Edward and go back to the cottage. There are hens to feed and eggs to collect and the sheets to press.'

'Mistress Turner! The master is restless and Mrs More needs help.' Michael looked frightened. 'She asked for more laudanum as he spilled the last dose she gave him and spat out the rest.'

'Can I help?' Hope was already following her.

'Wait. Put these ribbons in your hair and stand by the door where he can see you.' With a shrug, Hope tied the red and pink bunch to her hair and walked slowly after

103

her aunt, half afraid although she knew that Sir William was helpless.

The Lord of the Manor lay low in the bed, his hair unkempt and his face pale after the third bleeding. Mrs More looked round with relief. 'He tries to talk and I can't understand what he wants and that makes him angry.' The two women lifted him higher in the bed and Ellen brushed his hair while he stared at Hope. She backed away, disturbed by the mixture of anger and disbelief in his eyes, then noticed that the doctor was entering the room.

The doctor put a finger on the limp wrist and smiled. 'Better, much better and no need for further bleeding. Can you hear me, Sir William?' The patient nodded and raised a trembling hand to point to Hope. 'Ah, you haven't lost your appreciation of a pretty face.' The doctor sounded hearty and not a little drunk.

Sir William made a growling noise in the back of his throat and pointed again to the dumbstruck girl. 'Not Hope,' he muttered, so low that only the doctor caught the words. 'Not Hope,' he slurred and Ellen heard the words too.

'Speaking a little, my dear sir? That's better.' He patted Sir William's hand. 'But pray don't lose faith. There is always hope and you are doing well, very well.'

'Not Hope!'

'I tell you there is much hope for you and a certain recovery if you do as Mistress Ellen tells you.'

Sir William saw the ribbons in the girl's hair and closed his eyes as if his thoughts were too confused to let him watch her further. Obediently he drank the herbal brew that contained his physic and slumped back on the pillows. Ellen smiled. Even if his speech returned, now that he had seen Hope wearing the bunch of ribbons similar to the ones found in his bed, he would never be sure if the girl he had raped was Hope or someone put there in her place.

Hope shuddered. If this degenerate man had taken her she would never again have felt clean. The blotchy skin and slack mouth and the claw-like fingers filled her with horror and she wondered how he could have sired a man like John. She closed her eyes and said a silent prayer. Please God let me be a good wife and grow to want my good strong clean husband as I do John.

'Go now,' Ellen said. 'Take your trug and knife and bring me more of the thistle when you have time and, if they are ready, some young bramble leaves.'

Edward was talking to the steward. Hope ducked back into the wood to avoid him seeing her and the low branches pulled at her hair. She decided to go home through the copse and started off slowly until she heard footsteps behind her. The steward came up beside her and grinned.

'There are pretty things to find caught up in a snare, Miss Hope,' he said. 'Look what I found on a branch back there.'

She snatched the bunch of ribbons that he dangled in front of her face and snapped. 'I'm no longer Miss Hope, I'm Mistress Fletcher now.'

'And was the first bedding everything a young girl could desire, *Mistress* Fletcher?' His mockery made her furious.

'What passes between husband and wife are not for common ears,' she said.

'If that was the first time,' he said. 'Your husband had little to say when I asked him if all was well. You and I know how you spent the night before the wedding.'

'What do you want from me?' She tried to hurry on but the trees grew dense at the bend in the path and the shade was darker under the overhanging branches. A last year's bramble clung to her dress and she had to pause to free herself and found the steward close behind her, breathing heavily.

'I swear I'll never tell what I know if you come to me,' he said. 'But why should I watch like a eunuch procuring women for a harem when I have feelings of my own?' His hand on her arm was shaking and hot, and Hope knew that she was far from help, far from Edward and had to defend herself. 'Come on,' he said. 'Nobody misses a slice off a cut loaf.'

'Edward!' she called, but the only sound was a flurried flight of birds disturbed by her cry. Furness laughed and her anger was like a mist before her eyes. She shook him away and he grabbed at her bodice, then fell back, moaning.

'No!' she said and looked down at the man writhing on the ground with blood on his doublet. Hope stepped back, her head suddenly clear. The knife she held shook and there was a drop of blood on the tip of the blade. She let the knife fall and the blood was lost in the brown and green floor of the copse. She bent over him and saw that although his doublet was badly ripped, the padding had saved him and he was more frightened than wounded and the bleeding had stopped.

'Get away, you bitch,' he said between clenched teeth. 'I'll see you hang for this.'

Hope picked up the knife and stood over him. 'Perhaps I should kill you now,' she suggested. 'Before my husband finds you or Master John returns and knows that his steward rapes defenceless women.' She saw that he was badly shaken. 'Do you remember the barn that was fired the night after Abigail told her husband what happened to her?' He nodded. 'If Edward and a few more had not held them back, the men of the village, and some of the women too, wanted to lynch you and set fire to the manor with Sir William inside it. I have only to say you raped me and your life would not be worth a candle, so I think we are equal, *Mister* Furness. You have nothing to say about me and I have nothing to say about you, but I shall carry this knife with me wherever I go.' She wiped the knife on the leaves and walked away, leaving him to struggle up and go in search of a salve for his skin-deep wound.

She found two more rabbits in snares and defiantly took them home although they were the manor's property, and when Edward came home at three in the afternoon for dinner, he could smell rabbit stew and herb dumplings. 'I thought we had food from the wedding,' he said.

Hope smiled. 'You may be hungry in the night, my love,' she said. 'We can eat it then, but I was hungry after my walk to cut Holy thistles and this is better for now.'

'Did you cut enough?'

'Plenty, but I'll go again and take a knife for the young bramble leaves that Aunt Ellen wants tomorrow.'

They ate in silence until Edward sighed and pushed away his platter after wiping the dish with the last of the bread. He glanced at the dingy walls of the kitchen and the cracked slate surrounding the sink. 'I should have done better for you Hope.'

'We have a place to live and you have good work and enough to live on,' she reassured him. 'You can do more here now that we are together and I can help you. The walls need but a wash of lime to cheer them up and once I have scoured the old table and floors, we shall be comfortable until you make more chattels. When I go to the dunes I must fetch more sand.' She saw that he was pensive. 'What is it, Edward? Has marriage fallen short of your needs?'

'Never that,' he said, fondly kissing her hand. 'I want you now but I must get back to work while I have the strength to saw wood.' He smiled. 'I want the world for you, my love. I want to take you away where we can find adventure together and make a life for our children, in perfect freedom. Here, I am in the shadow of Deerwood Manor and the uneasy whims of Sir William and I have fears for you.'

Hope picked up the pewter platters and put them in the stone sink. 'You sound like the men who talk of the New World when they are in their cups,' she said slowly. 'But you are sober and I think have considered this for a long time.'

'It is only since you told me of your danger that I came to want to leave so badly. A pall of disease and wickedness hangs over that house and we are too close.'

'Danger for me is over,' she said. 'Sir William is unable to talk and if he does, nobody will believe him if he speaks about that night. Furness can say nothing, or Aunt Ellen will swear that he was too drunk to lock up or to know what went on in that room, and when she went to Sir William he was alone. She has Deb as a witness and Deb doesn't know that Aunt Ellen drugged the steward's ale. Anything that Sir William says would be dismissed as the ravings of a sick man. This has been my home for all my life; I don't want to leave.'

'There's only an hour or so left of daylight, so I must go back and use the light,' Edward said. 'The last two stools are finished and I must take them to the manor.' He kissed her and smiled. 'I'm glad the nights are long. We can walk by the dunes and maybe find a crab or two in the traps I set, then shut the door against the world for the rest of the night.'

Hope washed the dishes and wiped the greasy scum from the sink using grey wood ash to break up the dirt and fresh clean water to wash the ash away. She swept the stone flags and sent the cockroaches scurrying, then took her mending to the window and tried to think of Edward and his love and to forget her one great passionate experience. Perhaps if we went away, far away, I would forget sooner, she thought.

Alice came in carrying the dry sheets. 'You want to have these in before the dew falls,' she said and laughed. 'I saw them this afternoon, all nice and clean. Did you use the liver?'

'I burned it,' Hope said, shortly.

'You are lucky not to need it as that means you can carry a child,' Alice said. 'I've never been moist there so I can't bear children and I've been married for three years.'

'That's an old wives' tale,' Hope said. 'I may not have children either. Only time will tell.' She filled a pewter mug with cider and handed it to Alice. 'Edward comes from a family that have few children and I was an only one after my brother died.'

'See what I bought? Your aunt gave ribbons to Sarah to sell and I bought this one. It was hard to chose between the colours so I chose blue but I wished I had the red like you have there.'

'It's crumpled, but it might recover if you leave it over some steam,' Hope said. 'Take mine and I'll have more from my aunt if I need them.'

She closed the door after Alice left and laughed softly. Now, Alice and Bessie, Mistress Hamble the spinster woman and Hope Fletcher all had similar favours to wear, so who had been in the manorial bed that night?

Chapter 6

Edward Fletcher carried the last of the stools into the great hall of Deerwood Manor and sat on it. His glance wandered to the small room by the entrance and its closed door, and his face stiffened with controlled fury. He got up and began to walk slowly towards the room where Sir William lay helpless. He clenched his hands and paused, unsure of what he must do.

'No!' a voice said, with quiet authority. 'If you confront him you will do harm to many people. His fate will be sealed when he meets his Maker.'

'Master John!'

'Yes. Now that I am back again and have had time to see what is happening here, I know that my father is sick and unlikely to recover, so I beg you to say nothing and to keep away from him.'

'Hope told me,' Edward said with emotion.

'Told you what?' John's reply was sharp.

Edward smiled. 'Please don't pretend that you did nothing to save her. She told me that you paid Sarah for Bessie to go in there.' He jerked his head to indicate the closed door. 'I shall be in your debt for the rest of my life, Master John.'

'You owe me nothing, Fletcher, and you must promise not to mention this again to me or any other person.' John tried to smile. 'Hope was worth more than a degenerate's arms.'

'I know her to be chaste and true and our wedding night was even better than I had dreamed possible.'

John turned away to the fire so that Edward couldn't read his eyes. 'Pray that mine will be as blessed,' he said in a low voice. 'You are a fortunate man.'

'Do you think Sir William will recover and harass my wife?'

'He shows signs of moving more and tries to speak, but Mistress Hannam who came back with me was shocked and refused to see him after the first meeting. I think you have little to fear from him.'

Edward frowned. 'I am uneasy about him and think we may have to leave Little Deerwood.' He sighed. 'I am a freeman and skilled and can work anywhere they need a good craftsman, but Hope loves the village and may not want to leave, unless we have to go.'

'But you sound as if you would like to go? Where would that be?'

'To America.' Edward regarded John with doubt as if he expected to be mocked.

'So far away?' John looked sad. 'I have been there and found it good now that settlements have been made, and many of the Indians of New Hampshire and New England are friendly.' He sighed. 'I have land there, but when I marry my duty will be here. Mistress Hannam refuses to travel by sea further than the Isle of Wight where her uncle has property at Godshill.'

'Where is your land?' asked Edward. 'Is it on a map?'

'It is on an island called The Vineyard because of the vines that grow wild all over the trees and bushes and give sweet small grapes. It is like this country in many ways, but the summers are hot and the winters are harder and the seas rough except in summer.'

'Is there good timber?'

'Enough oak and maple and more pine on the mainland that is towed on rafts to the Vineyard and the tall straight trunks make fine masts. The Indians fish in long boats with turned-up prows, and bring back whales killed by stabbing with long harpoons and arrows, so there is no shortage of oil for lamps and candles and meat that they dry and smoke for use in the winter.'

'It sounds a good place,' Edward said eagerly.

'It will be soon,' John said. 'But there is much to be done and the land has to be tamed into giving good harvests. Many of the crops that the native Indians grow are strange to us and it takes time to accept them. Many families died and more were left penniless when the first wave of settlers landed. Even now cholera takes its toll and there are never enough men to do the work, but sometimes transported criminals are put to the harder toil and often make good and earn their freedom if their crimes were not violent ones.'

'Why did you leave such a fine place?' asked Edward.

John's smile was hard edged. 'I left here to travel the world because I hated my father, and I left New England because I was homesick for the fields of Deerwood and the faces of my friends. I had a feeling that my fate lay here, and I wanted to find if it was true.'

Edward looked delighted. 'And you found your fate! You met Mistress Hannam and fell in love.'

'Yes,' John said slowly, 'I fell in love.'

'John?' Judith Hannam stood by the stairs dressed for riding. 'If you insist, then I obey,' she said with a smile. 'Here I am ready to be taken for a ride; a short ride,' she added.

'You are very brave,' John said with a solemnity that was belied by the laughter in his eyes. He kissed her hand. 'I have ordered a small calm pony for you and you will grow to love the saddle, but if you feel unable to face the ride back to Southampton tomorrow, I shall take you in the carriage.'

She looked at Edward Fletcher and saw his working apron and leather jerkin. 'You are the carpenter who was wedded?'

'Yes, my lady,' he said and backed away to the door.

'Is your wife pretty?'

'Yes, my lady.'

Judith gave John Halben a coquettish glance. 'Then I am glad that she is taken so that other men might not be tempted by her charms.'

'Who could compare with you, my dear?' John said, and Edward wondered how many times he had been made to say that to keep the lady sweet.

John Halben picked up his riding whip and escorted his bride-to-be to the stables. The small grey palfrey stood demurely by the mounting block and Judith was installed on the side-saddle without too much fuss. She draped her dark-green velvet habit and adjusted the feathers in her hat to the best advantage and glanced about her to make sure that everyone who saw her was impressed, but already she was hot in the heavy velvet under the bright sunlight.

John clicked his tongue and the pony walked slowly towards the gate of the stableyard. John swung into the saddle of his bay mare and followed, keeping a tight rein as the horse seemed to want to be as free as she was when John took her out alone. 'Steady,' John said, softly. 'Later we'll gallop over the shore, but not until my lady rests after her ride.'

The pony ambled along the path to the dunes and over to the shore. 'I find this saddle uncomfortable,' Judith said, crossly.

'It is well padded,' John said shortly. 'You rode when you were a child, or so your father told me, so why not now? This is the first time I have managed to persuade you to come riding with me and we could have much pleasure in each other's company when we are out like this alone.' He smiled and bent over to touch her hand and she blushed. 'You are a pretty woman, Judith, and we are to be wed, but I wonder if you really want to come to me.'

She looked startled, almost afraid. 'Do you not love me, John?'

'I am as fond now as I was when you agreed to give me your hand in marriage,' he said flatly.

'Please don't be impatient with me, John. You look so angry that I am half afraid of you.'

'We are betrothed and yet you draw away when I kiss you. You keep your servant in the room when I want to be alone with you

117

and you show no promise of making my bed warm with your love,' he said bluntly. 'I am a man with a man's desires, Judith.'

'Desires that you have indulged with other women?' she asked petulantly. Her eyes filled with tears.

'I have travelled the world and taken pleasure where I found it as all men do, while waiting for the perfect wife, but I go with no whores. I have chosen you, my dear, to be mistress of Deerwood.' He curled his lip and looked ahead at the surf. 'Besides, your father made me so welcome that I knew he wanted me to ask you. We have a good arrangement with wealth and lands and social position. What more do you want?'

'I am very happy,' she said, through tight lips.

'Then show your happiness and make me happy,' he suggested gently. 'I need a wife to love me and to give me heirs. I want no sterile marriage with no laughter or affection.'

'I am shy,' she said, with an arch look.

He laughed. 'Marriage will change that.' He dismounted and hung the reins over the mare's neck to make her stay, and before Judith could demur, he had lifted her down from her pony and embraced her. She stiffened and then relaxed long enough for him to kiss her on the mouth, but as his hands caressed her velvet-clad body, she moved away. Her foot caught in her habit and she staggered back against the mare, making her plunge away from them and John watched her gallop over the dunes and vanish from sight.

'Oh, what can we do?' Judith said in a tragic voice.

'We can do this and this and this,' John said, kissing her again and again with rising warmth tinged with irritation. 'Forget the mare. She will find her way home safely, or someone will bring her back. She at least is biddable,' he added bitterly, letting Judith stand away to pin her hat more securely and to smooth the ruffled feathers. 'Give me your foot,' he said. 'I'll walk back with you, leading your pony.'

Judith found herself propelled up on to the saddle with rather more force than was necessary, but seeing his angry eyes, she dared not complain, and they returned to the manor in silence. 'Will you take chocolate with me, sir?' she asked, as soon as the pony had been handed over to the groom and she felt more secure with other people around.

'No, madam. I have a horse to catch and matters to attend, and I need exercise, not the fragrant empty air of your parlour while you ply that infernal needle.'

John strode away, trying to forget the

humbling lack of response he had endured. Perhaps she *was* shy, having been brought up in a family of females with no brothers and only one male cousin, which made the union of the two families important if male heirs were to be provided for the two estates.

He sighed. She had made an effort to dress to please him, but seemed uncomfortable in the rich garments that were fashionable, preferring the dull dresses that were relics of Cromwell's time.

The sky over the estuary was pink-clouded with a turquoise edge where it met the sea and sea birds rested on the calm water. A log of wood floated down to rest on the shore and the tide came high over the sand and shingle. John Halben kicked a shell and saw a wooden trug full of bramble leaves lying to one side of the path as if left there for collection later. From the distance came the thud of hooves on sand.

He climbed higher to see into the distance and saw Dark, his bay mare, galloping along the ridge of the dunes as if propelled by a storm. The girl rider, seated as a man would ride, leaned over the horse's neck to urge her on and the soft, pale-blue cotton of her dress flowed behind her with golden hair unbound and free over her shoulders.

John stood transfixed and stared as Hope drew rein and patted the heaving neck of her mount. She laughed with exhilaration. 'I knew she was yours. How did you lose her? Did you take a toss? She goes like the wind.'

With effortless grace, Hope slipped from the saddle, kissed the nose of the horse and handed the reins to John, her bosom a gentle tumult and her eyes bright but shy.

'When did you ever see me thrown from a saddle? Do you have to live on nettles, now that you are married?' asked John solemnly, as he handed her the trug.

'They are bramble leaves to ease the pain when Deb has her courses. Aunt Ellen makes a broth of them.' She regarded the mare with anxiety. 'Did I wind her? She must be rubbed down before she chills.' John stepped towards her and she shook her head to dispel the tension between them. 'No,' she said, softly. 'Never again, John, my love.'

'This can't be,' he said. 'You and I are one, my sweetheart, and we must be together. It's too late now to give up.'

Hope tucked her skirt up and ran with the trug to a circle of gorse where John dared not take the horse. She stood behind it and smiled sadly. 'You are right, it's too late for us. Never again. I thank you from the bottom of my being that you saved me from your father. I thank you for everything and I would change nothing,' she whispered. 'But now I must make a home for Edward and give him my love.' He made a protesting sound and she became angry. 'Keep away, John, or you will destroy us both.' Her mouth trembled. 'How can I bear it if I see you in the village, at the manor, or on the shore?'

'Hope?' he called, but she had gone, running down the loose sand and sliding to the path. She stopped only when she reached her own cottage and flung herself on the bed, her shoulders heaving with the effort of running and her inner anguish, then brushed her hair and washed her face before walking along to the bothy to meet her husband, keeping to the lane and avoiding the shadows of the copse.

'Your aunt asked if you had brought the leaves,' Edward said. 'I've finished here and we can take them up to the kitchens together.' He put an arm round her waist and kissed her. 'You've been running.'

'I was later than I thought on the dunes. I found John's mare wandering and caught her. She broke away when he took Mistress Hannam riding and he was coming back to find her when I handed him the reins.'

'And you had a good gallop first, I'm sure,' Edward said, with an indulgent laugh. 'It's more than Mistress Hannam had. The pony was hardly exercised when they returned and Miss Hannam looked as if she had been through torture.'

Ellen unpacked the trug and insisted that they took a pot of her good venison stew. She smiled happily, seeing the flush on Hope's cheeks and the pride in Edward's eyes. 'Go out by the front door as the midden is overflowing and the path at the back will be foul,' she said.

Hope hesitated in the great hall, half-afraid that she would see John. The door to the small room was open and Sir William sat propped up in bed, watching her. Edward had gone ahead and saw nothing amiss, but Hope knew that the man in bed was trying to mouth her name. Ellen gave her a push to make her move and almost ran her out of the house. 'The doctor says he can be brought out here by the fire tomorrow,' Ellen said in a hurried whisper. 'Keep away, Hope. He is deranged, but has you on his mind. Forgive me. I thought that door was shut fast or I would never have brought you this way.'

Edward took her hand. 'First hot and now cold, my love?' he said.

'Oh, Edward! I saw Sir William through the open doorway and his eyes were like hot coals burning into me. He knew me and beckoned and I am afraid.'

'Nothing can harm you now that I am here and we live together. I can protect you,' he said, firmly.

'Not when you work and I am alone in the

cottage,' she replied and was tempted to tell him about her confrontation with the steward, but closed her mouth over the words. 'I wish we could go away,' she said, more to herself than to him.

'We can! I thought you'd want to stay here with people you know and love,' he said eagerly.

'Where would you go? I often thought it pleasant on the island when my father took us in his boat, but even that is so close to Southampton that I would live in fear of Sir William!'

'The New World! America! We could make a good life there. I can earn our living anywhere and you can keep house. Master John said that they need skilled men and that land is cheap.' He caught her hand and turned her to face him under the blossoming apple trees.

'Leave Little Deerwood and my friends in Elney?' Hope looked up at him with sad eyes. 'Leave everything I've held dear?'

He kissed her cheek. 'We shall take with us what we hold dear,' he said. 'We are married and have no need for other people until we make new friends. We are one.'

'Yes, we have exchanged vows and are married,' she said, softly. The breeze caught the trees and a single petal from the apple blossom fell gently on to her cheek like a delicate pink tear.

'I have a little money,' Edward went on. 'I saved the money I had from the boxes I sold in Southampton for a good price and we have enough goods from setting up house here to last us for months.' His face was eager.

'You dream too much, Edward,' she said. 'That is not enough. The Pilgrim Fathers made the mistake of thinking that the Good Lord would provide and many died because they lacked money and supplies. If we go, it must be with some security; perhaps next year. I will limewash the cottage while you make more trinket boxes to sell and perhaps I can sell preserves in the market.'

Edward shrugged, the light dying in his eyes. 'You're right, Hope. It was a dream that we can never fulfil.'

'It isn't impossible. It takes effort and courage to make dreams come true but we can do it together.' They went into the cottage and Hope looked at the kitchen with a dispassionate regard, seeing afresh the lack of care that her mother had hinted at before the wedding. She pushed back a shutter that was hanging loose.

'I was going to mend that before the wedding but I was too busy at the manor,' Edward said.

She ignored the other things that she knew would annoy her after a while, like the ill-fitting door and the table with uneven legs.

'You are a craftsman, not a labourer, Edward, and I know it's hard to have to mend things when you want to make new and pretty furnishings, but we must work out what brings in more money, working for Sir William or setting up alone, here.'

'I can't leave my bothy. What would Sir William say if I left him now?'

'He can say nothing and Master John would encourage you.' Hope shook her head ruefully. 'When it comes to choice, I don't think you have the courage to break away, so how can you talk of going half-way across the world? Is it just the dream you want? Would it trouble you if that dream came true?'

'Everyone has dreams,' he said with a sulky frown. 'Even you, Hope, for all your practical ways.'

'Yes, I have my dreams.' Her expression hardened. 'But I make sure that I discard the ones that can't be and make the others work!'

'You are strong enough to do so,' he admitted.

'As you can be with me by your side,' she said, firmly. She reached up and kissed him. 'Come, my dear husband, we must get to bed and be up early. We have work to do.'

Edward curled up as if back in the womb after his almost desperate loving and Hope lay awake experiencing *la petite tristesse* so common with women after sex. Why sadness when Edward loved her and now made her more satisfied than on her wedding night?

Dawn came bright and the song birds were truculent and noisy. Hope pushed away the arm that lay over her chest and Edward woke and yawned. 'You have two hours before you begin work for Sir William,' Hope said. She gave him warm ale and bread. Edward was still half asleep when he walked along the lane to the bothy. He called goodbye and said with humour, 'I didn't know I married a slave driver.'

As always, the scent of pine and sawdust pleased him and he worked hard, making two boxes which he thought Hope might line with bits of velvet if Ellen Turner had any to spare. That would put the price up and the boxes would sell easily. With a sigh of resignation, he put aside his own work and began to repair a gate that had fallen in the storms and was needed to pen the sheep. The gateposts had also suffered and he decided to replace them with stouter ones, well tarred to stop wet rot. Michael loaded the cart with the timber and tar pots and Edward carried his frail of tools out to the field.

The sun came up hot and the breeze dropped and Edward stripped to the waist to keep cool while he dug and hammered to remove the old posts. With a grunt, he shifted the last piece and threw it clear and Michael dug out the loose earth to make the hole deeper.

'I'll light a fire for the tar,' he said. 'You bring ale and bread from Mistress Ellen and tell her what we are doing in case the steward has other ideas and accuses us of slacking.'

Michael left him cutting twigs for kindling and when he had put flint to tinder and made a spark, Edward blew on it gently until a small flame appeared and the dry grass under the twigs caught light, then he added a handful of resinous knots from a pine log which spitted flame and subsided into a steady heat. He added wood and put the black tar cauldron over it, suspended from a tripod of iron, waiting for the sluggish mass to liquefy.

With the fire going well, Edward was able to stretch out on the grass and shade his face from the sun, easing his aching arms and back after the hard work of the morning.

Michael brought a flagon of ale and a basket of bread and cheese and they sat in friendly silence while they ate and drank. The tar began to bubble and Michael stirred it with a long paddle-shaped stick, then carefully removed the pot from the fire. Together, they lifted the first post and plunged the base into the seething black tar.

The wood hissed and threw up smoke and they rammed it deep into the prepared hole.

'Best do the other while it's hot, as it soaks in better and we'll have no trouble later for years.' They repeated the manoeuvre and Michael wiped his brow with a hot hand.

'Rachel should bring her baby here,' he said. 'They say the smell of tar is good for whooping cough and I remember my mother holding me over a vat when I had it.'

'It's a good clean smell,' Edward agreed, then placed the still boiling pot on the cart, wedged with pieces of wood. 'No, don't touch it as it must stay until it's cool before we take it over rough ground.'

They finished the ale and Michael stamped on the dying fire to make sure that it couldn't set light to the gorse and grass, then eyed the cauldron with apprehension. He stirred it with the stick and left it in the pot. 'It's too hot to move,' he said. 'We could leave it by the hedge until it sets and come back for it later.'

'We'll wait for a while. We can't leave it here. What if a cow knocked the cart over? It's too dangerous to leave unguarded. We've worked hard this morning and can do with a rest.' He sat in the shade and Michael followed his example willingly, rapidly becoming drowsy after the physical effort and the fumes of the tar. Edward heard the sound of footsteps on the hard ground and sat up to see who was coming.

'So this is how you use Sir William's time? It's way past the time for a na-meat. Did Mistress Ellen give you too much ale to pass the time?'

Edward sprang up and faced the steward. 'We've worked hard and now we're waiting for the tar to cool before we take it back to the bothy.'

'A fine excuse! We'll see if it's cool enough,' Furness said, and tried to pull the stick from the tar. It came away with a jerk, splashing hot tar over the cart and, as it swung, the coated wood hit Edward on his bare chest. He gave a cry of agony and backed away. Furness grinned. 'Serves you right for malingering. Go to your saintly wife and make her kiss it better.'

'Put that down and get out,' Edward said through gritted teeth. 'I swear I'll kill you if you are here for another minute and sneer at my wife.'

Furness backed away, seeing the livid weal on the clear skin and the glowing blisters coated with tar. His expression changed and he looked furtively at Michael to see his reaction. 'It was an accident. You saw that, boy! And you heard him threaten me!'

'It was no accident,' Edward said. 'I'll make you pay for this.' He picked up his shirt and told Michael to stay with the cart until the tar was cool and could do no more harm. He walked slowly towards the manor and Ellen Turner's help, the pain growing worse with each step.

Ellen took one look at him and called Deb. 'Go up on the leads and pick a handful of house leek leaves, girl, and be quick.'

'It was hot tar,' Edward said faintly and sat heavily on a stool.

'I can see that,' she said, drily. 'No, don't pull away. I'll try to be gentle and I can take away some of the anguish.' She saw that Deb was back by the table. 'Bruise the leaves in the mortar and bring them here,' she ordered.

The fleshy leaves made a wet pulp which Ellen spread over the burn and Edward sighed with relief. 'That's better,' he said.

'Better for now but you must put fresh on it every time it dries and leave the scabs of tar or you'll take the skin off. The tar will keep the burn clean and will drop off when the skin underneath heals. Have you house leeks on your cottage roof?' He nodded. 'Hope can do this and you must stay from work and dust for a day.' She held out a cup. 'Drink this to take away some of the pain and try to keep your hands away from the weal or it will hurt the more.'

He told her what had happened and she tightened her lips. 'When I see Master John I'll tell him, but you must keep silent if any other person asks you. That man is dangerous when he knows he's in the wrong and will lie to justify his actions.'

Edward moved cautiously and half smiled with relief as the pain subsided. 'You are a witch, Mistress Turner.'

'Never say that, even in jest,' she said, urgently. 'There are people who might believe you, just because I know my herbs.' She bound strips of linen over his chest and helped him into his shirt. 'When Hope goes by the dunes again, tell her to bring the broad ribbons of brown seaweed to bind under the linen as it's healing and cool.'

Edward called in at the bothy on the way home to tell Michael where to find him if he needed advice. The boy picked up a piece of wood and put it down again, refusing to meet the gaze of his master. 'What did he say after I left?' Edward asked gently.

The boy was close to tears. 'He said that if I didn't swear that you attacked him first, my family would be thrown out and have to beg for a living.'

'He is a wicked man, Michael, but you will be safe. Tell Mistress Ellen what you have told me and don't be afraid, as Master John would never allow such an injustice.'

He walked home and had time to think of the future. If he stayed in the village of Little Deerwood, he might bring danger to many people, not least to Hope and the boy, Michael, and even to Ellen Turner.

Chapter 7

The priest had left and Ellen helped Mrs More to settle her patient more comfortably. John Halben stood by the window, staring out at the swaying green of the copse.

'Fetch his gruel and honey and I'll wait here until you come back,' Ellen said. Mrs More picked up a soiled towel and closed the door behind her.

'Now what is it you tried to say, Father?' John asked. 'When you whispered, I could hear nothing. Now we are alone but for Ellen who is one of the family.'

Sir William shook his head and Ellen withdrew into the great hall and left father and son together.

'Now, we are quite alone,' John assured him. 'You are much better and not about to die so you hardly needed the priest! I know you can speak a little, so tell me what worries you.'

'Hope.' He spoke in laboured small phrases as if he had two tongues in his mouth and had to struggle with them. 'I have done wrong.'

'We all sin, Father, but the priest absolved

you in the old way that you now favour, so you may rest.'

'I could not confess. I told him of small things.' His eyes became angry. 'He thinks I am mad, but my mind has cleared.' He sank back and closed his eyes.

'I am not a priest, Father. I want none of the burden of your sins on my mind,' John said sternly. 'Each man must bear his own guilt or be absolved in Holy Church.'

'I took another girl before her wedding night.'

'Who?'

'Hope Clarke, and afterwards, I saw her lying by the fire and believed her to be a whore sent to mock me and give me more pestilence. She looked like Sarah when she was young, and yet the girl I took was a virgin.'

'You have been ill and fanciful,' John said.

'I *did* take her, my son! Yesterday I saw her as she left with her husband and Ellen and I knew that I must make amends.'

'I think you imagine it,' John repeated. 'But it is as well to talk to me and to no other, as I will say nothing and so cause no pain. If this rumour was spread in the village it would do more harm than if you *had* raped the girl.'

'Rape?' Sir William seemed to relax and sink into his pillows. 'That was the wonder and the mockery of it as if it was a dream.

She came to me in the dark, murmured but said nothing and was willing.' His thin hand caught John by the sleeve. 'Was it a dream? Was I spared that fresh sin?'

'You had the woman from Southampton here for several nights. You were taken ill and confused them.'

'I may relapse and be able to say no more. Even if what you say is true, I have to ease my mind before the Devil takes me. You will fetch the box from my desk and bring it here with quill and ink.'

'Now?'

'Yes, and keep away the prying eyes until we have finished.'

John brought the ornate carved box inlaid with ivory and placed it on the table. 'It's here, Father.'

'Unlock it and take out the leather purse. There should be fifty pounds there unless that scoundrel of a steward thinks I am dying, and has taken it.'

John smiled. 'You are recovering well, Father. You are right; there is that amount.'

'Give it to Ellen to give to her niece and give her the paper under it. Write a note and hold my hand so that I can sign it to say that this is a gift to her from me with no restrictions. Ellen and you shall witness it.'

'This paper?' John looked up in amazement. 'These are the deeds to a patch of land and a cottage.'

'On the Isle of Wight where my grandfather lived and died helping King Charles when he tried to escape Cromwell. If it is true that I took her that night, and whatever you say, I swear it is true, then she should go away where scandal can never touch her.'

His face was drawn as if in pain. 'In my dreams I saw Hope and you as you were when young, playing with the goats and horses and laughing. If she had been born into another family, higher than a yeoman's, you would have had a worthy bride.' He shook his head when John seemed about to interrupt. 'I saw you with that puritan from the clutch of female Hannams today and you didn't smile. If Hope stays, you may want her more than your wife, so send her to the island and forget your childhood.'

'You see too much, Father, and imagine more. The blood-letting makes men fancy they see the future, and the valerian gives elaborate dreams.'

John called Ellen to sign the paper and then her helper brought a bowl of gruel. He left them to feed and turn their patient. 'Call me when he is to be set down by the fire and I can carry him,' John said.

'I must see if Edward is better.' Ellen went to fetch fresh linen bandages and salves.

'Tell him to stay at home and rest for another day but if he can walk that far, I will see him in the bothy later to appoint a man to replace his other craftsman and to hire another villein or a serf.'

'You could see him at home,' Ellen suggested.

'No, he must come to the workshop and when he is there, you may give this to Hope when you are alone. If she cares to tell her husband of this bequest, then she shall, but if not, then Edward Fletcher will be none the wiser until she decides what to do.'

'Hope is a married woman and her husband has the right to her property.'

'I knew them both when we were children and I know their natures. Hope is married to a man who loves her but if he saw this now, he might suspect that she was lying about the night at the manor with my father and is being paid handsomely for it, as indeed, my father thinks she is!'

'You are right. Edward is a good man but weaker than Hope. There are many women who hold the purse strings in marriage and make a good home with no wastage. Edward needs a wife like that as he jumps from one idea to another and loses time and money.'

Ellen collected her herbs and dressings and a pot of thick vegetable soup and left Mrs More to stay with Sir William who now seemed fatigued after the visit of the priest and his efforts to talk to his son.

The clothes-line outside the cottage was

heavy with washing and a bucket and yard broom stood by the open door.

'At last I've washed away the grime on the floor. I heated water for washing and when the line was full, I had water left so I used it on the floor with soapwort.' Hope stood back to let her aunt pass into the house. 'I doubt if the floor has seen brush or water since the flags were laid, and every corner was full of spiders. I'll gather rushes today and make it comfortable.'

Edward appeared in the doorway. 'Come into the other room or you'll have wet hems and wet feet,' he said and laughed. 'Hope gets the bit between her teeth at times and there's no stopping her. I was nearly washed away into the midden!'

'You seem well, Edward?' Ellen noted his bright eyes and easy stance.

'I should be, after your care, and Hope renewed the poultice last night and gave me the physic that took away the pain and made me sleep. I'm stiff, and sore if I touch the place, but there's no need for me to stay here idle.'

'Good. Master John asked to see you at the bothy to talk about another craftsman to replace your last man. I'll dress the burn now and then you can go. I've brought soup for Hope and you can eat in the manor kitchen. Tell Deb I sent you.'

The wide line of solidified tar gripped the

burn, pulling the skin tight, but there was no other inflammation and Ellen put a fresh mucilage of house leek and butter over it to keep the skin from drying and contracting further. 'I found a tight jerkin that covers the linen and protects the burn when I move,' Edward said.

Ellen nodded. 'It's healing well, but you'll be scarred as if branded by irons, like the poor creatures they ship from Africa and send on to Bristol.' She shrugged. 'They say they have no souls and can be bought and sold as slaves, but I can't think that the Good Lord had that in mind for them. I've never seen one, but they were made in God's image and I'm told they suffer as we do if they are parted from their families.'

'That feels good.' Edward sighed as the bandage was put on and the jerkin laces eased tight. 'I can't brace myself against a bench but I can do simple things and oversee Michael.' He walked away with an easy stride and Hope went on making the cottage wholesome and clean, scouring the slate shelf in the larder and washing the grimy window sills.

'I'll warm the soup,' Ellen suggested. 'I have to talk to you before Edward returns.'

Hope pulled off her sacking apron and dried her hands. 'Is it about that night?' she asked fearfully and told Ellen what the steward had said when he met her in the wood. 'I cut him with the knife I had for gathering the Holy thistle or I know he would have done me harm.'

'So that's why he came to me for salves for a cut he made when his own knife slipped?' Ellen smiled. 'I put on a salve that heals but burns and he howled like a baby. At least it convinced him that he'd have no sympathy from me.' She stirred the soup and looked worried. 'That man is dangerous. I tell Master John, but Sir William depends on him and he is a good steward so long as he keeps to his orders and does no wickedness.'

'What did you have to say, Aunt Ellen?'

'Master John gave me something for you.'

Hope looked startled, but relaxed when Ellen said that he refused to come himself but wanted her to see Hope alone. 'What is it? He gave me some silk for my wedding present and some money, so he's under no obligation to give me more.'

'Did you give the money to Edward?'

'No.' Hope looked uneasy. 'I should do, but I wanted to keep it until we have a child, so I put it under the clothes in my dowry chest.'

'Put this with it and say nothing. Edward is good but you have the better head on your shoulders and it's best to have something put by for a rainy day.'

'There's a paper with it, witnessed by John and you but signed by ... Sir William!'

'He asked the priest to call for his confession as he dreads meeting the angels and his conscience tells him to make amends to you.'

Hope thrust away the document and sat staring at it. 'But I wasn't there!'

'Listen carefully. He took a virgin to bed and still believes that it was you, although in his dreams he saw you as Sarah when she was young. Bessie is like her. She went to sleep on the floor in firelight and when he saw her, his sick mind was confused and tortured by what he thought was a mocking devil.' She handed the documents to Hope again. 'Read it. If you have to leave here, at least you will have a piece of land and a home far enough away to make you breathe easily.' She handed over the money. 'Put this with the other as a safeguard for the future. Keep it safe as it's a tidy sum, more than most freemen can save in a lifetime.'

Hope lifted the linen and put the document and the money under the piece of heavy silk, and they ate their bread and soup and talked of other things, although Hope's mind was flooded with doubts and sudden bursts of happiness. John has done this to make us safe, she decided. We must never be together and this may be the answer. I can look across the water on a clear day and imagine I see him, but I shall be a good wife.

Ellen walked back and called in at the

bothy. Edward was polishing one of the small boxes and she promised to bring him velvet to line them.

'If Hope can take some cow heel glue and stick the material down, I could take them to Southampton tomorrow,' he said. 'Master John ordered me to do my own work for two days before I start again here. In Southampton, I can hire more help and there could be a room for the men over the stables.' He held the box up to the light and admired the sheen on the wood and the fresh smell of beeswax.

'Has Sarah gone?' asked Ellen. 'There was no smoke from the chimney.'

'She left early when the carter went to Southampton. They were going to walk, but it's a muddy track by the two streams and Sarah is weak.' He grinned. 'She was dressed in her best and said she could afford to pay the carter so it seems that life may take a turn for the better for them now.'

'If you can say that the life of a whore is good,' Ellen said drily.

'She seemed in a hurry to leave and said she might never come back. She will pay her sister for a room in her inn until she finds out if she can afford a bigger one. Working from an inn will be better for her than plying the streets in all weathers, so long as there is no plague.'

'Be careful tomorrow, Edward. The groom

142

said that the press gangs are rife along the south coast and a friend of his disappeared last month.'

'They wouldn't take me. I am a freeman under the care of Deerwood Manor,' Edward said in a condescending voice.

'A belaying pin is a good way to convince a man that he wants to go to sea,' Ellen said. 'They take a man and ask questions afterwards when they are far out in the channel!'

'I'll go early as soon as Hope has dressed the burn and I'll go straight to the market to sell the boxes. I can eat there and come back late if I can find another traveller coming this way, but if I am alone, I may stay for a night to avoid footpads.'

At dawn, Hope fussed over him before he left, thinking that the scar was too moist under the wet dressing with all air excluded by the leather jerkin.

'I know it looks bad, but it's comfortable and I can let the air get to it when I come back,' he said. 'With this on it, I am not afraid of knocking the scab.'

'It doesn't look like a burn,' she said. 'But Aunt Ellen won't hear of me picking away the tar.'

He saddled the horse and walked it slowly to the first bridge, then found the lanes solid and made more speed. He was happy and knew that he was a very lucky man. The

143

loose ochre woollen doublet was comfortable over the jerkin in the early morning but
the sun rose high and hot and he wished he
was free of the cumbersome linen many-
tailed bandage that Ellen had made to
secure the house leek mucilage, but vanity
made him keep the doublet on, in case he
was thought to be a common serf in
worker's leather.

He heard the sounds of voices from an
inn, but passed by, eager to sell the boxes
and bent on finishing his business of hiring
labour before he took a morning draught of
ale. As soon as he reached the market by the
docks, he put his nag into the next inn
stable and ordered pigeon to be cooked for
him in two hours' time.

The noise and bustle of the market was
harsh on the ears of a man who heard
nothing louder than the bleat of sheep, the
lowing of cows and the thud of horses'
hooves, but it was exhilarating and he stood
by the inn door, watching the scene with
interest, wishing that he'd asked Hope to
come with him.

'Mr Fletcher!' He swung round to see
Sarah.

'Is this where you are living?' he asked.
'You look well.'

'And you look hot,' she said, eyeing the
thick woollen doublet with amusement.

'I'll finish the business I came to do and

then take it off,' he said.

'You could unlace that tight leather,' she suggested and he told her of the burn from the tar.

'Sell your boxes and come into the inn,' she said, and laughed when he looked askance. 'No, I don't offer myself or Bessie, but you may rest in a room and eat your dinner in peace without all that stuff on you.'

'I have ordered pigeons,' he told her.

'I'll tell my sister that you are a friend who needs a room and the potboy will show you where to go. I have to see that Bessie gets to a house by the river, as she is working there today with two men who like the fact that she is clean and can't tell their wives!'

'Is it safe to leave her?'

'Yes, I have known them for a long time and they will be kind. I shall collect her later and be well paid,' she said with satisfaction. 'Bessie is very happy and has some pretty clothes and plenty to eat, so I am happy too.'

Edward wandered through the market and held up a box from the sack he carried. A merchant stopped and fingered it and smiled when he saw the neat velvet lining. Edward asked a price that he thought was too much but the merchant nodded and made no attempt to beat the price down, so Edward offered the next one at an even higher price until all were sold quickly. He was bemused by the money he'd made after so little effort.

With the empty sack over his arm, he hired men for Deerwood who would go there the next day, then went to the various stalls and found fresh butter and eggs, and live geese cackling in wooden crates. A litter of puppies cried softly and begged to be taken to a good home, but he saw the big feet and long hocks and pale eyes and the signs of worms round their vents and knew they were mongrels from bad and possibly vicious stock, and passed by.

Women in bright skirts and head kerchiefs, sold mats made from rushes and wooden clothes pegs that they had made all the winter and now brought to the market from their gypsy wagons on the dunes. One seized his hand and asked for money for his fortune and he laughed and let her hold it to read his palm.

'You have a good woman,' she said, slyly watching his face and seeing a contented man. He nodded. 'You will go over water,' she went on more seriously.

'To the Isle of Wight?' he asked, mocking her. 'That's not far.'

'Further than France,' she said, as if anywhere further was beyond her comprehension. She looked up suddenly. 'You are in danger here. Go away and hide.

There are evil men.' She thrust his hand from her and turned away without demanding her money and ran swiftly into the crowds calling to the men of her family who came and disappeared along the lane to the woods.

'She is never wrong,' a woman said who had been listening. 'She saw the press men and told her men to run away until they have gone.'

Edward looked about him at the lively scene. 'I see no bullies,' he said.

'She saw them in your hand,' the woman said, and gathered up her bags of turnips and carrots and made for her small cart. 'God have mercy on you,' she called as if his fate was doomed.

A man with a wide black hat strolled among the stalls and as he turned, Edward saw the tarred pigtail worn by seafaring men. Two other men dragged a poor wretch in chains to a cart and left him under guard with blood running from a blow on his head.

Edward hurried into the inn and the potboy took him to a room upstairs where Sarah was sitting. 'Your pigeons are almost ready and I will eat with you, Mr Fletcher. Take off the hot doublet and unloose the laces on the jerkin.'

'The press men are here,' he said almost in a whisper. 'They have taken one man by force and are looking for more.'

'You must pretend to be with me if they come here, and they may pass this room.'

Heavy footsteps came up the wooden stairs and loud voices called to the inn-keeper to tell them if there were young men staying there.

'Quickly!' Sarah said. 'Loosen the bandages and show the wound you have.' She pulled the thin curtains across the windows so that the room was only dimly lit and undid her bodice, showing her still curved breasts. 'They have orders to take only men who are fit and have no visible infection, or they fester and die at sea. Say nothing and leave them to me.'

The door was flung open and a man stood there, grinning. 'Having a bit of entertainment before you offer yourself for hire?' he asked seeing the leather clothes of a humble workman and Sarah's state of undress. 'Well, His Majesty will give you a hammock on board one of his ships and if you come without a struggle you'll be treated fair.'

'I am a freeman,' Edward said. 'You can't take me.'

The man laughed and raised his baton as he approached the bed. 'Freemen don't come to market in worker's clothing.'

Sarah began to whine and put a hand as if to caress Edward's chest, then drew back, screaming. She rushed to the seaman and flung herself at his feet. 'Take him away! Take him away!' she shouted. 'He has the plague!'

She fell as he pushed her roughly away and stepped towards the bed to see better in the badly lit room. Edward exposed more of the black scar and the mixture of sweat and crushed leaves and the man backed away again, suddenly afraid.

'The flower of the plague is blossoming,' Sarah muttered, rocking herself on the floor. 'The black buboes have formed,' she added for good measure. 'Take him away from my room before he dies or I can never have customers here.'

'Whistle up the men,' called the seaman. 'And get back to the cutter ready to cast off!' He paused by the door and looked back, his face contorted with fear and loathing, then clattered down the stairs, shouting that the man they had captured must be released as they had been in the market and may have touched the one with the distemper.

Sarah buttoned her bodice with an air of false modesty and laughed. 'We'll not see their like for months,' she said. 'They had a few die of the plague on one of the ships and they are more careful now.' She took his hand and pulled him from the bed. 'No, don't cover it. You must show yourself to be clean or you'll ruin my trade.' One by one, more of the market traders came to see the man with the unsightly scar that was no more than a burn, and a wave of relief and amusement swept through the docks. 'You saved my life,' Edward said.

'You would have survived, but your bride would have suffered from your absence,' Sarah replied.

'You were wrong,' Edward called when he saw the gypsy who had read his palm. 'I am not going far across the sea!'

'I will tell you the rest and now you can pay me,' she said, her dark eyes hard and compelling. 'You will, as I said, go far across the sea with your wife. You escaped today, but there is one man who hates you and will try to harm you and yours, so go soon and grow strange crops, and fish for monsters out of the sea.'

'What of my wife? Do you see children?'

'I see her bearing a son and two daughters.'

Edward laughed with pleasure. 'I shall have a son!'

She eyed him in a strange way. 'You will prosper and there will be a son and two girls,' she said, and closed his hand over his palm.

Edward decided to ride home later and not spend the night in Southampton when he found two men who were going as far as Elney. He ate the pigeons and cheese and bread with Sarah before she went to fetch Bessie. She dismissed his thanks with a shrug.

'I'll eat up now if you pay, and get more strength, as I shall have a lot of business soon when men come asking how I sent away the press bullies. They'll talk about it all over Southampton and Portsmouth and when they come to the docks they'll remember me and want me above all other whores here, and brag that they slept with Sarah.'

Edward walked by the waterfront while waiting for his companions and looked up at the stern of a ship that was loading for a long voyage. He spoke to one of the sailors and learned that it was leaving in two days for America. 'How much is it for a man and his wife and chattels to go there?' he asked.

'Working or passage?' the man asked, eyeing his broad shoulders with approval.

'I'm a carpenter and a freeman with little money, but I wouldn't sign on as ship's crew and slave before the mast.'

'A carpenter?' the man consulted an officer who shook his head.

'He says we have a full complement and need no more skilled men.' He pointed to a building on the edge of the water by the Customs House. 'Go there and put your name on the list if you are serious about leaving. From time to time crews desert or fall sick and they supply replacements, but an ordinary voyage with some comforts would cost ten pounds for two. When you reached New England there would be more to pay for land and timber for a house. If you can pay, there is room for two with space for your belongings on this voyage. There is no other passage for two months.'

Edward rode home and put the horse in the stable with hay and a good bed of straw. He told Hope of his adventure and laughed about Sarah's part in it, but she sensed that he had been frightened and wanted to go away where no man could try to imprison him in a stinking hold.

He went to fetch wood and she quickly opened the chest and took out fifteen pounds of the money that John had given her on the night before the wedding. 'I also have something to tell,' she said. 'When you had gone, Furness came and tried to make me go to the manor as his master wanted to see me. I refused, as I didn't believe him. I think he wanted to take me himself as he threatened to do the other day.'

'He tried that? You didn't tell me!'

'You had your own worries,' she said, looking at the soiled and loose dressings. 'I hoped he would give up but I see that when you are away I could be in danger.'

'I'll kill him,' Edward said, with such force that Hope backed away.

'No, that would solve nothing. We must go away, my dear. Aunt Ellen told Master John and he was angry.' She took a deep breath as she knew that what she said was only half true. 'He sent money for us to go far away, to that place you told me about in America.'

'What money? We need ten pounds to go on the next boat,' he said, eagerly. 'I have a little but we need so much more.'

She handed him the fifteen pounds. 'That will be enough to give us food and lodging for a while once we are there, after paying for the passage. What money you have will buy things we'll need for our new home.'

'I shall never be out of my debt to him. I must go now to thank him and tell him we leave in two days on the evening tide. If I stay and see Furness, I know that murder will be done!'

'Master John is away with Mistress Hannam, visiting her relatives, so if we go now, we shall never see him again.'

'I shall leave a letter for Mrs Turner to give him, but we must leave now or there will not be another ship for two or three months. Don't look so upset. We have each other and that is all that matters.'

'Yes, we have each other for the rest of our lives,' she said quietly, as if making a vow.

Chapter 8

Ellen Turner swung the black kettle away from the fire and infused the herbal tea. She was exhausted, not by the physical effort of riding to Southampton in the bumpy coach, and back with John Halben in his carriage, but because she knew that she might never see her niece again.

Hope's mother had refused to go to the docks to see her daughter off to the New World. 'You'll die out there, eaten by savages,' she said. 'You won't have a roof over your head and your husband will go off after another idea, once the newness has worn off, leaving everything he touches unfinished.' She sniffed at the pretty new table that now was hers as a parting gift and ignored the fact that it was beautifully made.

'A married woman must follow her husband,' Hope said, her temper flaring. 'I want to go away. I can't stay here and be raped by that worm at the manor! You didn't know that he tried to take me in the woods, did you, Mother? He tried again here when I was alone and he is determined to have his way if we stay here. Since my father died,

154

everyone thinks you must be protected from bad news. Nobody tells you anything that you might not want to hear and you live here as if in a squirrel's drey, never seeing what goes on and never hearing anything that might upset you!'

'I'll come with you,' Ellen had said and she had arranged the coach to take Hope and Edward and their belongings, Edward's tools and the two dowry chests firmly sealed and strapped up to make them safe from sea-water and thieving hands.

Edward left brief letters to old friends and one stilted note to John Halben thanking him for all his care of them, but as he wrote, he found the words wouldn't go on paper and he couldn't think what to say. Hope wrote nothing and tried to hide the bitterness of her deep sense of loss by keeping busy and appearing indifferent to leaving Little Deerwood.

The docks were bathed in sunshine and the water was calm. White sails, heavy with brine, stretched over kegs of oil and ale to dry on the quayside, and sailmakers examined them for flaws that if mended soon would not present the hazard of splitting under heavy weather.

Gangplanks sagged under the steps of men carrying sacks and boxes of stores and the air was filled with shouts and the cries of vendors selling herbs and tinctures guaranteed to keep away everything from scurvy to the Devil. A cow and two pigs and crates of fowls were put with the fodder in the stern of the ship under a roof of canvas. Sacks of root vegetables, and turnip tops that might last for a few days before they wilted, were put near the galley, and it was obvious that the ship was nearly ready to sail.

Edward and Hope signed the papers necessary for the voyage and paid what was due, then Hope left her husband to see that their baggage was safely stowed away and that the quarters were neat and dry, before he joined her and Ellen for food in the inn.

Sarah came down from her room briefly to see them, but she was busy with sailors from a Dutch boat who found Bessie pretty and eager and with whom they had no language barrier as few words were needed. 'I've two rooms now since your husband was here last,' she said with pride. 'One for Bessie and me to live in and the other for work. Soon we may rent a house and have more girls there.'

Hope felt cold and dispirited. She drank some ale that tasted very bitter and tried to eat some of the lamb stew that was put before her, but the greasy skin that formed on top of the tureen looked grey and un-appetizing.

'Take these with you and make sure you have some every day,' Ellen said. 'It wards off scurvy and you may be at sea for several weeks. This other one is for seasickness. Your grandfather used it every time he went fishing and was never sick, even far out in deep water.'

Hope gave her a grateful smile and felt that she might need all the help she could have if the weather turned foul.

'Take some strong waters, mistress,' the innkeeper suggested. 'You look a bit green round the gills and that's best for it.' He poured a generous amount of brandy and she sipped it, feeling the colour return to her cheeks and the warmth to her whole body. She brought a flagon of the harsh spirit to take with her.

Gypsies with baskets of gaudy trifles and ribbons wandered through the inn parlour and the woman who had read Edward's palm looked at Hope with almost malicious eyes when she refused to have her fortune told.

'I'll say this for nothing, lady. You'll arrive where you are going with more than you thought you had, that is yours and not your husband's, and you'll prosper, but there's trouble in the future of your own doing.'

Hope looked guilty, knowing that she had hidden most of the money and had said nothing of it to Edward. Impulsively, she gave the woman a coin. 'Is there happiness where we are going?' she asked.

'Busy people make their own content-ment,' the woman said. 'Idleness makes for discontent. You will have much to do for a very long time.'

'I saw you the other day!' Edward came up behind them. 'Tell her what you told me.'

'I said that your wife would bear a son and two daughters.'

'And this voyage?' Edward, who had said that gypsies were false prophets and he believed nothing of what they said, seemed tense as if he needed her reassurance.

'You will make a safe harbour,' she said, took the coin he offered and disappeared into the crowds outside.

'That was short,' Ellen said. 'Usually they speak of so much that it's impossible to remember half of it afterwards. I should have asked when my rich and handsome stranger is to appear, as I was promised ten years ago!'

'What did she tell you?' Edward asked.

'As Aunt Ellen said, she was not willing to say much.' Edward frowned and she added hastily, 'She said nothing bad. We shall be busy and contented.' She took his hand. 'We shall have work to do and in it find pleasure,' she said.

'When we have children, we shall indeed be blessed,' he said. 'And a safe harbour is all we can think of until we start our new life.'

'Did you buy the fish-hooks?' Ellen asked. 'The man who came back from New England last year told me that they were like gold out there and even if you don't need them all, you can sell them to other settlers.'

'I have nails and fish-hooks and nets and snares and some good knives in with my musket,' Edward said. 'I can build a smoke house if we find game and we have saltpetre for preserving and a box of flints to make fire until we find flint-bearing rocks.'

It was an oral inventory that gave him satisfaction and Hope added the fact that she was well supplied with sewing material and needles and thread. 'I have a book, too, in which to enter what we spend and make and what we do from week to week,' she said. Her lips trembled. 'If we come back, it will be a journal of our time there and interesting for you to read, Aunt Ellen.'

'Remember that you have a home here,' Ellen said. It gave her pleasure to think that Hope could come back and live on the Isle of Wight if she needed to leave America.

'We sold our cottage,' Edward reminded her, and she wondered if Hope would ever tell her husband that she had a property on the island, now to be rented out under her aunt's care. 'If we came back, we would have to start again, which might be hard if we fail in the New World.'

Hooters sounded and whistles blew to

warn passengers to board the ship. Hope gathered her parcels and followed Edward who carried the box they would need on the voyage and which would not be stowed in the hold. At the gangway, Ellen embraced them and tears began to fall. Hope went on to the ship, her head bent and her shoulders shaking, trying to stop the urge to leap ashore and run back to the life she had always known and had once thought to be enough.

Edward and the other men embarking stood silently and pale-faced while sailors heaved on warps, and sails were untied ready for hoisting once they were free of the jetty. He almost wished that he had the hard physical work of hauling up the gangways to do instead of standing feeling sick at heart and watching the docks recede in the evening sunlight.

'Have they gone, Ellen?'

'Master John, what are you doing here?'

'I brought Mistress Hannam home and came to see a shipwright on the docks,' he said. 'I saw Edward Fletcher, but lost him in the crowd. When I asked for the names of passengers on the bill of landing, their names were there.'

'Hope had trouble with the steward,' Ellen said. 'They felt that they must get away quickly before he caused real trouble. There's no other ship to New England for another two or three months so they had to go now.' She sighed. 'It's for the best, as truth will out and Furness will be a threat to any he thinks is under his thumb.' She smiled. 'Now, thanks to you, he can hurt no one. I feel safe for the future in the house you gave me and I can leave Deerwood to work for the doctor if Sir William dies or goes mad.'

She laughed. 'Sarah has come off well as she is free of Little Deerwood. She is making a name for her and Bessie here, and will soon run her own brothel.'

John seemed not to listen. 'It's leaving,' he said, softly. He gazed at the ship as it slipped away from its moorings and sluggishly sat on the tide. Several of the passengers lined the rails and Ellen waved vigorously when she saw Hope's white fichu and pale-blue dress, but John Halben stood silent, staring at the girl who seemed to grow smaller as the gap between jetty and ship increased.

'I think she saw us,' Ellen said, but Hope had waved only once until she saw who was standing by Ellen's side.

'I'll take you home, Ellen,' John said.

'You look pale. Did Mistress Hannam not give you a good dinner?'

He grinned and she saw in him the impish boy she had loved since he was born. 'Nothing as good as comes from your kitchen,' he said. 'We'll eat first and I'm thirsty.' He told the coachman to wait and go for his own food, then led Ellen back to the inn where he ate little but drank enough to dull his anguish.

Hope turned away from the rail and stumbled along to the stairway leading down to her cabin, half blinded by her tears. He was there! It was cruel to watch her leave when her heart was with him, but he must be suffering too.

'We are fortunate, Hope. This is the best cabin and we have a window.' Edward was excited. He held her in his arms and kissed her tenderly. 'This was the right thing to do,' he assured her when he saw her tear-stained face. 'We must look ahead and plan what we have to do when we arrive. I met a man who had been there and knows all about it. He says he can arrange a house to rent before we build our own if he is convinced of our good will, and he can advise how we buy our stocks and tell us which people are honest.'

'All friends of his?' Hope said, crossly. 'He sounds like a fairground barker. We'll wait until we get there before we part with a penny to any one.' She eyed her husband with an attempt at humour. 'He *did* ask for money, I suppose?'

'Just to establish our good will, but I didn't give him any,' Edward said defensively. 'I said I'd talk to you about it.'

'I'd like to meet him,' Hope said. 'Is he on deck? We can see him now and be rid of him when he sees that we are not interested in schemes that we have not seen and decide may have no base.'

'He seems honest,' Edward said, 'but you can see for yourself.' Hope washed her face and felt better now that she had a problem to solve. They went on deck and ducked under the ropes that were loose from the sails as the men raised them up to hold taut wings already filling as the craft sailed down Southampton Water.

A group of men stood round a small upended barrel that was being used as a table in the bows of the middle deck. A smooth voice invited them to chance their skill in a game of cards and Hope laughed as one after another, men produced money to put on the table. 'Is that the man?' she asked and Edward nodded. 'He's started off early,' she said. 'He'll be a rich man before we land, and those idiots will be poor.'

The man looked up and saw Edward. He beckoned as if he knew that Edward would join them, but saw Hope and found the level gaze of the grey-green eyes disturbing and turned away. She watched the men play for five minutes and then put her hand in Edward's and smiled. 'He'll get nothing from us,' she said firmly.

He grinned and shrugged. 'I wish I had

your talent for knowing what people are really like,' he said. 'We must never deal with anyone without discussing it with the other.'

'Remain friends with him, but keep a tight hold on our money,' she said. 'This is a long voyage and we don't want enemies. If he does know the country then he can be useful, just giving us information about the people there and their way of life. I shall note it all in my book and have a few names to draw on when we get there, even if the names are ones we need to avoid! What is his name?'

'Joseph Rigsby. He left a wife out there, so he must have roots of a sort.'

'Poor woman to be left alone in a heathen land,' Hope murmured. She turned back the quilt of her cot and yawned. Edward sat beside her. 'This is a good cabin considering the space in the ship,' he said. 'But it gives no room for husband and wife to be together.' He glanced up at the narrow bunk above hers.

'This seems strong,' she said, demurely. 'I'm willing to share it with you for an hour, sir, if you wash off the last of the dressing and let it dry. It's healing fast and will do well with no further attention, so long as you don't knock the scabs.'

He went outside to wash and tossed the now stinking linen into the sea, while Hope undressed and lay naked under the quilt. Edward closed and bolted the door and glanced at the small square window and felt secure as it looked out on open sea and not the deck, so they were alone.

It was warm and dark and the sound of water under the keel sang a sweet chuckling song as they lay entwined. Hope responded with passion as she sought comfort and forgetting. She caressed the raised burn and knew that whenever she saw the scar, she would think of Deerwood and remember the events that led to their leaving the village. At last Hope urged Edward to go to his own bed and she stretched out in the cramped space, wide awake, to consider what was happening to them.

She smiled. There was no going back and life in the future could be exciting. Even their lovemaking was more satisfying now. I'll have to keep an eye on Edward, she decided. He's a babe in arms when it comes to swindlers as he has met mainly honest folk in the village. It's as well he knows nothing of the money I have safely packed in the bottom of my dowry chest.

She shut her mind to all thoughts and memories of John and fell asleep as the ship reached open sea, with nothing but the Atlantic and America ahead. The Isle of Wight lay lost in darkness as the emigrant ship sailed by and the property that she now owned but had never seen, was forgotten.

The clatter of wooden dishes and pewter mugs roused her and a knock on the door told them that there was ale and bread available. Hope blinked and looked out at the sea. It was still calm but she felt that food in any form would make her sick, so she buried herself in her quilt again and murmured that she wasn't hungry.

She slept and woke two hours later, suddenly famished, and was glad that Edward had brought her some ale and bread when he had his. The day passed easily, with gulls flying out to them until they left the last glimpse of shore; then they deserted the ship and flew back to England. One of the cooks trailed lines for mackerel and the stiff blue fish were cooked for dinner.

One by one, the faces of the other passengers became separate and recognizable, and Hope sat with a woman who already had two children and was going to join her husband who worked for the governor of the Massachusetts Bay Confederation.

'That sounds very important,' Hope said.

'It is fairly new,' Mistress Chilton said. 'It was started up in 1643 to link several states round Massachusetts Bay under one governor to help trade and protect the people against their enemies. My husband worked for the governor when he was in

London and he sent for him to help with the clerical side of his office,' Mary Chilton said. 'He decided to stay and sent for me and the children.'

'So everything isn't as primitive as we thought,' Hope said.

'Indeed not. In Plimoth and much of New England there are good houses and shops and the farms produce fair crops. The land abounds in game and timber and they send back beaver skins and sassafras to their agents in England with tithes to the men who supported the first Pilgrims and who now have a percentage of all their gains.'

'It sounds as if the agents do well with little effort,' Hope said.

'They do, but you must remember that for the first few years they had no return on their loans, and many of the first Pilgrims died or starved and the rest had nothing to send back as they had no strength to work.'

'Is it like that in all the new towns?' Hope asked.

'The early settlements are good but some have trouble with local tribes of Indians. At first, the Pilgrim Fathers made fast friends with the chiefs and were helped by them in time of famine. Samoset and Squanto were two who helped them to survive and served them faithfully for years, but people like Captain Miles Standish, who did a lot of good, also did a lot of harm as he decided that guns were more important than tools and parley and he showed strength and subdued many of the local tribes.'

'Is there strife everywhere?'

'No, I hear that the islands are better in safety but poorer in worldly terms. As yet, greedy men haven't tainted the friendship between immigrants and the natives. Good religious people settled on an island called The Vineyard after many of the towns were built in New England and New Hampshire and Massachusetts. They were not as rigid and bigoted as the Pilgrim Fathers as far as religion went, although they quietly converted many Indians to Christianity. They made friends and were given good advice and help when they thought they would starve. They found and were shown stores of corn and oil in empty places, where Indians had lived but whose tribes had been wiped out by an epidemic of cholera.'

'Are there houses there?'

Mary Chilton smiled. 'Of course. I haven't seen Martha's Vineyard but I hear that it is beautiful and not unlike the Isle of Wight, but smaller. There are settlements there and plenty of sweet water, and land that the Indians are willing to sell. As yet, there is a good life for the taking if you work hard.'

'You said Martha's Vineyard. Does it belong to someone of that name?'

'The island has had many names. It was

once called Neope by the Indians, which means, "in the midst of the sea", but later they called it Capawok. It was called Vineland by Norsemen who landed for water and game there a thousand years ago but made no settlements. Later, I believe it was called after many people, including Claudia, the wife of a French king, but when Bartholomew Gosnold landed, blown off course from his intended landing in America, he was much taken with the island, settled there and called it Martha's Vineyard after his mother.'

'How do you know all this?' asked Hope.

'My husband has maps and sea charts of the area and I am interested in the New World and mean to make a document of all the history of Cape Cod and the islands.' She smiled and put down her knitting to pull her shawl more firmly over her shoulders. 'If I am to live there, I must know what I am seeing and experiencing and take pleasure in it. So many people are blind to what surrounds them and wear blinkers in new surroundings. They wonder why they do not settle and so are unhappy! Where do you intend making a home?' she asked.

Hope smiled. 'Having met you I wish it was to be Plimoth, but we are bound for the islands where we were told land is cheap and they need skilled carpenters.' She hesitated and then said, 'We know a man from the manor house of our village who has property on The Vineyard. Are you sure that it is the same as Martha's Vineyard?'

'It is the same. Tell me, who is this man? Has he been to the New World?'

'He is John Halben, son of Sir William Halben of Deerwood Manor.'

'I must ask my husband about him and about his land. A name like that is a useful introduction so when you get to The Vineyard, mention that you are a friend of his.'

Hope laughed. 'He is the son of the lord of the manor and very wealthy, and my husband is only a carpenter, although he is a freeman and I am the daughter of a yeoman,' she added proudly.

'You will find that there is less difference where you are going. When people toil together and even have to suffer a little, it is a great equalizer.' She smiled. 'Rank loses its importance. If you can make a man happy and keep him well with good food and care, you can make a home even in a tent, or in one of the deerskin tepees of the Indians, and hold your own with anyone.'

'I thought they had hard winters in New England. How can they exist in tents?'

'They have shacks as well, and a tepee can be warm and dry even in storms.'

'We were told that the ship goes to Plimoth first and then on to the islands. Would you advise that we buy land unseen from a broker in Plimoth, or wait until we can see what we are getting for our money?'

'My husband's office deals with land and with honest brokers. It would be safer to buy and have all your documents safely witnessed before you leave Plimoth, and a copy lodged with a lawyer there in case someone tries to swindle you out of your land.' She looked serious. 'We buy land from willing Indians, and never try to take it from them, unlike the men who came after the Pilgrims and live in Boston and other places, who take what they want by force if necessary and bring shame and suffering to everyone.

'The settlers on The Vineyard have grown close to the local population and they help each other.' She frowned. 'Whatever you buy will need hard toil as it is virgin land and often rocky and unmanured, with bushes and trees that will have to be cut. If you buy close to the sea you can fish and use seaweed as well as wood ash to break up the soil.'

Edward had joined them and was listening intently. 'We don't have much money for land, but a piece by the sea would be best,' he agreed.

'We can buy a small plot and build a house and add to it later, or move away to a bigger plot when Edward has made more money,' Hope said.

Once again, she was tempted to tell him of her store of money but something held her back. With the money from the cottage and the rest of the sum she had handed over to Edward from John Halben's purse, they had enough for a small plot of land and for enough timber to build a house. She knew that Edward would work well if he knew an end to his toil was in sight, but after a while, he would want to make more artistic things than wooden fencing and door lintels. To buy something bigger would be unwise.

Am I wicked? she wondered when she was alone again, gazing out at the endless green water that merged with the pale-blue distant skyline without a break of land. The penetrating stare of the dark-eyed gypsy was clear in her mind. She told me I had something that wasn't Edward's. How did she know? And she'd said I'd be in trouble of my own making. She sighed. It's too late now. I know I must protect our future and if men like Mr Rigsby pour out that evil friendly charm on Edward, I'll need to keep a close watch on him.

In the distance, the sky was darker now and the wind changed, making the sails flap and the ship to lose speed. Shouted orders brought men scurrying to take in sail and the captain took the wheel. 'Best go below, madam,' he called. 'We're in for a blow.'

The canvas strained and sagged, then

strained again and the ship pushed through the water, sending up walls of white foam and leaving a flurried wake as the wheel turned the prow across the troughs to keep an even keel, to pitch and not roll. Hope clung to a strut and staggered below, nearly falling down the steep companion-way. The airless cabin was far worse than being on deck and she could watch the water cover the window, recede and come back again as if trying to get at her.

'Are you all right, Hope?' Edward was nearly flung across the cabin.

'I think so,' she said in a small voice. 'I've never been sea sick, but I feel sick now.' He put the night pail by her bed and she sank back and closed her eyes.

'I'll go aft,' he said. 'I'm hungry.'

Hope shuddered. 'No food for me,' she murmured. 'Just some of the herbs that Aunt Ellen gave me and a draught of spirit.' She sipped the raw brandy and felt warmer, but her head ached and if she opened her eyes, she wanted to reel down through the bed into a well of giddiness.

At last she fell asleep and when Edward came back, she was unaware of him standing by her cot. He smiled at her as she lay there. 'You are so beautiful,' he whispered. His pleasure was tinged with pride, but his smile lacked a certain sympathy. For the first time since they had decided to sail to

Massachusetts he felt superior and in charge. He was fit and enjoyed the motion of the ship, and at least for a while, Hope was weak and dependent on him completely.

The wind howled and the timbers creaked as the ship plunged through the waves. Hope slept, drugged by the spirit and the potent herbs that her aunt had given her. Dawn came with no respite from the storm and the cattle penned in the stern moaned and tried to break away, but were constrained and tied to stop them injuring themselves or doing damage to the ship.

Hope opened one eye and saw the green water across the window. She shuddered and almost prayed for death. It was madness to think that they could survive a voyage of weeks or even months on this terrible boat and then have the energy to make a home in some inhospitable wilderness.

'Am I the only one sick?' she asked feebly when Edward came in scattering seaspray and objectionable good health.

'There aren't many out of bed now,' he replied. 'You'd feel better aloft, out in the air, and it's a wonderful sight. The waves must be twenty feet high.'

She gave him a withering look and eyed the mug of ale that he handed her with distrust. She gnawed the corner of a piece of hard tack. 'Why do they bother to make ships-biscuits?' she said.

'They're so hard that it keeps the weevils from boring into them and they last for months at sea,' Edward said. He took out a penknife and cut a raw onion in half, added a slice of cheese and crunched it with a piece of biscuit.

Hope turned away. 'Is Mistress Chilton abed?' she asked.

'No, she's on deck with her children and they are all in good health, but she's the only female on deck.'

'She's the kind who should build New Worlds,' Hope said, with a tinge of rancour. 'If I ever get to shore safely, I'll never set foot on a boat again as long as I live.'

'It isn't only the women who are sick,' Edward said. 'Mr Rigsby will make not a penny today as he is prostrate and most of his cronies are too.'

'Go away,' Hope said, feeling a wave of nausea as she smelled the raw onion when Edward kissed her cheek. 'I dislike all men who can stand upon a bucking deck and not feel ill!'

'The captain says that it will blow itself out tomorrow. In spite of the weather, we've made good headway and managed to stay on course.'

'I want to sleep again,' Hope said. 'Give me more of the herbs.'

'Only a little,' he said, seeing her eyes were

still showing signs of belladonna, overbright and dark-centred. 'Try the peppermint. That settles the stomach.'

'Goodnight,' she murmured.

'Sleep well, sweetheart.' Edward closed the door behind him, grinning to himself. She must be stupefied if she wished him good night at twelve noon!

Mistress Chilton greeted him with a smile and enquired after Hope's well-being. Her two boys hung on the rail and tried to catch the spume thrown up by the waves laughing and rosy-checked. 'She'll be better soon,' she said. 'A ship like this is far worse than a small fishing boat for some people, but we are not affected; I feel sick only on small boats.'

'That is a relief, Mistress Chilton,' Edward said. 'Hope has never been sick even in rough weather when we went fishing.'

'I was sick once on the boat to Ireland,' she said, thinking back with a frown, 'but I was carrying George then so it was not really seasickness.'

'I wish that we were expecting a child,' Edward said. 'A boy like yours would make life complete.'

'You may have girls,' she said, with a smile. 'I pray that I may have a daughter one day.' She gave a wistful smile. 'That for me would make life complete.'

'We shall have a son and two daughters,'

Edward said, then blushed. 'Or so the gypsy told me, so by next year if she is right, I may have a son.'

'Did she tell you which would come first? It could be a girl,' Mary Chilton said with a teasing smile. 'That would be wonderful.'

'I hadn't thought of that,' Edward said. He looked crestfallen. 'I was hoping for a son.'

'As you have been married for such a short time, wait until your wife is expecting before you make plans!'

'Hope has never said if she wants a family,' he recalled. He shrugged. 'All women want babies, or they wouldn't be married.'

'We have no choice once we are wed,' Mary Chilton said with a sad smile. 'I married late and have less child-bearing years, and they say that I have been fortunate to have two sons.' She gazed out to sea with a fixed smile. 'There are three years between my boys, and no other on the way, but I pray each night that I may yet have a daughter.'

'Surely that is unimportant. If we have two sons as healthy as yours we shall be blessed.'

Mary Chilton looked at him with strangely cold eyes. 'How can a man know a woman's need for a girl?' she said, and Edward felt repelled by her vehemence.

Chapter 9

Three weeks of fairly rough weather followed the storm, during which time most of the passengers recovered enough to go on deck, and some even found their lost appetites. The sea lost its white caps and the captain made the most of the brisk following wind and put on all sails.

The motion of the vessel was now bearable and for the last time, Hope put arnica on the bruises that Edward had suffered when walking the decks and being flung against gunwales and hatch covers, and oil on the scars left by the tar burn now that the area was healed. He was exhilarated and ate heartily, urging her to do the same.

'You look like a ghost,' he said, and she knew that she had lost weight. She breathed deeply as she walked slowly across the deck and felt the fresh sea breeze in her hair.

'I've been away from the sun for too long,' she said, but knew that her lassitude was not due to that alone. It was made worse by the nagging homesickness that haunted her in her weakened state. Her skin was fine and almost transparent and her breasts were sore, but that was nothing new since the wedding, as Edward found them fascinating and irresistible.

Fresh fish was caught again and many of the passengers trailed a line to add to the day's harvest and it made a welcome change from the dried stores and cheeses that had been the diet of the past weeks. The cows decided that they could let down their milk again and their swollen udders were saved from mastitis by careful milking. Junket and cottage cheese made an addition to the diet and one man produced a small butterchurn to use up the milk and the whey went to the pigs.

Hope began to eat and enjoyed the fish, sitting again with Mistress Chilton who seemed unaffected by weather and food. Mr Rigsby appeared, wan and shaky from his cabin, but brightened when he found men ready to bet on the day's catch of fish. Most of the crew and many of the passengers made the bets with him.

'Why does the captain allow him to do that?' Hope asked.

'He says it keeps men interested and stops them from being aggressive,' Mary Chilton said, and certainly as soon as dusk fell each day and the last line was drawn in, there was muted excitement among the passengers and great arguments about the chances the next day of guessing the weight caught. Winds and ocean currents were studied, and older men in the crew who knew the Atlantic, were paid to give hints as to the whereabouts of shoals of fish and the conditions in which they thrived and could be caught. Hope smiled when Edward obviously wanted to join the others. He placed a small bet which he lost, to Hope's relief, as he then shrugged away all efforts to persuade him to put up more money and ignored any further betting.

'I've had my eyes opened on this ship,' he told her. 'Do you know that Mr Deane over there, the one who looks like a very pious parson, bribed one of the crew to swear that there would be a shoal of huge fish like sturgeon on the current yesterday and everyone bet on large catches except him and he won! Even when Mr Rigsby took his share from the bets that failed, Mr Deane made a lot of money.'

'If we learn such things, the experience will be good for the future,' Hope said. 'It is impossible to judge people by their looks. I thought Mistress Chilton was a delicate lady who did nothing but knit, but she is as tough as most men and has a fund of knowledge that any schoolteacher would envy.'

Lines of washing hung everywhere as clothes were freshened with the water collected in buckets and tubs and anything that would catch rainwater during the storms, and an air of optimism filled the ship. But Hope was depressed and even on calm days felt nauseated by some smells and some food, but by evening she was unusually hungry and ate mashed carrots and swedes as if she couldn't have enough.

Mary Chilton allowed her boys to run about in pantaloons and no shirts and they became brown and lively under the sun, fishing or playing card games with the other two children on board.

At night, Edward was eager to have Hope alone and delighted in her firm warm body and the physical passion that was growing between them. She was content to make love as her feelings were easily roused now that she was used to marriage, and she convinced herself that she now loved Edward as much as she had loved John on that one afternoon of misguided abandon.

She walked along the deck and avoided some damp washing. As she bent down she saw another string hidden from casual view as if it was a private thing. It was laden with small linen towels that she recognized as those a woman used when her menses were fluxing. She leaned against the rail, suddenly weak. So much had occupied her mind that she had forgotten when she was due, and she realized that she had missed a period.

Mary Chilton smiled and removed her knitting from the bench on which she sat, making room for Hope. 'You look pale, my dear. Are you ill?'

'No.' Hope leaned against the bulkhead and closed her eyes. She was adding up the days and weeks, and the more she counted, the faster she knew that she was expecting a baby. 'No, I'm not ill, but I think I know why I have been so sick.' She looked at Mary Chilton with wide eyes as if there had never been a woman in her condition before now and she couldn't believe it was happening to her.

Mary chuckled. 'I wondered, when you were sick long after the sea calmed,' she said. She held out her knitting and laughed. 'If I'd been a gaming woman I'd have wagered with Mr Rigsby that you were in that condition. I hope to finish this before we land and you shall have it for your first born as a remembrance from me.' She held up the shawl that was half finished and said wistfully, 'I make garments suitable for girls, but each time I have had a boy. If you have a girl you must bring her to Plimoth to show me and stay for a long time.'

Hope was suddenly shy. Edward would be pleased but she wanted to keep it to herself just for a while. She touched her still flat abdomen and wondered how a child could fit into a space that wasn't there! Her friends and relatives who had children hid the fact under the voluminous skirts and smocks that they wore for working so that they appeared fatter but much as they usually did. She had never seen a woman naked who was with child.

'How much longer are we at sea?' she asked.

'Long enough for you to rest and be used to the idea, but short enough to let you have your child ashore, when you have settled in a home of your own,' Mary said firmly, seeing the rising panic in her eyes. 'You won't have it on the ship and you have many months in which to prepare.'

'I'll be alone,' Hope whispered. She looked across the empty sea and shuddered. 'I shall know only my husband and have no goodwife to deliver me.'

'There are women there who have had babies,' Mary said, in a bracing voice. 'Most of the children survive now that there are better supplies and good food.' She glanced at Hope's taut breasts. 'You should be able to feed your babies.'

'And what if my milk doesn't come?'

'Be silent!' Mary Chilton looked angry. 'You are healthy and young and there are many months before you need think of that.' She faced the almost hysterical girl and looked into her eyes as if she would compel her to obey, the force of her personality almost frightening, showing that she would stand no nonsense. 'Consider what's ahead.

183

You will have a child and feed her as women have fed their young since the world began and you will raise a healthy child. If, however, you have no milk, then there are wet-nurses even in New England who will care for you and yours.'

'Women who have lost their own?' Hope said with renewed apprehension.

'Sometimes,' admitted Mary. 'But there are many who have too much milk for one and feed two babies.'

'Did you feed yours?'

'I fed one and had a wet-nurse for the younger one. I had to follow my husband to France and he made me leave the children with servants under the care of my sister who is unmarried.' She bent over her knitting again. 'Don't be afraid of where you are going. If it is God's will that you have an easy birth, then it matters not where in the world you are. I became pregnant too soon after the second boy as I wasn't making milk, and miscarried in France even though I was attended by the best doctors there.'

Hope saw her almost hidden distress. 'It was a girl?'

Mary nodded. 'Since then I haven't conceived and Henry is almost five.' She laughed as if she threw away her grief. 'If you have a girl and don't want her, give her to me!'

'If I have twin girls, then one is yours,'

Hope said lightly. She kissed the woman's cheek. 'Thank you, Mary. I am calm now and can tell Edward without bursting into tears!'

'All women weep at these times but have happy moods, too. Eat well and I'm sure that your Aunt Ellen, whom you talk of so much, has given you herbs to help you when the time comes.'

The ship's bell jangled to announce that food was ready and Hope took her share of fish soup and bread and ate it with a good appetite. With hot water begged from the gallery, she made an infusion of tea from dried scurvy grass and insisted that Edward drank some, too.

'You look better,' he said.

'I'm well, and I am hungry. When we land I want fruit if we can find some and good broth if we catch wild fowl or rabbits.'

'I was right. We shall make a good life, Hope, for us and for our children when they come, but that will be later, of course, when we have built our home and I have found work.'

She regarded him with amusement. 'We have been married for almost three months now and you have taken me in bed every night. Don't you think that something might have happened in all that time? If it did not, you would accuse me of being barren and now I know that I am not! Don't look so shocked. You've talked enough of having children and now you seem put out.'

'We didn't want one so soon,' he muttered. 'There's work to be done first.'

'We'll manage,' she said quietly, and knew once more that Edward would depend on her, as he hadn't thought beyond the idea of a family. I must make sure that his heart is in it and then he'll be a tower of strength, she declared. 'If we are to have a son and two daughters as the gypsy promised, we must start at some time, and I am in good health,' she said, as if she had babies with no trouble, every day of the year. She was glad that he hadn't seen her when she was talking to Mary Chilton.

The sickness left her even when the sea was uneasy and Hope walked the deck and filled her lungs with good salt air. The sun rose hot and brilliant each day and sunset was a fiery glow across the endless sea. As most passengers now looked less at the water and kept to their quarters, out of the sun, Edward and Hope often sat in the bows in peace and silently urged the ship on to make a landing, trying to stifle their impatience.

Mary Chilton finished the shawl and started sewing baby clothes from the material that Hope had with her, edging the garments with lace she cut from her own petticoats.

'My son won't want to wear frills, Mistress Chilton,' Edward teased her, but he was secretly pleased that she took such pains to please Hope.

'Your daughter will wear this and more,' she replied. 'When she comes to me she shall wear silk.' She looked at the tiny garment tenderly as if there was a baby there in its folds and Hope began to wonder if Mary was quite as sane as she appeared. The idea of the child being a boy seemed to annoy her in an unreasonable way and Hope asked Edward to stop talking about it to her.

'She lost a baby girl,' Hope explained. 'If we have a girl, she wants us to take her to Plimoth to show her. She's been so kind to me that I feel that she is more like a sister than someone I met on a ship. I feel that we have a friend in the New World and that we shall see her again.'

Edward studied maps and couldn't decide where they should settle, but Hope refused to consider renting a house until they did decide where their home should be, as she wanted to make her own nest quickly for her child.

'Have you been talking to Mr Rigsby again?' she asked.

Edward's face turned red. 'He says that the lawyers in Plimoth are dishonest and he knows the people who matter in Martha's Vineyard.'

Hope tightened her mouth and picked up her diary. She walked on deck and found Mr Rigsby and smiled at him as if greeting a dear friend. 'Edward says you want to help us,' she said. He looked surprised as Hope had avoided him on deck, and when he saw her watching him when he played cards, he had a very uneasy feeling that she knew exactly what he was like under his charm.

'If I can be of service,' he said with an ingratiating smile.

She opened the book and held the pencil ready. 'If you would give me the names and addresses of the men you say have houses to rent and land to buy I can make a note of them and we can see them all when we land there. Tell me where the best sites are available and we can at least decide on the area we want to live in.'

'I must repeat what I said to your husband, that I expect a certain sum of money in advance if I am to act as your agent in this matter.'

'I'm not asking you to act for us until I know where these plots are to be found. We have maps and wish to check the suitability of each one and then if we find what we want, on paper, you could act for us.'

His smile died. 'They are spread over the island and I have no addresses to give you without payment.'

She shut the book with a slap. 'I heard it

said that you will not be going to Martha's Vineyard, Mr Rigsby. Mistress Deacon was very pleased that you had offered to find land for her family outside Plimoth and that you would be there to help them. Also, the family going to Cape Cod have been assured of your care, but I find it hard to believe that you can be in three places at once.' She looked at him with scorn. 'Have you ever set foot on Martha's Vineyard, Mr Rigsby?'

'I have been there,' he said defensively.

'And you know some of the settlers living there? Some of the main families? Like the Daggetts, the Folgers and the Nortons?'

'Everyone knows them,' he said.

'Is the land where they live good to buy? I forget the name but I'm sure that you know the town if you know the families.'

'People move about,' he said with a shrug.

'No, these were early settlers who stayed and are known to Mistress Chilton's husband as leading citizens of Great Harbour.'

'It's a while since I was there, but I do have good connections,' he blustered, and added spitefully, 'Wives should do as their husbands want and not have stupid ideas of their own.'

'Is your wife like that?' He looked puzzled. 'You told us that you had a wife on Martha's Vineyard. Is she a ghost, Mr Rigsby, like the wife you said you have in Plimoth and the other you told someone was in Portsmouth?'

'That is untrue,' he said with dignity. 'I said I wanted to find a wife in any of these places.'

'Rest assured, Mr Rigsby, if we need your help we will ask for it, but until then, please leave us alone to make our own plans.'

'You are very unwise,' he said slowly, and she felt the threat under the words.

'As you are,' she replied quickly. 'I could tell the other families what you have promised the others and when you reach Plimoth, Mistress Chilton could tell her husband, who is a man of authority. I wouldn't vouch for your safety after that.'

He scowled and turned away and Hope watched him go. She sighed with relief and went back to Edward and told him what had been said between them.

'He would make a dangerous enemy,' Edward said. 'To many people he seems to know a great deal more than they do. He treats them as if he is better than they are. I think that's why men take notice of him. I saw him when someone refused to pay a gambling debt. He said that Rigsby cheated. He was made to feel as if *he* had been the guilty one and had to say he was sorry, in front of the other men. Rigsby hardly raised his voice, but he was frightening.' Edward looked worried.

'He reminds me of the steward at Deerwood Manor,' Hope said, and smiled, secretly savouring the moment when she had defended herself with her knife and had stabbed him and, when he came to the cottage, had been forced to jump clear of the door when she threw boiling water at him from the wash tub. 'He can do us no harm now, and bullies are usually cowards, too. The captain says we should sight land soon and be in Plimoth by Sunday.'

'Look!' Edward put an arm round her shoulders. 'Over there!' He pointed beyond the piles of coiled rope in the prow and she saw a bird, flying out to the ship. It circled the masts. Other passengers saw it. They cried out to the ones who had stayed late in the cabins and in the main communal mess deck, and faces that had almost forgotten how to laugh, now were wreathed in happy smiles.

'The first ones to land in America must have felt like this,' Hope said, tremulously. She looked about her at the sea-battered scuppers and the rusty chains on the anchors and the piles of ropes where she sat on fine evenings. It was home and safety, and she wanted to stay with the things that had become familiar and safe.

Families grouped together as if they were ready to disembark, even though land was still far away; the bonds of easy friendship

191

made on the voyage seemed transient, easily lost now that they would go their separate ways. A few began packing clothes into bags and pulled half-dry washing from the lines until the captain announced that they must wait for at least seven days as the wind had dropped, so the washing went back on the ropes.

More birds appeared and seals and dolphins dived close to the ship. In the distance, a humpbacked whale was sighted as it up-ended its huge tail and disappeared down to its feeding grounds off the coast of a tiny island where small fish abounded.

Mary Chilton folded the last of three gowns that she had sewn and gave them to Hope. 'Remember,' she said, 'you may stay at the Lobster Inn in Plimoth while you arrange your business, but I shall expect you to visit me each day and tell me of your progress. I shall tell my husband about you and he will advise your choice of land. I wish you would stay in Plimoth, but you seem set on Martha's Vineyard even though you haven't seen it.'

'Mr John Halben has land there and we feel that if he liked it, then we would too,' Edward said. 'He is a good friend and has done more for me than I can ever repay, so if he needs someone to be near his land, we can look after his interests.'

Mary shrugged. 'I know men who have

bought land in New England or Massachusetts as an investment, in the hope that their sons will inherit it and make a life out here as they have faith in the future of the New World. There is also the uncertainty of life in England under a changing monarchy and laws that might be harsh on many religious orders. After Cromwell, there has been a swing away from puritanism. They say that the old religion may come back and everyone might have to bow to the Pope and the inquisition again.'

'The plague is also a threat to life, especially in London and Oxford and many other big cities, like Southampton which is close to our village,' said Edward. 'That is enough to make people want to leave England. I want my son to grow healthy in pure air in a place where he may fear no man.'

'If we have a daughter,' Hope said, seeing the vexed expression returning at the mention of a son, 'she will be free of men who think they have the power to take her against her will. The good people on the island will protect us all.'

The captain sold much of the spare stores now that the ship was close to land and many of the passengers bought stale food and hard biscuits in case they starved ashore, but Mary Chilton prevented

Edward from doing so and assured him of good food and fresh vegetables in Plimoth.

Hope began to wonder if the idea of living on Martha's Vineyard was a bad one as Mary Chilton was very persuasive, hoping that they would come to live close to her home. 'Stay for a week or so and then decide,' she begged. 'You can sail on a smaller boat round to the islands and have time to buy what you need to take there.'

Edward agreed that this would be wise, especially as Mr Chilton would be able to advise them and show them deeds and sketches of properties on The Vineyard, but Hope began to feel trapped in Mary's warmth and the way she was harping on about the baby being a girl. Mary constantly told her what to eat and what to do to make sure the baby came quickly when the time came for the birth, and made Hope promise again and again to bring the baby girl to see her in Plimoth.

'If you don't come to me, I shall come to you,' she vowed. 'I feel that I have a part in this child as I was the first person you told.'

'We shall come,' Hope said, wearily, 'but as you said, there are months ahead of us when we must prepare a home for the child.'

'If it is a girl, you shall be godmother,' Edward said, as if that was a light duty and more of a compliment than a holy commitment.

'I wish you had said nothing of that,' Hope said when she was alone with her husband. 'Mary is a great friend, but I sense that she wants to take over our lives.'

'Your condition makes you have idle thoughts and baseless suspicions,' Edward said. 'If Mary Chilton hadn't been on the ship you would have been lonely for female company.'

Hope shook out her best shawl and packed it in the dowry box. The weather was very warm and she felt hot even in the thin cotton gown that she had taken from the box. Edward was bronzed and he looked almost handsome, his light-blue eyes bright against his darkened cheeks and his hair bleached by the sun. He trimmed his beard with the small scissors that Hope used for needlework and polished his best shoes and the silver buckles on the toecaps.

'Are we expecting company?' she teased him, but was pleased to see how eager he was to land at Plimoth, and at last, after being maddeningly becalmed for five days, they sighted land and the wide sweep of the bay where buildings could be seen clearly.

The gangways creaked after being stowed for so long in salt conditions and the tethered beasts could hardly walk when they were released and led ashore to pounds and fresh grass where they could wait for their owners to collect them.

Mr Rigsby was first ashore and left his luggage on the ship while he went to the inn. Mary was met by her husband who kissed her forehead and merely touched the hands of his sons. He shouted to a man driving a cart to come to take off her baggage.

Mary introduced her new friends and he was immediately interested in what they wanted. Hope decided that he was more interested in business and possibly politics, than in his family and felt a twinge of remorse that she had felt impatient over Mary's care of her. She glanced up at Edward's good honest face and the affectionate looks he exchanged with her even when other people were present, and thanked God for a good and loving man.

'Come to the house as soon as you have put your luggage in the inn,' Mr Chilton said. 'Mary was wise to ask you to see me as there are many charlatans about who try to sell land that isn't theirs to sell or doesn't even exist.'

It was bliss to sit on a broad bench with cushions and to drink ale that had not been soured in the heat of the hold. A sad-looking woman in black was with Mr Chilton, and her eyes were those of a beaten dog. 'Mistress Butler wishes to sell her land on The Vineyard,' he said. 'Her husband died when out in a small boat, fishing, and she needs to go back to her family in Ireland.'

Hope took her hand in hers and found it cold and unresponsive. 'I'm sad for you, Mistress Butler,' she said. 'Have you no desire to stay here?'

'I thought I was in heaven when we came last year, but now my husband is dead, there is no place for me here.' She looked tired and upset. 'As soon as I said I wanted to sell, I was surrounded by men who tried to make me sign away the land for a few pounds or even shillings until Mr Chilton heard about me. Now he is going to sell quickly so that I can return on the ship you sailed in, as soon as she is revictualled and cleaned.'

'Can you tell me a little of the land you own?' Hope asked, gently. 'Is it difficult to build a house there?'

'There is a house, small but free of damp and cold and it has a stove and fireplace and a good sink that my husband cut from rock.' She began to cry. 'I must go back to Ireland now or I'll have to wait for months and it will be cold and rough on the water when the year ends.' Her voice sank to a whisper. 'I am expecting a child and need my family round me when it comes.'

Mr Chilton produced the deeds of the land, and Edward saw that there was an acre of land close to the sea and a small boat with a sail. 'They called it Clam Cottage because of the shellfish they found there in the bay,' Mr Chilton said. 'I know the area. The soil is hard and untilled as yet but would respond to manuring with seaweed and wood ash. It's a bargain if she'll accept a fair but low price,' he added to Edward so that the woman couldn't hear.

He named a sum and Edward was pale with excitement as it was far lower than he had imagined. 'Is it a fair price?' he asked anxiously.

'It's far higher than she was offered at the inn,' Mr Chilton said bluntly.

Edward led Hope away and told her what had been said, and she found herself smiling. 'We wouldn't have to build a house and we can add to it later,' she said with satisfaction. 'They liked it very much there and I can work on the soil until the baby is due, but are you sure that we are being honest?'

'We need to buy stock and stores and at this price we can do so easily,' Edward said. He saw that she was unconvinced. 'This offer is the best she will have and she can go home quickly, which is what she wants,' he argued.

The sale was agreed and Edward went with his host to sign documents and to read all the details about the property.

Hope was pensive and saw the resignation in the other woman's eyes. 'It isn't what you paid for it, is it?' she asked, and saw her shake her head. 'Are there other things in the house?' Hope asked. 'Is it secure against thieves?'

'It is safely locked up. I left a table and a bed and some stools and a cupboard that needs finishing that I'd hoped to sell, but I can't do so from here so I must let them go with the house.'

'I will buy them,' Hope whispered. 'I shall say nothing to my husband or the Chiltons, but take this and use it for your child.'

She gave her enough money to bring the total up to the price that had been paid when the young couple first went to Martha's Vineyard and put a finger to her lips. 'Bless you,' she heard, and hoped that her blessing was important for their future. If we had bought low, we would deserve to be unhappy there, she thought, and smiled wryly. Now Edward could boast that he had made a good deal and the widow could return to her family and be independent, all due to Sir William's gift of conscience.

Chapter 10

It was almost like being back in England except that the early houses were made of wood rather like clinker-built boats with overlapping planks making the walls, or were constructed of whole logs, the joints filled with soil. Only the grander buildings were partly brick built. Many open spaces were covered with unfamiliar grasses and shrubs, but gardens were full of apple and pear trees brought over to add fruit to the grapes and wild berries that fought for survival, growing over trees and bushes.

'There's a boat leaving tomorrow for The Vineyard,' Edward said, bursting in on Hope and Mary as they sat by the window of the solid house that Mr Chilton had bought for his family.

Hope tried to stem her rising excitement, as she knew from the sudden stiffening of her shoulders that Mary was not pleased. 'I'm ready,' she said, softly, and gave Edward a warning glance.

'The weather is good and the wind fair and the captain has put our things on to a smaller boat that will call in at several places on Martha's Vineyard and leave us at Oak

Bluffs where a stage will take us to our home,' Edward said firmly. 'It isn't as lacking as you led me to believe, Mary. There are horses to hire and a regular stage linking most of the settlements once a week. The local Indians are very helpful, willing to sell corn and game and they can hew wood for me when I'm ready.'

'I think you are unwise,' Mary said, but the sudden slackening of her body showed that she recognized defeat.

'I shall miss you,' Hope said, impulsively. 'But Martha's Vineyard is not far and we shall meet again soon.'

Mary seized her in a hard embrace. 'Promise me,' she said.

'There is no need to promise,' Hope said. 'We are friends, and if it is possible, it will be so, and not be a duty made by promises.'

'Come down to the jetty and see the boat,' Edward suggested, but Mary shook her head and Hope left her sewing a shirt for George. 'I'm glad she didn't come with us,' Edward said. 'But I think she will give up pouring cold water on our plans now that we have made up our minds to leave.'

'She hates to part from us as she has so few friends here as yet.' Hope frowned. 'On the ship she took to me but not to many of the other wives. There were two families settling in Plimoth but she made no attempt to ask them to call or to help them in any way. She told me that her husband likes her to mix with his friends and entertain only his business contacts, so she will be lonely.'

'With two fine boys, she will soon meet other mothers and forget you,' Edward said. 'Look! That's our boat and we leave on the flood at noon tomorrow. If you wish to buy anything, we must do so now.' He frowned. 'I spent more than I wanted on more tools and a felling saw and axes, so we have to be careful with the rest of our money.'

'I have a little money from the present I had from Aunt Ellen just before we left,' Hope lied. 'And I had some I'd made from making pies for women in the village. I saved it for the wedding, but Aunt Ellen would not be paid for the food she made.'

Edward's face cleared. 'If you can use that, then that will be a relief. I'm glad I married a thrifty wife.' He didn't ask her how much money she had and seemed content to know that she could pay for what she wanted.

Hope bought iron buckets and a wooden wash board, kitchen knives and spoons and six earthenware jugs, all of which she had sent to the boat. She paused by a selection of rugs woven in bright colours in strange designs, made by the local Indian women. She held one to her face and found it surprisingly soft and warm. On an impulse she bought two to use as blankets and another small one for a child's crib.

A bundle of cotton wicks for candles which she could use once she had mutton fat to make her own, and a gross of ready-made candles to use until she was settled, joined the stores of flour and loaf sugar and lard. Knowing that the stage brought goods to the settlements on a regular basis, she relaxed. Mary had hinted that life would be much harder than it now seemed likely and she went from the marketplace eager to see what lay ahead in Martha's Vineyard.

Edward met her in the inn and ordered food. He showed no interest in what she had bought for her kitchen and asked no questions as to what she had paid for her purchases.

The sad little widow came to speak and Hope asked her to eat with them. She sat down heavily and drank a mug of clear water that was a luxury now after the stale water on the ship and ate some of the mutton stew and bread that smelled tempting and was free of grease. 'When do you sail?' Hope asked. 'I heard that they had finished cleaning the cabins and the stores are on board.'

'I wanted your advice,' she said. Edward left them and went to speak to a blacksmith who had promised him a small pair of bellows, to remind him that the boat would leave the next day.

'You look worried,' Hope said. 'Is it money?'

'No, thanks to you, I am secure now. Mistress Chilton is trying to persuade me to stay with her as her paid companion until I find other work. In a way, I want to stay close to where my dear husband died but I need to get home to my family where they will care for me and help me with the baby.'

Hope felt a chill of fear and could find no reason for it. 'When did she ask you?'

'I told her that I was expecting and she asked many questions about my family and how many children they had.' She looked puzzled. 'She showed no interest in me before that, but now she asks daily and even offers to adopt my baby if I need to go away and work for my living.'

'Go home.' Hope's mouth was dry with a sensation of dread. 'Pack your things and get on board and don't listen to her.'

'But she is your friend!'

'Yes, I love her dearly, but she wants a baby girl and seems to be fixed on it in any way she can have one. If you stay and have a girl, you will lose your baby to her if you have no man to protect you, but if it is a boy, she will want none of him and you may suffer.' Hope shook her head. 'I can't know if this would happen to you but she is determined to make me bring my baby here to see her. Until I know if it's a girl or a boy,

I want to be far away when my child is born. I'm certain that she'll want to see the baby only if it's a girl, and then she might try to rule my life.' She laughed. 'If I have a boy, we can remain good friends.'

'Is she mad?'

'It is a kind of madness, just as some men are mad who demand sons from their wives and beat them if they give birth to daughters. Whatever is her intention, go home and forget the New World and take comfort from your family.'

'You give me strength. I thought I was being ungrateful, but in my heart I knew I wanted to go back home.'

'You owe her nothing and her husband even less as he made you sell to us for such a small sum.' Hope gave her a warning look. 'Never say anything about our private transaction. I paid for your kitchen things, and that is all. Keep away from men who offer to help you when you are on the ship and buy nothing from anyone even if they seem honest. If they think you have no money, they will leave you alone and you will be able to start again when you reach people you know you can trust,' she added. 'I will come with you and help put you in your cabin and wave goodbye.'

'You are so wise and yet you can't be older than me.'

'Not wise; just aware of what dishonest

men and women can do if they want anything badly enough. It is good to trust people but better to hold back until you know them better.'

'This will be useful,' Edward said, on his return. He blew cold air into Hope's face with the bellows and she took it from him and examined the leather and wood that made it work. 'It's simple and not really work for a blacksmith except for the air outlet which is made of metal. I could make the rest.'

'Buy some sheets of the metal and if you can make something like this we may have a basis for trade with the Indians. Everyone makes fire, and in bad weather, this might be a very welcome tool.' She called after him, 'I'm going to help Mistress Butler to board the ship. If Mary asks for me, tell her that I am talking in the inn, but make no mention of Mistress Butler leaving.'

Together they carried the small pieces of luggage and paid a boy to carry the big box on board. Hope stopped to speak to the captain while the luggage was settled in the cabin and asked when the ship was due to sail. 'Are you not tired of roving the Atlantic, Captain?'

He called to a seaman loading a box of beaver pelts to make sure they were well covered against the salt air, then smiled. 'I'm waiting for a rich widow lady to fall in love with me and take me ashore,' he said.

'You told me that you were married!'

He winked. 'I am, and that's why I rove. I've a shrew of a wife in Portsmouth, England. And I shall settle here, far away from her when I make up my mind, so I can have two wives; one there and one here.'

'What if she sails after you?' Hope was enchanted by the idea of this big strong man being pursued over the ocean by an irate wife.

'I'll tell her my last voyage is to Guinea or North Africa and she can scour the whole African continent and never find me.' He sighed but his eyes were merry. 'It's a dream I have on a night watch and I know I shall never have the courage to do it.'

'Have you seen any of your old passengers?' she asked.

'Only two who settled in Plimoth and, of course, the governor's men who came out a few months ago. Mr Chilton will be glad to have his wife again, I reckon. I saw Mr Rigsby yesterday and he seems to have landed in clover.'

'Is he going to Martha's Vineyard?'

'What? Not him. He's going back with this ship taking a sock full of money and a lot of deeds for property out here that's fit only for snakes and ravens and nothing else. He bought them dirt cheap and it's legal to sell for what fools like to pay.' He looked up at the sun. 'If they're all aboard I might catch an early tide as the wind's fair.' He glanced at the bill of lading and nodded with satisfaction.

'All stores on board and all passengers. Mr Rigsby is very anxious to leave as he thinks a few people might be wondering where he is in Plimoth and The Vineyard and other places where he promised to find properties.' He laughed. 'He thinks I'm leaving early because he paid me to do so, but I leave when I feel it's right and had made up my mind long before he put money in my hand. It does me good to make him pay something for nothing.'

'I'm glad that you go now. Mistress Butler was uncertain and I shall be happier when the ship sails with her on board. Look after her. She is sad and expecting a baby and has bitter memories of the New World.' Hope smiled. 'I don't think she is your rich widow, Captain.'

The ship's bell clanged and people ran to the jetty to watch the ropes cast off. Mr Rigsby came on deck cautiously as if afraid to be seen. Hope laughed and called out to him by name as if to say goodbye. She watched him dive behind the sail lockers and stay there until the gap between the ship and jetty was too wide for even his most enraged victim to cross. Mistress Butler waved and waved and held a kerchief to her eyes as she finally went below and Hope stood back and watched the ship that had brought her so far from home, drift away under full white sails.

Edward came to meet her by the inn. 'I thought I heard the ship's bell. Has it gone so early?'

'Yes, Mistress Butler and her baby will be safe now.'

'Why do you say that?'

'I don't know.' She shivered. 'I'm chilled. I talked to the captain. Mr Rigsby has gone back with him and will sell acres of rubbish to many hopeful settlers and they will come here and be ruined.'

'Mary asks us to supper to meet some friends of her husband.'

She shook her head.

'We must go if we are to leave tomorrow. It will be the last time and you know you enjoy meeting people.'

'The last time? Of course, I was forgetting. I wonder if she knows the ship has gone? If not, please don't mention it as she may be very angry when she finds that Mistress Butler decided to leave at the last minute.'

The last time, Hope told herself over and over again when Mary Chilton talked about the hard times that lay ahead in The Vineyard and tried to make her promise to come back to Plimoth and have the baby under her care.

Mr Chilton didn't seem to hear her or ignored everything she said and turned to Edward to fill his glass with good sack. 'I've looked at the details of Mr Halben's property and I'm impressed. He left it under the care of an honest servant who is now making the estate pay well, employing many newcomers and some local Indians who have set up their tepees and built huts in a compound close to the house. A very wise move,' he added. 'Loyal Indians know the country and guard a house and property better than any who come green to the country.'

'Does he need a carpenter there?' Edward asked eagerly.

'No, Edward,' Hope said in a low voice, when Mr Chilton turned away for more sack. 'We must settle in first before you take any work that will fill the days and leave no time for our home. Although we have a good start with a house already built, I want a secure and warm home before the baby comes, or we might have to come back to Plimoth for my confinement.'

Edward noted the sweet smile that told him that Hope had good reason for making sure he would do as she wished. He grinned and glanced at Mary who had taken him to task, saying that he had no right to set his poor wife down among wolves and snakes when she needed a safe and warm home.

'I'll not commit myself,' he said. 'But I'll need work soon.'

'Not on the Halben estate, Edward. We left all that behind and now we must be free of them all.'

'Even free of John Halben?'

'I want to forget everything,' Hope said, and knew that she would have no peace of mind if his concerns became theirs.

'I can't bear to see you go,' Mary Chilton said when they left the house to sleep at the inn and pack their last bags ready for the morning. 'I shall not come to the jetty, but remember, you must send word as soon as the baby arrives, or come to me before the birth.'

'I feel free,' Hope said as the sails bellied out in the wind and Plimoth lay behind them. 'I had a feeling of being pulled along a path that I would hate to take.'

'A path lined with flowers and easy living,' Edward said, eyeing her to see if there was any trace of regret.

'Flowers mixed with nettles,' Hope said firmly. She took his hand. 'Dandelions are pretty too, and gentler. Look!' They watched dolphins play under the stern of the boat and fancied they tried to talk to them, making them welcome. 'They are smiling,' Hope said, leaning over the side of the boat to see them better.

'Come away. You'll crush my son if you

lean out too far,' Edward said, half in earnest.

'Not a daughter?'

'For Mistress Chilton to steal?' Edward laughed and put an arm round her slightly thickening waist, his eyes misty. 'I will look after you, Hope. I want to sleep with you in our own bed and not in a bed in an inn or in a house where we would be beholden to someone like Mary Chilton. We shall love whatever God sends us, but I pray it's a son.'

The deep bay flattened out as the captain selected the landing. Small houses and one or two larger ones met their gaze as they approached Great Harbour. Men waited to take the mooring ropes and idlers watched the people disembark. A church with a cross on the starkly plain roof and a schoolhouse with children playing in the yard made Hope feel at home. 'Our house will be more lonely,' Edward warned her, but as they swayed in the coach to the tiny village where Clam Cottage lay, they looked about them with eager eyes and saw woodland like it was at Deerwood, streams of sweet water and vines covering every tree with small unripe pink grapes. The sun shone with shimmering heat.

A deer watched them from a thicket, and rabbits, unused to being disturbed, ran off with white scuts bobbing in the grass. Hope thought she saw a brown face peering at them but when she looked again it was gone and she found many other things to take her interest. They passed a lake covered with green leaves and a crimson carpet of something she couldn't recognize.

'That's a cranberry bog,' the coachman said. 'Soon we'll harvest the berries which are good to eat and make into preserves and pies.'

Everywhere, the promise of plenty was heartening and even the rather shabby little house did nothing to dim their enthusiasm.

The coachman departed, leaving Edward to unlock the door and carry in the baggage. Hope struggled to open the window in the kitchen and fresh air dispelled the musty smell of a house shut up for too long in hot weather. She filled a bucket with water from the stream at the back of the cottage and washed the table and shelves before bringing in anything of their own and Edward shaved off a sliver of wood to make the window shut properly. He went over the house with his tools, tightening a hinge here and easing a lock there.

'The last man was no carpenter but it's all solid and will do for a while,' he said.

'We need a floor,' Hope said. 'This is just dirt and not rock so you must order timber from the man the boat captain suggested and lay floorboards, or in bad weather the place will be full of mud.'

'I'll go tomorrow and fetch some to get started. He said it's but half a mile away and I can drag it unless I can buy a donkey to carry heavy loads.'

'There's a room above the kitchen,' Hope called. 'It's well floored and might have been prepared for the baby and for storage, as there is a division making it two rooms.' She sat down, suddenly weary and hungry. The food she had brought from the inn was unwrapped and they sat in near silence, eating cold meat and drinking water from the stream which they found to be sweet and sparkling.

Dusk found them spent of all energy but happy. 'Do you wish you were back with Mary Chilton in her fine house?' asked Edward, struggling up from his seat as if to go back to work.

'No, my dear.' Hope put out a restraining hand. 'No more work today. I have made the bed. It has a good mattress and feather overlay and I've unpacked the candles so we may have light for a while.'

'There's a lot to be done,' Edward said, stifling a yawn.

'Tomorrow,' she said. 'Go to bed and I'll wash this dish and leave all neat for the morning.'

He took a candle and when she went into the bedroom, he was fast asleep, half naked on the bed too hot for covering.

I should have made a fire in the stove, she thought, but the effort of even considering it was too much. She stripped to her shift and lay beside her husband, exhausted.

The night was starlit and quiet except for the unfamiliar cries of wild cats and the more recognizable bark of a fox. Hope slept and woke to find Edward bending over her to wake her with a kiss.

'Go away,' she murmured, but put her arms round his neck and held him close. He slipped the shift from her shoulders and she wriggled free of it. The scars on his chest were now hard-edged and dug into her tender breasts, but she remained passive and almost relished the pain as his desire made him hold her even closer and she gave herself up to his yearning. This pain was not like another she had sought and suffered one warm afternoon in spring, but it reminded her, and she opened her eyes, needing to be sure that the man now entering her parted thighs was her husband and not a lost ghost who must never be with her again. As she reached an explosive climax, she bit her lip to stop herself calling a name.

'You are crying.' Edward kissed her tears. 'I'm sorry if I hurt you,' he said anxiously. 'But we couldn't do this at the inn and it seemed so long ago that we lay together.' He touched her breasts and traced a blue vein in the creamy skin, then saw the bruise caused by his scar. 'You must never let me hurt you,' he said.

'It was a sweet pain,' she whispered, and the ghost fled.

'I'll strike a fire and light the stove,' Edward said.

'I'll make soda bread and put ale in the stream to cool.' Hope took down one of the big jugs she had bought in Plimoth and filled it from the barrel, wedging it firmly between stones in the shallows of the stream bank.

The new bellows brought the wood into flame and the stove heated quickly. Edward felt that he was not alone and turned. 'Who are you?' he asked.

The man stared at him for a minute without speaking, his brown face impassive, his dark hair heavy with oil and his body naked except for a small apron and string of leather trimmed with shells, and a mass of shell necklaces. Ochre and crimson stripes decorated his chest and face. He carried no weapons, but Edward sensed that this was a formal meeting of welcome.

'We have bought this land and house from Mistress Butler,' Edward said slowly, as he had no idea if the man spoke or understood English. 'Come inside.' He gestured towards the kitchen and the man walked slowly across the threshold, his eyes expressionless.

'I am Chiabos, son of the son of Hiacoomes,' the Indian said.

'I am Edward, son of Michael Fletcher,' Edward said solemnly. 'You are welcome to my house.' He smiled and saw that Hope had put fresh soda bread on the table and the jug of ale. 'Eat with us,' he said. Hope brought cheese and a dish of salt, as she had been warned that the summer heat brought on cramps if there was not enough salt eaten to replace that lost through sweat. 'This is my wife, Hope,' Edward said, and the man nodded. He tore off a piece of the hot bread and dipped it in the salt before he ate it. Hope poured ale into three mugs and watched this strange man, her eyes wide and full of friendly interest.

'You have a good squaw,' Chiabos said without looking directly at Hope. He picked up the jug and examined it, running a finger along the dark glaze inside the rim. He saw the others on the shelf and pointed. 'For one I bring two rabbits, a groundhog and a bowl of corn.'

Hope smiled and took a jug from the shelf. 'I can spare this one,' she said. 'The others must be kept to preserve meat under fat and for water and ale.' She looked inside to make sure that the glaze was complete and set it on the table.

217

'I fetch my barter,' Chiabos said and went swiftly out into the sunshine.

'I've heard of this,' Edward whispered. 'I'm glad you made him understand that we can't spare more of our jugs and I pray that he may be convinced that we have little to barter until we are settled here.' He thought for a moment. 'There may be others like him who want to visit us, but I think he's a kind of head man. Mary said that the ones in authority wear a lot of shell and bead necklaces and trimmings of shells on their garments.'

Chiabos grunted as he threw down two freshly killed rabbits and a large hedgehog. He went away again and brought a woven basket of Indian corn, scraped from the husks ready for storing or grating and Hope took a few grains in her hand, looking puzzled, as she had never seen hard maize, but she thanked him and offered him more bread.

'I can bring more for the winter and show you where to hunt,' Chiabos said. 'My woman will come and show you how to use it. She helped Mistress Butler and now you.'

'You are very kind,' Hope said. 'It's such a relief to know that you speak English.'

'I went to school,' he said with pride. 'The Reverend Mayhew took in children from our tribe to the school in Oak Bluffs and taught us the love of your God. I worship

Him and our Great Spirit.'

'You worship both?'

'Your God saved us from disease when many people died and left a village silent and their stores abandoned. He saved us when the Reverend Mayhew prayed to Him, so my grandfather, Hiacoomes, became a follower of your God and now we give thanks to Him, but the Great Spirit knows about the rivers and the woods and our friends the whales, and brings the harvest, so we give homage to Him or He would be angry and bring *bukadawin*, the famine.'

He picked up the jug and left, leaving Hope smiling. 'If only religion could be so simple at home,' she said. 'We must go to church in Oak Bluffs, Edward. It may take all day if we have no horse, but we shall meet people and find out more about this island.'

'They say that Reverend Mayhew owned many of the islands here under English law but he made people buy land from the Indians as he insisted that this was their country, and so kept their friendship. That's why there is no trouble here as there is in other parts of the New World. We must make sure that we remain good friends, Hope. They are good people even if they are half heathen.'

'I've met too many people who swear piously by God and our church yet do

219

terrible things,' Hope said. 'I wonder if his wife will become a friend?' She picked up a rabbit and took it out to the stream to skin it and gut it, then soaked it in a bucket of clear water to blanch it. 'Have you any hooks?' she called.

'I'll put some in the kitchen ceiling,' Edward said. 'The game should hang clear of the ground unless we want it infested with grubs.' He eyed the hedgehog with suspicion. 'That's gypsy food,' he said.

'Then we'll cook it as they do, wrapped in mud and cooked in hot embers so that the spines and skin come away in the mud when it is cooked,' Hope said. She laughed. 'Do you think our child will grow up to be a wild hunter?'

'You are beginning to talk of him as a boy,' Edward placed a hand over her rising fundus and felt the child move. 'He wants to be born and be here with us to chase the deer and go fishing,' he said, with pride.

Chapter 11

'Give me some food as I may be there until dusk,' Edward said.

'You'll take your musket?' Hope asked, trying not to sound anxious.

'A knife and my crossbow,' Edward said. He kissed her. 'Please don't worry. I know the woods and they told me the bears are not there now, only deer and wild turkey and maybe a boar and racoons. Chiabos will be there and others as they want to kill game.' He packed his tools on the stout wooden sled he had made and added the leather pouch of food that Hope gave him. 'I will bring more planks if they have split them and ask for a cedar log if I am to make a bigger canoe this winter.'

'Bring more chippings,' she said. 'If I'm to smoke turkeys and cod, I'll need more oak.'

He covered the sled with hempen sacks and pulled it away into the woods along a now well-trodden trail, dry after the hot summer, and Hope returned to the sweet-smelling kitchen, floored with pine planks and covered with rushes. She sat for a while, sipping a drink of cranberry juice and wild honey as she seemed to need more sweet-ness in her food now that ale gave her heart-burn.

Only the sounds of water running clear over white stones and the murmurs of the forest broke the almost total silence. Life was good, she decided. One day drifted into the next and she had lost her first sense of urgency. Everything had been done that needed to be done, and the store in the cellar under the floor and the shelves in the upper room were stacked with food for the winter. Circles of yellow squash, dried under the boughs in dry warm air, were strung high in the ceilings with whale meat and mutton dried in the Indian way as pemmican, beans overflowed wooden crates that Edward had made to act as granaries and there were packs of lard for cooking and bowls of whale oil and solid blubber for lamps and candles. She went into the back room for another string to loop along the kitchen wall to take dried herbs and garlic, and paused in the doorway.

She smoothed the mound that now reached her breast-bone. The child would be born when it was ready and there was no question of her going to Plimoth to be confined. Mary had written asking her to go back, but everything in Plimoth seemed unreal now and she knew that Edward was so in tune with nature and the friends they had made that he would never want to leave Clam Cottage.

Katsi, the wife of Chiabos, squatted on the floor, disdaining the comfort of a wooden stool. She picked at a rush and broke it into small pieces, her long brown fingers hard and restless. Hope watched her from the doorway leading from the back room. Katsi had several children, but seemed to be able to come to Clam Cottage every day to check that Hope was in good health as she couldn't understand any woman with child being alone.

The other women in the long house would look after her own children and cook for any of the family who .were sick or injured. There was a fire burning night and day to feed the twelve to twenty people who lived together in the log and wattle and daub dwelling.

'The men have taken a wigwam until the new moon,' she explained when Hope asked her who was going with Edward.

'A whole week? Two?'

'Until the new moon,' Katsi repeated. 'They hunt deer before the cold comes and the women must harvest the corn. It is the time of the ripe Mondamin and men do not gather the corn.' Katsi smiled. 'You will come but watch and not gather as your land is not yet fruitful. Next spring you will come and plant the three sisters with us and we will plant with you.'

'Edwards said he was going for the day,' Hope said.

'Chiabos will tell him that I have told you he will be away for the hunt. If you will not come to our lodge I shall sleep here with you,' she said calmly as if Hope had no choice.

'There is no need,' Hope said. 'The baby is not due yet.' She knew she could never face sleeping in the long house which was always full of smoke from choked chimneys and the odour of urine from young children, and where men smoked harsh tobacco in clay pipes.

Katsi looked at the swollen belly and put her hand over the rounded fundus. 'He sinks and will come soon,' she said, and Hope realized that she breathed more easily now but had more pressure on her bladder.

They shared fish and soft pumpkin and sourdough bread and Katsi drank the ale that all her family liked.

'Tonight, we go to the fields to gather the corn,' Katsi said.

'Why at night?'

'The full moon will light our way and give us blessing as she is female. First we pray and give thanks for good corn, then go without men and gather the cobs. While the men are away we strip the husks and hang the corn to dry or scrape it free and make meal. Keep the ashes from your fire as they cool, and do not put them into the ground for the planting as we shall need all for boiling with the corn we use now to make meal, and for the feast when the men return.'

Hope wandered by the sea-shore, but her cumbersome body prevented her from bending to gather seaweed. She sighed. Waiting was becoming tedious and there were many tasks she had taken for granted that she was now unable to do.

The clearings that Edward had made, burning off small shrubs and trees and chipping the hard soil to make beds into which they had piled ashes and seaweed and withered leaves, were softening, and after the winter frosts, should be lighter and ready for spring sowing. She returned to the house and scraped rabbit skins free of fat and rubbed them with ashes before stretching them to dry to be sewn together for blankets and mittens, as Katsi had warned her of cold weather after the next two moons. The last letter from Mary lay on the table. A girl from England had arrived in Plimoth looked for work. Hope could sense the triumph behind the words: *She is pregnant and has no husband so I am going to look after her.*

'Poor girl,' Hope said, and was thankful that she had escaped.

Evening came and Katsi came to bring her to the fields. The women prostrated themselves before the full moon and chanted old songs that Hope could not understand. Even Katsi seemed to have forgotten every word of English she had ever learned. The atmosphere was powerful and pagan and the women gave their minds to one thing, the harvest of corn and the reverence due to the moon and to Mondamin, the young man who had fought with Hiawatha and been slain and buried, so that his body would become Indian corn. So he had given his life for them to gather up food each year and be free of famine.

Hope insisted on helping to strip the cobs of their brown tassels, but sank back on a pile of deerskins after an hour. The chanting and laughter went on and the fields were left bereft and stubbly with broken stems, as the baskets were filled and the women dragged them away to their tepees or houses.

Dawn came with a paling moon and the work was done. Hope awoke from her soft bed of hides. She smiled up at the drifting clouds across the moon's dim face and saw the sunrise.

'Come,' Katsi said. 'We eat now and then sleep.' The women from the long house brought cooking pots full of deer meat and herbs and others brought bread and corn-meal biscuits out on the fields. Katsi helped Hope to carry a keg of ale that Edward said they would need when the harvest came home and they ate and drank until the day was bright and the rosy marks of dawn had gone.

At last, they went their ways for a few hours' rest before they tied the bunches of cobs ready to hang in the long huts, and pounded grain in huge mortars with logs as pestles, to make meal, leaving the torn fields to be burned by the men and so give back the ashes to the soil and make ready for the spring planting.

Edward had already negotiated a barter for a supply of corn and soon the woven baskets in the upper store were filled and dozens more of the cobs were ready for Hope to tie into bundles and hang to dry. Some she boiled with lye to soften the outer skin and then washed away the ashes and pounded the corn to make meal as Katsi had taught her.

Katsi and four other women came to collect the bellows and wooden bowls that Edward had made and the two cupboards with slatted backs covered with muslin in which they could keep meat safe from rats and flies. Katsi had seen the one that Edward had made for Hope and noticed that their fresh meat never harboured maggots from flies, so these would be a welcome addition to the long house.

Hope had made knitted gloves to go inside mittens covered with rabbit fur, to complete the barter, and the women went away well pleased.

Hope shook the tiny mattress stuffed with duck down and feathers and lay the blanket and beaver skins on it in the sturdy and shining rocking crib that Edward had made with loving care, then sat by the fire and waited alone.

News from Aunt Ellen and Little Deerwood had arrived on the last boat but told her no real news. The village church had celebrated its harvest festival and a man had brought a bride from another village. Hope smiled wryly. Did he have to go so far to escape his bride having the fate of Abigail and Bessie? She read on. Sir William was much better but not able to walk far and his temper was worse. Of John Halben she said nothing except that he had married Mistress Hannam and left her to make unwelcome changes to Deerwood Manor while he went hunting.

Poor John, Hope thought, but he seemed like a wraith as she slipped deeper into the role of a woman waiting for the birth of her child and had no thought beyond her own hearth. Her letter must wait until she was delivered and had news to tell.

At night, Katsi slept before the fire on her deerskins over a bed of dried moss, and each day she went home to her children and to help with the cooking. Hope no longer protested and secretly enjoyed being with a woman who spoke little but shared the experience of pregnancy. If I was with Mary Chilton, she would be fussing around me enough to drive me mad, she thought, as she glanced at Katsi's impassive face and the strong arms that pounded corn in a hollowed-out tree stump. Even Edward would watch her anxiously if he thought that she might give birth soon, but Katsi murmured softly, prayers or incantations that had their roots in pre-history, and merely felt the taut skin once a day.

On the third day of Edward's hunting trip, Katsi brought herbs which she infused in boiling water and gave to Hope to drink.

'What are these?' Hope said.

'It will come soon now,' Katsi said. 'Not today, but soon, and this will make you happy.'

Hope drank the brew and shuddered, but after a while she felt calm and lost the restless need to pace the kitchen, and the odd cramps that she'd experienced over the past few days seemed unimportant. She brought in logs and made corn bread as if laying up supplies for a siege, and spent some time wandering by the sea.

'He will catch whales,' Katsi said. 'You watch the waves and he will watch them too. She eyed the small canoe that Edward had made, with a smile. 'Your man must build a bigger boat to catch your brother whale and learn to respect the sea.'

'If I walk in the fields does that mean he will be a farmer or a hunter?' Hope asked, almost believing what Katsi said, just as she had almost believed the gypsy in Southampton.

'He will love the sea as you do now. The moon rules the tides and you were asleep in an open field under the full moon when he started on his journey to the world.'

'What of the new moon? The men return at the new moon and then after that my baby will be born.'

Katsi smiled and said nothing. She gave her more herbs and Hope slept for most of the next day and night.

She woke in pain that hardly disturbed her but made her cry out in wonder. Katsi gave her broth and she slept again in fitful intervals until the pains grew deeper and she lay on the floor where Katsi had laid a bed of moss. A stool of dark wood on low legs was brought from the long house and Hope raised herself to sit on it as the pains came rapidly, until she gasped and held on to Katsi's leather-covered shoulder and felt warmth and wetness and a feeling of release as the baby slipped from the womb and joined the human race, shouting his defiance as he left safety and comfort.

Katsi wiped the creamy vernix from the tiny face and tied the cord with two strands of softened leather, then cut between them with a sharp knife and put the baby to Hope's breast.

'A man child,' Katsi said with satisfaction. Her hard hand probed the now flaccid abdomen until the womb tightened, the after birth came away and the blood stopped. She wrapped the baby in the clean cotton sheet that Hope had ready by the crib and placed him under the covering of soft blanket.

'A boy!' Hope said, joyfully. 'He will belong to us and Mary Chilton will have no time for him. My husband has a son!' She tried to imagine what Edward would say but more herbs were given her and she dreamed of nothing but deep calm water and sunlit meadows and only vaguely heard her baby cry.

Edward followed the trail and the loping Indians. Some carried wigwams and some stores, but no cooking pots except for one iron cauldron. If they were to be away for a week or more, they were travelling very light. His own pack was on the sled but the heavy crossbow and bolts dug into his shoulder and his clothes were hot, even though the sled was light and smooth in its progress. He strapped his crossbow to it. He envied the near nakedness of his companions as they silently padded along on soft moccasins and carried quivers of arrows tipped with flints and light bows of hard but supple woods.

They came to a clearing where the wigwams were erected and food was prepared. Tough pemmican was cut and chewed and bread was made and put on pieces of bark from chestnut trees to bake on the fire. The men took their bows and followed the prints of a large buck, its size and weight assessed by the depth of its prints.

Chiabos ignored a female deer he saw in the bush as he said it might be feeding young. 'If we kill the mothers we shall weaken their tribe and they will not be able to feed our families. The buck is older and may well die in the snow if the wolves find him, so we ask his pardon and tell him that he will give much life to our young. He will die with dignity.'

The prints were wet now as they found a stream and the buck stood upwind of them, gazing across the water. He was a fine healthy beast with spreading antlers with the remains of the rutting velvet on them.

With a feeling of superiority, Edward took his crossbow and reached for a bolt. Such a weapon would kill the beast quickly and quietly so that other game were not disturbed, and the fire would be accurate even from such a distance. As he raised it to aim, a faint swish of air passed his head and the buck fell, with frothy blood appearing from the one small arrow wound by his left shoulder.

Chiabos smiled. 'Arrows are a part of us and can fly swiftly where we will.' Edward put away the crossbow and helped to tie the legs of the deer over the carrying pole. He noticed that the arrow had gone into the lung and through to the heart, killing the beast instantly and keeping the hide whole.

The men had cut the beast to spill the entrails and Chiabos spread them over a bare patch of earth, calling the creatures of the forest to share their kill, but the heart and liver were cooked over their fire and eaten as if they attended a religious ceremony, the brave who had shot the arrow having the first piece.

The hunt went on with five deer killed and many turkeys, and Edward felt his pride return when his sled was used for dragging three of the deer. He shrugged. He had set out to buy timber, planks split from a living tree, but it made sense to stock up with game now and be secure for the winter.

He wondered how Hope was faring, but thought that she was not ready to give birth so stayed with the men to enjoy their carefree but ordered life. He practised shooting with bow and arrow, and cut the woods that Chiabos suggested, to make his own bows, light and tough and supple. By the camp-fire in the evenings he chipped flints to make arrow heads, trimmed turkey feathers to make flights and handled each bow that they used, to feel the tension and to test his own strength.

At last Chiabos looked at the crescent moon and announced that they would go home. The morning fire was stamped out, the sled piled high and the other game slung on poles resting on the shoulders of pairs of men who trotted through the forest as if they carried thistledown.

Racoons and other animals that had watched from the coverts and made quick sorties to eat the discarded remnants of the hunt, gathered to scour the camping-ground for food and left the forest clean.

Edward agreed to make a sled and more bellows to trade for a deer from the hunt. He knew that he had enough meat preserved for his own use, but had learned that he would be expected to give a feast if his child was a son. When the last stage had come to the village he had bought more ale and sugar with this in mind, but no strong waters like the harsh brandy that Hope had used on the voyage, as he knew that Indians were not used to it and were soon drunk if they sampled it.

They no longer had to bend under the branches, and the track widened to a familiar scene. Women ran from the long house and tepees and helped to bring in the deer, their sharp knives and flint scrapers ready to flay the carcasses and prepare the hides for leather. Edward took his share on the sled and pulled it slowly to his home by the water.

The smoke from the brick chimney was

diffused in a breeze that only hinted at the first chill of autumn, and the door to the house stood open. Katsi greeted him with more animation than he had seen on her usually expressionless face. 'Come,' she said and almost pushed him inside.

'Hope!' He rushed to her side where she reclined on a bed of moss and hides and then followed her complacent glance to the crib. 'It isn't...! You haven't...?' He took her in his arms as if she might break in two and found her more slender now, with full breasts and a very self-satisfied expression.

'You've come back after all the hard work is over,' she teased him. 'Don't you want to see what we have made between us, sweetheart?'

Katsi swept the baby from the crib and held him where Edward could see him. 'Now you have a son. I will help with the feast,' she said. 'Hope will make sweet cakes and puddings and the women will bring bread and cook the deer.'

'Was it painful?' he asked, and seemed far more concerned with Hope than with his own son.

'I don't remember,' Hope said. 'Katsi gave me herbs, the pain disappeared and I slept.'

He took the baby and gazed into the wide-open eyes. 'Hello my son,' he said. 'He looks like you, Hope.'

'He's good and hungry,' Hope said, 'so

that's like you.'

'We must take him to church to be christened before the weather turns bad.'

'What will you name him?' asked Katsi. 'He will be as tall as a pine.'

'How do you know that?' Edward asked with an amused grin. 'He's about the size of a rabbit.'

'He has big knees,' Katsi said as if this was irrefutable evidence.

'I would like Michael, after your father,' Hope said quickly.

'Or John, after our dear friend,' Edward said. 'I have thought about it and would like that.'

'Michael John,' Hope said, as if she had made up her mind. 'But to me he will be Michael.'

Katsi put the baby back in the crib. 'I must go to my man,' she said.

Hope smiled. 'Katsi has been very kind,' she said. 'There was no need for any other help and I feel free of everything from the past. Mary Chilton will not bother us again and now we really do have our own family and friends.'

'And a larder full for the winter,' Edward said. 'Are you strong enough to pluck turkeys?'

'Yes, I have been well since the day after Michael was born and if you collect the horse and trap from Oak Bluffs that Mr

Norris said was for sale, then we can show our son to the people there.'

'Do we have enough money to buy it?'

'Yes,' Hope said firmly. 'We have the money that you made from selling those three coffins, and Mrs Mayer bought a crib; the repairs to the meeting-house and the school brought in more than I thought possible and I told you that I had a little money put by for emergencies.'

'That money seems to be lasting well, like the widow's cruse of oil in the Bible,' Edward said.

'I have been careful and not spent it on fripperies.'

'That's one thing you have no need of here. The women dress soberly at all times and even flowers in your hat would seem out of place except in church or at a wedding feast.' He kissed her. 'You need no flowers. I've never seen you look so beautiful.'

The baby whimpered and Hope gathered him to her breast. He suckled greedily and Edward watched fascinated as the tiny hands punched the full breast as if he couldn't take the milk quickly enough. The small body squirmed with pleasure.

'Steady,' Hope whispered. 'You must wait or you'll be sick.'

'He'll take life by the hair and make it do his will,' Edward said. He touched the thick fair hair and the rounded cheek and then drew away, almost resentfully. 'Never let him take my place, Hope,' he said.

'He's a baby, not a man,' Hope protested. 'He is your son and will have a duty to you alone. I have a husband and a baby, and both will be dear to me in different ways, but he is here through our love, as much yours as mine.' She put the baby back and buttoned her bodice. 'Come here and tell me about the hunt,' she said, then made a wry face. 'Bring a turkey and I'll pluck while we talk.'

Chapter 12

John Halben dismounted and tied the reins to the fence. A dog barked and the door of the cottage opened and Ellen Turner peered out into the dusk. 'It's me, Ellen,' he said softly, and she opened the door wider.

'What brings you here, Master John? Is all well with your lady?'

'Well enough,' he said shortly. Moodily he stared into the fire, stripping off his leather gauntlets, and Ellen mulled ale for him as he sat sprawled along the wide bench. 'Are you settled?' he asked, and looked round the homely but comfortable room. 'Are you as well here as in your rooms at the manor?'

'Settled and content,' she assured him with a warm smile. 'I have my own house and the land is not too much for me to manage with help from a boy and a man to plough for the sowing. The chickens are fat and the pig went to market last week, so I have room for another to fatten.' She watched his face and saw the tension and a line or two of unhappiness that had not been there before his marriage. 'Are you hungry?'

He nodded and she brought out a piece of pork pie and pickled onions. 'This is all I have today,' she said. 'But there's apple cake in the oven.'

'I couldn't ask for better,' he said. 'You make the best pastry in England, Ellen. I never eat the rubbish brought to me by the new cook.' He grinned and he was once more the lighthearted man she loved. 'Sir William threw his on the floor the other night when my wife was entertaining her cousins. Even the dogs were not eager to finish it.'

Ellen blushed with pleasure. 'I can make a pie for you at any time, Master John.'

'I'll eat it here! Now that you have left Deerwood, I refuse to have you made use of only when it meets with my wife's approval.' He chuckled. 'Visitors ask after you and three have wondered if you would work for them, but I tell them you came into property and are a lady of leisure now, so isn't it time you stopped calling me Master John? You know how I dislike it coming from you.'

'I'll try to remember,' she said. 'I bake for the doctor and his family once a month,' she admitted. 'But I enjoy that and they are grateful. I also have news of Sir William and the ways of folk at the manor through them, so I feel I am still in touch.'

'My father hasn't forgiven you for leaving. The worse the cooking and the more surly the servants become when I am not there, the more he blames you for going, and he begins to hate the steward as if he has some hold over him.'

'Poor soul, he isn't the man he was years ago. I can't hate him even after he attacked me.' She hid the mark on her wrist where he had struck at her with a steel poker when she put her hand out to protect her face.

'He should have married you, Ellen, after my mother died.' She looked shocked. 'I mean it! Too much is thought of blood and position. You were the mistress of Deerwood in fact but not in name for years.'

'I never lay with him,' Ellen said, quietly. 'I had a good man of my own when I was young and couldn't take another, and blood tells, whatever you say in haste. You married Mistress Hannam because you both come from families that demand a tie of rank and

240

wealth and will go on doing so, raising heirs to marry again into rank and wealth.'

He stared at her and she felt the pain of watching him in sadness as she had watched with joy when he was happy. 'Heirs?' he said bitterly. 'My wife brought her cousins with their children and I've seldom seen such a pale bed of weeds in my life. One son amongst a half a dozen girls and he will never do more than sit and give orders to those with more intelligence than he has.'

'He is young,' Ellen said mildly, but she knew of the boy and secretly agreed with John.

'He is ten and does not ride!' Ellen laughed at his disgust. 'I took him to the stables and made the groom put him on the smallest pony, and he cried! One of the girls had more spunk but backed down when I wanted to make her gallop, as she said her mother had told her it was unseemly!'

Ellen smiled. It was easy to imagine the scene and the ensuing conversation among the ladies after the visit to the stables, condemning John Halben as a coarse and insensitive beast who bullied their precious offspring. 'Girls are not used to men like you, John,' she said. 'Did you ride here?' She started up anxiously as the evening was cold.

'My mare is fine,' John said firmly. 'I put her in your lean-to with a blanket over her withers and I haven't ridden her hard today as the ground is frosty.' He sighed. 'I must come here, Ellen. You are all that's left of past sanity. My father is mad for most of the time, when he recognizes nobody but me, with intervals of clarity when he accuses everyone of stealing from him while he has been sick. My wife is terrified of him because she thought he had no sense left, she changed the hangings in the great hall to those depicting religion and saints, and made the room by the entrance where he took his whore, into a sewing room.'

Ellen repressed a smile. 'I remember those hangings. They were a gift from the bishop who married your mother to Sir William and he never liked them, as he said they watched every mouthful he took and accused him of loose living and gluttony.'

'You see, you of all people know about my family and of the happy times we had before my father's mind was corrupted by disease.' He ate more pie with increased appetite. 'I think my most happy years were when I ran wild with the sons and daughters of the yeoman of the village and the huntsmen.'

'Most of them are gone away, some to the King's Troop and others married out of the village.'

'And Hope left with them.'

She recognized the irony. 'Only my Hope left. You have your own hopes now that your lady is expecting; and nearly due or so they say,' she added with a puzzled smile. 'She carries it well as it isn't showing in front. Mrs More says that when it is like that, the child's backbone runs with the mother's, but she is very small.' She patted his hand. 'Enjoy what is to be. You are too young to dwell on old memories. Leave them to your old age. You have time to make your own,' she upbraided him gently. 'You have everything a man could desire here: a good life, a wife of rank to bear your children, faithful servants and friends and more horseflesh than many a duke has in his stables.'

'You are right.' He drew on the gauntlets and riding cloak as if to shut out any further sentiment and stood by the open doorway to say goodbye. A breeze from the dunes came salt and seaweed fresh and he closed his eyes for a second, seeing again a girl in a pale-blue gown, astride his bay mare, riding like the wind with pure joy in her eyes.

The mare nosed his neck and smelled of warmth and fine leather as he removed the rug and led her out into the cold the breath from her nostrils misting on the hint of ice in the air. He walked her home and handed her over to a sleepy groom then went into the house. The assembled company looked at him with accusing eyes and he realized that it was late. Time had vanished as he talked to Ellen in the comfortable parlour and he had a fleeting sympathy for men who took other women if they offered warmth and amusement instead of the frosty stare of a frigid wife.

'My mare cast a shoe,' he lied, and despised himself for making excuses in his own home. 'I walked her home,' he added with more truth.

'Is a horse more important than hearing my cousin play on the viol and my nephew play the flute?'

'Yes, madam,' he said curtly, and swept past them to the stairs. He heard a girl's voice in his mind. 'Have I winded her, John? She must be taken and rubbed down before she gets chilled.' He looked down from the gallery to the group of women and two men which included the unmarried woman whom Judith had wanted to come to live with her as her companion. She had lank dark hair and a sallow complexion and no inheritance. He grinned. Judith would be safe with her in the house. No husband would want to dally with such a creature, even if her eyes seemed to follow him as if she was fascinated by him. Chastity Morgan, he thought: a name from Oliver's time from a family true to the Protector Cromwell. Sir William had sworn an obscene oath when he saw her, and now Judith kept her out of his way while she decided if she wanted to keep the woman.

244

He called for his valet and changed into a dark-blue silk jacket with golden facings and velvet pantaloons of an even darker blue, deliberately dressing in such a way that Mistress Chastity would be repelled by his extravagance and obvious loyalty to King Charles II and yet be drawn hopelessly to the man under the rich clothes. The only person to be pleased to see him dress well was his father, who still decked himself in all the fine feathers of a royal courtier and who despised the plain greys and blacks of Judith's family.

'Well, sir! Why do you dress up now after the evening is over?' Judith said.

'We have guests, madam, and you summoned me to listen to music.'

He glanced round at the drab company. 'Come then, Makepeace,' he said to the unwilling boy. 'Play me a gavotte so that the company can dance.'

'I know of no such music,' he replied, hesitantly, and looked at Martha, his aunt, for guidance.

'A minuet is slow and simple, boy. Play that metre and I will dance with Mistress Chastity unless my wife feels fit to dance.'

'Makepeace knows no profane music,' Judith said with a stiff smile.

'No music for joy and laughter? You must remedy that, madam, if the boy is to visit us often,' John said. 'When next you come, I shall have a music master here to teach you the music I like to hear.'

'He has a tutor who is well versed in sacred music,' the boy's mother said.

'I never dance to fugues,' John said. 'He needs another tutor who will teach the latest songs from the court. Leave the boy here for a month and you will see the difference. He shall ride and learn the harpsichord and look merrier.'

'Judith will be delivered soon and wants no noisy children round her,' Martha said.

John's laugh was explosive. 'Judith will have her own noisy child near, so a quiet boy would not even be noticed,' he said. 'Infants cry madam, day and night.' He fixed his wife with a stern regard. 'Boys cry more than girls, but it will be a blessed sound when you give me my heir.'

He called for wine and sat in the great chair that his father had used for years before his ill health overtook him. The saint in the tapestry above the hearth looked silently disapproving and John turned away. 'Is all ready for the birth?' he asked.

'The physician will be here and a woman from the village,' Martha said. 'I shall stay until it is over to give my cousin comfort, but I shall send the children home to their father with two maids.'

'A husband gives comfort, madam if his wife loves him,' he said. 'But if she thinks she needs you, then stay, on *my* invitation, but there's no need to take more of *your* time, sir,' he said to the other cousin, Makepeace's father. There was a poignant silence and Judith looked angry. I must show my authority, he decided. The party at the table looked like drab grey birds eyeing carrion and he sensed that Judith was trying to sap his will by bringing them into the manor as if to take over his domain; surrounding herself with her own kind.

'We shall leave tomorrow, if we are no longer welcome,' Cousin Arthur said, pursing his mouth in disapproval, tight as the vent of a chicken.

'It will be safer if you all go together,' John suggested, as if he assumed that everyone was leaving. 'There are footpads on the Winchester road and you need to be in a big party to frighten them away.' He smiled. 'When it is all over, we shall rejoice and entertain you and the gentry from Southampton. Bring your best clothes, and you, boy, learn the gavotte as we shall make merry and dance and sing with joy, to bless my son.'

'I had hoped, sir to have my family near,' Judith said with lessening conviction.

'And so you shall! I intend to stay close as I am your family now. Cousin Martha may stay, but you must let the others go back to their homes where they are needed more.

They can't afford to leave a cold hearth if ice is on the way, and the ways grow treacherous if frozen.' He smiled grimly. The servant boy Michael had sharp ears, and had told him that the family with most of the children had shut up their house in Winchester for the rest of the winter, thinking that they could live at Deerwood until they decided that the weather was warmer, and they would need no fuel for months.

Cousin Arthur tried to speak then closed his mouth and stood up. 'Come, Makepeace, we must pack,' he said. 'We have a great deal to do.'

'Yes, you brought far too much for a short stay,' John agreed, but made no effort to assure them of a prolonged welcome if they returned after the birth.

They looked at the elegant man lounging by the fire and saw that under the smile was a determination that could not be challenged. One by one, they made their excuses and left, and sounds of frenzied activity came down to Judith and John in the great hall.

'You insult me,' Judith said, sullenly.

'Not you, my dear. I dislike hangers-on who have no real affection for you, but are willing to eat my bread and talk behind their hands of my habits and dress. Before we married, you wore fine clothes to please me and I gave you silks to adorn your pretty body, but now you dress like them again and the silk is still put away.'

'I dress suitably for a matron,' she said.

'You dress as a dame in Oliver's house. Cromwell is dead, as are all his crew, or disgraced and scattered. We tired of restrictions,' he said, more gently. 'Our children must laugh and be unafraid of outdoor skills and pastimes and enjoy life.'

'You sound like Sir William,' she said, spitefully.

'I am his son and I was told today that blood tells,' he said mildly. 'In his youth, my father was a fine man who brooked no nonsense from such as they,' he said with a lift to one eyebrow. 'He was blessed with a loving wife and his infirmity came from missing her love when she grew sick and having to find solace in the arms of whores.' She looked startled. 'You say I am like him and so I am in many ways but I would swear fidelity to any woman who returns my passion, and hope it may be my wife.'

'I am nearly at my time!' Judith avoided his penetrating gaze. 'You would do me harm if we lay together now.'

'I think not, madam. You have made excuses for the past few months and now we shall see what can be done, with gentleness and care.'

'It will hurt the baby.'

'They say that when a fruit is set, it will not fall until it is ripe, however much the tree is shaken.' He finished the wine. 'Come to bed, Judith. When you are delivered it will be weeks before we can be together, so I ask you now to come to me.'

Judith took one look at him and saw an implacable will under the now smiling face. She felt a thrill of fear mixed with a reluctant anticipation and she followed him up the wide stairway into the bedchamber.

John kicked the logs in the hearth to make a blaze and lit candles. The warmth of the room and the light on the rose velvet drapes made a setting for lovers, but Judith lingered over undressing and tried once more to convince her husband that his attentions would be unwise. He stripped off the fine coat and pantaloons and stood in his cambric shirt waiting for her to lie on the bed. As she made no move, he took her shift by the ribbons at the throat and ripped it down until she was naked, her swollen body curiously beautiful, as a ripe peach is smooth and ready for the hand. She made as if to protest but he lifted her high and placed her on the bed with the control of a strong man. He kissed her taut skin and the soft hair at her pubis, revelling in the female smell and the movement within the womb.

Judith moaned but he couldn't tell if it was fear or desire, and he no longer cared. 'You are not gross,' he said. 'You are not even big.'

'It is not due for another three months,' she whispered.

'You lied and said that you were with child so that I would leave you alone!' He laughed bitterly. 'Then I took you one night against your will and it was so, after all.' He climbed on to the bed and placed his lips on hers until his desire came swift and urgently and she submitted to his passion. 'Judith,' he said softly, 'we could be happy,' but the pale face that turned away from him told him everything. 'Do I have to rape my own wife?' he asked. 'You married me to take my name and have this house and wealth. In return you offered to give me an heir, but with that I expect warmth and respect and some sign of affection.'

'I am not capable of acting the whore,' she said with contempt.

'Then you should have gone to a nunnery. I want a wife, not a whore. I want love, not duty.'

'You resent my family and send them away,' she protested.

'As I would any parasite,' he said grimly. 'They came to be with you in your confinement or so you said, so their visit would have been a long one if they were to stay for three more months!'

He pushed her back on the bed as she

attempted to rise and she felt the hardness of his sex again as he thrust into her in anger more than desire. At last he lay spent and vaguely ashamed but his anger was deep.

'Give me a son and you can be free of all this, and I'll not trouble you more, but give me a daughter and you can go to hell in any way you please,' he said. 'But even then we will try again and again to make a boy.'

He left her weeping quietly and slept in another room. In the morning, Judith appeared to say farewell to her relatives with downcast eyes as if she had been condemned to death.

'You would waste your time here,' John said heartily. 'We find that Judith is not due for three more months and so we can go on with our lives. I can spare my wife for a few weeks if she would like to visit you, Cousin Arthur.'

'No, that would not do,' Arthur said, then added hastily, 'A lady in her condition would find my house cold until we have been there for a while.'

'Surely the warmth of your family would compensate for lack of fuel,' John said and laughed when Judith said she had no wish to leave her home. 'You see, she is a loyal wife and cannot bear to leave me,' he said, but he knew that Arthur kept a comfortless house and poor larder and Judith was now used to the best of everything.

'What is it?' he asked impatiently as the carriage left and he was alone by the gate to the lane. Angus, his valet-secretary, handed him a letter. He tore open the seal and let out a cry of pleasure. 'It's from my estates in America,' he said. 'Come and help me. You have an eye for figures and a Scottish shrewdness that I value.'

'A ship docked yesterday, sir, with mail and beaver skins, sassafras and Indian blankets.' The young man's eyes were wistful.

'And you want to go to Southampton to see it all?'

Angus flushed. 'My uncle went out there with the Pilgrims but died. He was a canny man but caught a fever and so perished. I would like to go there one day to find where he died, but I have no desire to make my life in a new country, over so much water.'

'But first you must see the ship and imagine the life on her. It isn't easy, as I know from my own experience, and bad weather can make a man wish he was dead.' He laughed. 'Let's make holiday. Order the carriage and we'll meet with the sailors and eat in Southampton.'

'I have work to do, sir.'

'Not today. I must brush the cobwebs from my mind and think for a while, and where better than by the sea?' He grinned. 'I prefer your company to the steward's and the cleric calls today to see Sir William and

I want none of him.'

'Have you letters for me to write, sir? Orders for your estate overseer in America?'

'The ship will be in port for revictualling and so that the captain can have leave. We must examine the figures in this report before we write, but today we shall take our ease and perhaps learn more about Martha's Vineyard than words on paper can tell us.'

John dressed warmly in a fur-trimmed cloak over a worsted suit of dark red and supple thigh boots over long stockings. His hat was plumed and gave him the air of a rakish bandit. Judith refused to look at him but retired to her room with Chastity, to make more embroidery for even more fire screens and tapestry stool covers.

Fur rugs covered their knees and the coachman huddled in the open with so many layers of clothing that his weather-beaten face was almost invisible. The horses were restless and ready for exercise.

'What is it like over there, sir?' asked Angus.

'Like another world, but like here too.' John sank back on the cushions and pondered. 'Men work hard there but are free and there is hunting and fishing for everyone. No man would be hanged for taking a deer as might happen here, as the need for food for survival for the good of the settlement is accepted as a necessity.' He frowned. 'I met a man who had been sent by a humane English magistrate to do hard service there for such a crime, instead of hanging for poaching. I took him to work for me and I sent his wife and children over last year.' He shrugged as if excusing any act of charity. 'It was better so as they were a burden on the parish.'

'Is every man allowed to take what he wants from the countryside?'

'The native Indians cannot understand such a sentence if a man kills game to feed his family, as they have hunted all over the territory for hundreds of years and never kill for sport, but only for their needs.'

'You sound as if you envy them,' Angus said with a sidelong glance at the now sad face.

'There are times when I wish I was there. When I read my reports I can almost smell the sea and the smoke from Indian fires.' He shouted to the coachman to hurry before they froze. 'You are a free man, Angus. You can go where you will. There is work for men like you who are honest and capable of handling business, but now I am married I am a prisoner in my own estates and can only dream about The Vineyard.'

Masts and sullen limp sails stood out, high above the docks and the carriage stopped. John Halben ordered the horses to be stabled and fed and the carriage put under the care of a boy to protect it while the coachman went to rest in one of the ale houses by the waterfront. It was bitterly cold and the two men strode down to the ship and gladly accepted the invitation to drink sack with the captain in his snug cabin.

Barrels of ale were being loaded in the hold and sacks of stores banked up evenly and tight to trim the weight and make sure there was no risk of shifting ballast in bad weather.

'Do you leave soon?'

The captain nodded. 'The winter gales are nearly over and we may have good weather with enough wind to take us quickly. The cold will abate next week and I have a full complement of crew and many passengers ready to sail in five days' time.'

'You feel no call to go home for a month to take ease with your family?' John asked.

'I have a wife in Portsmouth whom I saw yesterday. It was enough! She hasn't grown more desirable over the past six months and as soon as I gave her money, she wanted to see the back of me.' He grinned. 'The sea is a good mistress and never answers back. As to women, I've found a pretty little girl who likes men and I shall have my fill of her before we sail?'

'Is she clean?'

'As driven snow! Her mother makes sure

she goes with no common sailors or men who go to the stews and the girl is quiet.' He tapped his head with one finger. 'She may lack brains but she likes her work!'

'And her name is Bessie?' The captain nodded. 'She comes from my village and her mother is a good woman. Are they at the inn?'

'No, they have their own bawdy-house. Bessie goes with only the ones Sarah chooses for her, while the other girls serve the riff-raff.' He smiled in a knowing way. 'Do you want to know where to find her?'

'No! I am happy that they prosper, but they are free of my village now and it is better so.' He thought of his father, and any desire to pay a woman for sex died before it surfaced.

'Eat with us at the inn and we can talk of The Vineyard,' John said. 'I haven't read the reports that you brought for me, but I will have replies here by Friday if that is time enough before you sail.'

The captain stood up hurriedly. 'I'll come gladly but first take this. I sent your mail by special messenger, but I have more for your village if you could take it with you.' He produced a packet bound with tape and addressed to Ellen Turner. 'I took her niece and her husband out there some months ago, and the girl wrote these and gave them to me personally when the ship picked up passengers from The Vineyard and sailed on this voyage.'

'There's more than paper here.' John felt the bulky package with curiosity.

'A present, I expect,' the captain said. 'From what she said, her aunt is the only one who will miss her.'

'There are others,' John said. 'She had many friends.' He took the package from Angus who was putting it away in his script. 'I'll take it to Ellen,' he said. 'I am anxious to know if Edward Fletcher prospers.'

Chapter 13

'It seems only last month since they went away,' said Ellen happily. 'This letter brings her close again. She's always been a good girl to me and she knows that if ever she has to return here she will be welcome.'

The package that John Halben had put on the table with a nonchalant gesture as if it was unimportant, lay unopened. Ellen seemed content to look at it and reminisce. 'Are you not anxious to find out how they are?' he said at last. 'Has Edward Fletcher obtained work? I shall write to my overseer and suggest that he employs him if times are hard.'

'I am forgetting my manners,' Ellen said and bustled into the kitchen to bring ale and bread and cheese. John moved restlessly in front of the fire, his gaze never leaving the package and his impatience growing. 'The knots look tight,' he said as Ellen poured ale and pushed the mug over to him.

'I recognize the tape as some I gave to Hope. It ties tight but neatly and I shall undo it carefully as I can use it again.'

'Cut it,' he suggested. 'It may be tainted with sea-water.'

She gave him a reproachful glance and insisted on untying most of the knots until the package could be slipped away from under the tape. 'I'll finish them later,' she conceded, putting aside the rest of the tangle and unwrapping the contents. Three letters lay on the table, one for Ellen, one for Hope's mother and one for Edward's family which she picked up. 'Do you think I should go there now and give them this?' she asked.

'No! Open your own and tell me the news,' he said briskly. 'Don't take all day, woman!'

Ellen laughed. 'I must stop teasing you,' she said, and opened the letter. She read for a minute in silence and then passed the paper over to John. 'Read it to me. My eyes are not what they were.'

Trying to hide his eagerness, he began to read about the voyage and the people they had met and an amusing account of their meetings with Mr Rigsby and with Mary Chilton. His mouth softened as he could almost hear Hope's voice making gentle fun of Rigsby and feel her warmth when mentioning Katsi and Chiabos.

His hands shook and his voice died. 'What is amiss?' demanded Ellen in sudden fear.

'Nothing amiss. Hope was delivered of a fine and healthy son before the ship left and she is well.'

The letter slipped from his fingers on to the table and Ellen took it, peering at the small writing. 'She says that they are to call him Michael after Edward's father and that Edward wants to name him John after you! Hope writes that he insisted as Edward said that he owed John Halben more than he could say.'

'John!' he said softly.

'Michael John,' Ellen corrected him. 'Read the rest.'

'Edward is well and busy bartering his skills for supplies and they have deer meat and mutton and corn enough for the winter, fuel and good fishing.'

Ellen unwrapped the beaver-lined slippers and the soft jerkin of supple leather and blushed with pleasure. 'She knows I suffer with chilblains in winter and these moccasins will keep me warm.'

'I must go,' John said abruptly. 'The

260

steward needs orders for tomorrow and I must look to the horses.'

'I shall write a little but I am not good on paper. Have you a message for them?'

'Only joy at their health and the birth of their son,' he said as if the words hurt him. He smiled sadly. 'I could add envy and frustration to that, but say nothing of it.'

'My dear,' Ellen said touching his arm gently. 'I wouldn't have done, you know. Leave her to her husband and the happiness she has found over there and take pleasure in your own family.' She smiled. 'It can't be long now, and I pray that it is a boy.'

'It will be three more months,' he said, harshly. 'I have been cheated, but I've sent the crows packing and my wife knows that she can trifle with me no longer.'

He stormed from the house and his horse whinnied as he mounted roughly. Ellen was reminded of Sir William in his youth when something angered him. I am not there to smooth the tempers now, she recalled, and her heart was full of dread.

The hooves bit into the thawing ground and John Halben eased the reins, patting the horse's neck in apology for his brusque handling. He went back a longer way, knowing that he would find solace in the movement and closeness of his stallion, newly bought and needing exercise. The dunes opened up before him and he rode fast on the soft sand, horse and rider breathing heavily and facing into the wind.

She doesn't need me, he thought. Would I be happier if they didn't thrive in their new country or had bad luck and a mealy-faced daughter like Judith's cousin's children? Hope's child would be fair and beautiful. Even Edward was a fine figure with strong pleasant features, so the child could not fail to be handsome.

The frozen shreds of last year's brambles were trodden and crushed under the hooves and it seemed impossible that new growth could ever replace them, but John knew that the birds had left the shore for their breeding grounds and small buds were appearing on cold branches, so life must be reawakening.

Judith drew back, away from the gust of cold air that surrounded John as he tossed off his hoar-frosted cloak. 'Mulled wine, boy,' he called, and Michael ran to take the cloak from the stool and hurry to the kitchen to hang it to air and to bring the wine.

'You ride late, son,' Sir William glanced at his daughter-in-law to enjoy her reaction. 'What female sent you out so late? Were you driven away, or enticed to a warm bed?'

John laughed. 'I see that you are well today, Father. It's good to see you downstairs. Did the priest give you comfort and shrive your soul?'

Judith looked alarmed. He had not denied that he had met a woman! Sir William laughed and she noticed how alike the two men were now that Sir William was in a sane spell and well dressed.

'I am bound for Hell, John, but not yet I think. The physic that Ellen gave me does good. Tell her I need more. The doctor has no need to bleed me for the other condition and my mind is clearer.' He raised his silver mug in both hands to help the weakness of the left side which was the only remaining outward sign of his apoplexy.

'Ellen has left you,' Judith said harshly.

'No! Ellen would never leave me. You lie, woman!' He began to tremble. 'Send her here and tell her to bring her herbs so that I sleep tonight.'

'Ellen is not here, Father,' John said. 'She lives in the village.' He saw the flaring of anger and added tactfully, 'I am married now and have a wife to see to the household arrangements.' He smiled. 'But Ellen still cares for your welfare and I can bring your physic from her tomorrow. I saw her today and she said she was making more.'

'So that's where you were tonight!' Judith sounded annoyed but relieved.

'Yes, Ellen has a warm heart and has been like a mother to me.'

'And could have been if she'd married me,' Sir William said. 'I asked her after your mother died, but she'd have none of me as she thought I had the pox.' He sounded as if that was a stupid assumption and that his infirmity had nothing to do with the disease.

'And she said it wouldn't do.' John smiled sadly. 'I have heard her say that many times.'

'She's right. How could any nobleman think of marrying a common woman whose stock is no better than a serf's?' Judith's voice was shrill.

'That is not true.' John felt his temper rising. 'That family have good blood. They are yeomen and some say there is good blood there which brought them beauty and intelligence.'

'I want Ellen here!' The voice was slow and lacked strength as Sir William sagged in his seat and was suddenly insecure. 'She had no right to leave me.'

'I sent her away, Father, when you struck her. I could not allow that to happen again. She was not safe with you,' John said bluntly, no longer able to hide his impatience.

'I meant no harm. I was ill and knew nothing of what I did.' He looked sly. 'She has a daughter or a niece who could work here,' Sir William said eagerly. 'A pretty thing, if I recall.'

John wondered what the man would say

next and wished that Judith was absent from their conversation but she seemed fascinated.

'She is her niece and she is not here, either.' John hoped that the matter would not be pursued.

'She had enough sense to leave the village and go far away where you can never have claim to her,' Judith said, with the charm of a dog worrying a helpless rabbit. 'She may be dead by now as they went to a God-forsaken island in the New World. They will die in poverty like the criminals who are sent there.'

'That is not true.' John spoke reluctantly, but could not bear to hear what she said in such a scathing tone. 'I was with Ellen when she opened a letter from Hope today. She and her husband Edward Fletcher are well and prospering.'

Judith looked as if she didn't want to believe him and Sir William began to weep quietly. 'So far away,' he said. 'And because of my sin.'

'You have nothing to do with their leaving,' John said, as calmly as possible.

'What sin?' asked Judith, who seemed to find him entertaining.

'I took her virginity.' Sir William shook his head as if to rid it of clouds.

'You had a woman from Southampton here, Father. You had her here each week until your seizure.' John smiled grimly. 'You used the small room over there for your trysts, where Mistress Judith now sews under the tapestry of Holy Catherine as peacefully as if there had been no bawdy happenings there.'

'You did not tell me!' Judith was furious.

'You arranged that room when I was away for a few days and refused to give it up when I said it was unsuitable,' John said mildly.

'I can believe that the girl might have gone in there too,' Judith said with venom. 'I heard she was friends with Sarah, the whore. Why did she need to write if she has turned her back on Deerwood? Does she really flourish or is it a pretence to gain sympathy and to get money from her aunt to help them through the winter?'

'They are secure,' John said. 'They are happy and have more than many men of rank have here.' He watched her turn pale as he said, 'She gave her husband a holy gift. They have a fine son in good health. I pray that you may be so useful, madam.'

'A son? I must send her a present.' Sir William seemed to diminish in size. 'Who has a son?' he asked. 'I want to go to bed.' He began to undo his doublet and took it off. 'Is she in there waiting for me? Tell the steward to bring her as soon as she comes and get her warm, as the road from Southampton must be icy and I can't bear cold hands on my body.'

He shuffled towards the small room by the entrance and Judith gave a muted cry. 'Stop him,' she begged. 'There is no bed there, sir! Take him to bed and tomorrow put a lock on that door. All my best embroidery is there.'

'It is his house, madam,' John said mildly, but his eyes showed his amusement. 'Perhaps you would have been more comfortable with your cousin, Arthur. I suggest that you retire now and leave him to Michael and the steward, who will carry him to his room and see that he does no harm.'

'And you will wait with him to see that he falls asleep and doesn't wander?' Judith asked, with a hopeless wish that she could be left alone.

'There is no need. I have a woman to sit with him now, quietly by the door, with laudanum if he is restless, mixed with some of Ellen's herbs to make him calm and give him sweet dreams. Go now, my dear. I shall not be long here.'

Judith walked stiffly to the stairs as if her legs were unable to support her weight, then quickened her steps as she thought that she might be asleep when John came to bed and so escape his lust.

He watched her go, almost reading her thoughts and sighed. Any transient pleasure he had from their unions was cancelled by the weariness he felt after he lay with a statue who had no feelings for him except revulsion.

He called for the girl to douse the candles and to take fresh ones to his library. He carried a jug of wine with him and went up to the comfortable and wholly masculine room where he sat by the fire reading far into the night and drinking the good red wine until he forgot the ache that had grown ever since he read Hope's letter.

He studied the papers from his agent, Lubbock, in Martha's Vineyard and was impressed by what he read. The orchards were bearing good fruit and the harvest of squash and beans was enough to use for the workers over the winter, with plenty more to sell in Edgartown for a good price. Local Indians bartered pelts and baskets for tools and sugar and the market value of the furs and sassafras when sold in England made it worth sending them overseas.

He suggested that John Halben should check the goods against the list submitted and to send further orders on the next ship as he wanted to enlarge the compounds and surround them with tall fences to protect his labour and to make their long houses safe from bears and other marauding creatures.

The horses arriving on The Vineyard were making work easier and giving good riding.

Maybe breeding them would be profitable as they were in short supply, if a man could be found to see to stables. The agent stressed that he was not good with horse breeding and would need help, but the market was good and he saw a future for such an enterprise.

John wrote his letter, suggesting certain improvements and acquiescing to Lubbock's requirements. He sat back in his chair for a long time, thinking, then wrote, 'Have a care for any who come to you from this village as I know them all and have known their families for years. Send me news if you hear any concerning them but do not intrude on their lives as they may want to forget Deerwood Manor for ever. If hard times overtake them send word to me so that I may help them.'

He wanted to say so much and yet there was nothing more to say. Wearily, he yawned and climbed into the narrow cot he had put in his library, as unwilling to sleep by Judith's side as she was to be near him. He thought of Hope as he fell asleep, not as a mother with a child at her breast but as she had been when they made love and she had robbed him of his peace of mind.

'Angus?' The young man started then pulled back the drapes in the dark library. 'I had work to do so I stayed here last night,' John

Halben said. He rose from the bed and rubbed his eyes. 'I'll put on fresh linen and meet you here. Order ale and a pasty for us to eat while we work. No! Order bread and cheese. No pasty unless we want heartburn all day!'

'Sir William had a bad night, sir. I have just seen his nurse and she talks of leaving.'

'Can she not control him?'

Angus hid a grin. 'He thought she was his woman from Southampton and wanted to take her to bed.'

'She should know that he is no threat to her! Since his seizure he has been weak and so forgetful that he would forget what she was there for after two minutes!'

Angus frowned. 'The steward went to him and talked in a low voice, making him look into his eyes. Sir William seemed afraid.'

'Listen to what they say Angus. I have thought lately that Furness rules my father through fear. The boy told me so and I have seen my father become sober when Furness talks to him, trying to gather his wits, but unable to retort.'

Angus coughed. 'You asked me to look at the accounts, sir. Mr Furness refused to show me the books and told me not to meddle, as he had his authority from Sir William who is still Lord of the Manor and has given no orders to undermine the authority of the steward.'

John went quickly to his desk and unlocked a box full of papers. 'When I returned from the Tour, I saw that my father was ill but not at that time mad, and insisted that if I lived here I must have his powers transferred to me as his heir. Here are the documents. Mr Furness knows about them.' John gave a short laugh. 'He also knows that I have copies resting with lawyers in case these are lost, or are destroyed by some criminal person.'

'You do not trust him?'

'He is a good steward, or was,' John admitted. 'I think that now he aims too high and lines his pockets with my father's wealth.' He handed over a bunch of keys. 'These are keys to the bureaux in my father's study. Go there now and bring me the red leather box and the black lacquer drawer from the escritoire.'

John Halben dressed and returned to the library. He drank his first morning draught as Angus set the boxes on the table. Together they checked accounts with the entries made by the steward and it was increasingly clear that Furness had been quietly taking regular sums of money over a long period.

'What is to be done?' John asked.

'Faced with this he can be dismissed or arrested,' Angus said. John turned to look out of the window, a sullen rage welling up in his heart, mixed with a sense of fore-boding.

'Now that you are here, sir, the estate can manage without him.'

'For the sake of my mother's memory and the good work he did before he turned sour, I would not have him hang. In many ways my father is to blame. He fell into profligacy and Furness procured women for him and was ready to follow and aid him in all things, even to falsely accusing men who displeased Sir William and seeing them hang.'

He examined one of the papers without seeing a word. Furness believed that Hope had been deflowered by Sir William and knew that if he told the villagers that it was so, there would be trouble, both for the manor and for Hope's family. He could never prove it, but when had truth ever been a match for rumour?

'Take these back and say nothing,' John said. 'I must consider what is for the best, for my father, for the estate and for the peace of mind of many people.'

They settled to the business of Martha's Vineyard and Angus wrote out what his master ordered. At last it was done and John sealed a letter he had written to the landlord of the inn where Sarah's sister lived. In it was a note to Sarah with the request that it should be taken to her at once.

'You must show nothing in your manner to make him think we suspect him,' John said. 'Find him and bring him here. I shall send him to Southampton today to take the papers to the ship's captain and to buy harness for my latest stallion. I want you to go with him as far as the docks but to come back alone. You will lead a young in-foal mare to be shipped to my estates on The Vineyard. She is from the same sire and dam as my best mare and has the same colour. She will start a strain of value that may well be profitable is she survives the voyage.'

'Where will Furness go? He will expect to return with me.'

'You will finish your business first and say that I need you back here. He enjoys a day out and will go to an inn and maybe a whorehouse. He will be glad to see the back of you as he knows that you never frequent such dens.'

'I'll tell him before I dress for riding,' Angus said.

'Carry this letter to show your position here and wear your finest cloak. Pickpockets are not anxious to be caught by men of rank especially when they are armed as you must be.'

John went to the stables to fetch the mare. 'Goodbye, Russet,' he said, softly. 'You will be nearer to my love than I shall ever be.' He packed her saddle-bags with good blankets and bags of carrots and made sure that Angus would check that on board she would be well fed. He watched the men leave and saw that Furness was wearing fustian breeches, complaining that the saddler kept a dirty workshop even though his harness was the best in the south of England.

The men rode in near silence, Angus keeping to the rear with the mare so that she trod gently and without harm. 'Meeting a lady?' asked Furness with a leer, as he eyed the good clothes and plumed hat with amusement.

'No, I thought I might visit a lawyer,' Angus said with wry humour.

'On whose business?' Furness said sharply.

'My own. Every man should make a Will,' he replied, and was amused to see the steward relax.

At the inn, Sarah's sister took the note, drew her shawl about her shoulders and hurried away. The men ordered sack as a preventative against the plague and before they had drunk a glass, Sarah appeared, feigning surprise at seeing them. She was well dressed in a gaudy manner and had regained much of her former looks. She asked about the village and the manor as if it didn't really concern her and told them of her house with the seven girls she now employed.

'I am always pleased to see old friends,' she said, as if Furness was her second-best friend. 'My girls are clean and pretty and you can eat with us if you come when you finish your business here.'

'I have to go back. Mister Halben will be anxious to know how his mare managed the ride here.' Angus spoke sternly as if he disapproved of Sarah and everything she did. Furness winked as if Sarah and he shared a joke at the expense of this pious fool.

'I'll be but an hour,' said Furness. 'I'll be hungry for food and a pretty wench.'

Angus shrugged and led the mare to the ship where she was put in a compound ready to load at the last minute. He gave her a carrot and smoothed her silky nose. 'I wish I was going with you,' he said, but shuddered at the thought of the wide sea, then started for home.

Furness left the new harness with the saddler to be collected later and left his horse in the livery stable. The air was warm now and when he reached the wooden house where Sarah lived, he looked up at the new paint with a certain admiration. Sarah had chosen well as the road in front of the house led directly to the ships, and ships brought sailors, hungry for everything that could give them pleasure.

Sarah was waiting for him and took his

warm coat, saying that it was far too hot to sit at table in it, so he reclined against a high-backed settle wearing his shirt and trousers. She served him with more sack and a dish of mutton with sweet herbs. The stew was salty and he drank more and more as Sarah kept talking.

Half fuddled, he asked where Bessie was and Sarah told him that she was away with friends. She hoped that she was not brought back from her gentlemen until Furness had left. 'Pretty girl, Bessie, but I want a girl with dark hair and plenty of flesh.'

'I know who will please you,' Sarah said. 'She'll be here ready for you in half an hour so you have time for another drink.' He drank again and she glanced out of the window. The sack was strong and Sarah had been steadily filling his tankard all the while they talked. 'Come, drink some more. There is plague in Portsmouth. As yet we are safe, but men come from the ships each day and it is never clear who will bring it next.'

Three men strode up the road and stopped in front of the house. A girl beckoned and they laughed, but had other business than love on their minds. The front door opened and Furness saw them through blurred vision. His head was heavy and his brain seemed asleep. 'Give him his jacket, mistress. He'll need that where he's going.'

'Who are you?' Furness sensed that they

meant him harm, but his legs refused to support him.

'We come in the name of His Majesty to take you as a willing recruit into the navy.'

Sarah gave a small scream that came too late and too soft to have effect and hastened to help the drunken man into a jacket that had seen better days and stank of ale, left by a man who had been too drunk to take it with him. The good cloth coat that would mark the steward as a man of importance lay hidden in the corner of the room. The press men didn't even ask his name.

'Thank you, ma'am,' said one man. 'We'll leave your house alone in future. We're always ready to rid you of riff-raff like this and you know where to find us if you need us again.'

Sarah watched them go, her face set and her eyes cold. 'Enjoy your new life, Mr Furness,' she said. 'Suffer as you made others suffer and may you drown in foreign seas.' She shook out the coat and folded it carefully. Now that the steward could never touch her, she would visit the village and return the coat that was part of Deerwood livery and tell them that Mr Furness had been taken by the press gang.

They could go by stage coach, leading the nag behind it. Bessie would enjoy meeting old friends again and John Halben would want his horse back. It could stay in the livery stables for a night as that would give time for Mr Furness to be far away before anyone missed him. She laughed. 'I pay my debts,' she said, and the girl who came to clear the table looked puzzled. A good customer had been dragged away by navy men before he had paid, and madam was smiling.

Chapter 14

The baby lay in a woven basket in the shade and Hope hung out the bedding in the fresh air. She stopped to watch the sun on the sea and smiled. It was so like home but in many ways different, the main one being that she felt free. Edward was very contented with their life on The Vineyard and the baby was healthy and grew bigger almost as she watched him, eager for her milk and ready to laugh at everything.

Katsi and the other women wondered at his vivid blue eyes and fair skin and the restlessness of the firm body. Edward had been proud when they went to the church in Edgartown to have the baby named, as many people had admired his son and invited them all to their homes.

Hope had lifted the pale-green silk from

278

the chest and looked at it, remembering that she had thought to make it into a gown when her first born was named, but she had put it back and covered it once more with simple linen shifts, choosing to wear a fresh cotton dress and a plain straw hat with a trim of wheat ears to the church.

Somehow here, among the hard-working communities and the half-naked Indians, she felt that silk would be pretentious and it belonged to another world. The Vineyard wasn't like Plimoth or the other early settlements like Boston and had a lot to do to catch up with the sophistication of such places. In any case, she told herself with a sad smile, it had nothing to do with Edward, and to wear John's present here as Ellen would have said with pursed lips, 'Wouldn't do.'

Apart from the churchmen and their families who seemed to think they had a certain superiority over all others, there was little attention given to the former status of the newcomers from the Old World, as they soon realized that everyone depended on each other for something whether it was goods to barter, boats to share, or just company and care in bad health or accidents.

Men who were sent from England as prisoners soon became absorbed into the communities if they worked hard and were willing to be loyal servants. For many, transportation was a deliverance and not a penance. A full belly and a roof for his family usually tamed the most hardened petty thief, and poachers had the pick of game that surrounded them on every side, so there was no need to disobey any law.

Katsi squatted by the basket and chewed dried pumpkin seeds. 'The men are fishing and the women are ready to plant Sister Corn. Our fields are ready and you have made your land ready for birth,' she said with a smile, and Hope felt pleased that all the hard work met with her approval. Edward had dug in the rotted seaweed that they had gathered laboriously from the shore in the handcart, together with the wood ashes from the fire before the winter frosts made digging impossible so the soil was lighter and easily worked now. They had made narrow mounds of soil at intervals on which they were to plant the seeds, following the example of Chiabos and his family and trusting them to know what was right.

'Why today?' Hope asked. 'How do you know when to plant?'

'The oak leaves are free of their winter coats, and the whippoorwill has been heard,' Katsi said patiently, as if any child would know that this was the time to plant corn.

'Do we plant squash now?'

Katsi smiled. 'We plant Sister Corn now,

and when the stalks are strong we plant Sister Squash to spread under the corn and kill the weeds and Sister Bean to grow up the corn maidens and keep her safe from winds and withering sun.'

Hope smiled. 'I feel strong and ready for work. Where do we gather for the planting?'

'We gather at the far fields first, then go to the next until we come here, then start again over many days so that all is done and nobody has fields left unplanted, and all seed corn is shared equally.'

'So everyone has some corn ripening at the same time and more over several weeks? It doesn't have to be harvested all at once?'

Katsi nodded as if it needed no reply. She swung the baby she was carrying in her leather sling on to the ground and when he whimpered gave him a piece of whale blubber to suck as a comforter. 'He is ready to leave the breast,' she said. 'I must take medicine to stop another child until I have less work to do.' She looked at Hope's full breasts. 'Tell me when he is no longer filled by you and I will give you medicine to stop a child being made.'

'I shall feed him for a few more weeks,' Hope said. 'But he is a lusty boy and will need other food soon.' She smiled fondly as Katsi touched his cheek with one brown finger and he laughed up at her. 'I shall not worry if I have more children quickly,' Hope said. 'I feel that I need to make my own family here as I am far from my relatives.'

'You have no news?'

'Yes, I have news. My aunt writes and my mother sends messages in her letters and Edward's father writes occasionally, but I feel that his family think he has deserted them and they have no further interest in us.' She paused while she considered what to say, then added cautiously, 'Mr John Halben's agent here met us in Edgartown when we went to church and brought us news of Deerwood Manor in the village where we lived. He asked Edward to visit him at Ostungo the Halben estate, and we may go there soon.'

'Soon or many moons?' asked Katsi shrewdly. 'You do not wish to go there.'

'I think he may write to Mr Halben with news of us and I think it might be unwise.'

'Edward says many good things of this John Halben,' Katsi said.

'Yes, he is a good man but unhappy. His wife gave birth to a daughter and John wanted a son to carry his name. I think his wife does not love him as he needs. My Aunt Ellen says so and she knows about them.'

'His woman may bear better fruit,' Katsi said, and picked up her child. 'Today I bring a sling for your baby if you are to work for a long time. It soothes them and they are no trouble when they are safe on a mother's back and sleepy.'

'Are you sure that you can do this?' asked Edward when she explained that she had agreed to plant the corn.

'I am strong now and I have to do it as it is woman's work,' Hope said simply. 'Not just because the men make women do this work but because they say that a female must plant female things like the Three Sisters or the crops will not be fertile.'

'That is Indian talk,' he said, laughing. 'Surely a man who knows the work can produce fertile crops? I think that it should be Brother Corn, as the legend says that it came from the body of the youth that Hiawatha killed and buried to make Indian corn for his people!'

She regarded him with a mocking smile. 'Hark at the superior English man who refuses to believe in superstition and gypsies! Who did I hear asking the pardon of the spirit of a hare that he killed?'

Edward blushed. 'I do it to please Chiabos and to respect their customs.'

'Even when he isn't there?'

'It seems right,' Edward said. 'I have never enjoyed killing for the pleasure of it, even if it was to kill rooks and pigeons and other pests.'

She regarded him with affection and held up her face to be kissed. 'You are a good man, Edward,' she said.

'More fortunate than many I know. John Halben would give much to have a son like Michael,' he said with pride. He gazed down at the now sleepy child and laughed. 'Perhaps it's as well that we have the ocean between us or he might try to take our baby as Mistress Chilton wanted to do if this child had been a girl. I would be happy with either,' he said, forgetting his longing for a son when first he knew that Hope was pregnant. 'But I know that some people think it important to have a son at all costs.'

'The Reverend Martin has four daughters and his wife has another child on the way,' Hope said. 'She looks as if a puff of wind would blow her away and yet they try for a boy.'

'It is the way of life.' Edward shrugged. 'Marriage brings children and unless a man agrees to be continent which is against nature, then it follows that babies are made.'

'The squaws seem to avoid it when they are too busy and want an interval between children, even when the men do not curb their passions.'

'They may be less fertile than we think,' Edward said, dismissively. Hope smiled and decided not to tell him that Katsi had offered to give her medicine to prevent a child.

'I shall not conceive while I feed him,' she said. 'It is as well if I am to plant Sister

Corn. Go fishing,' she added laughing. 'We need no men today and in the days to come until the planting is over.'

'What will you do with Michael?'

'Katsi is bringing a sling to carry him on my back as she does with her baby.'

Edward looked at her eager face and sparkling blue eyes. Her skin was clear and smooth and her body was slim and supple once more. 'Be careful that you don't turn into a squaw,' he said. 'Mrs Martin disapproves of settlers wearing baby slings. She dislikes us to copy the Indians.'

'Mrs Martin has servants to hold her children but she has no real friends here. I am glad that Edgartown is too far away for her to visit us often. I like my life here and if what Katsi teaches me makes sense then I accept her advice with gratitude. We live here now, not in a village with a bigoted cleric to frown on everything we do, and my mother to tell me I dress immodestly! I go to church, but I have no wish to make a friend of Mrs Martin!'

'I have been invited to Ostungo again and this time you must come, Hope. I can't think why you are so reluctant to see the place. It is beautiful and very well run and they asked to see you.'

'We came away to escape Deerwood,' she said.

'Escape? John Halben is our friend. We

285

have known him since we were children and he has our interests at heart. Mr Lubbock said that he asked for news of us and it seems churlish not to visit his estate.' He looked serious. 'I said we would go there for dinner at four after the next ... two Sundays.'

Hope laughed. 'Now who is following Chiabos? You were going to say, after the new moon!'

'He is my friend,' Edward said, his face reddening.

'As Katsi is mine, above all women here! She delivered my baby and gave me love and care. Never let that be forgotten! She is worth a dozen Mrs Martins or Mistress Chiltons!'

'Calm down! I have nothing against Katsi and you are right: we must do as we please, not as the reverend lady says is right and proper, but old ways die hard and at home the influence of such women was great.'

Hope eyed his leather jerkin and breeches with amusement and watched him sling the quiver of arrows over his shoulder. The strong but supple bow that he selected from the four he had made had a leather hand grip that was already worn by use. His hunting skills had improved. The crossbow lay under a pile of skins, forgotten.

'When the new moon rises, you must wear English clothes to visit the English estate,' she said, gently mocking him. 'And I shall wear a hat and sit in the pony trap, holding our son in a shawl!'

She sniffed. 'Wait and have fresh bread,' she said, and put the bread paddle into the oven to withdraw the salt-risen bread. 'I made enough for a few days as I shall be busy in the fields and have no time to leave the cornmeal to sponge.'

'I can make bean bread if you are not here. Leave the meal and beans and soda where I can find them and I shall cook them with pork and greens ready for when you return at dusk.'

'Catch me some crabs and cod and we shall not starve.' She packed bread and dried meat into a leather pouch and when Katsi came with the sling she put Michael on her back and walked freely on her moccasin-light feet.

They passed the boat that Edward was making and Hope noticed with amusement that he had followed the Indian custom of decorating it with porcupine quills and strips of silver birch round the prow. It was a big boat that could go far out to sea with a sail and oars. Edward had been advised to make stout timber joists on the sides to hold nets and spare sails and to give purchase if a man had to brace himself to bring in a big fish. The prow curved upwards in the manner of the canoes used to hunt whales and several boys looked at it in awe and the hope that they might be allowed to sail in her.

'Soon we shall need oil and the men have seen Brother Whale clouding the sky with his breath as he hunts the shoals of small fish near the island outside the bay,' Katsi said.

'When will they go? Edward's boat isn't ready for deep water,' Hope said, and secretly wished that he had made a much smaller canoe for inshore fishing.

'They will go when the women are not busy in the fields, so it will be ready,' Katsi said.

'But the women don't fish out there.'

'We lie quiet on our beds with our feet pointing away from the sea. The men dress in paint and wampum to give reverence and pray to our gods and to Brother Whale to give us meat and oil and to preserve our men and children from the sea. We rest still so that the whale does not get restless and swim away and we lie straight to show the whale the way to the shore.'

'Who cooks and looks after the children?' Hope asked.

'The old women who can no longer bear children and whose men have died or are not fit for the sea.'

'I will make bread for you,' Hope said. 'And the old squaws from your long house may bring the babies here so that you rest quietly.' Katsi nodded but gave no indication that she was anxious about the men who would hunt the whale nor did she mention that Chiabos would be with the hunters.

'It will not be soon,' Katsi said, and Hope recognized a hint of relief that this was so.

Hope remembered the days when she had helped with the harvest in the village of Little Deerwood. She put on thick stockings knowing that biting insects were universal and there were as many here as there had been at home. She filled the wicker baskets with corn that had soaked in the liquid that Chiabos had brought them that would keep away mice and chipmunks, and put the baskets on the handcart. The spring day was warm but the breeze cool enough to make work easy as the women set out for the far fields.

Katsi put the baskets belonging to a pregnant girl on the cart and she grunted her thanks. Hope wondered if more carts would be acceptable for the women when Edward had time to make them, as they worked hard and carried heavy loads for long distances.

The first field looked bare and charred after the men had fired last year's corn stubble, but the earth was light and easily worked and soon the narrow mounds of soil had seven seeds planted in the top of each one. The women moved on when they had filled a certain number of rows and started on the next field.

When it was time for food and to feed the hungry children they sang and shared everything they had brought, as they shared the seed corn, and the days passed happily until all the fields were sown with corn and it was time to sow the squash.

'My back stopped aching after the first week,' Hope said when Edward became anxious about her. 'Michael loves being on my back and listens to the singing as if he might join in.' She looked at her sunburned hands and laughed. 'I am like a gypsy and my hair has been bleached by the sun. Katsi finds it strange to see how fair my hair is now and how Michael has such blue eyes. She can't resist touching Michael's hair and cheeks and seems fascinated by him. I'm afraid that Mrs Martin would be shocked to see my brown face, but I can't go to Edgartown until the sowing is through, so there's no need for her to see me.'

Edward held his son in his arms and gazed at the small face. 'He gets more like you ever day, Hope. Anyone can see that you are his mother.' He sighed. 'Perhaps our next child will be darker like me.' He kissed the baby and smiled. 'I'm wrong to grumble. I have a handsome son and a beautiful wife and enough work and food to last a lifetime.'

'You aren't dark,' she said. 'Darker than me but I think he has your smile,' Hope said without conviction. 'And didn't your aunt have fair hair on your mother's side of the family? He may grow darker. His hair isn't as fair as mine. Already it is darker, more like ripe wheat.'

'That's right.' He seemed to have forgotten the lank mousy locks that the lady had hidden under a cap for most of her life. 'If you are fair and I am darker, then he may come in between.'

'I'm not fit to be seen at Ostungo,' she said.

'You look well and happy and you are going there on Sunday.'

She laughed. 'How do you know it is the right time? There was cloud over the moon for the last three nights so how can you say that it is a new one?'

Edward ignored her teasing. 'Do you think we should take a gift?'

'Has Mr Lubbock a wife?'

'Yes, but she's not pretty like you.' He put Michael back in the crib and took her firmly in his arms. 'I love you even more than I did when we married,' he said. He fondled her body and kissed the white throat and her breast where the sun hadn't caught it, marvelling at the softness and the warm smell of milk. Hope responded with passion and they went into the bedroom and lay for a while making love until Michael began to cry. 'I'll fetch him,' Edward said. 'I have to see to the horse and the pigs but I'll wait until you start to feed him.'

Hope put on her shift but left the front open. Michael clung to her and began to suck impatiently, as if hungry and annoyed at being kept waiting. 'Oh, you monster,' she said affectionately. 'You are as strong as your father, but these are not love bites! I'll have to start giving you cornmeal and soaked bread, and dried meat to chew to bring your teeth through.'

Edward sat for five minutes as if in a dream then rose to leave. 'Is something the matter?' Hope asked.

'No.' Edward seemed to wake up. 'It's nothing.' He gave a nervous laugh. 'Suddenly Michael seemed like a stranger. I could see him growing big and strong and not looking like our baby. Promise me that he'll never come between us, Hope?'

'My dear! He is a baby and all babies are selfish beasts who want food and warmth or they cry for it! When he has brothers and sisters he will have to share us and it will be a good time, watching them grow up and become loving and sensible.' She touched her breast where the baby had marked her. 'The sooner I put him on real food the better I shall be and I can dry up my milk.

If he has as happy a childhood as we had, when we played with the other children and rode John's donkey, he will be fortunate.'

Firmly she patted his back and put him down in the crib in spite of fretful cries as he hadn't finished his feed. Usually Edward enjoyed watching her give the breast to Michael but today he seemed to think that he was a threat. Can a man be jealous of his own son, Hope wondered, and decided that she must try to feed the baby when Edward wasn't there.

The clothes that she had bought in Edgartown were now too small for the growing child and Hope sat late, sewing small shirts and trousers by candle-light, wishing that she had the nerve to let him go naked as the Indian babies did, but as she had no idea how Mrs Lubbock would react to such outlandish behaviour, Michael had to suffer the indignity of being dressed on the day of the visit.

Ostungo was set back among cherry and pear trees and the cedar shingles were mellowing to a light silver. Steps leading up to the entrance were flanked by the windows of the two main rooms and above them were the sleeping quarters of the family. Other rooms and the kitchen were at the back and in the yard was a big smokehouse built of coarse local bricks bonded together with hard mortar made from sea shells and bone ground to a powder and mixed with sand. The deep fireplace was also made of brick and stone and a huge pot of venison stew simmered gently over the log fire.

A young Indian unhitched the trap and led the horse to the stables at the back of the buildings and Edward and Hope were taken into the timber house. 'Do you see?' Edward said. 'I can make another room at the side as they have done with wattle and daub and a facing of planks.'

'It's beautiful,' Hope said and Mrs Lubbock looked delighted to see her.

'We needed more room as the family grew, and if Mr Halben comes over to see his land then we shall have to make even more improvements,' she said. 'I have never seen Deerwood Manor but he must be used to much more than we can provide here.' She laughed. 'When he came here first, there were only Indian long houses. We lived in one for a year, but he seemed not to care and slept happily on a pile of moss and deer skins in a tepee.'

'That sounds like John Halben,' Edward said with approval. 'He is a good man with none of the puffed-pride of many men of his rank who flock to the court of King Charles now that there is more freedom from puritan restrictions.'

A girl of about twelve took Michael to see

the chickens and Thomas Lubbock offered to show the visitors round the estate. Hope looked about her eagerly and envied them the prolific blossom on the fruit trees.

'Our trees are small and as yet bear no fruit,' she said. 'The blueberries and cranberries make good pies, but I prefer raw fruit from a good pear tree.'

They walked to the back of the house and heard a mare whinnying.

'She's talking to your horse,' Thomas said. 'She foaled a couple of months ago and has a fine colt.' He opened the high wooden gate that led into a paddock surrounded by tall posts woven with laths to make a firm fence. A bay mare lifted her head and walked slowly towards them.

'You beauty,' Hope whispered as the mare came to her eager hand.

'Mr Halben sent her over in foal to start a stable of thoroughbreds and she settled well.'

'I knew her dam,' Hope said. 'I rode her before we came away and she went like the wind.' She caught her breath and almost smelled the gorse on the dunes at home. Dear God, let me forget, she silently prayed, and knew that if she visited the Lubbocks too often she would remember bitter things that lay hidden in the pleasant life she now shared with her husband and their child.

Edward patted the mare in a desultory way, but was more interested in the oxen that Thomas Lubbock used for heavy work in the fields and to drag timber. 'Two are ready to drop their young and we want to sell them when they are weaned,' he said.

'Can we afford one?' Edward asked Hope and told her what Lubbock was asking for him.

She hesitated. Edward left most of the business to her now and seemed willing to accept that she was the better at the management of money, as he was inclined to buy on impulse and regret some of his purchases. Sometimes he wondered how she did manage so well, but she was careful not to show the rest of the secret store that still lay hidden under the green silk.

'We can if we wait until the autumn after we have the money from the skins we sent over on the last ship,' she said. 'We may have beans to sell, too, and the beaver skins that Chiabos will barter for your help with the boats.'

She let the foal nuzzle her neck and laughed with delight. 'He's wonderful. Look how strong he is, Edward! What good legs he'll have. And see that deep chest for speed and endurance!' She turned to Alice Lubbock who had brought Michael to see the foal and to ask them to come to dinner. 'You are very lucky,' Hope said. She looked back but Edward was walking away to the sheep pens.

'I see that you would rather have the foal than a heavy beast of burden,' Alice said drily. 'I like the look of horses, but I never ride and Thomas isn't the best of horsemen. I regret having them here but Mr Halben was adamant that we should try to breed and sell over here.'

Hope regarded the warm hut and the fragrant straw bedding with pleasure. She admired the wide paddock where there was room for the foal to play and cavort with her mother and she sighed. 'You are doing well,' she said. 'Nobody could find fault with the care you lavish on them. You must have a good stable boy.'

'That is easy. We have two men who have been with horses at home and can look after them day by day, but when the foal is ready for breaking in we have nobody who is skilled or interested enough to do that and we need people to ride them and make sure they are well trained and well exercised.'

'Perhaps Mr Halben will send someone out to take over the stable if you tell him how well the first foal is doing.'

Alice looked at her and sensed her deep pleasure when the horse came near. Hope took Michael and held him up to touch the soft nose. He gurgled with delight and tried to pull the flickering ears. Russett came closer, unafraid of his exploring hands.

'Grow up soon,' Alice told him. 'You will

love horses as your mother does.' She smiled. 'I can always tell: it's bred in the bone. Your husband is like mine; they use horses but never have real pleasure from them but Michael takes after you. My children are like Thomas so I can't expect much help from them. If you can spare the time, you will be more than welcome to come here to ride, and when we need help next year with the halter and bit, will you come and give orders to the stable hands?'

Hope blushed with pleasure. 'I did help John Halben once when he tamed a very wild stallion,' she admitted. 'He became a good mount and a fine hunter. John rode him until he broke a leg and had to be destroyed. John left for Europe soon after that and I think that was one of the reasons why he needed to get away.'

Her eyes misted with nostalgic tears. 'They called him Satan but he wasn't wicked.' She saw Russett through a blur and saw where the sun caught the gloss of Michael's hair as he leaned forward to pull the mane. Hair like ripe corn, the wheat that swayed like a living tide under English skies when the summer breeze sent it rippling like water. Hair like John's, on a neck that even on a baby beginning to crawl and hold himself erect, was held proudly as if he knew that he was born to be one of the world's elite.

Chapter 15

Lady Judith Halben bent over the tapestry frame and carefully inserted two stitches to match the lavender in the petals of the flowers in the picture. The faint cries from the next room seemed not to bother her. She wanted to finish the flower before her cousin Arthur and his family arrived to visit her.

'My Lady?' Her companion, Chastity, hovered in the doorway.

'What is it now?' Judith said sharply.

'The child is crying and Nurse is worried about her.'

'Do I have to see to everything in this house?' Judith asked, reluctantly leaving her tapestry.

She walked slowly into the next room where the nurse sat by a roaring fire holding the child on her lap. The air was stuffy and dry and, in spite of her love of warmth, Judith drew back. 'I told you to keep her warm, not to bake her,' she said acidly. 'Sit back and let some air get to her.'

The nurse carried the little girl to a seat by the window and gave her a wooden doll to hold. 'She will not eat and she cries when I give her the physic that the doctor ordered.

I think it purges her too much,' the nurse said.

'Another chill?' Judith took the child by the hand. 'She is cool and her eyes are not dull,' she said as if passing judgement on a pet rabbit. 'She is better without the physic and you must make her eat some gruel with honey.'

'Sir John gave me herbs to boil for her,' the nurse said. She reddened as Judith looked angry.

'When Sir John isn't here to upset the household, you take orders from me and give her nothing from the village,' she said.

'He will ask me,' the nurse said unhappily.

'You will do as I say,' Judith repeated. 'He is in Southampton for two weeks talking to lawyers about his inheritance and I am in charge here.' She looked out of the window impatiently for the sixth time. 'My cousins are due today to keep me company while my husband neglects me.' She turned to Chastity. 'See that the kitchen is ready for them.'

Chastity regarded her mistress with unease. As soon as the master was away she assumed his harsh manner and made everyone jump to her orders. It made all the servants of the manor edgy and this time she was as bad as Sir William had been when in a foul mood. She sighed. At first this had seemed a wonderful life. Sir

William had died in his sleep even though he was wicked enough to endure a terrible death, and when the baby was born the whole household relaxed as if better times were ahead, until it became plain that all was not well between Sir John and his wife. The birth of their first born had not healed the breach.

She went to the kitchen and gave orders about dinner. How could Lady Halben not rush to her husband's side as soon as he lifted a finger to beckon? She sighed. One look from those deep-blue eyes made her own knees like water. Each time he said a kind word to her she was so aroused that she had to retire to her room to flagellate herself and bring enough pain to dull her yearning.

'How long will he be away?' asked the housekeeper whom John Halben had brought from Southampton in place of the woman who menaced his digestion.

'Two whole weeks,' Chastity replied.

'I'd rather he stayed here,' Marjorie, the housekeeper, said. 'He demands the best but he's a good master and we all suffer when he's away. You'd think that now she's near her time again she'd want to rest and enjoy his company, but they sleep in separate rooms, as if he has done his duty in making her pregnant and has no further need of her.'

'It's so strange,' the companion said. 'He is

301

so much a man; they are married and can enjoy each other until she is delivered, but they seldom touch.'

Marjorie stirred a sauce and hid a smile. For a woman who spent half her life in church, the companion knew all about carnal urges!

'Maybe he has a mistress,' she said, just to tease Chastity and make her angry.

'No, that isn't possible; we would have heard of it,' Chastity said. 'The only woman he visits in the village is his old nurse and housekeeper, Ellen Turner.' She picked up a wooden spoon and turned it in her hands so that she need not look at Marjorie. 'I call on her sometimes to see how she does. She lives alone and welcomes company. Once,' she said with a faint smile, 'Sir John was there and brought me home in his carriage. We were quite alone,' she said, almost over-come by the memory.

'What happened? Did he fumble you?'

'*No!* Sir John would never take advantage of a helpless woman, even if he desired to do so,' she added hopefully.

'That's not what I heard. He was quite a rake when he was abroad but settled down when he took his responsibilities here I supposed he didn't want to die of the pox like his father. They say that Sir William took a girl on her wedding eve and she bore a monster.'

Chastity gave her a look of utter condemnation. 'I know there were old customs, but I'm sure that those things never happened here. Even if some men might try to take that right, Sir John would never do anything like that.'

'If you ever get married, let me know who slips into your bed the night before you are wed.' Marjorie laughed at the idea that the woman would find a husband and, more important, that any man of rank would ever fancy her enough to rob her of her virginity.

'Is the gruel ready for Miss Mary?' Chastity asked with offended dignity. 'I'll take it now as Lady Judith was asking for it.'

'Poor mite. She needs to get some colour in her cheeks, and gruel isn't the answer. Take it now but she won't eat it. I'll make some good mutton broth, well skimmed and hearty with vegetables. Tell the nurse to bring her down here for an hour and I'll try to tempt her with some of the dainties that I made for Lady Judith and the visitors. When she has a new sister or a brother she may find an interest and a playmate. Lady Judith never allows her to go near the animals and she has her father's love of them.' She winked. 'I'll take her out the back tomorrow and let her scatter meal for the fowl.'

'Don't let Lady Judith catch you.'

'Never fear. She doesn't both me much

303

here since her legs swelled and she can't get down the stairs easily. She spends most of her time in the boudoir, sewing.'

'She will be downstairs today if her cousins come,' Chastity said. 'Her cousin Arthur who is married to a distant cousin of my own sings sacred music and his son plays to accompany him. I am looking forward to hearing them.'

'No wonder that Sir John left in a hurry,' Marjorie said when she was alone. She knew that there was time to go to the village before the gentry took dinner at half past four; even later if Cousin Arthur had not arrived as punctually as Judith hoped. She hurried down the lane and saw four horses being led back to the stable by a groom after exercise and wondered if they missed their master. When she reached Ellen's door, she stepped briskly up the path and tapped on the door.

'Come in. You are in time to try the ale that Sir John brought me. He left it here before he went to Southampton.' Ellen made Marjorie sit down although she said she couldn't stay long. 'They won't be there yet,' Ellen said. 'They are afraid of robbers and will ride behind the afternoon coach for safety.'

'Why not come by coach instead of using their own carriage?'

'Lady Judith isn't the only one with child

and the coach bumps enough to make any woman give birth after two miles. She nearly lost the last one. It was a girl again so I pray that they will both have sons.'

'Sir John will be free if that happens,' Marjorie said. 'And Lady Judith will be free of the marriage bed.'

'Is it so plain to see?' asked Ellen sadly. 'They have a child and a pretty little thing she is if Lady Judith would let her have some amusement. When they're all dead what will it matter who has the manor?' She laughed. 'It's good that some people are happy. My niece in America is pregnant again and they are building more rooms on to their house and making a barn to store crops. They have a son, but I don't talk about him to Sir John as he is envious and it saddens him.'

'Are those the slippers they sent you?'

'These are the first ones and I have more in the closet that Hope made, using the methods that the Indians taught her. They sell readily over here and Hope is making money fast. She pays women to make them and sells them at a good profit, what with the moccasins and the beaver-fur hats. She wrote to me telling me all about it and she mentioned the horse that Sir John sent over. Hope helped break the colt that was born there but now her husband forbids riding in case it injures the baby.'

'She's very brave to be delivered out there in a pagan land,' Marjorie said.

Ellen shivered. 'I feel cold weather coming and out there it will be a cold Christmas. They have more ice and snow than we have here and sometimes see no English face for weeks on end in winter.'

'If they have wood to burn and food to keep them going, they should thrive and a baby needs only warmth and its mother's milk. It's better to wean a baby in the summer and let it kick in the sun. Do they have candles?'

'They can buy them or make their own. Hope says that the ones made from whale fat smell sweeter than those made of mutton fat. They have lamps with cotton wicks dipped in whale oil so they are never in darkness even in the darkest days.'

'I came to ask you if you have herbs to help Miss Mary to eat. If she doesn't eat soon, she'll fade away. I think she is sad because the family wanted a boy and she can never please her father because she is a girl. I know she's too young to know why it is, but she must feel cast out at times as if she has done wrong.'

'Lady Judith will be angry if she finds out that you used my herbs,' Ellen said. 'Sir John displeased her by forbidding me to help at the manor after I left. He said that she would use me and try to make me cook for all their visitors.'

'So they had to find someone who could cook and make good pastry?' They laughed and Ellen gave her a small amount of powdered chervil and dandelion root to be used sparingly to sharpen the appetite.

Ellen lit candles to push away the dark early winter evening and read the letter again. *I am not as well this time,* Hope had written. *I am big for my time and awkward and have cramps in bed, but Michael is a fine boy who plays with the children and is walking well. He is no trouble.* Ellen sensed that Hope was unhappy under her cheerfulness and could find no reason for it other than the depression caused by a heavy body and the inability to do the things she normally could do. She noticed that Hope said very little about Michael, compared with the early letters that had contained reports about the first tooth, the first step and the first mouthings of words, all radiating joy and pride.

Marjorie went back to her warm kitchen and soon heard the sound of wheels as the visitors arrived. The kitchen maid raked the fire to make it glow and the pots began to sing. The suckling pig on the spit needed but a few more turns to bring it to perfection and the bread came from the oven hot and fragrant.

As soon as the family were settled in the great hall with Judith and the cleric who had been invited to eat with them and the judge who was staying at Deerwood on his way to the Assizes, the nurse brought Mary down the back stairs to the kitchen. Marjorie sat at the table with several dishes of sweet-meats and bowls of broth, and snippets of bread and meat as if she intended eating it all. She smiled and hugged the little girl and praised her blue velvet dress, secretly thinking that a paler colour would suit her better.

Mary eyed the food and then Marjorie, but was not offered any. In fact, Marjorie began to sip some broth from a small cup and took a tiny piece of bread which she ate with evident enjoyment. She spoke to the nurse, but still kept a comforting arm round the child and shifted along the bench to make room for her to join her. 'This is nice broth,' Marjorie said to the nurse. 'Help yourself if you'd like some; there's plenty in the pot.'

The nurse took some and sat on the other side of Mary. Marjorie passed the nurse a dish of meat and chopped green cabbage in front of Mary, and went on to eat her own, taking tiny titbits from the dish and savouring them. Both women ignored the child when she reached out and took a piece of meat and they went on talking and telling Mary about the number of eggs they had found under a hedge where the fowls laid away from their pens, and of the small calf that Marjorie had seen on her way to the village.

Mary smiled and took more food, choosing the pieces that Marjorie seemed to want and making her exclaim, 'You're eating all my supper!' until she was laughing and stuffing her mouth with food.

The outer kitchen door opened and the nurse gasped, but Marjorie didn't see who was standing there and had been listening to them for a full minute. Mary took an almond biscuit and leaned against Marjorie, looking very pleased with herself.

'Poor lamb,' Marjorie said. 'You can eat if you're not made to eat what you don't like. And a good hug and a few words of love are what you need, my precious.'

'And you give her that.' John Halben smiled. 'I knew I chose well when I brought you here. You are like my nurse, Ellen.'

Marjorie blushed scarlet as Mary began to drink barley water from a mug. 'It seemed a good time to bring her down, with the company busy in the great hall and Mary with nothing to amuse her.'

'You did well. It would be better if she had food here with you than alone with her nurse in her room.' He walked across the room and sat on the other side of the table. 'How time goes. She'll be three when my son is born.' He regarded her with interest.

'I seem to know so little of her but she is a pretty thing. She has my mouth, which is a relief,' he said wryly. 'You can't help being a girl, and tonight I have been shamed.' He stretched as if weary. 'I came back for papers I need and left Angus in Southampton to work towards the meetings tomorrow.' He smiled and Mary laughed as if he smiled just for her.

'Shall I send word to Lady Judith?' Marjorie said. 'They have only now begun to eat as the visitors were late.'

'I'll eat here if you'll try to tempt me with morsels,' he teased her. 'My daughter and I are both in need of pampering. I shall sleep here tonight and be gone before first light, so my wife need not know I am here now. Stay here with the child, Nurse. I shall enjoy her company until she falls sleepy. Put her before the fire with wooden spoons and dishes I played with nothing more when I was an infant, until I had small animals to feed and donkeys to ride.'

'The best of the meat has gone in,' Marjorie said, but John Halben peered into steaming pots and helped himself to what he fancied, exclaiming that the pieces of suckling pig that had dropped off on to the table on the way from spit and board were the best as they were crunchy and sweet.

The kitchen maid brought empty dishes from the great hall and took in syllabubs and fruit and soft cheeses. She looked scared when she saw Sir John and was told to keep quiet about his presence in the kitchen. Michael, who was now a manservant, fetched more sack and ale and he, too, was told to make no mention of his master. He grinned and picked up the full decanter of sack.

'Cousin Arthur keeps a frugal table in his own home,' John said, 'but he makes up for it when he comes here, and I am not sorry to miss eating with the judge. He tears at his food and eats nothing daintily. I hope that the food lies lightly on his stomach or he'll send a few poor devils to the gibbet tomorrow.'

He took more sack and sat relaxed by the fire with Mary playing at his feet. 'Do you realize, Marjorie, that your cooking may have an influence on the good judge tomorrow? Think of all those wretches who will live or die because of you!'

Marjorie looked anxious. 'I'll make sure he has a soothing posset in the morning before he leaves,' she said.

'Put some laudanum in it!' suggested John, who was enjoying himself more than he had done for weeks. He yawned. 'It's early but I can't face them tonight, so before they move from the table and Arthur and his son start caterwauling, I'll retire and sort out papers for tomorrow.' He picked up

Mary and kissed her. 'We must get to know each other,' he said. 'Take her to bed, Nurse, and make sure she comes here each day for dinner when my wife is otherwise engaged.'

He went up the back stairs and into his library, closing the door tightly behind him so that no light showed, and used a taper from a candle flame to put a light to the kindling of the ready laid fire. Half an hour later, Michael tapped on the door.

'I brought warm water and a jug of wine, sir,' he said, softly and set the water bowl on the slate shelf. He coughed and looked embarrassed.

'What is it?'

'When you go away, Mistress Chastity comes here to borrow books and she may want to do so tonight after the others are in bed.'

'I thought to strip and refresh myself,' John said with a laugh. 'Should I leave the door ajar and give her pause for thought?'

'Not if you don't want her to have the vapours, sir!'

'Would it be kind to spare her the sight of my body, or do you think it would lighten her dreams?'

Michael grinned. 'She'd want more if she had a glimpse of Heaven.'

'That, I can't provide,' John said seriously, but with a wicked sparkle in his eyes. 'But I wish that someone would take her as I weary of her entreating glances and the way she is always there when I go downstairs.' He sighed. 'She's as ready for plucking as a ripe fig, or perhaps a ripe but sour gooseberry! Women are strange cattle. Some could be loved but have no fancy for it, and others who are deprived, want it enough to drive them mad. A few find and give happiness.'

'I'm to be wed soon, sir.'

'And is she willing and hot for you?'

Michael blushed. 'That's why we want to go to church. She is three months gone.'

'So I can't pay you to take on Mistress Chastity.'

'Not while you are here, sir, and she'd need a dowry to get a husband.'

'Then I must go away and leave her with a dot,' John said lightly. 'Tonight I'll lock the door before the lady has a chance to cry rape or swoon at the sight of a man.'

He found the papers he needed and locked his desk securely. With Angus and he both away, he wanted no meddling fingers in his affairs. He locked the door and washed, taking delight in his clean virile body. 'What a waste,' he said, as he snuffed the candles. 'But I balk at the thought of taking Chastity's maidenhead.'

He lay in the state of sleeplessness that comes after being too weary and his thought taunted him. Judith was near her time. Would this mean an end to their marriage or would they have to endure the misery of merging their bodies again to make a son? Did Hope find passion with her husband? Had she forgotten what had happened just once in Little Deerwood, now, as she became deeply involved in the adventure of her new life? He tossed under the quilt and gazed into the dying fire, remembering the last letter he had received from Thomas Lubbock.

'Mistress Fletcher is big with child. My wife thinks she may have twins, so she will have a handful to look after. Their boy grows tall and handsome with deep-gold hair and a laughing manner. He already fishes with a small rod that his father made for him, but he prefers to come with his mother to see the horses and we put him on a pony.'

He went on to tell of the progress of the farm animals and the need for a man to take charge of the growing stables. John had been restless for days after he read it. Hope had a son who loved everything that she loved; everything that he loved. He should have been mine, he thought bitterly, as he slipped into sleep and didn't hear the door being tried or the gasp of dismay when Chastity realized that he was at home.

The judge waited for his carriage and his clerk, and John Halben decided that he must be diplomatic and greet him. He was amused to see the judge sipping the mixture of wine, spices and cream and water that Marjorie had given him.

'Your cook is good,' he said. 'She put herbs and leaves of Goat's Beard in this to make me belch and my stomach is soft this morning.'

'What have you today, sir?'

'Nothing of the moment. A few poachers and a felon or two. No murders nor much of a violent nature, so I shall not be long at Winchester.'

'You need not hang them?' John asked.

'I think not.' Obviously Marjorie had worked magic! 'Two might go to the Americas and the others to hard labour or the navy.'

'I heard that a man I know is coming up before you soon. Is he on the list today?'

'Local man? Amos Birch? A farrier by all accounts.'

'Yes, I know him to be a good worker. Of what is he accused?'

'Trespass and poaching, but no violence of arms or words when arrested.'

'If he is to be sent away, might I not buy his release and take him on here? I might send him to the New World later at my expense if that is acceptable.'

315

The small eyes in the flabby face glinted. A fee from Sir John and the fare to New England which he could claim was paid for by the state would make a nice contribution to the judge's income and would have no need to be noted down by his clerk. 'I must see,' he said portentously.

'You will return here to stay for the rest of the assize?' John said with great courtesy. 'I shall be away on the business of my inheritance but please make this your home.' He smiled. 'If you send Amos Birch ahead in the stage, tell him to go to Mistress Turner in the village and she will look to his needs until I return.'

Before leaving for Southampton, John walked to Ellen's cottage to tell her to expect Amos Birch. 'I prayed for him,' Ellen said simply. 'He is a good man and I trembled to think of him taken to the gallows.'

'The judge is in good humour and Amos is safe.' He smiled at her stricken expression. 'Take heart, Ellen, it will be so as I have offered to pay for his release, but if he is condemned, then I shall send Mistress Chastity to offer herself for a gallow's wedding and so obtain his freedom!' He thought for a moment. 'No, that would be too great a penance for any man. He might prefer a quick end!'

'You never change, John,' she said

affectionately. 'You have a kind heart; always generous and with thought for others.'

'No, I grow hard. Last night I saw how badly I ignore my daughter and I found her soft and sweet.'

'Praise God for that,' Ellen said. 'I wish I could cosset her, but Lady Judith never lets me near her.'

'Marjorie will take your place with her. She loves the child and is good for her, but if anything happened to Lady Judith or me, you would see that Mary didn't suffer?'

'Yes, but you are both hale and healthy and can look to your own.'

He paced the room. 'We shall see. If I have no heir, I may visit my estate in the New World.'

'Leave Deerwood?'

'Deerwood would wait for me as it has for a hundred or so years. Angus makes a good steward and we have a well-run farm and stables.'

Ellen regarded him with sad and slightly accusing eyes. 'She is married, John. She bore a son by her husband and now carries his next child, or perhaps twins.'

He looked away. 'I shall go to see my horses and Amos can decide if he wants a new start there in charge of the stables. I shall see Hope and Edward Fletcher but keep my distance.'

'And what if this baby is a boy?'

'That's more than I dare dream,' he said, pulling his velvet plumed hat closer on his head. 'When Amos comes, tell him what I have in mind for him and he can think about it until I return from the lawyers.'

'He has no wife now as she died of cholera last year, so he may want to leave England.'

'Look after him and see Marjorie often to ask about my daughter.'

He walked back and climbed on to the box of his carriage, taking the reins and driving in a silence that the coachman dared not break until they stopped for food and to water the horses, then John rode the rest of the way inside and looked at his papers.

The sea air was cold and people hurried about their business on the docks. Pedlars looked blue-cheeked and doleful as few stopped to buy their wares.

'Mr Halben? Or is it Sir John now?'

'Captain! It's good to see you. I thought you were on the high seas.'

'Repairs had to be done and a few improvements made so I am taking leave for a week or so.'

'What did you bring from Martha's Vineyard? Come to the inn and tell me later when I've seen my steward.'

John strode away to the lawyer's office and felt light-hearted. The sea captain had been there, trodden the same soil and seen the same shore where Hope lived. On the

318

horizon a ship with full sails came slowly across the distance, ready to dock. He felt a thrill of excitement. It might be from France or Guinea, Tangier or the New World. John turned away. First there was business to settle.

Chapter 16

Katsi opened the kitchen door and closed it as soon as she was inside. 'A man is coming here,' she said.

Edward looked up from the arrow shafts he was smoothing. 'Hope is resting,' he said. 'Do you know this man?'

'Chiabos has seen him once when he went to buy a horse from Ostungo, but this time he comes here.' Katsi sat on the floor and sorted turkey feathers from the heap on the floor into matching bunches for Edward to use as flights on the arrows.

'Do you know his name?' he asked.

'Mr Chilton. He sailed from Plimoth with his woman and left her in Edgartown while he did business with the people in the long houses by The Place on the Wayside near Timsbury. His woman stays with people in Edgartown and asked about you.'

'You seem to know their business Katsi!'

'We listen,' she said, calmly. 'The woman will come later.'

'Here! To our house?' Edward looked disturbed.

'She knows that Hope will be a mother again,' Katsi said, her eyes guarded this time, as if she wanted to keep her own counsel.'

'Hope has told you about her?' Katsi nodded. 'What more do you know?'

'They say that she smiles and is empty inside. Bad spirits have taken her mind away even though it does not show.'

'Perhaps if she sees Hope she will feel better. They were friends on the ship coming here and she and her husband were kind to us.'

'Do not tell Hope,' Katsi warned. 'Hope's spirits are troubled and she is near her time.' She took Michael in her arms and hugged him, saying softly, 'There, little man child, little hunter, Owaissa, little blue-bird, see where your sisters will lie.' She rocked the two cradles that Edward had made as it seemed more and more likely that twins would be born.

'Why sisters?' Edward smiled. 'We may have more sons.' He put down the arrow and looked thoughtful. 'Is that why Mistress Chilton is here?' He gave a nervous laugh. 'I know they talked about babies on the boat and Mary Chilton said she wanted a daughter, but after we had Michael we lost touch and though never to see her again.'

'She has a long memory and can have no more children of her own.' Katsi shrugged. 'Sometimes a squaw bears only girls and dies when her husband blames her and beats her, and some fade away if they suffer in their minds after birth.'

'Thomas Chilton never beats his wife and he has two boys so he is satisfied.'

'I will come to stay with Hope until after the babies are born and the woman has gone away.' She stood up. 'The man is coming.'

Edward heard nothing until a minute after Katsi slipped away, then brittle twigs broke from the trees as a horseman rode by. He went outside, drawing his deer-skin cloak round him and saw Thomas Chilton dismount. 'Put him in the lean-to. There are blankets there,' Edward called.

'Were you expecting me?'Thomas Chilton looked surprised. Edward nodded briefly and invited him to sit by the fire. Thomas Chilton cleared his throat nervously. 'Mary asked me to call and enquire after you and your family,' he said.

'As you see, we have a fine son,' Edward said.

'Mary heard that Hope was expecting another baby.' He looked about him at the warm but small room and the two cribs. 'We were sorry that you and Hope didn't come to see us,' he added. 'It is a pleasant ride now that the roads are better, to go by land along Cape Cod in fine weather, with a short crossing by sea to The Vineyard.'

'The days are not long enough for us to fritter time away on visits,' Edward replied shortly. 'We have animals to tend and our crops to sow and harvest.'

Thomas Chilton nodded gravely. 'It must be hard to make a living and be subject to almost eternal toil.' He sighed. 'One extra mouth to feed is bad enough but more children will put a great burden on you.' He eyed the cribs with interest. 'It seems that the gossips are right. By the looks of things you expect more than one.'

'We have a full store of food, more work than I can manage and a good life,' Edward said firmly. 'Whatever children we have will be welcome and we shall have enough for all.' He regarded his visitor with suspicion. 'How is your wife?'

'Well enough in body, but a trial in other ways. She had a pleasant companion in the lady who came to Plimoth from the boat carrying an unborn child, but when the baby was a male, Mary turned on her and accused her of cheating her.' He looked down, obviously upset. 'I had not realized that her need for a daughter was so deep and I sadly neglected her as she seemed sane. For a time she was restrained in bonds, but for the past month she has been quiet and happy.'

Edward felt colder than the air outside. 'Why are you here?'

'In her ramblings she swore that Hope had promised her a girl if she had two. She heard of your wife's condition from the crew of the last ship to anchor here.'

'If anything like that was said, it was in jest! What mother would part with her own?' Edward laughed. 'It seems that I breed boys, so what will she do when they are born?'

'She will go mad.'

'There are ways of buying a baby,' Edward began.

'Since her madness, the doctors here refuse to allow it. Our own sons now are old enough to be safe as she loves only young children, and they have a tutor who fills their time. The doctors think that any young child might be in danger, but that's not true! If she had a girl, I know she would be well again and love it deeply.' He looked at Edward with a desperate plea in his eyes. 'Hope talked about giving her a baby girl, and even if for Hope it was said in jest, Mary pins her whole future to that promise.'

'It was no promise and whatever we have is ours for life.'

'We could give a child much more than you can ever give her. I swear that if you help us, you will be rewarded and never regret it. I have been a bad husband, but now I know how much Mary means to me and I beg you to help.'

'I think it is you who is mad,' Edward said. 'I want you to leave now and I shall not say anything to Hope about this, but I warn you to keep away and take your wife back to Plimoth.'

'I could ruin your trade here,' Thomas Chilton said in a bullying voice. 'I have a great deal of influence.'

'If you made one move to harm us I would write to Sir John Halben and the Governor of New England. It wouldn't do if the governor's representative had to restrain a mad wife from stealing another woman's baby!' Edward opened the door. 'Go, before I am too angry to control myself.'

He heard the horse clatter down the icy lane. Hope came in from the bedroom, still fuzzy with sleep. A minute later, Katsi came back and silently sat by the fire. Michael ran to her, scared by the men's anger. 'Who was it?' Hope asked. She held her taut stomach and winced.

'The snow broke a branch and it fell,' said Katsi.

Hope yawned. 'I thought I heard voices.'

'I was here and came back,' Katsi said. She brought out a leather pouch and a woven basket and put thin strips of deer skin to warm and grow supple in a bowl of spring water. 'It will be soon,' she said, and patted the thick pile of dry moss that would be Hope's couch. 'Wenono will be here soon to help. Take Michael to my mother,' she ordered. Edward wrapped the boy warmly and put him on the sled with toys and a small bow and arrows.

The long house was full of smoke and Edward stayed to clear the chimney to release it, then saw a shutter that swung away from the window where the old women sat. As the men were out looking for bears, he stayed longer to fix the shutter and then to eat with the women as they seemed to want to show their gratitude. Michael played happily with his friends, and they made room for him to share a bed of dried leaves and skins.

Edward stayed until Michael was asleep then walked back leaving the sled behind him. It was new and he had promised Hope that he would give it to Chiabos when the babies were born, instead of giving a feast in the bitter cold weather.

Darkness made the moon seem extra bright as he went home. He thought of Mary Chilton and shuddered. She must be in another very unhappy world if she imagined that he would give away any child of his. A wolf howled across the frozen cranberry bog and the sea was sullen and grey.

He paused as he came near to the house and saw the smoke from the chimney, the light from the window and smelled cooking. His hand was on the latch when he heard a baby cry. He opened the door and rushed inside, bringing a cold breeze with him that Wenono quickly shut out.

A baby lay in one cot and another was making its debut into the world. Hope lay exhausted and the Indian women worked on her to stem the flow of blood from the slack womb. Hope sighed. 'Is it over?' she asked.

'Drink this.' Katsi held a cup to her lips and Hope drank the bitter brew. She felt her womb contract and the two women grunted with relief as the blood flow stopped.

'What are they?' Edward could hardly speak as emotion and a kind of fear engulfed him.

'Two girls,' Katsi said. Her face was impassive as she threw the afterbirths on to the fire after making Hope eat a small piece of each one. 'We must guard you,' she said softly and Edward knew that she had listened to what Thomas Chilton had said and understood everything. 'My people will watch the path and if she comes I will take the babies to our lodge until they are gone.'

'What is it? Why speak in whispers? Am I ill? Are the babies whole and well?'

Edward took her hot hand and calmed

her. 'They are beautiful,' he said and Katsi held one so that Hope could see the tiny face.

Hope yawned. 'I'm glad it's over,' she said, and giggled. 'She looks just like you, Edward.' Katsi held up the other one. 'And she is like my grandmother. We must call her Melissa and the other one Edwina. I thought that twins looked alike, but these are different, and different again from Michael.'

'Sleep now,' Katsi ordered. Both babies began to cry and she smiled and wrapped them tightly in blankets to make them feel safe. Hope was helped from the now soiled bed of moss and put to bed in her own room and Edward swept the moss into the yard and burned it. 'Go,' Katsi said to Wenono. 'Tell our families and ask the women if they will feed these babies.'

'Why?' Edward asked sharply. 'Hope had enough milk for two last time so why not now?'

'She needs rest,' Katsi said. 'She was heavy before, and now her spirits need lifting.' She glanced into the room where Hope now lay asleep. 'If my people feed the babies we can take them to the long house when we hear of the woman coming and they will not be here when she comes. It is better if she does not see them.' She looked at the babies again and smiled. 'They are well. Give Hope this when she wakes to harden her womb and I will bring Michael here tomorrow, but the babies need no food for a day, as a mother's milk does not flow so soon.'

Katsi strapped on her snow shoes and picked up her leather bag. It was heavy and she looked at Edward in surprise. 'It is nothing,' he said. 'I made some small boats for your sons as they admired Michael's and Hope made the sails. Is it too heavy? Take the other sled and use it to bring Michael back tomorrow. I told Chiabos that the new one is a gift to give thanks for my children so keep it by your lodge and use it well.'

He sat by the fire and began to fix flint-heads to the arrows as he was too restless to sleep. He looked at the babies and was filled with love for them and a sense of belonging that he had never experienced with Michael. He had felt pride and love for him, but he wanted to hold these babies, to bury his face in their softness and to shout his joy at fathering them.

He gave Hope cornmeal bread and honey when she woke and she fell asleep again, exhausted and relieved of her burden. Edward went to bed and woke early, kissed his wife and made cornmeal mush and heated ale. Hope sat up and ate hungrily, asking where Michael had gone. The twins lay asleep and warm by the fire.

'They are girls,' Hope said as if he might

be disappointed.

'I have never been so happy,' Edward said. 'I have a son whom I love, and now I have two beautiful daughters.' He laughed. 'They say that men need sons, but I feel more kinship with these babies than ever I did with Michael.'

'Michael loves you,' Hope said. She looked sad. 'If he was not your child, would you still love him?'

'You are being fanciful,' he said and brought one of the babies to her.

'You mustn't make this one your favourite because she looks so much like you,' Hope said, smiling now as if she had cast off a hidden grief. 'Michael will be surprised when he sees them.' She winced and sat more comfortably and sipped more of the liquid that made her womb contract. She felt her breasts. 'I seem empty,' she said.

'Katsi says that you will not have milk for a while and suggests that as there are two, her cousins may help to feed them.'

'I would like that,' Hope said. 'I feel so tired and all I want to do is sleep.' She smiled. 'With a baby on each arm, and that smile on your face, anyone would think that you were the father!' She was suddenly pale. This was no time for teasing. Of course he was their father and he was Michael's father too, but now that the babies were clean of the birth fluids she could see that they were not going to have the bright corn-coloured hair that Michael had.

Katsi brushed the snow from her hood and Michael ran to Hope and flung himself on the bed. 'I saw a deer and two squirrels this morning,' he said. 'The squirrels should be in bed but they were looking for nuts. Katsi says it means that the cold is nearly over.' He looked anxious. 'I want to slide on the ice before it breaks.'

'Come and see your sisters,' Edward said.

He climbed down from the bed and followed Edward obediently. He stared at the small faces and laughed. 'They are too small to play with me,' he said and turned back to his mother.

'Stay and rest,' Katsi said. She washed the babies and held linen dipped in water for them to suck, then held them to Hope's breast so that they could take the first colostrum which was rich and purging before the milk came. 'Tomorrow, the women will come to feed them, and sometimes I shall take them to the long house to them while you rest.'

'I feel better now,' Hope said, but she didn't protest and during the next three weeks, she busied herself with sewing and mixing food and let Katsi take over the babies, with the two women with milk enough for their own and for another, who came and ate the sweet cakes that Hope gave them while they fed the babies.

Edward split wood for the fires and tended the animals, watching the weather with relief as the snow fell and blocked most of the main paths. Another week went by and Hope was full of energy and regretting her lack of milk as she fed the babies only at night. Her body gave what was needed and no more.

'Look, Michael,' she said one morning. 'The snow is melting and the birds are singing. Soon you and your friends will be able to sail your boats on the cranberry bog even if the lagoon is too rough and cold. Your father will clear a patch of weeds and cranberry plants to make a shallow lake.'

When the ice melted, Edward cleared the water and tied long strings of leather thronging to Michael's boats and to the boats of his two friends so that they could be sailed but not lost. He grinned as the fathers of the Indian boys watched and then took the strings and set the sails, in spite of their sons' objections, as all men do when wanting to play with children's toys.

Katsi came to the house with two baskets on the sled. 'Today while you cook and feed the boys, the babies can come to the lodge with me.'

'There is no need. Their nurses like my sweet cakes and ale.' She saw Katsi's set expression. 'What is it?' she asked quietly.

'Something is wrong, Katsi.'

'Is she coming?' Edward asked, as he had heard what Katsi said.

'My people have seen them making the carriage ready now that the roads are clear and heard hard words spoken between husband and wife but they will be here soon.'

'Who?' Hope asked.

Katsi regarded her with satisfaction. 'Hope is better now and can be told,' she said. She picked up Melissa and wrapped her in a blanket that almost covered her head and put her in one of the baskets. 'Come, Omene, little pigeon,' she said as she lifted the other baby into the other snug nest. She turned at the bend in the lane and looked back. 'May the warm winds of Heaven blow softly on this house, and the Great Spirit bless who live here,' she murmured, then dragged the sled over the muddy ground to the long house.

'But it was all a jest!' Hope said, when Edward explained what had happened when Thomas Chilton visited them.

'Not to her,' Edward said grimly. 'You suspected that she was mad when you told the little widow to leave for Ireland and go back to her people. I wonder if she is well? She had little enough from the sale of this place; I wish we have been able to pay her more.'

'She had enough to take her home and had a good family to take care of her,' Hope said quickly, unwilling to talk about her as she remembered that she had given her money enough to make up for what Edward had not paid for the house.

Edward's face was serious. 'It was Thomas Chilton who made that deal and I felt guilty even then, but a loving family was what she needed, not a life of dependence with Mary Chilton.'

'That is past now. Today we have other matters to consider.'

'Are you strong enough to meet her?' he asked. 'I shall not leave to go fishing until I am sure they have gone for ever.'

'Go back to the boys,' she said. 'You will see the carriage from there and come with it. Look pleased to see them if you can and show surprise.'

'First I shall put one of the cribs in the store upstairs and she may be convinced that we had but one child. I told Katsi to bring Melissa here after three hours if Mary refuses to leave before she sees our baby. Be careful, Hope. I think she is a dangerous woman.'

'I shall bake bread,' Hope said. 'Bring the two hares ready for eating from the store. I'll put them in the pot with some venison, and we shall offer them food and ale.'

Edward lifted the largest cauldron on to

333

the trivet over the fire and Hope put in water and vegetables and herbs with the game, and when the carriage arrived, the kitchen was welcoming, with a savoury smell coming from the pot.

Edward called from the lane and Hope hurried out to greet the couple who now stepped down from the carriage. Thomas Chilton looked cautious as if unsure of his welcome, but Mary ran forward and embraced Hope with every sign of affection. Her unlined face was placid and showed no sign of inward turmoil and she looked about the warm room with eagerness, her gaze resting on the wooden crib.

'You will eat with us?' Hope suggested.

Thomas peered into the steaming pot. 'You were expecting visitors? Mary thought to find you alone.'

'No one but you,' Edward said enigmatically.

'When the thaw came we thought of old friends,' Hope said hastily, 'and we knew that some of our friends would be calling.' She put wooden platters on the table and pewter mugs for the ale.

'Where are they?' Mary said almost violently.

'Where are what?' asked Edward.

'You gave birth to two girls,' Mary said, her voice now hard and accusing.

'My dear,' began her husband nervously.

'You agreed that if I brought you here, you would be quiet. This is not the time to talk about such matters.'

Mary ignored him. 'One crib? That is too small for two babies.'

'We have a lovely daughter, Melissa,' Hope said in a quiet voice. 'One baby, who is with the wet nurse while I do my housework and cooking, but will be here after we have eaten.'

'You are lying. Where is the baby you promised to me?'

'I made no promise. We talked and laughed about my pregnancy and you know we had a son. Now, we have a daughter but she is ours and not to be given away.'

'There were two! I sent a man to ask about you and he said that you expected two!'

'Not every birth is safe,' Edward said. 'We have one daughter.'

'One died? Dear God, tell me that isn't true!'

Hope looked away unable to lie, but ready to accept what Edward hinted. Mary turned pale and seemed to shrink. She was silent when Hope served the food and she ate a little and drank copiously of the ale.

At last when the tension in the room was bearable, Katsi came to the door with the sled, and Hope saw that she had come to the house from the south, the opposite way from the long house. The tracks in the mud

335

were fresh for a long way into the woods.

Edward took the baby and unwrapped her from the blankets but held her away from Mary's pleading arms. 'This is Melissa,' he said solemnly. 'Please put her to bed, Katsi.'

Mary stared at the baby and then turned to the Indian woman who stood by the crib. 'Where is the other one?' she asked roughly. 'Tell me, woman!'

'Michael is with the boys by the bog,' Katsi said.

'Not the boy! Where is the other baby?'

Katsi looked blank as if she didn't understand, then smiled. 'My baby is here.' She swung the sling from her back and held out her younger cousin's baby. 'She was born on the day after Melissa so they will be sisters. Already they suck from the same breasts and so are bound by more than friendship.'

'I don't believe you!' Mary seized her cloak and ran to the door. 'You have hidden my baby.' She opened the door and looked at the tracks left by the sled. The path to Katsi's lodge was well trodden and showed no signs of recent use, but the way to the woods was muddy and seldom used except for setting snares and following game on foot. Mary glanced back and laughed as if she had solved a problem. 'I shall find her,' she said and ran along the path, following the tracks.

Thomas Chilton watched her go, uncertain what to do. 'She will find nothing in the long house,' Katsi said. 'There is only one path so she will come back.' Edward opened his mouth then shut it again. Mary was heading for the long house belonging to the brother of Chiabos which lay a mile along the lane and through a copse. Hope made Katsi sit down and drink warm ale, realizing that she had come swiftly a very long way round, to throw Mary off the trail.

'I'll go after her,' Thomas said, as Mary didn't return. He walked quickly through the glutinous mud, his boots soon caked and making walking a labour. Edward brought one of the unhitched horses from the Chilton carriage and saddled it, walking it slowly after the man who now dragged his feet and stumbled as he used more energy than he usually did in a week.

Edward heard voices and slapped the horse into a brisk trot, but he held back when he came to the long house as he wanted Mary to be convinced that there was no English baby there.

'You are lying!' Mary screamed. She climbed the wooden ladder into the house and ran about the room looking everywhere. The Indians stood in polite but bemused silence as she ranted and looked in every corner, until she sank to the floor and wept.

'Put her on the horse,' Edward said, and helped Thomas to lift her on to the saddle, her muddy skirts heavy over her now shoe-less feet, as the mud had sucked the light shoes off in her raging progress to the long house.

The two men walked, one on each side of the horse to keep her on the saddle as she sagged with exhaustion and the loss of all desire to live. 'My baby is dead,' she murmured over and over again and when she was put into the carriage, she sat passively in one corner. Hope hurried out, followed by Katsi who stood on the carriage step and pushed a soft blanket into Mary's hands.

Mary felt it and looked up.

'Mourn for your baby,' Katsi said gently. 'Keep this blanket to remember her and let your grief heal your mind.'

Mary leaned back, the blanket by her cheek, and fell asleep. The men hitched the horses and Thomas nodded curtly as he drove away.

'What will happen to her?' Hope asked.

'She will mourn and believe that she lost a baby,' Katsi said. 'The man may be different so I will keep Edwina with me until two days.'

'They have gone for ever,' Edward said.

'Wait.'

The next day, a man wearing Chilton livery rode by, pausing for water for his mount and saying that he was on his way from business in Ostungo, but it was obvious that he had not come from that direction. Edward invited him to eat with them. Melissa was crying softly and Michael rocked her cradle. Edward made sure that the man saw everything in the house before he left, and the man became more forthcoming. He told them that as Mistress Chilton could not find a baby in the New World, she was leaving for England where she had been promised a baby from a family where the mother had died in childbirth. He winked. 'They know nothing of her illness there and she will bring it back here or die in England in a madhouse.'

'Is her husband going with her?' Hope asked.

'No, but he's sending a companion-nurse with her, a woman who came out here with female prisoners and is more warder than nurse. They'll stay for a while in their property in Salisbury.'

'Poor Mary,' Edward said as he watched the man go down the lane. 'How can she want a child that is not her own? She has two fine boys from her and her husband. For me, I ask no more than my son and my two daughters: flesh of my flesh, bone of my bone.'

Chapter 17

John Halben leaned back in the leather chair and listened to the ship's captain. He heard of storms and near mutiny and the peace and beauty of the New World in summer. 'A few more voyages and I shall settle down out there. A man can't sail the seas for ever and I yearn for a home with a hearth and fresh meat when I want it.'

'How does your wife take to the idea?'

'My wife?' the captain said as if it had nothing to do with her. 'She has a house and money enough to last her and two children to look after her in old age, so I am free,' he said firmly. 'We give each other nothing now and she'll be glad to be rid of me.'

'Is it that easy?' John smiled wryly. He gazed out across the square to the rigging of a tall ship. 'I envy you, Captain. I have land over there that begs a master and stables that are making good foals.'

'You can visit it and come back again. When the tides are right and the wind fair, it takes less time now that we navigate more skilfully and manage to land in the right places!' He laughed. 'I made my own charts of the islands and their shoals of rocks and I can take Nantucket Bay with full sails.' He looked bashfully pleased with himself. 'I had a visit from gentlemen from the Navy Office sent from the Navy Secretary himself, Mr Samuel Pepys, who wanted copies of the charts. I have to finish them before I sail again.'

'You could make a living making charts,' John said.

'That might be,' the captain admitted. 'The Navy Lords offered to pay me well for such charts and they want more details of the rocks round Nantucket and the islands as well as Plimoth and Cape Cod.'

'Martha's Vineyard?' asked John quickly.

'Is that where your land is, sir?' John nodded. 'As fair a place as any I know. I've taken several settlers there who are making good, and others who have not been fortunate.' He sighed. 'There will always be men of low character who fleece the unwary and some have bought land that has no value from them.'

'I may have a passenger for you,' John said. He told him of Amos and the fact that he was to be released into his care.

'Are you sure he may leave without an escort of someone to speak for him when he arrives in the New World?'

John stared at him. 'He would go to my agent Lubbock on Martha's Vineyard.'

'The authorities might say he is a felon

who could run away and go elsewhere than to your estate to be in your employ.'

'I suppose that is true. Every man released into the custody of a private person isn't as honest as Amos. When do you sail?'

'In ten days if the wind is right.'

'By then I shall know if my wife gives me a son. If she does, then I shall stay for a while, but if not, I shall sail with you and come back in six months' time to try again! I shall keep Amos with me and take him to the New World when I go there.'

'I shall expect word from you by next week, or the cabins will be taken,' said the captain. He levered himself from his seat with reluctance. 'I have stores to check and paper work to do and the charts to finish so I must go back now. I hope to see you with me to lighten my days with conversation and maybe a hand at cards.'

John Halben went back to the lawyer's office in a contemplative mood. Someone would have to escort Amos out of the country and see him settled with all the right papers signed. Angus had most of the day's work done and ready for him. He signed agreements and negotiations with other landowners in Little Deerwood and Southampton, and nodded to several suggestions about investments.

'Is there a play or other entertainment here?' he asked when they were done with documents for the day.

'There is, but I heard that it would be unwise to go there as one of the players died of the plague last week,' Angus said. 'None of them stay at the inn where we lodge so I think we are safe, but two more died who had supped with the actor in his lodging. I called for fresh herbs and garlic to be put in our rooms, and sack to drink before we retire.'

John sighed. 'I wish my business here was over.'

'We made good progress today, sir. Another day might suffice and you can go home and leave me to settle minor accounts.'

'Do you enjoy your work at Deerwood enough to make it a permanent way of life?'

'Yes, I like figures and making things tally and you give me the responsibility I crave.'

'Could you manage to rule my affairs at Deerwood if I went away for a few months? I mean rule!' he added. 'I would give you free rein, but are you strong enough to resist other influences?'

'Yes. None of the people at Deerwood know about legal matters and I would let no one bring in outside authority without consulting you, even if it took months to contact you.' Angus looked at him with level grey eyes. 'Can you trust me with a power of attorney, sir?'

'Yes.' He smiled. 'I couldn't wish for a more thrifty man to handle my finances. I think we have our evening planned now. There will be more documents to be perused by my lawyers tomorrow. I have made you my steward but you live at Deerwood. Now, you have earned your privacy and need a cottage of your own in case you want to be married. Tomorrow, I must find a chandler and buy seeds of grasses to send to Ostungo for pasture, and the other items on Lubbock's list. When I read about my horses there, it seems but a mile away, and not far across the sea, and I long to be there.'

'If The Vineyard suits the mares and even if you cannot go there soon, you could send more bloodstock to await your arrival and run down the stables at Deerwood to a manageable size that three men can handle.' Angus smiled bleakly. 'If you have too many horses here, I think that some of your relatives might want to borrow them for an indefinite period, but if you keep only brood mares and a stallion and coach horses, they cannot interfere.'

'You are very observant, Angus. I have noticed my wife's cousins looking at the stables and complaining of their own poor mounts.' He took pen and paper and made a list of the animals for sale and decided to send two mares and a stallion of a famous strain out to The Vineyard on the next ship. 'I shall go back and arrange it,' John said. His eyes sparkled. 'I feel that I shall see the New World again, Angus; that is unless you want to take my place?'

The steward looked alarmed. 'I will serve you well here, sir, but never will I set foot on another ship. I was sick and wished to die the only time I sailed on such a vessel, and I have no love of foreign shores.'

'And will you find a wife and breed sons?' John asked a trifle wistfully.

'I shall marry when I find someone who will be a true wife, but I will accept what children the Good Lord sends,' Angus shrugged. 'That will never be a worry. I am an orphan and have no inheritance to pass on.'

John pushed aside the documents and picked up his glass, drinking deeply of the good French wine. 'You are a fortunate man,' he said. 'All this is a burden. Responsibilities and duty! Duty and responsibilities make a prison for a man. You can marry for love and have no thought for the future as I shall make that secure, but I must bite my lips and wait for a son made from a bitter coupling.'

Angus eyed the carafe uneasily. The wine was talking in a way that he would rather not hear. 'It is chill but bright, sir. Shall we walk by the docks for a turn before bed?'

'You are a good gaoler, Angus. Come with me and save me from cut-purses and whores, for I am weak tonight.'

John breathed deeply as they stood by the capstans and the piles of rope that smelled of the sea. Smoked fish and whale oil had come on the last ship from Plimoth and sailors boasted of huge catches of cod and of whales that spurted steam as they rose from the deep. He talked of what he had seen when he had bought Ostungo, the game and dolphins and the bear he had chased but not killed as he was overcome by the sight of such strength and beauty.

'Come Angus, I shall sleep now and work tomorrow. I know that I must go there, and soon.'

Even the shouts of sailors carousing on their way back to their berths kept neither man awake and they drank the first draught of the day early while they laboured over papers.

'Is all this necessary?' Angus asked with mild apprehension. 'I shall serve you well and honestly, but you give me more power than you give your own.'

'My father was a sick man, and in many ways evil, but from him I learned that everything must be on paper, sealed and witnessed and left with lawyers if justice may be done. There is no need to advise Lady Judith of the contents of these documents unless trouble comes to Deerwood when I am away, and you shall hold copies of everything we do today. Now take this down in a clear hand.'

Angus listened, then gasped. 'But what if your wife gives you a son this time?'

'He will inherit Deerwood, but as Lord of the Manor I look to the future of my villagers,' John said, simply. 'My father did much harm to some families; harm that can never be put right but I owe a duty to others. Edward Fletcher is a friend as well as a neighbour; his wife is the daughter of a yeoman whom my family respected and I wish to help them. They have a son who was born on Martha's Vineyard and so is a new American who should inherit his future there, so write as I direct. The said Michael John Fletcher shall on the death of his legitimate father, Edward Fletcher, become my heir to all properties and lands, money and produce of Ostungo, on Martha's Vineyard.' He paused. 'Add to that in legal terms, that his mother Hope Fletcher shall enjoy the property and revenue with him for as long as she desires to live there.'

Angus sought for words. 'If you do this, sir, people will say that he is your son.'

'You are direct, Angus, but you flatter me. I wish with all my being that it was so. No harm will come to them through such gossip. I may be under the ground long before he inherits and they need know nothing of this document for years. Hard work will make a man of him if he thinks he must make his own way, and they are comfortable as they are. Edward Fletcher is healthy and the boy may well be into middle age before he hears of this.'

The lawyer frowned with disapproval at some of the clauses both in John's Will and testament and the ones pertaining to Martha's Vineyard. 'You leave Lady Judith with little that she can oversee freely,' he said.

'She will be comfortable for her natural life, but I make no provision for hangers-on and parasites,' John said firmly. 'My daughter must have means of her own to avoid being sent into a marriage that she dislikes.'

The lawyer pursed his lips. 'Young blood runs over-warm at times. She could marry a very unsuitable man if she has independence.'

'She would need my consent, but if I was away, she would not be forced to accept a man of my wife's choosing.' He laughed. 'As she is but three, I feel no immediate anxiety over her.'

'In the unlikely event of your untimely demise, sir, would these powers revert to your wife? Who would be your daughter's guardian?'

John laughed. 'I have no intention of dying before my daughter comes of age, but if we are to be so solemn, then name my housekeeper, Marjorie, as her duenna when Mary becomes a woman at fifteen, and make out a pension for her to sweeten the responsibility. You disapprove?' The lawyer nodded. 'You are mistaken,' John said softly. 'Love cannot be bought and that woman loves the child.'

Angus folded the papers neatly and put them in a leather pouch, leaving the copies with the lawyer to be locked away safely. They retired to eat a late dinner at half past four, of lobster, a fine loin of beef, roasted ducks and braised vegetables, with syllabubs to whet the appetite and cheese from a local farm.

Even the lawyer seemed less stiff-necked after several glasses of red wine, and when John went to find the chandler and to ask the market overseer to collect the horses he wanted to sell, he felt as if he was almost a free man. 'Please God may it be a boy and I am rid of her,' he murmured.

The farrier greeted him with a distracted air. 'Your harness chains are ready, sir. The boy will bring them to Deerwood tomorrow.'

'What are you doing?' John stood back as sparks flew from the red-hot iron on the anvil.

'Do you see the navy vessel out there? They want shackles made in a hurry to keep the pressed men secure in port. They lost two in Guinea and there are a few from hereabouts who might think that home is more comfortable than a life before the mast!'

'Who from Southampton?'

'Two felons taken at the Assize a year or so ago and a man from your way, sir; Furness by name, who tried to jump overboard when they docked, so this is for him, ankle shackles and heavy wrist bands with a length of chain between them to link up and hobble him.'

'I know the man,' John said. He looked out to sea and felt a fleeting sympathy for him, then recalled that he was responsible for procuring Abigail for his master and plotting the deflowering of Hope Clarke. He was stunned by the rush of emotion the memory brought him, and he hardened his heart. 'Do you take them aboard?' he asked.

'Not me! They say that there was a plague death on that ship in Guinea and only the captain and three of his crew are allowed ashore. The sailors are near mutiny as they thought to have drink and girls here, but they sail tomorrow and we can all breathe easier.'

'Where are they bound?'

'They've supplies for six months or so, and

the rumour is Tangier in North Africa where they are building a mole to harbour men of war to fight the pirates and make a base by the big inland sea.'

John nodded. 'The Mediterranean Sea,' he said and sighed with relief. 'A long voyage in unfriendly waters,' he said. 'I wish the captain safety.'

Angus came looking for him. 'The last of the papers are ready for signing, sir.'

'Good. I've finished business here and must go back to Deerwood tomorrow. There are matters to sort out there before I leave.'

'You really are leaving?'

'Sooner or later. I must,' he said, simply. 'I need to go there.'

'I ought to stay here for a day or two,' Angus said. 'I can come back by stage unless you need me now.'

'Finish here so that I know that everything is settled and order furnishings for Willow Cottage ready for you to take over. Make it fitting for my steward to occupy,' he said with a smile. 'If I go away, life might not be easy, but I promise you that you will earn everything I give you!'

The carriage went through lanes soft with a spring morning and new life. John closed his eyes and thought of a girl riding fast, her hair loose and her cheeks pink with effort and delight. He smelled the grass and saw the fine dust of gold from the hazel catkins and wondered if she had ever worn his pale-green bird's eye silk.

Chastity ran towards the carriage. 'Lady Judith is near her time,' she said.

John jumped down from the carriage and told the coachman to go on to the stables. 'I shall be in my library,' he said, brusquely.

'Will you not see Her Ladyship?' Chastity was shocked.

'Why? I am not a midwife! She needs women near her. Men are out of place at such times and I have urgent business to finish.'

'She asked for you.'

'To make sure I came back?'

'She is your wife!' Chastity said with a dramatic air of tragedy.

'Has the doctor come and the apothecary? Is Mistress More in attendance and the female cousins?' Chastity nodded. 'Then there is no room for me. Send Miss Mary to the library. You may have her nurse,' he offered generously. 'I will see to my daughter. Make sure she is dressed in an hour, ready for an outing. I shall be here for dinner at five.'

John studied the documents that Angus had given him and grunted approval. Do men feel like this when they are dying? he wondered as he read of the arrangements he had made for all his worldly goods. He took the letters regarding the inheritance of

Ostungo and put them sealed in a package in his personal desk which he locked. If I go there, these must lie in the vaults of a reputable lawyer in Edgartown, and the copies will rest in Southampton.

Satisfied at last, he waited for Mary and took her to the stables, oddly touched by the trusting way she allowed him to hold her hand as they walked through the copse. He put her on the small pony he had bought for her and she laughed, digging her heels into the beast's flanks to make him go faster.

He led the pony to Ellen's house and tethered it to a post. Ellen beamed when she saw Mary and took them inside, unbuttoning and removing the child's coat and sitting her by the fire.

'You've been away,' she said.

'To Southampton on business, but I may go further.' John set his mouth firmly when Ellen looked anxious. 'I have land to see and I must take Amos if he is to work there. He may not go unescorted. Has he come to you?'

'He's mended my fence and is splitting wood in the yard,' she said. 'He seems to want to work hard and feels grateful for his release.'

'I'll see him later,' John said. 'First I must tell you of my plans.' He touched her swollen hands with gentle fingers. 'Keep warm, Ellen. We need you to be here for

Mary if I go away. You must write to me, sending news of her and Deerwood in every ship bound for Plimoth, but your hands could never manage a child again, so Marjorie will see to Mary and if necessary become her duenna when she is ripe for marriage.'

'Marjorie a duenna? Lady Judith will never allow it!'

'Lady Judith will do as I bid her. If my father asked you to marry him then why can I not choose a housekeeper to care for my child? She loves Mary as you do and will care for her as you cared for me. I have made it legal and have many documents tying up my property as I want it, and making sure that Cousin Arthur and his ilk never touch it.'

'You look like your father in his young days,' Ellen sighed. 'You have his stubborn ways but he was a good man in business and a kind one until his sickness turned mind to madness. Lady Judith is in labour, or so I heard. Surely you must be there, John?'

'I have no place there. I shall take Mary home and they will tell me if I am a father again. When I know, I can make my own future. I need to go to Martha's Vineyard and take Amos there to manage my stables. Keep Mary here while I talk to him and I will take her back to dinner.'

Mary sat eagerly on the pony, her cheeks

more pink than John remembered. 'If I go away, you must ask Angus to ride with you every day,' he said. 'I shall tell him that I wish you to ride well.'

The great hall was deserted and John sent Michael to order food. He sat with Mary and ate, dimly hearing sounds of activity upstairs but he showed no curiosity and, when an hour later he was sitting by the hearth, he sipped wine and tried to muster his thoughts. Mary drowsed after the unaccustomed fresh air and Marjorie came to take her to bed. 'I think it's over, sir,' she said. 'The doctor asked to see you.'

He passed a maid carrying a basket of soiled linen and heard a feeble cry. Judith lay still, her face parchment pale and her brow beaded with moisture. Mistress More wiped her face and tidied the bed clothes then walked over to the crib and picked up the bundle that held the new-born child. 'You have a son, Sir John,' she said in a voice that lacked enthusiasm.

The doctor put a hand on John's arm. 'He had a rough passage,' he said. 'Lady Judith was very brave, but she also suffered as the child lay across her and I had to turn it. She lost blood and the afterbirth was ragged.' He looked more directly into John's face. 'I fear she may be unable to bear more children.'

'No matter! I have a son!' John picked

away the blanket and regarded the small head with concern. The soft caput caused by the baby's head pressing down and becoming distorted, made the infant look strange, and there was a yellow tinge to his face.

'The colour will improve,' the doctor said hastily. 'The swelling also will disappear in time and he will be a handsome boy.'

As if remembering that she was there, John went to his wife. He took her cold hand in his enveloping warm grasp and bent to kiss her cheek. 'Thank you, my dear,' he said. 'You have kept your part of our bargain, and now that you have given me a son, you may have no more fears of me.'

She shrank back from the impact of his masculinity and swallowed hard.

'Don't you understand? I swear to you that whatever happens, I will never force myself on you again.'

'You swear it?' she whispered.

'You may stay celibate or take a paramour, it's all one to me,' he said carelessly. 'But now you must have everything you need and want. You may even have the minister here if that pleases you.' He turned to the two female cousins who stood apart watching them, dressed in dark clothes as if ready for a funeral instead of a joyous birth.

Triumph gave him leave to speak his mind, long suppressed in the interests of harmony. 'Give my condolences to Make-peace and Cousin Arthur,' he said. 'I doubt if this birth will echo happily in their minds as I now have my rightful heir. Look after him well, Mistress More, for one day he will be Lord of Deerwood and must grow big and strong to make him ready for that care.'

'My cousin is too weak to feed him,' Arthur's wife said.

'Bring a wet nurse and make sure she is clean and has no disease,' John said. 'She must live here until the weaning and I must know of what her own child died before she touches my son.'

'She may have a live baby,' she said.

'I want no other baby here,' he said firmly, then smiled. 'Today I am a happy man and we shall feast tonight. I shall refuse no reasonable request from friend or tenant and a gift of money will go to every servant on the estate.'

His wife's cousin Dorothy came closer. 'I rejoice for you both,' she said bleakly. 'But poor Makepeace will lose a great deal if he is not your heir. You have other properties that your son would not miss and yet would serve to secure his future, so if you are indeed generous now, may we expect something for him?'

'You have thought of these properties, madam? Had you already chosen them if the die was cast against you?' He smiled but his eyes remained cold. 'What had you in mind, madam?'

'There are farms on the Isle of Wight and houses there,' she said eagerly.

'My father disposed of many there before he died,' John said, wondering what they would think if he told them that Hope Fletcher had the deeds of a good farm and house, now rented to a yeoman and his family.

She hid her resentment well and went on. 'If not the island, there is the New World! You have interests there and I am told you breed good horses at Ostungo.'

'Would Makepeace survive the sea voyage?' he asked with a lazy smile that hid his dislike of even the mention of the boy's name. 'Would you dispatch him there for good? He seldom rides and hates the sea and boats.'

'You manage the estates from here as many landowners do,' she said. 'He need never set foot in New England.'

'You are too late. I have disposed of Ostungo, or shall do in time. Before that I must go there to see for myself if it prospers. No blade of grass can grow unless nurtured, and men who are paid have not the same interest as owners.'

'You have sold Ostungo?'

'No, madam, but I have plans for it,' was all that he would say.

Marjorie was red-faced from the heat of the kitchen and Michael brought in boys from the village to turn to spits and baste the meat. The servants were summoned to the great hall to drink to the health of the new-born heir and he was shown to them with his poor little bruised head hidden in a lace cap. Purses of money were handed out to each servant and when Angus walked from the stage by the spinney on the way home, he heard the church bells chiming a message of joy such as had not been heard since before Cromwell stilled their clamour.

He took his case of papers to the library and locked them away, wondering if John Halben would now regret his impulse to make Hope Fletcher's son his New England heir.

'The vultures are gathering, Angus,' John said to him. 'They take for granted my generosity and mean to benefit from it today as I must follow the traditions of the house.'

'How did they know?' Angus asked as he saw Cousin Arthur's carriage arrive, spilling out the rest of the family including a morose-looking Makepeace.

'Michael found baskets of pigeons not destined for table and yesterday they flew home to their roosts with news of the impending birth.'

'I'll be away about my own business,' Angus said with a grin as Arthur hurried towards them.

'Good day to you, Arthur,' John said heartily. 'And it is a good day. It was kind to come now to rejoice with Lady Judith and to see my son. I have a feast ordered and tonight you shall drink fine French wines and have anything you desire.'

'It is a day to spread largesse,' Arthur agreed eagerly. 'Makepeace is anxious to see his cousin and to wish him good health.' He gave the unwilling boy a nudge and Makepeace mumbled his rehearsed speech.

'It is a pity that you do not ride or pursue any of the manly sports,' John said lightly. 'My son will need a companion who will share his love of the country and the animals.'

'He may prefer books,' Arthur said. 'And sacred music, which Makepeace loves.'

John laughed. 'He is my son,' he said.

'He is Judith's child too.'

'That's so.' John looked at the pale-faced boy standing by the florid man and had a moment of doubt, then said, 'He will learn to follow me. He will be given the right companions and receive a good education.'

Arthur saw the tightening of his face and knew that the moment had passed to ask for favours. 'You may not find it comes out as you wish, John. Blood tells!'

'And your blood must be calling you to your cousin's side. I note that you didn't hurry first to her today, but wasted time in idle talk with me.' He gave a grim laugh. 'Is your need for your son's preferment greater than your affection for Judith? I can put your mind at rest as I know that you are disappointed. When Makepeace comes of age he shall have a gift of money, but no invitation to make this his house or influence my son in any way. It will be enough to buy a house in a town and provide a modest income.'

Chapter 18

'That is the third time we have been told that,' Hope said impatiently. 'First he says he'll come to Ostungo and then the ship arrives without him and the poor Lubbocks wonder what is happening.' She shrugged. 'I think he puts off his visit because he must hate to leave his family. He has a girl and a boy and Deerwood takes a lot of managing.'

'He has a wife, too,' Edward reminded her. 'If she is afraid to face the sea voyage, then he will want to stay with her.'

'I think he will come here, as more and more horses have arrived for the stud farm and Deerwood stables must have very few horses left of any worth. John couldn't let them go to strangers without making sure that they are in good hands.'

'You've worked hard with the horses,' Edward said. 'John would be pleased, but now you seem to want to have done with the place just before he is expected.'

Hope pounded the linen in the tub with vigour. 'He will bring a new manager with him if he ever gets here,' she said. 'I don't know the man, but he has been with John Halben for several years now and must know his ways. I believe he is a good farrier and has an eye for horses, and we need more skilled men who can make wrought iron and shoe horses. I wanted to leave everything ready for him and then keep away. I find that the thought of meeting people from England makes me restless and I hate the way that some of the newcomers in Edgartown speak to the Indians. Why can't they leave us alone!'

'Why? You sound as if you dislike him. John will want to see us. We are old friends and he has said how much he appreciates the care you showed last winter when that mare foaled badly and nearly died.' He gave her a faintly accusing glance. 'You and Michael spent more time there than in your own home and left Wenono and the girls to me.'

Hope laughed. 'You liked being with them and having them all to yourself. I've never known a man so besotted with his daughters as you are, and Wenono has learned to cook all the things you enjoy.'

'I didn't lack for food,' he admitted, 'and the girls help her a lot now.' He took the log that Hope used for pounding the wash. 'Let me take a turn,' he said.

'I am strong again,' she said. 'The Lubbocks won't let me do anything heavy for the horses, but I rode last week and felt no adverse aches and pains.' She laughed. 'Michael beats me easily when we race together and he can catch a loose horse better than most men.'

'I still believe that you rode too much and that brought the miscarriage,' Edward said.

She shook her head. 'I rode sidesaddle when I was carrying and never galloped. It was soothing.' She took the wood from him. 'I think that I shall never bear another child, Edward,' she said.

'We are still young!'

'A gypsy once told me that I would have a boy and two girls, and that is what we have. I had a fever when I lost the baby and Katsi thinks my womb will not grow another child.'

'She may be right,' Edward said. 'We have lain together for eight months now since you recovered from losing her and you are

363

not pregnant.' He put the log away and kissed her. 'You are a pretty woman and show no sign of anything amiss and I find my flesh hardening each time I touch you.' He held her close. 'Was any man more fortunate?' He bent to kiss her breasts through the muslin gown and she clung to him, then pushed him away.

'Even if I could have more children, we seldom have the opportunity to make love during the day as we did not so long ago! The children are coming back from fruit picking and I must make pies before the fruit turns mouldy.'

Michael threw down a hare and two squirrels on to the stout deal table. 'I thought you were helping your sister to pick fruit,' Edward reminded him.

'I picked as much as they did but I spent less time picking flowers and gossiping!' He saw that Hope was not pleased with the squirrels. 'I'll clean them and prepare them, Mother. You know you enjoy them when they are cooked.' He gave her a sweet smile and his deep-blue eyes danced with pleasure. 'It was good out there. I saw a doe and two possums. I left them alone as she was in foal and I don't like possum flesh.'

'We need more fish,' Edward said brusquely. 'Take the small canoe and bring only big fish for smoking.'

'I'll prepare the squirrels first,' Michael

said and Edward turned away to the girls who were trundling the handcart along the lane.

'You annoy your father, Michael. You must do as he says. Leave the squirrels and do them later.'

'They should be done now,' Michael said. He laughed and kissed her cheek. 'I'll be good,' he whispered. 'I'll fish for an hour and come back here to work with Father if you'll promise me that I can go to Ostungo tomorrow.'

Hope moved uneasily, crumpling the hem of her apron. 'You spend a lot of time there, Michael, and I think your father resents it.'

'I do what he wants first,' Michael said quickly, his face hardening. 'But he doesn't understand horses as we do, Mother, and I feel at home there.'

'This is your home, Michael.'

'I know, and I am happy most of the time, Mother, but there are times when Father looks at me as if I make him unhappy.' Michael frowned. 'I have done nothing to displease him and yet he does not care for me as he does the girls.'

Hope forced a laugh. 'You are a big boy now, almost a man. In the wild, you have seen how the young threaten the older ones of the pack. Even if he would never feel threatened by you, he is a man who likes to be head of his household and rightly so, as

365

he has worked hard to make this a comfortable home for us all. He does love you, Michael, and until you are old enough to make your own home, you must obey him.'

He nodded seriously. 'You are right, Mother.' He turned at the door, fishing rods and nets in his hands and a large basket of woven grass on his back. 'But when I leave here, I would like to work at Ostungo.'

Hope leaned against the table, suddenly short of breath. 'Dear God,' she murmured. 'Keep John away, but if he comes here let him be changed so that his smile is not like Michael's. Let Edward remain blind for ever.'

Her tears fell into the washing. Just one passionate afternoon before my wedding she thought. It can't be possible! She sighed and wrung out the linen ready to hang outside. Edward was proud of his son and had taught him to fish and hunt and to make wood obey his ready hands, but he eyed the boy with a puzzled air at times and Hope held her breath, waiting for him to have doubts as the corn-coloured hair grew lustrous and heavy and the boy's body sturdy and arrogantly proud.

'Weeping?' Edward took her into his arms and she closed her eyes as she felt his love and the peace that he gave her.

'I finished reading Aunt Ellen's last letter, and suddenly I was homesick,' she lied. 'She asks Marjorie to write for her now as her hands grow more stiff and swollen. It's better so as I have more news that way.'

'What news is there?'

'Just that Lady Judith is more of a recluse than ever, and rarely leaves the house. Her cousins visit less as there is nothing for them now that John has a son, and apart from John's hunters there are not many horses in the stables that they can borrow. They call the boy William after John's father, which displeases her as she wanted a name from her family. She has little interest in either of her children.' Hope told him of the births and deaths and marriages that had happened since they left the village but he only half listened.

'Would you go back there if anything happened to me?' he asked.

She looked startled. 'You are my husband and this is our home. I like to hear of my old home, but everything that happened there seems unreal now; behind a veil of mist. It is impossible to go back to the past.' She wound her arms round his neck. 'I am yours till death,' she reminded him. 'And you are not going to die until after you bury me!'

'It's just that I feel that you are miles away at times. You are closer to Michael than I am to him.'

'Is that all? You wouldn't be the man you are if you agreed with everything that a rising young stallion did. He is young and has a lot to learn and you teach him well.' She smiled. 'You haven't clashed antlers yet, but it that comes you will at least respect each other and give a little each way. Besides, I seem to find you and the girls laughing about secrets that I don't share. It's natural and I am happy about it.' She saw his face brighten and teased him. 'You will have your troubles when they come to maturity and lust after boys! No man will be good enough for your daughters.'

She went into the store-room where the two chests were filled with clothes. 'I must turn out the chests,' she said. 'I found a patch of mould on a shirt that I put in the closet and some shirts are old and shabby so I shall turn them out to make room in the boxes for the new ones. As you lined them with cedar they suffer from no damp or fungus.'

Edward followed her and sat by the bed while she unpacked his box, advising her which of the clothes were now too old to keep and watching her fold the new ones.

She put the box tidy and opened her own, removing the top layer of shifts and simple cotton gowns. Her hands met the hidden silk and absentmindedly she brought out the material and laid it on the bed, realizing too late that Edward had seen it. She sniffed at the inside of the box and said briskly, 'No smell of damp here.' She began to put the clothes inside again and bundled the silk up to follow the rest as if it was unimportant, but Edward stopped her.

'What's that?'

'I've had this for years, but never made it up as our life here doesn't demand frills and fine clothes.'

'I've never seen it before now.'

'It was part of my wedding gifts,' she said, smiling to hide the fast beating of her heart. 'Lady Judith had many pieces like this, but this colour didn't suit her as her skin is sallow, so it came to me.'

'I suppose Aunt Ellen wouldn't let it go to waste,' Edward said with approval. He thought for a moment. 'All this time you have had that lovely cloth and never worn more than cotton in summer and heavy woollens in winter. Do you ever crave for pretty things, Hope?'

'Please don't look sad. When would I wear it here? I am content, and soft muslin and fine lawn are pretty and cool.'

'Do you have time to sew it?'

'Yes, but there is no need.'

'Susannah Lubbock is to be married and we have been invited to the wedding in Edgartown. You must wear the silk and I shall be proud to have you with me.'

Hope folded it and put it to one side.

'When we go to Edgartown to shop, you

must buy what you need to sew it and what you need to trim and dress your hat.' He looked so pleased that Hope couldn't refuse. She decided to ask Alice Lubbock for help as she had many reels of thread and good scissors.

'I shall take it to Alice tomorrow and Michael can come with me and bring the fish we promised them.' She saw Edward frown and she added hastily, 'I shall need him. You promised a load of shells to crush to make mortar and we can put two sacks in the pony trap.'

'So I did. I meant to take it over sooner but now Michael can make himself useful. After tomorrow I'll need him to help rig the boat.'

'The canoes are seaworthy,' Hope said. She looked anxious. 'Do you mean the whaling boat?'

'I've put it off long enough,' Edward said. 'Chiabos used it last year after I had to repair it when the storm beat it against the jetty, and it was very successful, and now I must show faith in my own work. The next time they go whaling I must be there.'

'I shall not have a moment's peace if you go out there.'

'It will not be soon. I shall have many skilled hands to help me, and the prayers of everyone in the village to help us return safely.'

'Do you want me to lie still in bed as the squaws do to make the whale tranquil?' Her smile was tremulous.

He laughed and shook his head. 'It will not be until after the wedding, so make your dress and forget about sewing sails!'

'Where are you going now?'

'I have to collect the moccasins and beaver hats from the workers. Chiabos promised to send his son with a pack mule and our cob with panniers to Edgartown, in time for the ship bound for England.'

'We are making a lot of money from such things,' Hope said, secretly relieved to find she no longer needed to use the money hidden in the bottom of the chest. 'And Katsi's family are pleased with their share of the profits.'

Edward laughed. 'I was beginning to think you could perform miracles when everything we needed was paid for so quickly.'

'I had a little put by for emergencies and I am a very good manager,' she reminded him.

'And a wonderful wife.' He regarded her with concern. 'If you no longer bear children, will that mean the end to our pleasuring?'

'No my dear.' She kissed him on the lips and pressed her body close to his so that he felt her breasts soft and warm against his chest. 'In one way I am glad to be free. If a baby comes then we shall love it, but now, each time we are together I no longer have to think that perhaps in a few months' time I may have to stop working and riding for a while and grow heavy and sick.' She smiled. 'You have proved your virility with a fine family and so any fault will be in my body.'

She heard Michael whistling by the stream at the back of the house and smelled the smoke as the oak chippings flared before subsiding into a hot bed to smoke the fish. He is so sensible, she thought with affection. In many ways quicker than Edward to see what must be done and in which order he must do the work. Edward would have caught the fish and then have to leave them to get limp as he would not think to make the smoke-house ready while he was away in the canoe.

She picked up the two squirrels and a sharp knife and went out to the stream. Michael was gutting six large cod and putting them to drain on a wicker tray. 'I was coming to fetch the squirrels,' he said.

'I don't mind gutting them, but you'll have to do the rest.'

Michael took the fish guts and the squirrel entrails and put them on a patch of grass away from the house. 'Come little brothers,' he said. 'Share our bounty from the Great Spirit.'

Hope felt slightly uneasy. 'The Lubbocks

say that we should not copy the Indian ways,' she said. 'Many people in Edgartown say the same and in Plimoth they have trouble as they say they made close friendships in the beginning and their children learned too many pagan ways. When they kept their children away from their friends it made trouble.'

'Do you believe that?' Michael was shocked. 'My best friends live in long houses and I learned to use a bow from Chiabos who also taught Father! Katsi loves us all even though she never says so,' he added with a grin. 'I hate going to church in Edgartown with all those stiff-necked people.'

'That's because I make you wear a jacket and real shoes.' Hope laughed. 'I feel the same at times, but you must remember that it was members of the church who opened up this part of the world and did much good on Martha's Vineyard when the Reverend Mayhew was here and brought friendship and trust. Katsi still goes along the Indian trail by Timsbury and leaves a white stone on the pile at The Place by the Wayside, where the son of Reverend Mayhew gave his last sermon to the Indians. He preached there to a great crowd who wanted him to stay, then left on a ship and was drowned. Katsi's father added that story to the ancient ones that the storyteller tells when they sit by camp-fires at night. It speaks of hundreds of grieving Indians passing The Place with their heads covered and walking in file back to their homelands.

'You see, Mother, you love them as much as I do. All your friends belong to Katsi's tribe, apart from the Lubbocks.' Michael shook water from the squirrels and took them into the kitchen where he flung them into the fire. When the moisture had hissed dry and the fur singed away, he raked them out and set them to cool and rubbed them white in a dish of cold wood ashes.

Hope could now watch him when he put them in a baking dish with onions and herbs, but she hated to see skinned rabbits and singed squirrels as they reminded her of dead babies. 'May I go to Ostungo tomorrow?' Michael asked.

'Yes. Your father wants you to take the shells there and some fish and I have to look at one of the colts.'

'Can we go early?'

She looked at his eager face and they shared a conspiratorial glance. 'Be up early and bring in firewood and hitch up the pony trap and we can go as soon as your father has eaten breakfast.' She looked serious. 'Make the most of tomorrow because you will be needed to help with the boat and have no time for Ostungo for a week or so.'

'Are we going whaling?'

'The men are.'

Michael blushed. 'I am twelve! In three years' time I shall be a man and married!'

'In England you come of age at eighteen,' she told him.

He glowered. 'That is too old. Mr Lubbock knows of youths who marry at fifteen and have their first houses then if they join the deep-sea fishing boats, and English boys go to sea in the navy at twelve!'

Hope hugged him. 'Don't grow up too soon,' she begged. 'Boys grow up faster here by necessity, and I have already begun to lose my son.'

'Never!' He kissed her cheek. 'Father may lose me but never you, Mother.' He fingered the heavy silk. 'Is this for you? It's pretty.'

'I shall wear it to the wedding,' she said, and knew that now she must make it into a gown and be seen in it.

'Did you buy it in Edgartown? It looks far too fine for the ladies there.'

'I brought it with me when we first came here,' she said.

'You are a sly one, Mother,' he teased her. 'What other secrets have you hidden away?'

'None.'

'I don't believe you. You look very guilty.' He threw back his head in a way that she remembered too well, and he laughed. Her heart seemed to die a little. Soon, very soon, Edward would know and when that happened, she might as well die.

Edward came back from the shore and looked inside the smoke-house. The fish hung in strips on tenterhooks above the smoking oak chips and he grunted his approval.

'You've done well,' he said, and Michael flushed with surprised pleasure. It had been weeks since he had been praised by his father. 'Sometimes I think I expect too much from you. You are only a boy and yet you do the work of a man.'

'I am nearly a man, Father. I can fish well and hunt and manage horses and I could help you in the big boat when you go whaling,' he said eagerly.

'No!'

'I would obey every command you gave me and stay safe if the boat rocked,' he pleaded.

'Whaling isn't like sailing a boat for fishing. It takes skills that I have yet to master and more strength than you have, son.'

'When will you go?'

'Not for many weeks; that depends on the work I have to do on the boat, and the sacred preparations that Chiabos must make.'

'I shall be older by then.'

Edward regarded his son with amused exasperation. 'A few weeks older, but not yet a man. When your voice deepens, you can say you are grown.' He tousled the bright hair. 'I didn't know that we must expect it so soon! I must take you to Edgartown and Plimoth to look for a wife!'

Michael tossed his head. 'I'll want better than Maisie Hanford or Doris Fleet!'

Edward stared at him, wondering at his arrogance, half amused and half afraid. 'I am a carpenter and you are my son,' he said. 'You must not reach too high.'

'Mother comes from yeoman stock and they say that one of her forebears was gently bred, even if it was on the wrong side of the blanket.'

'Who told you that?' Edward's brow creased with anger.

'You did, Father! When Mr Lubbock was drinking with you and he was boasting of his family in Wales, you said that a great grandmother of your wife had been taken to bed by a nobleman.'

'I remember now.' He smiled wryly. 'It was a tale that Hope's mother told and it may have no truth in it. I am ashamed now to have boasted of it, but I was full of strong waters that night, as we had sold a lot of skins and received our returns from England.'

'It must be true. Mother said that my great aunt Ellen has a look that isn't seen in her family, and I have something besides my mother's looks, and your broad shoulders.'

Edward laughed. 'Yes, your shoulders are

like mine,' he said with relief. 'Good, honest, artisan's muscles that will thicken to strength in time, so I do have claim to you! But you grow more like her every day, and I can see little of me in you. The other looks that have puzzled me for a long time must be a throw back to that time. I recognized it as familiar but could put no name to the connection.'

He looked serious as if weighing up the possibilities. 'Be warned, you may have inherited more than looks. That family were lecherous and loose-living until John Halben was born. He is a fine man with none of his father's vices, and saved an innocent girl from a fate that would have brought her disgrace and unhappiness. I owe him a great debt and I thank God he was untainted by the disease that drove his father mad. He now has a son who is heir to Deerwood.'

He sighed with a relief he had never known he needed, and silently admitted that he had been ready to misjudge his own dear wife. At last I can look at my son without the feeling that at some time Hope was unfaithful or may have been taken by Sir William.

Hope served the braised squirrels with fresh bread and blueberry dumplings and wondered why Edward looked so cheerful.

'I promised to help to sew up the sealskins

to make air bladders for the whaling,' Edward said. 'I have sharp metal awls and glue that will make it easier for the women.' He took his tools on the sled and whistled as he disappeared down the lane.

'Have you been a good obedient boy?' Hope asked. 'Your father is in a very good mood, and says that you may spend a night at Ostungo.'

'It seems that I resemble your forebear who he boasted about that night at Ostungo, and he seems pleased to know where I get my fair hair.'

Hope spilled her ale and went to fetch a cloth to mop it up from the table, fighting to stem the panic that his words caused her.

'Was it a bad disgrace?' he asked when she returned. 'It was before Cromwell, who made many things a hanging matter, or so the schoolmaster told me.'

'People were more kind,' Hope said. 'They looked after their own, and a child born of such a union was never cast out.'

'Father was pleased to know of the link as it had been worrying him. He couldn't make out who I was like, apart from you.' He grinned. 'I told him I had his shoulders and the sturdy body of a workman and that pleased him.'

Hope packed the silk in a linen case and put it in a leather saddlebag. Her throat was dry as if she had been running fast and she gulped air to force her mind to calm down. For the first time for years she felt gratitude to her mother. Aunt Ellen Turner had been more of a mother to her and had given her love and made her wedding day a success, while her mother did very little for anyone outside her own home. She lived in a dream world where she invented fanciful stories, like the one she had told Edward, to impress him as to the value of his bride-to-be, and make sure he didn't forget that she was a cut above his family.

Slowly, she recovered and began not to dread meeting John Halben again. He would know that the story her mother had told was a lie, but even if he saw a family likeness he was in no position to mention it, as he was Sir John Halben, Lord of the Manor of Deerwood, with a wife, a daughter and a son. As far as the rest of the world knew he had never taken Hope Clarke to bed, but had defended her in a most chivalrous manner from the steward Furness and his father Sir William.

Passion is dead, Hope decided. I love Edward and my children, and John and I can meet as friends. She raked out the fringe of grey ashes from the fire. Love died and turned to calm affection and a deep caring, she told herself firmly. There would be nothing left between them but a thin smouldering of memories.

Chapter 19

William Halben sat on the dry stone wall and watched his sister Mary. 'Hide!' he called and Mary ran with him to the stables and climbed the ladder to the loft where Mistress Chastity couldn't reach them. Mary hugged the protesting puppy that she had been playing with when William called the warning, and it stopped whimpering.

'Mary?' The voice was shrill and hard. Chastity walked carefully on the stones avoiding the ordure in the stableyard. 'William? Your mother needs you in the house.' She looked about her and listened. The children stifled their giggles and sat quite still while she went on to the bothy where the mason was making a dust over stone for a hearth. He blew on his work and sent fine powder on to her dress and up her nose and Chastity glanced hurriedly into the bothy and walked on, her thin shoulders set in resentment at the duties she was asked to perform.

Her voice faded as she went back to the house. William stretched out on the straw. 'You'll get your hose covered with dust,' Mary said in a tone reminiscent of Marjorie in a censorious mood.

'I don't care! I'm not going in yet.'

'That's not the way a gentleman speaks,' Mary said with dignity, and then threw a handful of straw over his head.

'And that's not the way a lady behaves,' he retaliated, and they fought happily until they had straw in their hair and dust all over their clothes. The puppy danced about, yapping, and made a puddle on Mary's skirt.

'That's Father's carriage!' William said, as wheels creaked over the gravel of the sweeping driveway.

'Quick, brush me down,' Mary ordered. 'Oh, you little beast,' she said as the wet patch spread on her dress.

'We'd better go in the back way and ask Sophie to help us,' William said. 'She hates Mistress Chastity so she won't tell her about us. She'll do anything to protect us from her so she will hide these dirty clothes and make us neat again.'

They climbed down the swaying ladder and ran to the kitchens, and in fifteen minutes they emerged looking clean and well dressed with sweet smiles on their faces, ready to meet their father.

'Well?' John Halben eyed their crisp linen and spotless velvet with amusement. 'It must have been a very dirty game to have you so clean at this time of day!' Mary giggled and William looked self-conscious, then smiled. His thin face and narrow shoulders belied the humour in his eyes and the wiry body that made riding easy. 'Did you ride with Angus today?' John asked.

'Yes, Father. He allowed me to jump a much higher log and said I would be the right shape to be a jockey for the races approved by King Charles.'

'And so you might be,' John said, 'but not yet before your bones are harder. You must learn more, but say nothing to your mother. As you know, she hates all horseflesh and thinks you are in mortal danger each time you sit on a pony.'

'I wish I had a better horse, Father,' William said. 'You've sent the best away across the sea.'

'I have a good stud farm there and I need less here,' John said. 'Tell Angus that I am home and ask Michael to bring ale to the library. I have to see Angus first, then I want to see Mistress Turner and give her letters from The Vineyard, but that must wait until later.'

'Shall I tell Mother that you are back?' Mary asked.

'No, another hour will be of no consequence, as I've been away for a month.'

'Did you see the king? Were the ladies dressed in silks and fine brocade?' She regarded his silk doublet and the slashed sleeves showing crimson under dark ochre, with envy.

'Poor Mary. You are taken nowhere but to church and see none of the wonders a girl should see.'

'Mother says the court is full of wanton women and the king does nothing to prevent evil,' William said.

John eyed his son with a frown. 'You'll make a preacher yet, my boy,' he said.

'That's what Mother wants,' William said reluctantly. 'But clerics have no fun, Father. Some of them never ride and they spend too much time indoors and I don't enjoy prayers.'

John laughed. 'What can I expect from our union?' he said. 'You are torn between your mother's pious bigotry and your love of freedom to ride and take a part in the farm life here, but thank God you love Deerwood.'

'You do too, Father, although you spend so much time away.'

'I may go away for six months or more. I have to see what my horses are doing over in Martha's Vineyard.'

'May I go with you?' Mary put her hand in his and smiled appealingly.

'I wish I could take you, but someone must stay and look after your mother.'

'She has Chastity and the priest and has nothing to do with the housekeeping any more,' Mary said. 'She stitches and prays and hardly ever leaves her room. She would not notice my leaving.'

'I want to go too!' William said in alarm. 'If I stay and you are not here to prevent it, she will make me assist the clergy in church as if I am a sacristan, and I am frightened when I am in the church alone with them.'

'I can tell him that you are not to touch vestments or the chalice nor swing the incense,' John said firmly. 'Such practices are creeping back and I want no part in them.'

'Mother would be cross and make him take me,' William said.

'I think not. He depends on me and not your mother for his stipend!' He grinned. 'You are thirteen now and maturing. You ride well and fence a little, but have you not found it pleasant to look at girls?'

'No, Father!' William looked shocked and very like his mother.

Mary giggled and John turned to her.

'Time flits by and soon I must find a husband for you, Mary. At court, they marry early and many of my friends have daughters wed at fifteen.' He laughed. 'You are old, madam!'

'I can find no husband here, sir,' she replied. 'Are there no healthy handsome men in Massachusetts?' Her smile was mischievous. 'While you were away, Mother invited Cousin Makepeace to stay and made me walk with him.'

'S'death! Did he touch you?'

'I walked with him as far as the stream beyond the dunes where the mire is covered with pretty green algae.' She looked demure and John began to laugh. 'I forgot to tell him that the land was insecure and he sank in the mud,' she said with satisfaction. 'He went home and I think that even an easy life here would not make him want me.'

William scratched a bite from an insect that had found him in the loft, and the scratching made it tender. 'No good man would want her,' he said, in a voice that was only half teasing.

'Oh, sir! So you know all about it, do you?' Mary looked pugnacious and reverted to childhood as she taunted him. 'Who was it cried when Daisy Amise tried to undo his pantaloons in the hay field and didn't want to see her breasts when she offered to show them?'

John blinked. 'It's time I considered what is to become of you,' he said. He recalled how Daisy was made, with high firm breasts and a bold expression and a mouth that promised every vice under the sun. 'Go to your mother and say that I will take tea with her in half an hour. I must change into something more sober for her company.'

'I have been blind,' he said to Angus. 'My children grow and become adult and I think of them as infants.' He waved aside the books. 'Tomorrow will do for business and talk of property. I looked briefly at the farm and it is in good heart. You work hard and can now take a little time to be with your wife.'

'You have no need to worry,' Angus said. 'Mary will not be forced into any match that she dislikes although she is now ready for marriage; or a liaison.' He coughed. 'I sent away the newest stable lad, who looked after her with too much yearning and she was beginning to notice him. He now lives over the water on the island where a friend of mine has a farm, so he has not suffered by the change.'

'And William?'

'Keep him away from the church,' Angus suggested mildly.

'His mother has influence there but I will nip it in the bud. He needs to learn of life. He is thirteen and his voice has deepened but he refused to pleasure a girl from the village who wanted him!'

Angus helped him into his grey coat edged with black velvet. 'He may not go to church so often now but they come here,' Angus said, hesitantly. 'I make sure he is not alone when Her Ladyship asks the priest and his curate to dinner.'

'What is it? You keep something from me.'

'I thought I was shrewd but my wife, Nancy, notices more than I would ever do,' Angus said, with an unhappy shrug. 'She suspects that the curate is a threat to your son, and it was she who alerted my attention to the stable lad.'

'I owe her a debt,' John said warmly. 'Does she also think my son is not man enough to resist such overtures?'

'He is young and needs a man's company but not that kind of man if he is to make a happy marriage and sire heirs for Deerwood.'

'If I take him to The Vineyard for a while, do you think it might be wise?' Angus lifted a disbelieving eyebrow. 'I know,' John said impatiently. 'I've blown hot and cold over that visit for years and you must think I never intended to go there, but I have been away from here for long periods over the past few months and find that life goes on without me under your care and the ministrations of Marjorie. I am glad that she has made a friend of your wife. They are good women who will protect my interests whatever happens to me.'

'Do you make plans?'

'Yes, I shall go soon and take Mary with me.' He considered that prospect. 'No, they shall both come with me. A spying sister makes a good gaoler and a brother who loves his sister will keep away parasites.'

'What of Lady Judith?'

'I am to take tea with her now and I shall tell her; then make Chastity cope with the vapours!'

'And I continue to keep authority here?'

'Completely. If you have trouble, consult the lawyer in Southampton and he will come here to lay down the law to my wife. All we have left between us is a legal marriage with legal agreements and as she is frightened of all legal matters, she will need only a hint from you to bring her to heel.'

'I am not her warden!'

'You are, but a kindly one whom she respects. There will be no trouble now that the relatives have flown, including Makepeace!'

'You heard of that?'

'Mary told me with great glee, the false minx! Tell me, is she pretty to a man? I see only my daughter and my son but others like you have no mist of fatherly love before their eyes.'

'Mary is like you in nature and is pretty in a fair way with a body that promises beauty.'

'And my son and heir? Is he a true man?'

'He will be if taken from here, sir, and given his head and healthy friends, but life is stifling him under his mother's influence.'

'So they come with me next month, sailing

on a new vessel just launched, which is more comfortable than any I've seen.' He stood up and tweaked his cravat into place. 'Now to break the news to my wife!'

'Why don't you go away again and leave me in peace!' Judith said. 'You must not take my children among savages.'

'They need to see something more of the world than Deerwood and Southampton, madam. London is still tainted with the pestilence and I was glad to be out of it, and Oxford is no longer fashionable since the king left.'

'They can stay with my cousins in Salisbury,' Judith said eagerly. 'There is much sacred music there and a fine community of pious men who would instruct them in the ways of the world.' She showed more spirit than he had seen for a long time. 'I could take a house there and go with them to church soirées and other entertainments.'

'They need more than that.'

'What better influence than that of the righteous?' she asked solemnly. 'Immortal sin finds the unwary.'

'That's what I want to avoid,' he said coarsely, thoroughly irritated by her sanctimonious manner. 'Your precious curate has ambitions to take my son when he is unwary and trusting!'

'What do you mean, sir?' Judith's face was flushed and her hands trembled.

'Does he come with me, or stay to be buggered by the curate?'

She saw his anger and the hard expression that had grown over the years, and she shuddered. 'It shall be as you say,' she conceded with a sigh. 'Leave me alone to face a lonely old age without those I hold dear.'

'You may have anyone here for your comfort, madam. Entertain a little and see the play, but the accounts remain with Angus who has my sealed commission giving him power.' His face softened. 'I do not take them away for ever. We shall be back before you realize that we have gone.' He stood by the window and seemed to fill the room with healthy force. 'Marjorie remains here even if Chastity resents her influence. If anyone leaves, it shall be Mistress Chastity, so make no changes here when I am away. Marjorie will chaperone Mary at court once we return.'

'You raise her so high?'

'Long ago I learned that rank is often a weak vessel to hold contentment and Marjorie would defend my daughter with her life, unlike a white-faced virgin like Chastity!'

'So, she is a virgin?' Judith smiled maliciously. 'She hints that you turn to her now that we no longer have concourse.'

John laughed and his mirth echoed from the room, bringing the companion along from the gallery to hover in the doorway. 'I keep my door locked, madam, to avoid such temptations.'

'Perhaps you have no need of her,' Judith said with a sly glance to note his expression.

'Perhaps not.' His face was bland and he gave no sign of his suspicion that his wife had put spies to find out if he had a mistress. 'Our union wasn't such an experience that I want to repeat it,' he said, and left the room abruptly, nearly knocking Chastity to the ground. He saw her ingratiating death's-head smile and felt a frisson of disgust. He would be free of women, all women, if he went away; free of his wife, her soft-footed companion who followed his path whenever she could, and free of Lady Beatrice from the court of King Charles II, who of late threatened his peace of mind and his reputation with her husband as she grew more demanding.

'They will need new clothes,' Marjorie said, when she realized that this time Sir John was adamant and was really going to take the children to the New World.

'New, but not too fine,' he said. 'I recall how the women dressed there and they wore dun-coloured gowns with no trimmings.'

'That was when the Pilgrims landed and

had sway over them but you haven't been there for years and fashions must have caught up with them.'

He shook his head. 'They work hard and many have little money, but I agree that in the main towns there must be changes. My agent asked for pretty material such as they cannot buy there unless a French boat brings lace and silk for the matrons of Plimoth and Boston, where they have entertainments to rival London. His daughter's dower chest needed pretty things as she is marrying soon, so the guests will wear more festive clothes than I remember, but for the main, they dress simply. My children must not put on a show that marks them as something apart and which might invite disapproval and envy.'

Marjorie watched him as he sat on the edge of her kitchen table, his strong body relaxed and his silk-clad legs swinging free of the floor. He put a finger in the dish of gravy and licked it.

'They are good children and will not disgrace you by making enemies,' she said. 'Have you thought of what you will find there?'

'Changes of a minor nature and for the better.' He shrugged. 'Lubbock has built a house for me which stands empty this five years, and the stables are thriving, but crying out for a skilled manager. There is room for Amos over the stables and he can build a smithy and house to his own liking. I wish for nothing more.'

'Ellen's niece sends a lot of slippers and leather bags to market here and does well. When you see her, would you give her this bag as a pattern to copy, as I think it would sell better here, being smaller and finer than the ones that servants take to market.' She sensed his lack of will to do so, and added, 'Or it can go with Ellen's letter and the small presents she sends to the children.'

He gave her the bag again and nodded. 'Let it go with the rest. I shall be busy for a while and may have to postpone meeting the Fletchers.' They discussed baggage and clothes and Marjorie looked sad. 'We shall come back and you must be ready to put Mary in the way of society, Marjorie, so fine clothes must be ready for both of you on our return, when I shall take her to London if the plague has gone, but for now, a few gowns of simple style and hard-wearing clothes for my son.' He took a pasty hot from the oven and bit into it. 'I shall miss your good food, Marjorie, and Mary will miss your care, but I need you here to look after my interests, with Angus and Ellen Turner to help you.'

John wiped his hand free of pastry crumbs and went to see Angus, already making a mental list of what would be needed on the voyage. He tried to avoid any thought that had nothing to do with practical matters, but he was shocked to find that the mention of Hope's name had found a raw spot in his sensitivity.

What is she like now? he wondered. I must take more shoes and thick stockings. She has had a boy and twin girls and Ellen mentioned a miscarriage so her health may have broken and she will be fat and unwholesome. Books and paper and ink may be in short supply. He scratched a note to obtain them, letting the ink drain down the quill to the table as he held it over the ink pot. She must be in good health or she couldn't help with the foals at Ostungo. Was her skin still clear and fine as a dragonfly's wings? Had she forgotten everything about him? Had marriage and childbirth brought happiness, or was life for her a passing show as his had been, seeing all and living well but feeling as if he had no part in it?

'It is dead!' he said aloud.

'What is dead, Father?' John looked into the face of his son and saw Judith there.

'The past, William.' He smiled. 'We have a new life to make. Ask Sophie to see to your clothes and what mending must be done before we sail for the New World.'

'Truly, Father?' William's eyes sparkled and his cheeks dimpled with excitement and John saw only his own image in the boy.

'May I tell Mary?' He paused, looking guilty. 'The curate asked me to study with him, but I hid. I conned my books early today so that I could ride with Amos. Did I do wrong?'

'You need him no more, William. He reeks of the pope. I wonder if he is fit for this parish.'

'Good. I hate being alone with him. He breathes down my neck when we study and smells of old damp straw.' He rubbed his cheek vigorously as if to rid himself of something foul. 'When I get work right, he tries to kiss me and his mouth is wet.'

'Never sit alone with him again. There is no need and you will have little time for Latin now,' John said mildly, inwardly wishing to see the curate in the flames of Hell. He smiled. At least William's repugnance augured well for the future. There would be heirs for Deerwood once William found a wife.

'You look as if you have lost a guinea!' Angus beckoned him into the library and closed the door. 'What is it, man? Is one of the horses sick?'

Angus looked pale. 'Furness has been seen in Southampton and caused an affray outside the inn where we stay when on business.'

'No, that must be a false rumour. He is far

away on the seas or in Tangier.'

'He has served his time and is free,' Angus said quietly.

'Did the militia confine him for affray?' asked John quickly.

'They were busy with a pirate's contraband and set him free when he sobered. They laughed at him and said the ale was too strong in Southampton for a man just free of the ship's hold. He shouted that he was looking for a whore called Sarah, and they made fun of him, asking if he could still make a woman happy.'

'Sarah?' John paced the room. 'If he finds her, he'll kill her. She caused him to be taken by the press gang and he's had long enough to decide that it was she.'

'He must have thought she was with her sister at the inn and can have no idea where she is living now.' Angus regarded his employer with anxiety. 'Do you think he'll return here to Deerwood, expecting a welcome?'

'No, after all this time, after disappearing without a word, even if it was no fault of his own that he couldn't send word to me, he must know that I have taken another steward and will have no time for him.'

'You are not convinced, sir?'

'No, I must find out more. Sarah is in danger. I hope I am not too late. Call for my carriage and fresh horses, if we have any left!

I will go to Southampton and find him, but as if by accident.'

'Let me go, sir.'

'No, Angus. There is more to this than you know.'

His mind slowly cleared as he drove back to the city. He was glad that he had dressed in dark, inconspicuous clothes when he went to Judith, as his bright court clothes and sweeping plumed hat would attract too much attention by the docks. The inn was quiet and he asked for the landlady, Sarah's sister, who came into the parlour cautiously.

'Sir John?' He sensed her relief and saw that her face was badly bruised.

'Who did this?' he asked, but knew it must be Furness. She told him that he had come there drunk a few nights ago and then again the next day before his behaviour had brought the militia and he was arrested.

'He came back again as soon as he was released and was cold sober and evil, but I wouldn't say where my sister is living and he went away after doing this.' She touched the swollen cheek and winced. 'He learned some rough ways in the navy.'

'He's gone away?'

She shook her head. 'I made the taproom boy tell him that she was in Portsmouth and he took a horse from the livery to go there.' She looked frightened. 'Men there know her and will tell him about her if he

398

says he is a friend.'

'Has Sarah protectors in her brothel? Bully boys to keep the girls safe?'

She nodded and managed a smile. 'She knows about Furness and is prepared if he goes there.'

'Make my man and the horses comfortable and lend me a nag,' John said.

He rode along the sea front to the big house where Sarah had her girls and noticed with grim humour that three men sat on the sea wall opposite the gateway. The tide was up and lapping against the wall, making spray, but they seemed not to notice the damp on their backs as they watched everyone who rode or walked by. They eyed him with suspicion.

John approached them. 'If you are from the house, tell Sarah that Sir John Halben is here,' he said. 'Look at me! You can describe me to her and she will know I am not the man she expects, but a real friend.'

One man went into the house after his face had been seen by the girl waiting by the squint window and he came out again quickly, beckoning John to go in.

'You look well,' John said, when Sarah welcomed him. She was dressed in expensive but gaudy clothes and her face was covered with paint and powder, at travesty of the style worn by Lady Castlemaine, the king's mistress.

'I have a clean girl from a farm,' Sarah said. 'I dress her as a novice and keep her for good friends.'

'I am tempted, but not now,' John said. 'I came because I thought you might be in danger from Furness.'

'I am,' Sarah said, simply.

'I can buy him off,' he suggested.

'Can you pay for all the years he's lost before the mast? He's had years to make his hate fester and come to a head, and he may believe he had something more to sell you as well as milk me dry.' She looked at him with determination. 'He must never be allowed to say that Hope went to your father. It wasn't true and she is safe and married now to a good husband, but people forget truth and a rumour would do harm to Deerwood and your family, as well as to Hope.'

'I am sorry, Sarah. I had no right to make you help me. You would not be in danger from him now if it wasn't for me.'

'You saved us from the poor house,' Sarah said brusquely as if she was about to weep. 'I still remember the good done to me, even if others forget, and I thank whatever god is up there, and the holy angels, if there are any! I was ill and Bessie a burden until you bought her for Sir William and set me on the road to Hell!' She smoothed her dress and the bangles on her wrists made an expensive sound. 'I have two houses and as many new girls as I want, as they know I never take the scrofulous or demented and I treat my girls well.' She smiled. 'Bessie is well and happy, with regular customers who like her, and I have bought security for her if I die. The wages of sin are security,' she said.

'I'll drink a glass of sack with you, Sarah, but I want no girl.'

'I hear that you have a better mare to ride.' She laughed at his dismay. 'I hear a lot about the court. I have men here from the Navy Office and servants from a duke's house who listen well, but are ignored as deaf and dumb where they work!'

'I am leaving England for a while, Sarah, so all that is over, but I must see that you have peace of mind and settle a few bits of business first.'

He told her about Deerwood and the children and about the stud farm on The Vineyard in Massachusetts. 'Give my love to Hope,' she said.

'If I see her,' he said lightly. 'Edward Fletcher is a busy man, and Hope has three children and a thriving leather trade, with Indian women to help her.'

'If any Indians want to come to me, I can use them. Novelty is always welcome; my Chinese girl rates highly among the richer men.'

'The Indians on The Vineyard have not been debauched and are good people,' John said firmly. He grinned. 'Darken a skin and add a few beads and you could charge what you liked,' he suggested, and Sarah nodded as if she might consider it.

'Madam!' The girl by the spy hole ran into the room. 'He is coming!'

'You say that my sister was badly beaten?' John regarded Sarah with concern. 'I have so much to lose here if he tried to take over and I will not have my sister hurt,' she said, her eyes hard and unforgiving. 'Leave me now. You were good to come here but I need no other help. I will see him but he must not see you.' A girl took him into another room and John stared out of the window at the man walking slowly along the road.

Furness was grey and his skin had the roughness that wintery seas and harsh winds give a man. He was lean and powerful and his mouth was set in a line that boded ill for his enemies. He wore thick sailor's trousers and sported a pig-tail, tarred and thin, but hint enough that the man had been taken for service in the navy and could not be pressed again.

He stopped by the gate and looked up at the house, grinning.

'Madam says that you must leave now by the back way where your nag is tethered,' the girl said. John wanted to protest but knew he must do as Sarah commanded. She was surrounded by her girls who were protective, and the three men outside were muscle enough to cope with one evil man. 'Wait at the inn and we will bring you news of what happens,' she said.

Chapter 20

'I came back the day before yesterday,' John said, 'but I had matters to discuss with Angus and couldn't come here.'

'And a hasty visit to a whore was a better way to pass your time than with an old woman with crippled hands?' Ellen laughed, enjoying his discomfiture.

'It was Sarah I went to see and I took no girl!'

'I know that. You never go with such women, but there's more that I know, John.' He looked apprehensive. 'I know that Furness was there.' He nodded. 'Sarah sent you a message by the seamstress whom Marjorie had brought from Southampton to make clothes for Mary. She was staying at the inn after fitting a lady for a wedding dress. Sarah's sister heard that she was coming here and told her to give me the note, away from the manor so that we could talk of it quietly when you came here.'

'Is Sarah safe?'

'Safe and happy,' Ellen said.

'She sent him away? Do you think he'll come here?'

'No.' Ellen regarded him with an expression that held relief mixed with fear as if what she had to say was unbelievable.

'How can you be sure he won't come to Little Deerwood and make trouble for my father's memory and Hope's family?'

'He went to the house and Sarah offered him wine as if she was pleased to see him. He was very taken with the house and the good trade done there and Sarah dressed up in silks and gold as if she had a fortune, but he hinted that he was home for good now and needed a comfortable bed and money enough to see him through, to make up for the time he had been at sea.'

'What happened? Was he violent? She was afraid he might want to take over her business, out of revenge, if she didn't stop him.'

'The wine was drugged, the tide high and he slipped over the sea wall and drowned.' Ellen's face was expressionless.

'Is this true? Was a body found?'

'An inshore fisherman found it that night when he was after a late shoal of fish. There was a half-empty bottle in his pocket and no marks on his body to suggest violence, so he was taken to the paupers' graveyard and buried quickly in lime.'

'So soon?'

'There have been many off the ships dying of the plague and he had a rash that was most likely scurvy after so long on board, but any marks, even a boil, make people shy away in fear and bodies are put in the ground without much delay.'

'So I can go away at last, knowing there is no threat to you, or Sarah, or to Hope's marriage and my family's reputation.'

'Was that what kept you here for so long?'

'That has some truth, but there were other matters that took time to resolve.' He looked at her cautiously. 'Am I right to take the children with me?'

'Yes, but not for ever. William must not be weaned away from Deerwood, but he will grow in every way if he goes now.'

'Have any letters you may want to send ready for the Fletchers, and some of your own cowslip wine to warm my stomach on the voyage.' He hugged her hard enough to make her bones creak.

'I have Hope's rents from the island,' she said. 'I can ask the bank to give them to you to take to her.'

'No, keep the money in safe hands as I have no idea if Edward Fletcher knows about the deeds, and money makes money, which she may need one day.'

John was lighthearted. Furness was dead and the last threat of discovery or any attempt at extortion was over. With furious energy he made arrangements for the voyage and packed what he thought might be needed for life on The Vineyard. Boxes and bags were stowed on board with a box of herbs that Ellen insisted were necessary to keep away seasickness and to foster appetite.

Judith refused to become involved, as if her lack of co-operation would stop the whole project, but free of her interference, the plans went ahead, with only Chastity getting in the way and bleating of the love she had for the children.

John knew that her tears were not for them but for him and her unrequited love, and on the day of departure when the carriage was piled up with the last of the baggage and the servants gathered to wave them goodbye, with Judith watching from an upstairs window, he took a deep breath and embraced Chastity and kissed her full on the lips.

'You'll have to leave now,' Angus said with a grin. 'Life here would be impossible for you after that! God speed you away quickly before she follows, but bring you safely home again!'

Tall masts and the smell of tar and wet ropes made William pale with excitement, and Mary gazed back at the shore as if unwilling to take her eyes from the scene that meant home and the country she knew. William begged for the work of feeding the tethered stock on board and Mary hugged the puppy she had insisted on taking with her. John rubbed the nose of the last of his brood mares as she was settled on board. That would leave Deerwood with only coach horses, a couple of hacks and the hunter he had given to Angus. He listened to the shouts of the sailors as they shifted ballast and battened down for the voyage and waved once more to Angus who had business to attend after the ship sailed.

'We sail within the hour, sir,' the captain said. 'The crew have a clean bill of health and we have a good wind to take us down Southampton Water.'

'You are new on this line?' John asked, seeing the young captain and wondering where his old friend was sailing.

'I've done this run twice and she's a sweet sail. We may find a storm out there, but the ship can take whatever Neptune throws our way.'

'Sir John!'

John clasped the hand of the old captain. 'Two captains on one boat?' he asked with a laugh.

'I am a passenger now. It seems the wind was in the right quarter for change. I'm leaving for good and want to settle in Massachusetts and make more charts. I think that you are being blown that way too.'

'At least I can offer you a roof until you find a place to live,' John said. 'I'm bound for Ostungo on Martha's Vineyard and taking Amos here with me to see to my horses.' He called to the children and, until late that night, when the ship had passed The Needles and the night mist closed over the Southern shore of England, William remained wide-eyed as he listened to the old captain telling stories of the sea and storms and bravery, and of monsters that grew in the telling and which John only half-believed.

'How far?' the children asked each day once the novelty of watching the sea had waned. The old captain taught them to trail lines to catch fish and soon they saw dolphins and heard the gulls from a distant shore. The one big storm was forgotten as the weather grew warmer and the breeze brisk and set fair for New England.

'I call at Plimoth with mail and goods,' the captain said. 'We'll stay there for fresh water and green vegetables and then sail for Martha's Vineyard.'

'We will go ashore while you victual the boat,' John said with satisfaction. 'I must pay my respects to the governor and make myself known in the colony.' He looked at his windblown daughter and smiled. 'You must make yourself fit to be seen, Mary, and wear a pretty dress.'

'Must I sit in a stuffy room while you talk to the governor?' she asked.

'You must for a while, but I will give you leave to go with Amos and William to see the town, once you have paid your respects.'

There was little time to explore, as the horses on board had to be taken ashore for much needed exercise. William and Amos were kept busy until the ship was ready to sail again. Mary stayed with her father and was fascinated by the wooden houses and the strange little shops. The governor's house was solid and the brick-built chimneys rose above wide hearths which opened on to large rooms, furnished as well as any in Southampton.

'Did you think they all dwelled in tents?' John asked when she showed her amazement. He was dressed in fine linen and a silk jacket and waistcoat embroidered with threads of silver. Mary glanced down at her own stiff silk skirt and tight bodice and felt disappointed. Would life here be the same as in any fairly large town in England? She saw two young men in sober garb who looked like secretaries. Would every man here be as boring as Makepeace?

She made an obedient curtsy to the governor and accepted a glass of wine from a liveried servant, then went to the window to look out over the bay. 'Everyone seems busy, so may I present myself?'

Mary found herself looking up into the eyes of a tall, slim man with dark-brown hair and brown eyes. He took her hand and kissed it, then held it for a moment longer. 'Mistress Mary, why are you making this pilgrimage and depriving London of your company?'

'I have never been to London. Who are you?' she asked.

'Richard Mace, the nephew of the governor. I hear you are bound for The Vineyard.'

She nodded and was bereft of words until he led her to a large painting and pointed out Nantucket Bay and the long houses and tepees of the Indians dotting the shore. In the picture, the trees were beginning to turn gold and red and the sky looked impossibly blue. 'Is it as beautiful as that?' she asked.

'This does it no justice. I know Edgartown well and the cliffs of Gay Head are pretty, but not as tall as the cliffs on the coast of England.'

'Do you know Southampton?' she asked eagerly.

He smiled. 'Not well, but you must tell me about it. I am to sail for England shortly, to begin the Grand Tour for a few months, and then go to Court at St James's, to meet the king in Westminster.'

He watched her eager face, the soft skin tinged brown from the voyage, and heard about Deerwood and the farms. He sighed as if he was sincere. 'How painful it is to meet and then part so soon.'

'We may meet in London,' Mary said eagerly, then blushed and turned away.

'Are you going back?'

'I have to follow my father to court and be presented when we return.'

'And find a husband?'

'That is for my father to decide,' she said demurely.

'Wait for me, Mary,' he said softly. 'We shall meet again.' He kissed her hand again and was gone when John called to her to make her adieus to the governor's wife.

John eyed the departing man with interest. 'So that is Richard Mace,' he said.

'He seems pleasant,' Mary said, as if dismissing him from her mind.

'Very.' Mary waited for him to say more but John refused to comment further, other than to say he didn't know the young man and could only judge him from his manners, which were impeccable.

'He's going on the Grand Tour and will be at St James's when we return,' she said.

'His reputation is excellent, I believe,' John said, but frowned as if his instincts told him that a man with such good looks and manners must have some vices. He laughed.

'I'm sure he's a fine man, but what Ellen said is true: it's hard for a father to think of any man making love to his daughter.'

'He only kissed my hand, Father … twice.'

A carriage was waiting by the docks at Edgartown to take the family to Ostungo. Amos waited to unload the animals and see them driven to the farm. The captain settled for the inn as he had naval men to see and a boat to buy for his work round the coasts. A string of mules was brought to carry the boxes and baggage, as rain had made the paths too muddy for oxen-cart wheels.

Free of the tight bodice she had worn in Plimoth, and once more dressed in a muslin gown, Mary looked about her eagerly from the carriage, the puppy asleep on her lap. William sulked because he had to ride inside instead of helping Amos with the horses, but gradually he forgot that he was ill-used and John was asked a barrage of questions as they passed cranberry bogs and sweet vines and many unfamiliar plants and trees.

John answered quickly, even impatiently, his throat tightening as he saw the place he had longed to see again. The original house of wattle and daub with logs to strengthen the corners and wooden shingles to seal the roof, was mellowed and softly coloured as if a wash of shadowy ochre had been passed over it. Rooms added as the Lubbocks' need

412

for them grew were more sturdily made of logs with the seams filled with hard clay. Fifty metres away the new house rose from the birch trees and they saw a double frontage, flanking wide shallow steps and an elegant porch.

'You've done well,' John said, his voice husky with emotion. 'If the stables are as good, I ask for nothing better.' William was already running towards the sound of a horse whinnying and his delighted shout brought the others to see what he had discovered.

The broad paddock was alive with mares and foals and two Indian youths waited by the gate to take the carriage horses and stable them. John looked at the tall pallisade of logs that surrounded the stable block and the long houses. 'We needed to build high because the bears come down in bad weather, sensing the fodder,' Thomas Lubbock said. 'They do little harm unless they grow bold and try to go into the long houses. We found one on our porch, which scared my wife.'

'I have hired two girls for you, who came out on a convict ship, but who are good workers and glad to be free here,' Alice Lubbock said. 'The poor wretches did nothing wrong except to steal a little food when they were starving; food that here we take freely and see no wrong in it. If the hens lay away then someone will eat the eggs and they will not be wasted, and a rabbit or two makes good common food for all.'

She urged them to leave the horses and eat in her house before unpacking anything, and set out fresh soda bread and roast hares and broiled fish. Mary noticed signs of sewing and fingered a piece of pretty cotton and some bright silk ribbons. A girl of her own age, or a little older smiled and told her that she was to be married the next Sunday in Edgartown. 'I'm Susannah,' she said. 'I hope you come to my wedding. We postponed it for a month until you could be here. We must invite our neighbours to meet you.'

'I have no wish to intrude on your celebrations,' John said. 'I know that our arrival must create curiosity that might take away the gloss from your day.'

'That is not true,' Alice said firmly. 'Our close friends will be there to wish them joy, and the other guests might not have made the effort to travel here if you were not coming, so you make this a special celebration, as many of our friends have not been here for over a year.'

'Do they come from far away?' asked Mary.

'Not so many now, as families we knew when we first came here have moved on to

Plimoth and Boston; some have gone back to England because they bought bad land and nearly starved.'

Mary ran a finger round the rim of her ale mug and tried to appear politely curious. 'Do you have friends in Plimoth? We visited the governor's house and found them pleasant.'

'No, we know of a family there who came to make trouble when Mistress Fletcher had twin girls. The wife was mad with an obsession to have a baby girl, and demanded to be given one of the babies. When she was sent away, her husband had her taken back to England on the promise of a baby girl there, but the child never existed and the poor lady died in a madhouse. The governor was embarrassed by the affair and sent Mr Chilton to a post in Boston and so we have no news of him.' She laughed. 'Of course, there is Mr Richard Mace.'

'Is he coming to the wedding?' Mary asked quickly.

'No, he is an asset to any social gathering, but I think the fish here are too small for his net. He will do better in England or France.'

'Why do you say that?' John said, his attention on Mary's flushed face.

'He is dependent on his uncle, the governor, and his only hope of wealth is to marry an heiress. He has charm and good looks and is an asset in any diplomatic situation, charming the ladies and entertaining the men, but he keeps no mistress and there is no hint of scandal attached to him, so we think he waits for a really big catch.'

'I wondered about him,' John said and looked at Mary. 'I hope you told him that in spite of my title we are only poor settlers who come to scrape a living from alien soil?'

'No. I told him about Deerwood and that you intend me to be presented to His Majesty.' Mary sounded bad-tempered. 'I'm glad he will not be there. I found him forward.'

Her father smiled. 'You will have many men wanting you for various reasons, but I think he liked what he saw before he knew your name, and you could trust him not to seduce you.'

'You mean I'm not a … big enough fish? I am not attractive enough?' Mary seemed to be on the verge of tears.

'Quite the contrary, my dear. If he wants you, we shall see him again and he will approach you through me. No seduction, no compromise, as he knows that fathers hold the purse strings.'

His smile was cynical. 'He may be poor but he knows he has charm and a good face to trade, and I think kindness. If he is as innocent of lechery as Alice suggests, then at least he has no pox!'

416

'Amos wants me to help settle the new mare, Father,' William burst in. 'I know I have to unpack, but I can do that later and help you with the boxes, but the mare is restless and on heat and the stallion got wind of her when she walked to her stable. Amos said she must not be mated now after the exhausting voyage.'

'Steady! You will collapse from loss of breath if you don't slow up.' John turned to Alice. 'The sooner we are settled, the better I shall like it, then I can look round my stables. You have both had a burden over the years and I hope that Amos will lessen it for you, but not take away your authority at Ostungo. He will deal only with the horses and build a farrier's work shed.'

'That will be a welcome relief, sir,' Thomas Lubbock said. 'We do our best, but horses were never my first interest and if it wasn't for the help of the Indian boys and the Fletchers, I could not have taken so many mares over the years.'

'Will there be ponies for my children?' John asked. 'The ground here seems fit only for stouter beasts than the thoroughbreds.'

'Edward Fletcher had two shaggy moorland ponies brought over, that are ideal here as they stand all weathers in the open except when it is really cold. He bred from them to sell to the Indians who find them to their liking as they are surefooted, small and can

417

be ridden bareback.' Lubbock smiled at Mary. 'I think they have two just ready for breaking that they would sell to you.' He saw that Mary was not excited by the prospect. 'You'll find them useful for getting about, but, of course, the other horses need exercising and they go on the beaches and through the water to make their legs strong.'

A flutter of dust from an upper window showed where the maid Selina was hastily making sure that everything was clean for the master and his family, and the other girl stood in the kitchen doorway smiling nervously.

'What do they call you?' Mary asked.

'Winifred, madam,' the girl said in a low voice, as if expecting a rebuke.

'Can you cook?'

'Yes, madam.'

Mary stepped into the kitchen and looked about her at the scrubbed tables and the polished wooden chairs. She lifted the lid of a pot hanging over the fire and smiled. 'I didn't know what meat you would have here but I'm glad you have cooked lamb today. It is my father's favourite dish. Can you make dumplings with herbs?'

Winifred nodded and she managed a smile. Mary sensed her relief and stayed with her, talking about the things available on the farm and what was not easy to obtain. She saw the fading marks of shackles on the girl's wrists and the way she rubbed her hands as if to rid them of the irons.

'Were you long in prison?' she asked.

'Six months before they put us on a ship and brought us here.'

'Have you a family?' Mary's horror grew as the girl told her how they were desperate for food when her father died and she had stolen a loaf and her brother had poached a rabbit.

'Where are they now?'

'My brother hanged and my mother and sister are on the parish.' She gave a shuddering sigh. 'They say they are fortunate to have a generous parish council who keep them from starving and don't turn them out to the next town.' She looked at Mary with pleading eyes. 'I have to be here for five years, but if I displease you I may be taken to gaol and never released.'

'And Selina tells the same tale?'

The girl nodded. 'Her family are all dead.'

'The house looks clean and cared for, and the smell of your cooking makes my mouth water. We must make this a home for my father so that he doesn't wish to take me and my brother back to England for a while.' She smiled. 'I think you have found a home, Winifred, if you go on as you have started, because when we go back, we shall need to know the house is safe and clean and ready for us whenever we need to come here.' She hesitated, then decided that sooner or later everyone would know that Amos was a convicted felon, too, so she told the girl and said how honest he had been all the time he had worked at Deerwood, waiting to come to the New World. 'So have no fear: if we are well served, my father will be kind.'

'Mary?' William called from upstairs. 'Father wants us to unpack some boxes and put our clothes away.' They worked hard until dusk and then sat down to eat, watching the fireflies on the edge of the wood. They slept in rooms still smelling of fresh pine and beeswax polish, waking only when the cockerels challenged the dawn.

William went at once to see the horses. Amos was examining the harness and saddles. 'If Sir John gives me leave I'll go to the town and order racing saddles for you and some better ones with more padding for general use.' He looked up from the tangle of harness and dull stirrups. 'There's work here right enough, and time to do it in.'

'We have to go to a wedding,' William said in disgust. 'You could come to Edgartown with us to buy the saddles.'

'So I could, but no slipping away for you from the wedding, mind! You'd get your fine clothes in a mess in five minutes.'

Mary selected a gown for the wedding from among the clothes that would have no part in her daily life on The Vineyard, and Selina pressed it, making the silvery ruffs stand out with stiffening of flour paste. John braced himself to meet the Fletchers, annoyed that after so long, the coming meeting could make him feel tense.

He sent letters from Ellen and Hope's mother, carried by the Indian boy who delivered mail, but wanted to be in a crowd when he had to meet Hope, so he made no attempt to contact Edward, in spite of his brief but enthusiastic note of welcome.

Mary was ready long before her father came down to the carriage, William dragging his heels after him. 'You must come, William,' his father said. 'If you turn into a savage here, your mother will make you go to the priests!' He grinned. 'I can think of better amusements, but tomorrow you shall ride along the shore and I will pace you. There will be other boys there and a few girls, so you may make new friends who can ride with you.'

John insisted that the Lubbocks should ride in the big carriage and he and his family followed with Amos driving the landau. The small church was soon filled with people; some guests and some curious members of the community. John looked round from his place in the front behind the bride's family, but saw no familiar face. Wide pillars obscured much of his view and he thought that Hope had not come to the church, but afterwards, when the assembly moved over to the meeting house for the wedding feast, he gasped.

'What is it, Father?' Mary asked in a whisper.

'Nothing,' he said, forcing a smile. 'Come, let me introduce you to some of my oldest friends.'

He seized Edward's hand and laughed. 'Just the same!' he declared. 'The years have not put a mark on you.'

'Nor you, John. It seems like yesterday!' Edward turned and took Hope by the hand. 'Isn't she even more beautiful?' he said with pride. 'And here are my two daughters, Edwina and Melissa, and my only son, Michael John. Children, this is Sir John Halben, my very dear friend from Deerwood Manor.'

Hope was pale and raised her glance to his with a fixed smile. 'John,' she said briefly and merely touched his hand.

He saw a slender woman with a high soft bosom and delicate sun-kissed arms, dressed in pale-green bird's eye silk that shimmered like an aspen as if she too trembled. Her eyes were pleading and gave a hint of warning as she drew her son towards him.

John saw the blue eyes and corn-coloured hair, the direct glance and generous mouth, and it was like looking at the miniature his mother had painted and set in an oval, diamond-studded frame when he was a boy.

Edward saw his expression and laughed. 'Hope's mother said that you were related several generations back by a liaison, and Michael is the living proof.'

John took Michael by the hand and they stared at one another for a moment. 'It is very like,' he said. 'I never believed your mother until now, Hope, but the sins of our forebears find us out.'

She let out a breath that had been imprisoned too long and her colour returned. 'And this is William?' she asked and saw Judith in his face but not in his eyes. 'Do you ride well, like your father?'

Chapter 21

Amos scratched his head and picked up his saw again. 'It's coming on, sir,' he said.

John Halben looked at the pile of neatly split planks that would make the walls of the new smithy and harness-room. 'Did you do all this?'

'No.' Amos grinned. 'The Indians are teaching me a thing or two. I ordered these and they took me up into the forest and I saw how it's done. They trim the twigs away and chop into a tree on one side up high beneath the bottom branches, then chop again near the ground. From the top, they force wedges into the sides, splitting the wood away to the thickness they want and go on down until the plank falls neat as you like. They still have the living tree and can go back when they need more. Better than felling and hauling heavy trunks to be sawn, and leaving half of it to the fungus and rot, and they set store by the birds that nest high up so they leave them undisturbed.

John led his mare into the shade. 'You think you'll settle here?'

'I'll never go back. If this is prison, then I like it! The girls in the house think they are in Heaven and I can even understand some of the local tongue now.'

John picked up the earthenware jug that was cooling in the stream and tipped the cool ale down his dry throat. He regarded Amos with amusement tinged with sadness. 'I am more a prisoner than you. I have to return to England soon and leave all this to face the idleness of court and the restrictions of my position.'

'You go back to a wife, sir, and friends.'

'Yes I have a wife,' John said in a flat voice. He grinned. 'If you are to stay you must have a wife, too, Amos. I frown on any who take a squaw to bed. We have no trouble with the tribes here as they have on the mainland.'

'I think Winifred may be willing,' he said. 'She's a healthy soul with a skill for the kitchen, but I'll wait until I've finished my cottage before I take her.'

'I'll hand the mare over and exercise another. They need the ride and the salt on their legs. Did I see William leaving earlier with the colt?'

'He led a string down to the water and the boys brought them back. Now William has taken two mares over to the Fletchers.' Amos seemed put out. 'Before we came, they say that Mistress Hope came here and did good work, and her son helped as often as his father could spare him, but now he seldom comes and she never visits the horses here. William spends a lot of them there. I could do with more help with the rides as none of the Lubbocks care for it and are glad to be rid of the chore. The Indians ride them with no saddles and go wildly, but the horses need schooling and discipline if they are to race.'

'It will take time to sort out a great many things,' John said. He left Amos sawing wood to fit the frame already erected, and knew that he needed a professional carpenter to advise him. 'I'll ask Edward Fletcher to come here and see to the plans before you do much more, unless you want an ugly, leaking barn to sleep in!' He saddled a fresh mare and took her slowly through the shady copse.

It was right to visit the Fletchers, he decided, but knew that he needed an excuse to go there after such little contact with them since he arrived in Ostungo. The building that Amos was struggling over was the way to approach Edward, and he must see Hope and the boy again, even if Hope had forgotten everything that had happened between them. 'But she wore my silk,' he told the chattering squirrels. 'She watched me take her son by the hand and saw the looks we exchanged, as if we knew each other, and yet we have not met again over all the time we have been here.'

'Father! Michael and I raced and the horses loved it.' William was animated and panting as he brushed the mare's heaving flanks and put her in the cool shed with the other one.

'Who is it, Michael?' Edward came from the house and he urged John to come in and have refreshment while the boys saw to his mare.

'Can you spare the time to help Amos? I want no lopsided shacks on my land and he is better with horses than with wood and nails! If it's impossible, I'll go to Edgartown for help, as I shall have to do for a labouring force, but from you I want advice, not manual work.'

'I'll come with you today. I've finished

caulking the whaler.' Edward looked annoyed. 'I missed the last trip as we had too much to do here, with Hope sick, but I am going the next time, and I hope we don't strike rock as they did before!'

'Bring Michael,' John said idly, as if offering an outing to a bored boy. 'Stay overnight and make sure that Amos knows what to do and what to tell the workmen.'

'There is work for Michael here,' Hope said.

John swung round at the sound of her voice. Her cotton dress was limp with the heat and her nose had a smudge of flour. She carried an earthenware dish piled with hot pies, which she put on a table in the shade and covered with a muslin cloth. She turned away to fetch cool fruit juice and ale and set the jugs on the table outside the kitchen.

Michael brought stools and poured the cold drinks and John tore away his gaze as the boy walked back to the house. He peeped under the muslin and selected a pie. 'You must have known I was coming here,' he said, smiling. 'Ellen always said I could smell her pies from a hundred miles away and this is as good as any she baked.'

'My mother was never a cook, so I must take after my aunt,' Hope said.

'And Michael takes after one very distant and tenuous connection with my family?'

427

His eyes were bold and his lips curved in mockery. He bent forward to take another pie and whispered, 'It was a connection that I never believed, but if your mother said it was so, then it must be true, and if your husband believes it, then I must believe it.'

Hope said nothing, but moved away and kept her distance while the men were talking. She sent Michael to bring lobsters from the long house as she knew that Katsi's son had caught some that morning and was boiling them, and she hoped he would stay away from the house long enough to miss seeing John Halben again.

'We are going back to England soon,' William was saying to Edwina in the kitchen. 'We shall take three horses and I am to train as a rider to race them on the courses made for His Majesty.'

'I shall miss you,' she replied, and added wistfully, 'I'd like to see England. Mother tells us about Deerwood and the country-side and I know I would like it as much as she does.'

'You can come, too. Father wouldn't object. Why don't all of you return?' he asked eagerly.

'Mother wouldn't go back now. I don't know why, but she wants to stay here and my father is the same.'

'You could come back with us.'

'That's impossible. Without my parents I

would have nowhere to live except with my great aunt whom I have never seen. Life would be very dull.'

William attacked a bush with a switch of hazel. 'Why can't you? I want you to come! Michael can come too.'

'He wants to stay here. What would your mother say if you arrived with a strange girl?'

'You are my *friend!* Why shouldn't I have my own friends to stay?'

Edwina blushed, and said in a voice that sounded like Hope and her aunt before her, 'It wouldn't do.'

'You do like me, Edwina?' he asked anxiously. He watched her pleasant face, so much like her father's but softer. He recalled the girl in Little Deerwood who had tried to make him love her in the bushes and his face reddened. Edwina was not as pretty or as demanding; her breasts were smaller, but close and upturned; her waist was slim and supple and he wanted to kiss her, his body disturbed by her nearness in a way that he had never experienced before today.

'Yes, I like you, William,' she said, and ran off, out of the house.

John pushed back his wooden stool. 'Edward, you go ahead with William and two of the horses. My mount hasn't had a gallop and I can bring her back later with some lobsters if Hope can spare them.'

'I can see what Amos is doing before the light fails,' Edward agreed. 'And tomorrow we can draw plans of a practical nature for your workers to start on as soon as you find men in Edgartown. I shall give him a note to some men I trust and you will have a fine cottage and a smithy in no time.'

John seemed to think deeply. 'No, take your own pony and leave two mares with me. I can lead one back and you will have your own beast to ride when you return here.'

'Hope can ride with you. She has not been to Ostungo since you arrived and must miss her rides,' Edward said kindly.

'No!' It was a muted cry that Edward couldn't hear. Hope put a hand to her throat as if she was choking. 'Amos is in charge of the horses now and might resent my interfering,' she said hastily.

'On the contrary, he would appreciate your help when you can spare the time. He knows how well you care for them,' John said smoothly. 'I shall saddle the other horse and we shall ride, madam.'

Hope took the last of the pies from the deep bread oven and splashed her face with cold water to cool down, trying to convince herself that it was the heat of the summer day and the baking that made her face pink. She brushed her hair and tied it back in a thick plait and put boots on her feet instead of her moccasins.

John held both horses and Hope went to the one she was to ride, smoothing its neck and breathing back into the horse's breath to establish friendship, and she was nuzzled in return. 'Hello Squant,' Hope said softly. 'I've missed you.'

'I heard that you named some of the foals, but the names are strange. What is Squant? And why Cheepi for my black stallion and Moshop for the other one?'

Hope laughed and took the bridle, leading the mare to a rock from which she mounted, making sure that John had no need to touch her. 'We hear many Indian stories. Squant is the daughter of Moshop so it seemed fitting that she should be Squant, the daughter of the giant Moshop who was big enough to eat whales!'

They walked the horses down to the beach. 'And Cheepi?' John sounded intrigued.

'He was another giant who lived in a cave and taught the Indians a great deal of crafts and was much revered, but Cheepi was wild, like your stallion, and ruled Massachusetts so harshly, he was sent here with his wife and seven daughters. His pipe made much ash which he put in the bay and it silted up to form Nantucket.'

John roared with laughter and urged his horse into a gallop as the sand stretched before them and the salt air brushed their cheeks. Hope forgot her fears and let her exhilaration have its way, the horses matching stride for stride, the sea now gently lapping their hocks.

'We should turn now before the ground gets hard and uneven,' Hope said.

John frowned. 'I don't want them winded. Do they usually go so far and then straight back in this heat?'

'No,' Hope admitted. 'They rest here. There's a stream and shade over there where I rest them before going back slowly.'

'Then why not today?'

Hope dug her heels into the heaving flanks and turned towards the shade. She dismounted and took a thick cloth from her saddle-bag to dry the damp hide and John followed her example. She sensed him watching her and her apprehension grew.

At last she knew that she had to face the man who had come back into her life. She sat on a log and John flung himself down on the dry leaves, as the youth had done so many years ago when they rode together and sank into weary contentment on the dunes near Deerwood: those innocent days before he came back from Europe and they found themselves in love.

John half closed his eyes against the glare. 'Tell me another story,' he said.

'We hear so many from Katsi and Chiabos and the squaws. The young braves are made to listen to them to keep the tales in their folk lore.' She smiled. 'Sometimes I think they must be true, especially when we women plant Sister Corn and Sister Squash and Sister Bean.'

'There are other stories,' he said. 'I enjoyed the one about a woman taken by a lord of the manor, maybe willingly, or as Abigail was taken, by *le droit de seigneur,* and who gave a heritage of Halben blood to your family.'

'It could be true,' Hope said in a low voice. 'You know these things happened.'

'If I had taken heed of the story, even allowing for the wanton fancies of your mother who told it, I would have sworn it was true and married you, Hope, in spite of my family and their concern for wealth and position, but I had never heard it told as fact before Edward told me. What a relief it must have been to him to think it true when each time he looks at Michael he sees me!'

'Edward is my dear husband and Michael is his son,' Hope said desperately. 'We are happy here and Michael loves the life and never wants to leave.'

'It may be true,' he said, his eyes mocking her. 'You look as if it could be true, and when you wore my gift of silk to the wedding, I couldn't imagine a more handsome, well-born woman, even in the Court of King Charles.'

433

She looked away from the anger and desire in his eyes, and stood up. 'The mares are drinking too much cold water. We must walk them gently on the way back.'

'Hope!' She turned as she tugged gently at the bridle. 'Michael is mine! He is more my son than William will ever be, much as I love the boy. I think I knew it when I heard he was born and Ellen said he had corn-gold hair. Our love was so deep and passionate that day that I hoped that my thrusting must have sired him, but I kept away for so long because I was afraid it wasn't so, and my dream would be broken.'

'Don't! Oh, please, John, don't torture me. Don't you think I have not suffered each day when I see him smile?' Her temper flared and she dashed away her tears. 'How do you think I have been all this time, wondering if you would see him and know, and knowing of the threat from Furness who would imagine he had proof that it was your father who took me as he intended? Go away and leave us in peace. I doubt if you spared a thought for me over all these years! You married and have two children and a fine estate and any woman who takes your fancy, and now you decide that you want to meddle in our lives.'

He swung into the saddle and Hope mounted from the log on which she had been sitting. 'Walk,' he told his mare. 'We

434

had to meet alone,' John said. 'It's not true that I forgot anything about you. I knew that I owed you a debt of love and to make up for any harm that might come to you from me.' She watched the dense hair on her horse's mane as it moved with the action, and would not look at him. 'I had to see you if only to tell you what arrangements I have made.'

She looked up sharply. 'You must not take him from me!'

'No, but I need to know that he is mine. I have made over Ostungo to him as his rightful inheritance after my death giving you the right to live there for as long as you wish.'

'You visited lawyers in Edgartown?' She felt cold. 'Some of them are far from discreet and their wives know everything about their transactions.'

'Only my family lawyer in Southampton and Angus know the contents of a sealed document, a copy of which, with my seal on it and on its many wrappings, is now lodged with a lawyer in Plimoth.'

She gasped. 'You did this in England before you saw Michael?'

'Yes. I hoped he was my son and even if he was not, I wanted you to be safe here for as long as you wanted to live on The Vineyard.' His face was hard as he stared out over the sea. 'If I have sinned, I have paid a thousand times, married to a woman with ice in her veins and a piety that stinks of the grave!'

'My poor John,' she whispered. 'But you have two children of that union, so God has not forgotten you.'

'They are a blessing,' he conceded. 'Even if I see Judith in William's face at times, and think he may be as cold as she is when it comes to marriage.'

'I see a different boy with much of you in him.' She gave a wry smile. 'If you wish to avoid another misalliance, take him home away from my daughter. He is waking up to a new warmth that puzzles him, but makes him find her desirable.'

'Is that true?' He smiled. 'The air of Massachusetts agrees with him, and yet I have to take him away, as my daughter expects to go to court soon and she needs us there. The plague has abated after the fire and the king is back at Westminster, with theatres opening and places of amusement thriving once more. The young need such diversions and Mary asks when we are going back.'

'Pleasure and vice thrive together,' she warned him.

'So it's better to wed early and give rein to passion in a clean bed,' he agreed bluntly.

'I heard that you have a mistress,' Hope ventured, as he waxed self-righteous.

'Did a seagull or Aunt Ellen bring you that news?' He paused to pick a ripe grape from an overhanging vine and ate it. 'A man must have a channel for his needs,' he said, 'so, I chose a married woman with no vices except her need for me.' He looked at her closely. 'After how my father died, do you think I could ever stomach a whore? After you, can you not believe that I thought of you each time I took another woman, and each time, I found her wanting?'

'I had forgotten you,' she said.

'With my face in that boy?' He gave a derisive laugh. 'If I mean nothing to you, the resemblance would not be important to you. Why are you afraid to come to Ostungo and talk as old friends?' He stopped and the mare moved restlessly, anxious to be back in the cool paddock. 'Nothing has changed, Hope. We still love each other.'

'No! Edward needs me and I love him for the good man he is,' she said slowly. 'I have done enough harm. My life is his for as long as he wants it,' she added simply.

'What if I can't stay away from you?'

'Then you must burn!' she said harshly, and kicked her mare into a trot. Among the bushes, she saw a slight brown form slip away, and knew that John had been unaware of being watched.

The girls were packing cooked lobsters in seaweed and a woven grass basket to keep them cool. 'Katsi suggested that these might be acceptable to you, sir,' Michael said.

'Can they be spared? Have you enough for your family?'

Michael laughed. 'They seem to know what to catch and are seldom wrong. Something told them to catch more than usual and there are hundreds of lobsters out there easy to take.'

'They didn't know I would visit you today.'

Edwina smiled. 'They have another sense that we do not possess. Katsi knows if one of us is ill or Mother needs help, and her sons are there to protect us when we go sailing and into the woods.'

'Then you are safe here for ever,' John said.

'They are like our own family,' Hope said. 'We ask for no better friends.'

'Do you find this life enough, Michael? There are many sports a boy can pursue in England that you cannot find here, and many other diversions.' John regarded him with curiosity.

Michael shrugged. 'I go to Edgartown and sometimes to Plimoth where I find all I need, and come back here to the farm and to Ostungo when I can be spared to work there.'

'If I asked your father, would you work at Ostungo and live there when I am away? The estate grows yearly and the Lubbocks say that they need more help to manage the place. Even if Amos is in charge of the wellbeing of the horses, his judgement is rough when it comes to breeding and he is only a bondsman until he has served his time. I know you are young, but you have known Ostungo since you were an infant and you have learned about race horses.' He glanced at Hope, who sat stiffly on the bench looking anxiously at her son. 'You share your mother's instinctive feeling for horses ... as indeed my own son does.'

'I love it at Ostungo and I enjoy studying blood lines,' Michael said eagerly. 'Father doesn't need me now as he has hired help with the crops and takes more and more interest in the sea and boat building.'

'Breeding *is* important,' John agreed solemnly, and Hope looked away. 'We must go over our stock together, and I will send for lists of pedigrees that will be useful if we want to breed valuable racers. There will be courses soon in America where they will need good mounts and have few available, unless we can supply them. What do you think of breeding more moorland ponies for a ready profit?' Hope went into the house, limp with spent emotion. The two heads, so close together, were painfully beautiful, and so right together.

'If you want the lobsters for dinner you must take them home,' Edwina said sternly and John laughed.

'Do you bully William like that?' She blushed under John's mischievous gaze. 'He will be returning with me soon,' he added and saw her distress. 'Why don't you come with us? Isn't it time you went to England and found a husband?'

'No!' Hope protested. 'The girls' futures are here.'

They walked to pack the lobsters in the saddle-bags and were alone for a minute. 'You have Michael,' he replied quietly. 'If I go away I may never seen him again. I promise not to take him from you, but if William wants your daughter, he shall have her.'

'Your wife would never allow it.'

His face contorted with rage and sadness. 'My wife? My family? Society in England? If only I had been deaf to them in the past we could have been happy together now. My son shall marry who pleases him and the rest can go to Hell.'

'I will not have her taken away into your house unwed, and thought unchaste,' Hope said proudly.

'Leave her for a year and if they want each other, they shall be wed at Deerwood.'

'I would have to be there,' Hope said. 'I don't know if I could bear that, and Edward is too devoted to the girls to see either of them go so far away.'

'Who knows what may happen in a year?'

440

he said lightly. 'I may tire of court and yearn for The Vineyard, or Michael might take a wife who hates horses and wishes to live in Boston.'

Hope smiled. 'I can't believe that could happen. He's too much like ... most boys brought up near stables,' she finished lamely.

'No, I agree that our son couldn't be like that.' He laughed softly. 'Our son, Hope! That beautiful boy is our son.' He bent from the saddle and kissed her cheek, then spurred away, his back straight and his head held at a defiant angle, the spare horse following obediently on the leading rein, as docile as many women might be when he beckoned.

The girls were preparing lobsters and Michael sat apart as if in deep thought. He seemed to come to life when Melissa told him to fetch a bucket of water and whistled as he dipped it from the stream. Hope knew that he was happier when Edward was away and the girls and he were alone with their mother.

The cornmeal bread and lobsters were finished and Michael ate two fruit pies, relishing them as John had done. Hope began to doubt if Edward could believe for much longer the tale her mother had told him. The bed was hot and she missed Edward's solid presence beside her. I do

441

love my husband, she told herself and knew it to be true. She walked in the dark, and drank cool water and found Michael sitting on the bench outside the kitchen.

'Couldn't you sleep?' she asked.

'I'm not alone,' he said, and she saw his teeth gleam white in the dim light of the kitchen fire.

'It's much too hot inside. Tomorrow, I'll let the fire go out and make one in the yard,' she said. 'We've bread and pies enough for days and can cook what we need over an open fire.'

'Come out on the water,' he said impulsively. He tugged at her hand. 'When I go fishing late with Katsi's boys, we sit and drift and trail our lines and the night is full of magic.'

'I'm not dressed,' she protested.

'You have a very respectable shift!' He laughed. 'Come on, you won't frighten the whales.'

Hope filled a bottle with drinking water and took a shawl with her. Michael was already in the canoe, untangling lines. There was a quiet excitement in the air as they pushed away from the shore. Hope took a paddle and they sent the narrow craft through the water with hardly a sound. Stars that she had seldom noticed now seemed bigger and brighter than any she had seen. Michael was a restful companion, and made no move to toss the fishing lines over the stern, even when they saw rings of turbulence where fish surface.

'I've never done this before,' she said.

'You should. I learned it from the young braves who often come here before they go hunting, to make them calm and rid them of aggressive thoughts. They kill only what they need and never in anger, in case the spirits of the deer haunt them.'

'Does my young brave need to be calm?' she asked, smiling in the darkness.

'Tonight I did, but we can go back now if you are tired.'

'Why tonight?'

'I love Father and would do anything for him, but why did I feel closer to Sir John today than I have done to any man?' The canoe lurched as he made a sudden movement to face her.

The darkness gave her courage, as he could not see her face clearly. 'You heard the story that my mother tells of a liaison between a member of my family and one from Deerwood, a long time ago? That means that you have Halben blood in your veins and so share kinship.'

'Then my feelings for him are not unnatural?' She sensed his relief.

'No. It is not unnatural to feel affection and respect for Sir John.'

Michael steadied the canoe as Hope

stepped out, then dragged it clear of the water. 'I'm glad. I wish he wasn't going away, but we shall write and he is to send me papers about race horses and breeding stock.' He picked up Hope's shawl that had slipped on to the damp sand. 'I'm glad we are related but today I wished that he was my father. Am I wicked, Mother?'

'Not wicked, Michael, but never neglect Edward for such feelings. Work at Ostungo and look on it as your home, and send a good account of your work to Sir John. It will almost be true: you can look after his property as if you are his son.'

Chapter 22

'The men are ready, so I must stay in the tepee with the other women and leave the children in the long house with the old squaws,' Katsi said. She unloaded the last batch of moccasins on to the table and Hope paid her.

'So there'll be no more of these until after the whale is killed?'

Katsi nodded and sat by the door. 'We have meat and meal enough and there is no need for work in the fields. We are free to ask the Great Spirit to help us and to will

Brother Whale to come to us quietly.' She glanced at Hope. 'Your man is coming this time so will you pray too?'

'Yes, I shall pray for many things,' Hope said. She smiled. 'I thought that the Reverend Mayhew had converted your tribe to worshipping our God, but you still pray to the gods of trees and animals and the sea as well as to your Great Spirit, Manito the Mighty.'

'Your God helped us when the sickness came, but our gods give us life,' Katsi said. 'We pray to them all.'

'Edward has a talisman which he says will protect him. When he was born, the caul from his birth was over his head and his mother kept it and made him bring it with him when he came here. It is dry and is sewn into a leather pouch. They say that a man born in such a way and who keeps the caul will never drown.'

Katsi hissed through her teeth. 'That is powerful magic. I am glad that my man and my son will be with Edward.'

'The boat seems sturdy enough, but what if the whale comes under the keel?'

'There are many boats gathered on the shore, with people from many families, all with sealskin bladders and harpoons, so it will be quick and the whale will not be able to dive under the boats. Chiabos has seen the whale spume flung high close to the shore and the whale footprint after he dives, like a round pool of peace on the waves. There are more out in the bay where the small fish gather.'

'Does Edward know when it is to be?'

'After three days,' Katsi said.

'Three days.'

'You are afraid or sad?'

'A little of each,' Hope admitted.

'You are sad because Sir John is leaving with William and his sister Mary.'

Hope nodded. 'We shall miss them.'

'Edwina will weep a little but she might see William again in his own country and Sir John will come back.'

'I wonder if he will.' Hope was wistful. She no longer considered him a threat and could treat him as a friend even though she knew that she must never let him come as close as he wished, but her heart ached for him when she was alone. The past weeks had been happy, with Michael now living at Ostungo and the tension of Edward seeing him with John far less, as Edward was hardly ever at Ostungo now that he prepared for the whaling.

'He must come back, to see his son,' Katsi said. 'And you may see him each time you look at Michael.'

Hope felt a kind of relief that Katsi had voiced the fact that she knew about them. 'Edward is still blind,' she said.

'Men see what they need to see,' Katsi said calmly. 'Even if they know it to be different.'

'What does Edward see?'

'He sees a good wife whom he wants to keep, a son who still fills him with pride when people praise him, as our men feel pride when their adopted sons became braves, even if they have been adopted after capture in battle with an enemy. He sees his friend who has helped him in the past and to whom he owes a debt,' she said calmly. 'That debt will remain whatever happens between them. Men have different values to those we consider important.'

'He says he believes the story my mother told him,' Hope said.

'He must believe it or lose you,' Katsi said. 'Never tell him the truth, or once spoken, the words will destroy.'

'What would I do without you, Katsi?'

'We are sisters,' Katsi sharpened a knife on a stone and cut long strips from a deerskin which she plaited into a thin rope and added to the others to make a strong tether of many metres in length. She piled the finished rope on to the sled and dragged it back to the long house to be fixed to the inflated seal skins and the harpoons. Hope took the girls to the shore to watch the boats assembling, taking food and drink for Edward and the boys who helped him make ready.

Out in the water, she saw a huge humped back rise like a grey bubble, glistening as it shed water, the wide, strong bifurcated tail hover as the spume from the blowhole shot into the air. The tail stiffened and the beast plunged and disappeared, leaving the ring of calm water that Katsi had said was the whale's footprint.

Edward waved and Hope smiled tenderly. Passion was too demanding for every-day living and Edward was a good and loving husband. She ignored the voice that told her that John would go away, perhaps for ever.

Edwina held up the basket and Edward climbed out of the boat and waded through the shallows to the shore. He was stripped to the waist and almost as brown as the Indians, and his body was firm and lean from hard work and the open-air life.

If John had never existed I would have known no better love, she thought, then remembered that if John had not saved her, she would have been tainted by his father and her children might never have been born.

Fires built to cook cornbread in pieces of chestnut bark, for families that had travelled far, were lit on the shore, and the women brought out jars of pickled beans and relishes of peaches and dried squash. The shore was covered with light tepees and men and women working to be ready for the hunt. Young braves fished in the bay from canoes and their women cooked the catch before it had time to dry and loose freshness in the warm air.

They ate, then Hope left the girls while she went back to the house. Edward climbed back into the boat and she knew that he was in another world, of men with instincts as old as time, in which she wanted no part. The sight of the magnificent whale had filled her with dismay to think of it being killed, and she knew that she would not join the party on the beach when they brought in a kill.

Two horses were tethered in the shade and John Halben came to meet her with William at his side. 'Mary is packing and will come to say goodbye tomorrow,' John said. 'But William and I must go with the baggage and horses to see it all safely on board today, so we shall stay in Edgartown tonight and finish our business there before Mary joins us.'

'You've come to say goodbye?' She felt drained of all emotion.

'Not goodbye,' William said firmly, with a quick glance at his father. 'You will come to Deerwood with the girls next year.'

Hope shook her head.

'You must.' William sounded agonized. 'I must see Edwina again. I want to marry her when I am a year older.'

John looked past him to Hope's pale face. 'Then we shall indeed be related,' he said. 'Edward raised no objection when I asked him and you must give us your daughter, Hope, even if I may not adopt your whole family.'

'Where is Edwina? I must see her before we leave.'

'She's on the shore with Melissa, watching the boats,' Hope said. 'It's a fine sight and you must see it, John.'

'Later, if at all,' he said.

William darted away, running to waste as little time as possible. 'Come back within an hour,' John shouted, and Hope breathed a sigh of relief that they would not be alone for more than a short time.

'Have you eaten?' she asked.

'You sound like Ellen.'

'I am like Ellen. I am like my family who were good yeoman stock but no higher. Here, everyone is equal except where possessions raise them above others, but when you return, you must face your family and society's opinion of rank.'

'I am my own man!'

'Judith will never agree to William marrying Edward's daughter as he came from a family of artisans.'

'Judith will have to accept what I say, as she has to accept my will in everything now,' he said harshly.

'And when you go to court, will you boast of your daughter-in-law there?'

'There will be no need. They will see a happy couple, untouched by family scheming to bring two young people together for convenience, but without love.' He hesitated. 'One matter has arisen and it does depend a little on rank.'

'What is that?'

'When you return to England, you will bring both girls with you as Mary has become fond of Melissa. She wants her to be her companion at court, with Marjorie acting as duenna to both of them.'

'So I must return?'

'You must return.'

'And leave Michael here? What of Edward? They will never live together again.'

'They will stay on The Vineyard and Edward will have his boatyard while Michael has horses, but living separately; Edward here and Michael at Ostungo, which will be his for the rest of his life and for his family after him. I could never hold him in my arms when he was born and call him my son, but I can give him this inheritance.'

'I can't leave Edward alone,' Hope said.

John shrugged. 'He might come with you as he loves his daughters.' He came closer, laughing. 'He must stay with you, or it will be thought that you are my mistress.'

'No, John.' She looked up into his face and her eyes were soft with a kind of grief. 'That must never happen again.'

'We could make another son.'

'I am barren, but even if I was not, it would break Edward and destroy us. If you took me now, just once, I would go with you and never look back, and I must never do that, my dear.'

She reached up and kissed him on the lips. 'We have Michael, and if Edward dies before me I shall tell him of his true lineage.'

'It isn't enough! I have watched you over the past weeks and felt a passion again that tears me apart.'

'It hasn't been easy,' she admitted. 'But I shall have a lot to remember when you are gone. Every time I go to Ostungo, Michael will be there with the horses and, as we ride, I shall think of you.'

'You never wrote to me after you came here,' he said accusingly. 'All my news was secondhand from Ellen, with a few brief notes from Edward.'

'I will write of matters concerning Ostungo, and Michael as your link with The Vineyard, but they will never be love letters, John, so you must remember me as Edward's wife and Michael's mother and no more.'

'I shall have nothing!' His cry was almost comical, and Hope regarded him with growing amusement. 'I go back to a grey life with no love and nothing for the future.'

'John Halben, you will have everything, or nearly everything! You have William who will bring you pride and joy when he rides for His Majesty, as I'm sure he will, and your horses will bring you fame, riches and prestige and women to love you.'

'I want no woman other than you.'

'Do you think I would fit into your life now, away from The Vineyard?' She held up the fish she was about to gut and her sacking apron was shining with fish scales.

'Not as a fishwife,' he admitted, with a wry smile. 'But dressed in silk with a hat that flops over your eyes in the breeze and your sweet lips parted with pleasure when we meet, yes, Hope, you would fit into my life.'

'Go back to Lady Judith and Deerwood,' she said sharply, to hide her pain. 'You married her for an heir and she has given you one who will bring you joy, and a daughter who is sweet and lovely in her own way. She deserves no scandal and neither do I! We have to pay for what we take wilfully.'

'So long as I don't have to take Chastity to bed,' he said and grinned. 'You look as fierce as you did when I wouldn't let you ride my donkey.'

'You promised and then mocked me when

you rode it away,' she replied, and the tension between them dissolved into laughter.

William and Edwina were walking along the path, their hands entwined. Hope stood back from the window to leave them unobserved and put a finger to her lips, but John frowned. 'We must leave now,' he said.

'A few more minutes,' Hope pleaded for them. She peeped out of the window and saw William kiss her daughter, tenderly, shyly and inexpertly. 'They'll do no harm. William lacks your passion, John, and their wooing will take longer!'

Melissa ran up to the house and the couple broke apart, flushed and awkward at being seen. Edwina had tears in her eyes as William brought the horses from the shade and led one to his father. 'You will bring Edwina soon, won't you?' he begged.

'As soon as we hear that she will be welcome at Deerwood and not made to feel that she intrudes,' Hope said firmly.

'Mary wants me to be her companion,' Melissa said with shining eyes. 'I shall see the fine clothes and go to the theatre in London and never have to gut fish again!' she said with feeling, as she glanced at the result of Hope's endeavours on the table. 'You haven't done that very well, Mother. Shall I tidy it up for you?'

'No, I'll do that when they have gone. I

had things on my mind that had nothing to do with fish.'

She took off her apron and washed her hands in cold water, then pushed back her hair and walked out into the sunshine.

'Goodbye.' William seemed close to tears and dug his heels into the horse's flanks to take him away before he wept. John followed slowly, with one last glance at Hope and no flicker of emotion in his eyes.

Edwina ran to her father who came into the yard carrying the basket they had used to carry food. He hugged her and saw her tearstained face. 'You will see him soon,' he promised. 'Your mother will take you back to Little Deerwood and you will be happy.'

'If I go back, then you must come too,' Hope said firmly. 'A wife is nothing without the husband and family she loves.'

Edward stared at her for a moment and she saw the sadness that he had concealed from her over the years. 'Do you really want that?'

'I have only one husband,' she said lightly. 'I married you and have not wanted any other since our wedding day.' She put her apron on again. 'My place is here with you. They've gone now and we have many matters to settle. Have you asked for more earthenware pots for the whale oil and do you think Michael should come down to set up drying racks for the meat?' She called to

Melissa. 'Have you the cotton wicks ready for candles?'

Edward kissed her. 'You smell of fish guts,' he said tenderly.

'We shall all smell of worse than that when Brother Whale is killed,' she said. 'I almost wish that we didn't need the meat and oil and whalebone. I saw one today quite close, and I shall not watch you hunting.' She felt the edge of her knife. 'Will you sharpen the knives before you go so that I can cut pemmican, and bring only as much meat as we can store.'

It will be a great adventure for me,' Edward said. He looked at her apologetically. 'As Chiabos and his sons will be in my boat, I must stay with them the night before and join them in their purification rites. I know it means nothing, but it pleases them.'

'It means a lot, and you know that you half believe it all, as I do when I am with the women, planting crops.' She looked at him in a teasing way. 'Who wears his caul round his neck when he goes to sea, even inshore in a canoe? The ladies of Edgartown would disapprove, but I value my Indian friends above all others.'

'I am envied for my talisman and I shall never be robbed as it might not work for another man, and could even bring him bad luck if it was stolen.'

Edwina scrubbed the deal table with enough vigour to scrub away her sadness. Hope hugged her and said, 'I know how you feel.'

'How can you?' the girl said passionately. 'You grew up with Father and have not been parted from him since you decided to be married. It's easy for you.'

'William will wait for you. You are both so young, and you must be patient. Take the pony and ask Michael to come to supper tomorrow. I shall be alone as your father will be with the hunters. Michael must tell me what he intends to do with the new colt as I shall be busy over the next few weeks and unable to go to Ostungo.'

'I'll see Amos next week,' Edward called, when Melissa fetched the moorland pony. 'If his forge is ready, he can shoe my beasts and save me the trouble of taking them to Edgartown.' He flexed his hands. 'I must wear gloves if I am to pull on ropes; the sinews on the harpoons may burn,' he said.

The girls were sewing and the house was clean and scoured.

'Walk with me down to the shore,' Edward suggested. 'Tonight we are free. They are gone.' He gave a sigh of contentment. 'Freer than I've felt for years.'

'We'll have work enough soon,' Hope said, deliberately misunderstanding. She followed him on to the shore and watched the ring of fires above the tide-mark and the tepees filled with families waiting for their winter food and the oil to light their long houses. The sea was calm and out on the rocks in the bay birds rested as if replete after fishing. The canoes were pulled high on the beach.

Edward's new whaler rested on chocks and he ran a proud hand over the smooth beams and the pattern of porcupine quills on the bow. It was the largest boat in the fleet and Chiabos was proud that he was to captain it, as it gave his family much prestige among his friends.

'Is nobody fishing?' she asked.

'Not until after the whale is caught. We leave him to have all the fish he wants, and peace at night.'

Chiabos stood in the doorway of his skin tepee, half naked, with paint on his face, and a belt of wampum hung with shells.

'I think you should go tonight, not to-morrow, Edward,' Hope said quietly. 'Katsi said that the men abstain from love now and I think we should do the same.' She kissed him and gave him a gentle push. 'I will bring your bow and spear and gloves when you are ready, but Chiabos needs you now if he is to be at peace and know that the old customs are observed.'

'Wish us well,' Edward said.

Hope laughed softly, as if humouring a

child. 'I'll wish you well, and when you leave in the boats, I'll lie quietly on my bed to make Brother Whale come closer, in tranquillity.'

The publishers hope that this book has given you enjoyable reading. Large Print Books are especially designed to be as easy to see and hold as possible. If you wish a complete list of our books please ask at your local library or write directly to:

Magna Large Print Books
Magna House, Long Preston,
Skipton, North Yorkshire.
BD23 4ND

This Large Print Book, for people
who cannot read normal print,
is published under the auspices of

THE ULVERSCROFT FOUNDATION